Hannah gingerly placed her leg d[c] handbag and rooted savagely f[c] found a couple in a zipped pocket insi hitched up her skirt to her thighs ar dripping foot onto the edge of a low _ _ tree, where many years ago a bough once protruded. Hannah used a scrunched-up tissue to dab at the self-inflicted fashion wound and then popped the tissue inside the dark hollow, as if it were a handy bin that nature had provided.

Leaning forward, she opened the bandage and carefully placed it across the blister, her nose wrinkling in its pretty way as a wet, honey like odour came from inside the guts of the tree.

She tossed the bandage wrapper onto the ground just as something with immense strength pulled her leg quick-fast into the dark hole of the tree. It happened so fast that Hannah bashed her head against the side of the tree and saw stars. She did not have even time to cry out in shock or pain as what felt like many small hands grabbed at her bare leg and pulled with bone cracking might.

Hannah's left leg flew up like a chorus girl's, with violent pain to her groin and pelvis. Her backside and tummy disappeared into the overly sweet-smelling tree. With one leg stuck out of the hole, with her hands and face for a moment before that was dragged inside. The loud crack of her bones echoing in her ears, and she saw the sunshine framed like an oval in front of her as darkness and clawed hands covered her young body.

Sharp, biting and tearing teeth followed, and then death.

HEDGE END

BY PETER MARK MAY

For Jane Ranasinghe

CHAPTER ONE

Simon Hay knew all about stress. It affected nearly every day of his life to a certain degree. Even on his weekends off, he dreaded the phone ringing, just in case it was work with another lame, it-couldn't-wait-until-Monday question.

It was ruining his time with Lucy, fucking up his sex life, causing premature hair loss and making him pig out on food's two years ago, before his promotion, he would never have eaten. He was a stone overweight, sweated too much, drank too much wine and hardly had time to indulge in his two lifelong passions. One was going for long walks in the country and the second was the book he had been writing for six years, on the local history of the town of Hedge End, where he and his partner lived in North Surrey.

Apart from the occasional phone-free romp with his live-in girlfriend of seven years, the book was the last vestige of his uncluttered soul. It was a secret place he could melt into and feel free from any outside pressures. He did it for love and it never nagged him about commitment, babies, quarterly sales reports or overdue staff appraisals.

There was only one other place he felt at ease and that was the woods he walked through up Hanger Hill Road from Hedge End to catch the early commuter train to Waterloo every weekday morning.

Every step was made with leaden gloom or brisk paced despair if he was running late for the 07:17 fast service to London, but this Monday morning he had a few minutes to spare.

Past the cricket pitch, past the shops and large houses brought up by the richer-than-he smarmy banker types was the road that went up and around Hanger Hill to the train station. Parallel to the concrete pavement was a small copse that had long ago been a forest that had been excavated, cut in half and raped by four sets of railway tracks. Yet a small triangle shape of trees bordered by a high Hawthorn hedge remained, with little woodland paths that had been walked into over the years.

Across the gulf and slopes on either side of the steel tracks lay an even smaller strip of the once same wood, divided for over a century; like a parting in a man's short haircut. Trees older than the railway, village or tall hedge that gave the place its name and had once stood on the same level were now separated by a polluted gulf and valley, and carved out of the hillside by Irish navies long ago.

Some of the more ancient trees now leaned towards the gap on either side and looked like they were reaching out for their long-separated fellows.

Here on leaf compacted paths between the trees that remained wedged in an ever-narrowing gap between the road and railway lines, Simon Hay walked every morning. It was his last reminder of what life should be, earth, trees of varying hues and bushes, in-between paths, winding their own natural way through ferns and holly. He still had hope here, where the birds still sang and the foxes made their dens. Once the soles of his leather black shoes hit the pavement to cross the road to the walk down to the station, he knew that packed trains, with noisy tinny I-pod music and sweaty bodies followed. Then miles upon miles of concrete hell into Waterloo station and then briskly onto work and the further dread and stress that brought.

Often in the woods he would have ideas for his book, or remember to buy flowers for Lucy, or when he felt really low, he felt like skipping work and throwing a sickie, just to stay in the woods all day and hide from the world and its adult responsibilities. He just wished for better things, foreign places to visit maybe sell the house and buy a farm and grow grapes to make into wine.

Lucy, old level-headed Lucy, always set him straight on these ideas, so much so he did not bother to share them anymore, where once they spoke of everything. Mortgage, bills, work;

there seemed to be nothing more for him, stretching on into infinity and then finally death.

A movement in the dappled shadows beneath a leaning tree caused him to snap out of his self-pitying daydreams and he bent his head and peered into the space under it, which was masked by a young sapling and a holly bush. Something fluttered and the old leaves moved and scattered. A frown crossed Simon's brow as he wondered what kind of animal was in there.

Then out flew a starling, not more than two inches from his left temple and he ducked and spun and cursed as the bird flew off into the morning sky.

"Idiot," he chided himself, and with a glance at his diver's watch, strode quickly down the path that lead out to the main road across the top of Hanger Hill and down the lane to the station.

Hannah Browning winced and rubbed at the back of her heel in an unlady-like crouch on the pavement on the way up to Hedge End railway station. She had her new shoes on and wondered if the £200 worth of fine Italian leather was worth the damage to her toes and heels. It would be worth it if Jack, the boss at work, noticed her. Well, more than he normally did.

She had only been at her first job for six months and already at eighteen she knew how things worked in the office and how people got on. Playground and college politics had been a skill she easily transferred to the workplace, where she knew when to be a bitch and when to be the sorry-I've-not-done-this-before new girl. She had seen Jack notice her. He was mid-thirties and still trim and handsome, but married. Not that that mattered much to Hannah. She knew her hazel eyes, long black locks and cracking tits, inherited from her Italian mother, would soon lure him in.

She had done it at school with Mr. Hodges to give her a leg up with her exams, and then Mrs. Bristow at college to get the tutoring and results she wanted. Her skirts had gotten shorter, her shoes higher and the buttons near her cleavage looser.

Hannah noticed a slightly podgy, geeky looking guy entering the small woods that ran beside the pavement and she vaguely recognized him from the train she caught every morning. Hannah was definitely not one for woods or the great outdoors in general, and she only ventured out in her garden to sun-bathe on the rare days the sun ever shone in this country. Not for the first time, she wished she lived in her mother's birthplace of Milan and not this arse-end of the stockbroker-belt.

Today she entered the copse, because the leafy paths looked dry and felt much softer to walk on and gave a bit of relief to her aching feet. A cobweb across her face made her vow never to take this path through the woods again, however painful her feet got. Give her cars and concrete every time.

She reached half-way into the small wood. At the deepest part the path led away from the busy road to her right. She could still hear the steady rush of traffic, but the trees, bushes and ferns blocked them from view. Hannah felt something wet on her right heel as she walked and she moved over to a huge oak tree that dominated the right-hand side beside the pathway. She leaned against the tree with her left arm and crossed her right leg up to take off her shoe. Out of a blister of white skin, blood oozed and Hannah gritted her teeth in anger and frustration.

"Fer fuck sake!"

She gingerly placed her leg down again, unzipped her handbag and rooted savagely for a plastic bandage. She found a couple in a zipped pocket inside her large bag and then hitched up her skirt to her thighs and placed her right blood-dripping foot onto the edge of a low hole in the trunk of the tree, where many years ago a bough once protruded. Hannah used a scrunched-up tissue to dab at the self-inflicted fashion wound and then popped the tissue inside the dark hollow, as if it were a handy bin that nature had provided.

Leaning forward, she opened the bandage and carefully placed it across the blister, her nose wrinkling in its pretty way as a wet, honey like odour came from inside the guts of the tree.

She tossed the bandage wrapper onto the ground just as something with immense strength pulled her leg quick-fast into the dark hole of the tree. It happened so fast that Hannah bashed her head against the side of the tree and saw stars. She did not have even time to cry out in shock or pain as what felt like many small hands grabbed at her bare leg and pulled with bone cracking might.

Hannah's left leg flew up like a chorus girl's, with violent pain to her groin and pelvis. Her backside and tummy disappeared into the overly sweet-smelling tree. With one leg stuck out of the hole, with her hands and face for a moment before that was dragged inside. The loud crack of her bones echoing in her ears, and she saw the sunshine framed like an oval in front of her as darkness and clawed hands covered her young body.

Sharp, biting and tearing teeth followed, and then death.

CHAPTER TWO

Catherina Di Marco loved the park. It was an open space in a cluttered world of brick, mortar and bullshit that surrounded the part of London where she lived. It was half-seven in the morning and she jogged around the trees, on the grass if she could, loving the fact that nature could still exist slap-bang in the centre of one of the world's greatest cities.

She had her dark hair in a ponytail and wore shorts today to show off her best parts, her long legs and olive tanned thighs. Matt, her boyfriend of three years, used to love her legs, normally wrapped round him in throws of passion. Yet as she jogged past an elderly gentleman walking his dog, she realized that those times had become less in these past few months.

She stopped by an old cedar tree and drank from the bottle of water she had purchased from Ted at the newsagents, like she did every morning. In her ears, light Italian opera played, its rhythm and beat were far more suitable for running than more modern music.

The rough bark of the tree felt good under her palm, and she moved her fingers slightly up and down loving the feeling of the hard outside bark against her skin. She felt hot and healthy and to be honest a bit horny. If Mathew hadn't left for work when she got back, she might try and re-ignite the spark that had been missing from his eyes for the past few months.

She knew it was something to do with the business he ran, but like everyone in lots of places, things were hard right now. She was feeling quite flush at the moment, having sold not one, but two of her paintings after an exhibition at a private gallery in Knightsbridge.

Maybe she and Mathew could take a break and head back to her home on the coast of the Tyrrhenian Sea, a lovely place called Amantea. It was the ideal place to kick back and take stock of their lives at a much more sedate pace.

She exited the park and waited at the crossing for the green man to appear before jogging off again past people off to work in the exhaust fume smelling streets. She entered the code on the gates to their eight-floored exclusive apartment block and passed a large white van next to the entrance hall.

Frank on the desk had his back turned to the monitor, or he might have shouted out a quick word of warning. In the end he only saw her once she was in one of the four lifts and heading up to the top floor, where her bright day would come to a sudden end.

Catherina popped the earplugs out, pulled her iPod from her waistband and fished out her door key, kept in the long sweatband that covered her left forearm. She didn't need it. The door to 8C was wide open and there were men inside and raised voices.

"'Scuse me, love." a short thickset shaven-headed man said, going past her in the long hallway, carrying a large cardboard box in his arms. She watched bemused at the bomber-jacketed man headed for the lifts and she hurried into the large living area to find a scene of utter chaos.

Another man, a clone of the one who had passed her in her hall, was unscrewing the large 40" television from the white stucco wall of their luxurious apartment while Mathew stood toe-to-toe with a third man in his late fifties. Her boyfriend was hurling obscenities, while the shorter older man was replying in a firm but calmer voice.

"Calm down, sir, you've seen the paperwork. Just let us get on with our job, please."

"Fuck your fucking paperwork. I want you out of here or I'm calling the police."

"Which is your choice, me old son, but pointless. We are official bailiffs with all the proper paperwork, with all the I's doted and the T's crossed."

"Mathew?" (Which sounded like Matt-chew because of her accent) Catherina asked confused, "What is happening here?"

"Shit, Cat, not now, all right?"

"I think you better tell the lady what's going on, mate, before we take her stuff as well."

"Do relationship counselling on the fucking side, do we?"

"Yeah mate." The older, much tougher man closed the distance between him and the younger man to inches. "But unlike this job, I don't charge for it."

The bailiff saw the twitch in Matt's eye and knew the younger man was weighing up the idea of trying to punch his lights out.

"Don't even think about it, son. Blood is real hard to get out of these cream carpets."

Mathew looked into the man's steely grey eyes and flinched inwardly, as if a shiver of cowardice had run down his spine.

"Mathew darling, tell me why these men are taking our things away?" Catherina pulled at her belittled boyfriend's arm, but he shrugged it off, making her own hand fly up into her face with a smack.

Not used to not being in charge, like he was, or had been of his debt-ridden firm, Mathew Reynolds ashamedly went red and stomped off to the bathroom and locked himself in. Safe knowing that there was not much of value here to take apart from Catherina's expensive beauty products.

"You got a right charmer there," the bailiff stated, lowering his clipboard as Catherina began to cry. "Don't cry, love, it's not your fault that your other half has gone bust owning hundreds of thousands of pounds. I'm sorry, but we have an official letter signed and dated, I'm afraid, to seize all assets, properties and personal items of any value belonging to one Mathew Ian Reynolds."

Catherina looked up at the man, who now had a kinder edge to his wide face. She wiped at her tear stained cheeks.

"What can we do?"

"Find a friend or relative to take you in. You can stay here for tonight. We'll leave the mattress, but the flat has been repossessed by the building society. You better be gone by ten am tomorrow. Sorry, it's the best I can do, I'm afraid."

"But we have had no warning. Surely this all takes a lot of

time. Do we not have more time to pay?"

"Your fellas had three months' notice to pay, love. Better take that up with him." The older man turned, as another younger man with a full set of wild ginger hair exited the spare room, carrying two of Catherina's paintings.

"What shall I wrap these in, guv?"

"No, wait, those painting I did with my own hands. They belong to me not Mathew." Catherina rushed over and pointed to a dark signature at the bottom-right of the painting.

"There's other painting and paint and brushes in that room, Jammer?" the older and obviously in charge bailiff asked his younger colleague.

"Yeah, loads of painting stuff and some only half done."

"Put 'em back and leave that room alone, okay?"

"*Grazie*, thank you so much. Those paintings are my life."

"You go and sit in your artist's room. We won't take any of your clothes and we have the key to Mister Reynolds's Porsche already. It's not personal. We have a job to do that's all."

Catherina nodded and went into the spare room that acted as her study, carrying back her paintings. She leaned them against the wall and went to close the door, just in time to see them lift up the sofa and carry it away. She closed the door with tears of anger in her eyes. Why hadn't Mathew said anything to her. Why had he left it to get so bad?

His cocky arrogance and good looks were what had first attracted him to her. His confidence rubbed off on her and she had painted some of her best pieces in the last three years. There seemed nothing he could not do or try his hand at, except one thing maybe, admit defeat.

Catherina sat on the stool in front of her easel and looked out across the sites of London and wondered what the hell would happen to them now.

CHAPTER THREE

Angela Pratchett normally reveled in her walks with Meisha, her cocker-spaniel bitch, but not today. Not even the warmth of the sun on her skin could let her drift back to the beaches of Scarborough, where she was born. Even that little thought, which usually brought up fond memories of Noel and his little quips, stirred nothing in her today. She was comfortably numb, on autopilot, walking the dog in Woodhouse Copse rather than the larger Leggett Woods or the park on the south side of Hedge End.

Something was terribly wrong in Hill House, their larger five-bedroom modern home, built on the slopes of Hanger Hill, in the second most desirable road in Hedge End.

She focused for a while on her surroundings. Meisha was off wagging her tail in the undergrowth, foraging and sniffing and peeing everywhere, because she knew this wasn't home and she could. Angela found she was at the centre of the long thin strip of trees, where the canopy of leaves and branches above opened up to let the full force of the morning rays fall upon her ebony face. She managed a half grin, wondering what Tobago was like now, for she had not been back for half a century, not since marrying Noel. He had been a junior member of the British High Commission in Trinidad then and they had met while she served drinks at a local government function on Tobago.

It had been love at first sight and even though their worlds were thousands of miles apart, they married they next year and moved to Hedge End, not far from where Noel had been born, in Weybridge. Noel had saved her from a life of menial work and she had not lifted a finger, apart from keeping a tidy home for him, ever since. He had never wanted children and she, house proud and teased as a child, wasn't too fussed either.

"Meisha, come on?"

She called over to her dog, who came running from around a large tree with a lady's shoe fixed between her jaws and an eager happy look on her face.

"Meisha honey, whatever have you got there?"

The bitch stopped before her mistress, dropped the high-heeled and quite new looking shoe at Angela's feet, and sat up on hind-legs and wagged her tail with proud delight.

Angela picked up the shoe by the stiletto heel and tossed it into the nearest bush, which sent Meisha pelting after it, thinking it was a new kind of game.

Angela Pratchett, formally Baptiste, was walking back the way she came down the natural path of leaf mold and thinking of the emails on Noel's PC, when Meisha turned up again panting, the shoe in her tiny mouth again.

"Naughty girl. Leave, leave it," Angela warned, her voice increasing in resonated menace.

Meisha had heard that tone of voice before, normally after gin fuelled dinner parties and the morning afters, where she usually didn't get a walk and was shoved un-ceremonially into the garden to do her business.

Angela picked up and threw the shoe harder this time, far into a patch of stinging nettles and gave her dog a stern warning not to fetch it again. In fact, she put Meisha's collar on again and headed back towards the southern entrance to the copse, by the main road that led halfway down the hill to her plush abode. A house that she would claim at least half of in the divorce courts when she confronted her husband of twenty-five years, on his return from work in Whitehall tonight.

The pictures of Noel and another younger man emailed to his account she had found by digging hard, fuelled by woman's intuition and tale-tale signs of a possible affair. She hoped to find nothing, expected to find evidence of an affair with a younger woman, but a man, not even her comfy life in leafy Surrey could let her take that lying down.

Maybe she would return to Tobago. With the money from a possible divorce she could buy a veritable Caribbean palace to live in and hire some fit young men to clean her pool. Noel had not cleaned her particular pool for a long time and now she knew why. She and Meisha exited the copse and headed for home, leaving the late Hannah Browning's expensive shoe hidden in a nettle patch, twenty yards from where it had originally been dropped.

CHAPTER FOUR

Lucy Gaskell walked out the door marked "staff only beyond this point," patted down her blue work shirt and cast her eyes around the empty shoe-shop she had worked in forever it seemed and sighed, seeing nothing had changed since Saturday. The stock was the same, her work colleagues and underlings, including the tired old glass displays and the frontage that really needed sprucing up.

She marched forward, past those shoes, the ones that she could easily kill a person for, with a sniff from her small upturned nose at the black leather and her eyes melted on the sleek Italian design. Some girl, probably seven or more years younger than her and taller and probably thinner, had bought a pair on Saturday with cash, using fifty-pound notes. Two hundred quid on a pair of shoes without a blink of her fake eye-lashed eyes or having to add up in her head if she could have a pair of expensive shoes or pay her half of the mortgage this month.

She exhaled, pushed a stray strand of her mousey-blonde hair back of her left ear, tied back into a pony tail at the back and headed for the window display. It was as bored and tired looking as she was and Lucy counted at least five dead bluebottles and one wasp lined up by the large frontage of the shop display.

She ordered the Polish new girl, Anna or something, to brush away the dead insects and the dust. Not that she had anything against the Polish, just that Anna was skinnier than her and had a huge bust. Lucy headed back to the rear of the shop as it was devoid of customers and hid away with a coffee in the stock room, putting matching pairs of shoes back into boxes, where the spotty Saturday boys and girls had just thrown them on the *can't be bothered to sort pile*. It was a task normally beneath her, but she didn't fancy facing the teenage gymslip mums today, not when her belly was empty of child. She wanted a baby so much, even more than a wedding or a fortnight in Tuscany she always badgered Simon for, and at the moment none of the three seemed that likely.

She sipped her coffee, put shoes into boxes and hoped not for the last time for a lottery win this Wednesday, Friday or Saturday.

CHAPTER FIVE

Catherina Di Marco had locked the spare room door from inside and wedged a chair up against the handle for good measure. Her fiery Italian blood had seen her go from stunned shocked silence, then into a simmer, now a boiling pot of hate, which she wished to direct at Matt.

Yet the artist part of the mind had told her to paint and paint she did, in oils, nearly ripping the white edged canvass with the stroke of her palette knife and cuts of her short-bristled brushes. She attacked the canvass without much thought or knowing what was going to come out. She just let her anger fuel the passion and something different from anything she had ever painted before appeared before her.

When Matt's timid raps came on the door, she finally left her zone and stepped back to look at what she had created, using mostly hues of green. The rectangular edges of the canvass had no paint on them, except for spits and splashes from the energy of its creation. It started oval in shape, with an outside tunnel of laurel and other green foliage, then entwined and seemed to spin up and around as she looked at it. Deeper into the picture and the green tunnel the colours melded into crimson and clarets and finally blacks. It shouted symbolism at her, vaginal in appearance and concept. Yet at its centre, caught in the reds, were two black cast shadows, like two children holding hands, at the pictures core. If her mother had been here she would have laughed and told her to hurry up and make some bambinos.

"Cat?"

The sheepish words from her lover and financial betrayer came quietly from the other side of the studio door. "Cat, let me in. I want to explain. I have to explain."

Catherina put down her paints and wiped her hands, which were splattered all over with green and red pinpricks of paint. Her rage at Mathew had somehow abated and a feeling of calm serenity had taken hold of her. She stared at the painting, her tongue nervously licking at the top of her lip. Catherina had been caught up and swept away by her painting before, but not like this. She had no idea what dark reaches of her Id this creation had sprung from.

Putting down her cloth, with her anger controlled, she turned with purposeful pursed lips, prepared to hear her lover's explanations. An hour earlier, she felt like throwing him off the balcony of their luxury apartment.

"Cat, open the fucking door. We have to talk."

Mathew rested his head on the door to the spare bedroom and pounded at the door with the soft bottom of his fist. He had really screwed up his life this time, and he knew he had to act fast or risk losing the only asset he had left, Catherina.

The sudden opening of the door made him rear backwards, his legs going from leaning to, shit-we-have-to-stand in milliseconds. He wavered like a drunk, taking a step back to stop himself from falling over like a tit.

Catherina stood before him, silent, a broody unreadable look on her beautiful Italian face. He saw from her blouse and hands that she had been painting and some green tinged work of art showed half-hidden behind her.

"I'm so sorry, Cat, I should have told you and now it's too late. I've lost everything, the car, the flat and the business." Mathew was laid bare now. He could not bullshit himself out of this situation. He had to give her the whole ugly truth and then just hope.

"Get me a glass of wine, if we have any left, then you will sit down and tell me everything from the start, like you should have months ago, you fucking idiota."

Catherina walked within a centimetre of him and stood by the window. Mathew gulped. This would be the hardest pitch he had ever made and the fact that she wasn't hitting him or shouting made him a . bit afraid.

He found one half-empty bottle of red that the bailiffs hadn't bothered to take, and the champagne glasses Catherina hid away in her handbag from her first gallery display. She was still standing tall and elegant against the London skyline, looking down at the cars and people going about their daily lives in the great multicultural city of London.

He gulped again and moved to her left-hand side and offered her a glass of the red.

She turned in a flash and sent a star-blinding slap across his left cheek that caused him to staggered and spill half the wine over his hand and onto the white shag pile carpet. Shock turned to rage and then quickly to remorse as he saw the tears and sadness in her brown eyes.

"That is for earlier, you prick!"

"I deserved that and much more. Hit me again if you like," he offered, "except not the face again, maybe, or the family jewels. I'm quite attached to them."

"You spilt the wine. Look at these carpets. Those stains will never come out."

"Bit academic after tomorrow really, as we are being evicted, hun."

Mathew looked from the carpet to his girlfriend, his left ear and cheek still ringing from the smack she had given him. A slight sniff of a grin flicked across her face and Mathew quickly pointed at her lips.

"Least I can still make you smile."

"You fucking stupid bastard."

"I accept all those things, but my parents would quip at the bastard comment."

Catherina grinned again in spite of herself, and took the wine glass from his wet hand and poured it in a line away from her, ruining the carpet even more. "I bloody hated this carpet anyway. Always it gets dirty too quickly."

"Look, I love you, Cat, and I know I've gone and fucked up everything, but give me a chance to make it right. You're the only thing I have left now," Mathew pleaded, his wine stained hand reaching forward to rub her bare forearm.

"If you want me and us to continue, you better start from the beginnings. How did you get into this mess, Mathew, and where are we going to sleep tomorrow night?"

Mathew Reynolds downed the remains of his wine in one gulp and threw his glass across the carpet. Then he recounted every little detail of the fall of his business, a familiar tale of bad unpaid debts, mortgages, loans and downturns and share prices that was scarier than any tale M.R. James ever told.

CHAPTER SIX

Mrs Puck wandered down her pea shingle drive, admiring the rows of yellow, white and orange daffodils she had planted in rows, which lined either side of the path to her front gate.

The air was fresh and the sun not quite warm enough, but later at around eleven, she would don her straw hat and gardening gloves and tidy up the weeds and self-seeding vegetation that had popped up around the base of some of the daff stems. Her immediate task now seemed less meaningful and more menial as she trudged, loving the crunching sound the path made under her shoes.

As she got closer to the tall holly hedge that towered over the low wall that marked the boundary of her drive she glimpsed through the lower and sparser parts of the hedge the trouser legs of a man standing on the pavement on the other side.

She spotted her blue recycling bin, with her food caddy on top near the edge of the five-bar swing gate and the hedge. On reaching the gate she pulled up the iron catch and pulled it slowly inwards, leaving a gap wide enough for her to retrieve her bins with minimum effort. She was still a little wheezy from the chest infection that had clung to her forty-nine-year-old lungs after three weeks and was only just abating. She rounded the bins to see a familiar man dressed in a long beige Mac, who stood with his back to her hedge, watching the comings and goings across the road.

"Back again, are we?"

The black and grey bearded man, only a year older than

her, turned and recognition turned his expression from patient concentration to polite annoyance.

"Mrs Puck, a pleasure as always to see you," the man replied, his hands still thrust in the pockets of his Mac, only turning his body at the hip.

"Just can't stay away, can you?" she continued, her voice not the most welcoming.

"I seem to be drawn to the place still, like it's unfinished business for some reason," he replied, but she wasn't sure if he was talking to her or the four winds or maybe even his god.

"I thought they sent you off to some carminative catholicon retreat to cure your addictions," she stated bluntly, with a twist of smile, enjoying the early morning sparring, that she had missed so much.

"I've missed you too, Rose." He returned her thin smile. "You must be so glad now, no bells to unset your sensitive pagan ears on a Sunday morning. I better warn Reverend Brown now. I'm sure he will be next."

"Father Carmichael—can I still call you that or are you priests without a church just called Mister—it's been a pleasure as always. Would you like to pop in for a spot of tea? I'm sure I have some gin or sherry somewhere to give it the kick you like."

Mrs Puck saw the flash of unholy anger in the eyes of the former priest of St Barnabus' Catholic Church and smiled inwardly. This was going to be a great day, as the daffs had signaled on her walk up the drive. She no longer felt the chill, and the tightness of her chest was eased by her words to her old and defeated adversary.

"You really are an evil old deluded haggard, aren't you, Mrs Puck?" Father Carmichael spat back, his brown eyes forced into slits as a truck with piles of sand trundled past, letting swirls of its contents loose over the pavements.

"How very ungodly of you, Mister Carmichael. Now please move along the pavement a bit. You're making the place look rather untidy." Mrs Puck turned to collect her bins, then stopped and turned half round to add. "Oh, and take any empties with you. The bin men have already been today."

Father Carmichael did not lower himself to reply. He just

thrust his hands deeper into his pockets and moved past her hedge and stopped just on the edge of her boundary wall. He heard her chuckle to herself and tried his damndest to turn the other cheek, but it was hard when he had lost everything that made him the man he was, or used to be.

A white van slowed as it neared him, then indicated and waited for two cars to pass before it parked outside the wooden fence that had been erected by the builders around his former church. After dwindling attendance, which were low to begin with, in this ungodly part of Surrey, the twenty-year campaign of hatred from Mrs Puck, the pagan across the road, and finally his drink problem, the powers that be had sold the church to redevelopers. Alcohol had solved all his problems in the end. It dulled the pain and gave the Bishop excellent ammunition to close the place.

It would have been better to have pulled the church down, but it was a listed building and now it was being turned into luxurious flats for the ungodly rich. Its gothic gargoyles seemed to mock him today, half-hidden by rising scaffolding, like he had let them down. He knew he had. The ever relentless Mrs Puck, the ever lowering of the holy trinity in everyone's daily lives had driven him and the Catholic Church from the area. Football, popstars, the internet and apathy were the new gods now. Other religions gained ground, but not in Hedge End. Older things like the hag Puck believed in were, he felt, always in the shadows at the edge of this town.

May Day and the winter and summer solstices were long traditionally celebrated here, but by Muslim, Sheik, Christian and Buddhist alike. It was all a bit of old cultural family fun. Surrey, he had learned, was the last county to recognise Christianity, and he was sure Hedge End had been the last place in the county to do so with great reluctance. Even in other places nearby the old religions had died out completely, but here they remained strong and he had no idea why. It made him fearful, and he craved the warm numbness of booze again, but losing the church was like a final straw somehow. He just knew the church was now an empty shell and the goodness of god was no longer inside, the bodies in the graveyard exhumed and moved to another place. He wondered without him and without the church, what would replace it. Nothing good, he assumed.

He wondered again if the knowing dread in his mind was the booze demon or the onslaught of some degenerate brain wasting disease that comes with old age. Father Carmichael took a last glance at his old church, thrust his fists deeper into his pockets and crossed the road, so as to walk near it again and skirt Mrs Puck's house. He walked past the boards and down to where London Road met Woodhouse Road and crossed over, passing the hawthorn hedge that had given the village its name. Most of it was gone now, dug up when the railways came or to put in more housing. A small bit remained here, a bit lined Bates Road and the longest part still ran down a part of Hanger Hill, dividing the copse there from the main road.

He crossed over the road heading over the railway bridge where London Road turned into the Woking Road and turned left to trudge down Station Lane and back to the railway station on the rise of Hanger Hill. He resisted the huge urge to head into town and visit one of the many pubs there and made for the trains and a trip back to the retreat his religion had dumped him in four months ago.

CHAPTER SEVEN

"This does not help our situation much, does it, Mister Ragazzo?" Catherina stated, lying across his chest on the crumpled sheets of their mattress, which looked very lonely on the floor of their rather empty bedroom.

"No, but it was needed, a pleasant distraction, like a comma in our shitty day." Mathew curled her hair in his fingers, staring up at the bare ceiling, where even the lampshade had vanished. "And tomorrow night we'll be sleeping in cardboard and drinking Tenant's Extra out of brown paper bags."

"I really don't know what you are on about sometimes, but we must think, darling, we must plan." She sat up on her elbow, the white sheets drifting down her lithe body, causing Mathew to stare at her dark brown nipples and rounded breasts with renewed interest.

"Right, a plan." He sucked on his teeth. Planning was his forte. "We need to get out of here, so we need to hire a van, something like a Luton van to take the mattress and what's left of our stuff, but you'll have to sort that, Cat."

"I am a capable woman, but why do I have to hire a dirty man's van?" Catherina rested on her slender right arm, all of her taut torso showing to great effect.

"Because you used to drive tractors and trucks on your uncle's farm back in the old country, 'cos I remember you telling me, and because all my credit cards have been maxed out cancelled by the banks for non-payment."

"How the mighty have felled." She smirked with a haughty air. He was sure she had royal blood in her somewhere.

"So, you sort the wheels and I'll pop and see Ted and sponge a few boxes off him to pack our stuff. See, plan coming along nicely, eh?" He reached his left hand from behind his head and tickled her ribcage.

"Hmmn, but my darling, where will we go in this van of ours?" She showed too much teeth, which detracted from her beauty, and put the long fingernail of her left forefinger into his belly button and wiggled it around. Mathew let out a rather girly cry and twisted out of range, his back showing to her,

"Get off." He turned over on his front, giving him distance from her probing fingers.

"Well?"

She cocked her head to the right as she spoke and he knew from her action that his next answer better be a good one, or she would quickly get annoyed and shout at him in her loud ear-piercing voice.

"I'll give the Colonel a call?"

Mathew blew out a long breath and his eyes met hers. She knew what that entailed.

"It is really that bad? When was the last time you spoke?"

"Great Uncle Jim's funeral, two odd years ago and we didn't speak then, we kind of shouted at each other and got into a fist-fight."

Mathew gave her one of his idiotic grins, but even he knew it was going to be a long shot.

"Maybe I will get two of those bags for sleeping outdoors maybe, huh, when I get the van?" Catherina shook her head and turned her body to sweep her legs from under the sheet and off the low mattress. Mathew watched her in silence as she went around collecting and putting on her strewn clothes. Watching her put on her bra was of always of interest to the technical side of his brain, but it wouldn't help him with his pleading call to his father.

"Good luck, huni," She kissed his cheek and headed for the door of their apartment.

"You not staying for moral support, then?"

"No," she replied, opening the front door. "The *I-tie Bint* thinks your father is a prick."

"Okay," he stated to the back of the closed door and wondered if there was anywhere else he could try before his Serving Army Officer father, who had called Catherina his *I-tie Bint* to their faces when they first met.

He exhaled again, reached for the landline phone and dialed his father's house from memory. Mrs Portis, the housekeeper, answered and was glad to hear his voice, but his father was at work at MOD Main Building in Whitehall today and she gave him the contact number. By now all the nerve he had to make the first call had ebbed away and only desperation made him punch in the MOD number.

"Reynolds MR7?" came the brisk and resonant voice of the career soldier as the ringing stopped after four peels in Matt's ear.

"It's Matt?"

"Who?" was the unexpected reply.

"Matt, your son, remember?"

"Mathew. Hmm, what do you want? I'm rather up to my eyeballs in it at the moment." The Colonel's voice wasn't cold. That would require some sort of emotion. It was like he was talking to one of his ruddy squaddies, but that had always been the problem between them.

"Look, there is no easy way of saying this, but I'm on my uppers at the moment and the business in a spot of trouble and I need a place to stay, well, for me and Catherina to stay." Mathew was not sure if he hated the Colonel or himself more for having to beg the stuffed shirt.

"Bit old for officer's training now, aren't you? What are you going to do?"

"I was wondering if we could stay at the Grange for a while. You only stay there weekends. We could stay out of each other's way, if you prefer."

"Oh, you want me to billet you and your little I-tie Bint at my expense, eh, rent free, I suppose, drinking my best porter and Mrs Portis at your beck and call. Think again, lad. We crossed that bridge and used incendiaries on it two years ago. Your mess, you fucking sort. Might make a man of you yet." Mathew could almost taste the contempt coming down the phone. He had forgotten that the Colonel never forgets those who trespass against him.

"I shouldn't have expected you to give a toss about me. If you see me on the street sleeping rough, you'd probably piss on me."

"You're such a disappointing wimp, Mathew, just like your mother. Try and be a man for a change. Anyway, you could always stay at your Great Uncle Jim's place. He left you the place for some soft in the head reason."

"What do you mean?"

"Well, if you had stuck around for five minutes or kept in contact, you would have learned he left his house in Hedge End to you in his will. My solicitors, Rardin and Keene, have all the details. Now I have a meeting with the Brigadier in five so off you go."

"Why didn't y-" The line went dead at his father's end, making the rest of his sentence redundant. "You cunting stuck-up old twat!"

Mathew put down the phone and went back to the bedroom, the mattress being the only place he could sit down in his apartment now. Why was his old man so much like hard work and so cold towards him? Then he sniffed, because he hadn't wanted to follow in his father's and older brother's footsteps into the army and Sandhurst.

Thinking of Tim brought a defeated tear to his left eye. Tim had followed his father into the infantry and where did it get him, apart from blown to tiny bits near Basra six years ago. He knew his father loved the military gravestone of Captain Timothy Reynolds more than his remaining living son. His brother had always done his duty, always done what Father had said, but where had it got him apart from dead?

Mathew used both sets of fingers to scratch the crown of his hair, trying to recall the number or address for his father's solicitors. Then something sprang to mind and he headed into the spare bedroom and was glad to see Cat's silver laptop on the floor recharging. He headed over to open it and get the information he needed off the internet. He wondered what state his great uncle's house might be in after two years without any occupants. It was a shithole when he used to stay there during the summers back from boarding school, when his father was serving overseas.

Tim never liked it, but Mathew loved the place as it backed right onto a set of woods, where his imagination could run wild. He had proper friends there, not like the boarding school fair weather alliances that he had made. Great Uncle Jim had been something wild and different to his military and boarding school upbringing and the black sheep of the family. Jim had never failed him as a surrogate father figure and even in death he seemed to be looking over him.

"Thanks," Mathew whispered and looked out the curtain-less windows of his bedroom, up at the clouds that had now gathered and covered the skies of London.

CHAPTER EIGHT

"Youse coming down the pub at lunchtime Tony?" asked Geoff the Geordie, as his unimaginative workmates referred to him.

"Sounds good, mate, if I can ever get this thing shifted," replied Tony McGann as he worked away in the crypts of the old church his firm were renovating into flats. Four new sets of water and sewerage pipes had to be laid into the foundations for the four different flats. Outside, the trenches had been dug and the pipes laid, but down in the colder by five degrees crypts something was blocking his progress.

Under the old wall foundations where the pipes would go through, something lay beneath. something buried under the foundations, something that wasn't in the architects' plans and so, pissing Tony off.

"What youse got down there then, canny lad?" Geoff asked, going down onto all fours to see what Tony had discovered. The flagstones lay up against the wall nearby and a sloping excavation lay going down under the braced church walls above. Right slap-bang where the pipes should come in was the top edges of an old stone block.

"Dunno, but it's about three feet wide and deep and it's in the bloody way."

Tony pulled his head back and leaned his body against the side of the pit to let Geoff shine a torch down at it.

"Maybe it's one of those time-capsules things?"

"Could be, mate, but it's different from the stone above. Kind of blue-ish and rock hard."

"Let me have a go."

Geoff got into the pit as Tony clambered out, glad to have the space to stretch his aching back. The Geordie picked up a trowel from the flagstones in level with his head and used it to loosen the dirt and rubble around the stone to get and outline of how big it was. It was revealed to be a near perfect square of the blue stone, which must have been chiseled square many hundreds of years ago.

"If we dig a space around it we could put straps around the thing and pull it out from the other side using a tractor like," Geoff suggested, taking off his hard hat and wiping his bare forearm across his sweaty brow and hair.

"And that might bring the whole north wall down on top of us." Tony pulled up his sleeve and his watch told him it was a quarter to twelve. His dream of a pub lunch was diminishing. "Don't think we have much choice here, mate. We'll have to leave it in Jackos's capable hands or we'll never get down the boozer in time."

"He's gonna love this," Geoff laughed and reached a hand up to his friend.

Tony grabbed his mate's forearm and pulled him from the ever-growing excavation and shook his head. No, the site manager would not be pleased at all.

"What the fuck is that?" Jacko asked, taking off his hardhat and running his fingers through his thinning black hair. He stood between Geoff and Tony, his hardhat now held to his hip. They were already behind schedule due to vandalism of the diggers and someone stealing their tools from a locked up shed on site. This with the developers breathing hard down his neck was the last thing he needed.

"Must weigh twenty hundredweight if it's a ton," Tony added, knowing it would make his boss feel even more stressed.

"Two ton maybe?" Geoff added with a raised eyebrow.

"Look, we don't have time to piss about. Dig out either side and above and brace the church wall, then get a jack-hammer to the bloody thing before a local council inspector sends in the archaeologists to shut us down for four months, okay?"

"Okay, we'll dig it out now and then have a crack at it after lunch," Tony replied, brushing some dirt from his sleeve.

"As long as it's cleared by today I don't give a shit, Tone." Jacko put his hardhat back on and left the crypts grumbling to himself and rubbing at a pain in his left abdomen. He was pretty sure he was getting an ulcer from all this stress.

The two builders cleared away as much of the earth and rubble they could in twenty-five minutes, then cleaned themselves up to head for the pub. The Highway's Head was only a few minutes' walk up the London Road and normally slow during the day and welcomed the influx of customers from the church site with open arms and a blind eye to the usual dress codes. The money they spent in one lunchtime could pay for the cleaners to come in every afternoon before the night sessions for a month.

Tony and Geoff were back clearing the block by five to two that afternoon, with beer and pie and chips inside them. Normally they would have asked for more help, but only two men could fit down the pit at once at the best of times. They cleared as much of the space around the block's top and side as they could and braced a small steel girder above it and under the church walls, with two poles of each side holding it in position. Geoff then chipped out a guide hole to the depth of three inches to stop the jack-hammer jumping around. Tony put the business end of the jack-hammer into the hole, set halfway down the centre of the blue block. What they wanted was a nice four way split that they could break down into smaller parts and lift out from under the braced wall above. It also gave them a perfect hole for the pipes to be laid through, with the girder support keeping the church walls from the new piping.

Tony turned on the jack-hammer and both he and Geoff were glad of the ear-defenders they both wore, for the noise in the enclosed crypt was deafening. The heavy tool did its work and sunk lower into the blue hard block, until there came a crack and a split shot down from the hole right to the base of the block.

Tony pulled the jack-hammer out and onto the dirt below to examine the crack when a silvery liquid oozed out of the crack at the base of the blue block and form a round pool in the dirt like someone had spilt a pot of silver paint on the floor.

"What the fuck is that?" Geoff asked from above the pit as more of the silver thick liquid flowed out of the cracked blue block and neared Tony's boots. He let the jack-hammer fall onto the side of the slope and scrambled back out of the pit, with Geoff's arms under his armpits.

"It might be toxic. Let's go get the gaffer," Tony said through his dust mask and pulling Geoff with him towards the stone steps of the crypt.

"What the fuck is with you poofs today?" Jacko the site manager asked, grabbing a face mask for himself and following the two men back down to the crypts. The two men were proper strong blokes and never this jumpy before. Maybe it was the cold crypt that put them on edge at bit. Jacko put on his mask and so did his two men and they followed him down into the crypt area again.

No more of the silver liquid had come out since they left and in fact some of it around the outer ring of the pool had seeped into the earth. Jacko picked up the dirty trowel Tony had been using and lent into the pit scoop some of the viscous silver liquid. It stayed on the towel, but when the site manager turned the tool slightly to the left, it ran off in beads back down into the small pool below.

"What is it?" Geoff asked from a safe distance behind his boss.

"Its bloody mercury, I think, which makes it hazardous to touch, which means we need a special crew to come in and clear it all away and we are fucked for another day."

Jacko shook his head, threw the trowel into the pit and turned and headed for the steps out of the crypts.

"What you going to do now, Jacko" Tony asked after his retreating boss.

"Make some calls. You two better tape this crypt off as out of bounds until the specialists get here," was their boss's gruff reply.

They two builders did as their boss had told them and then to their delight found out they had no more work and could slope off early today.

Inside the pit, down in the now dark crypts, the mercury seeped slowly away into the soil beneath the church. More cracks appeared unseen by human eyes in the blue stone and fell away in great and then smaller chunks. When the hazard waste team turned up the next day, all signs of the mercury were gone apart from a silver round scum mark in the earth and the blue block that had remained intact for two millennia was now a pile of rubble.

CHAPTER NINE

Mrs Puck was in her conservatory on the back of her largish house, partaking of a sandwich when a cold shiver ran down her spine like a team of headless horsemen were galloping over her future burial site.

She immediately stood, leaving her half-eaten homemade bread, with cheese inside and headed for the side conservatory doors. Outside in the April afternoon sun, it was still not-quite T-shirt weather, but just in her thin white blouse, long woolen skirt and with her knitted shawl left behind, she headed off across the lawn.

This was her formal garden and not a bad size to boot, given the pokey pocket-handkerchief sized squares of grass new-builds today got. She headed on to the centre where an ivy-covered door lay mostly hidden and where a wall long since lost to greenery and a Virginia creeper bisected the garden. Pulled out a large black key from her cleavage, tied around her neck with a leather thong, and tugged it over her head, unsettling her reading glasses from her left ear a little. She traced the line of her hair back over her ear, pushing the arm of her glasses down to make contact with her left ear again and then reached out to insert the key in the keyhole hidden behind daggling dark green flora.

The key made a solid rattle in the old lock and made a heavy lunking sound as it turned, which always satisfied Rose Puck deep down in her core. She pushed the door inwards and entered the garden that no one else saw. A rise and a high wall separated it from view of her only neighbours and on the other side of the wall was the long slope down to the railway lines below.

A small orchard of cherry trees ran down the centre of the long second secret garden and the borders and fences were lined by five old sycamore trees on each side. The cherry trees led on in a line for sixty feet or so and then met a ring of poplar trees that curved round each side to form a circle around a large and ancient wide oak in its epicentre.

The rough brown, almost grey bark of the tall oak, half covered in creeping mistletoe, split at the base and two great roots that had pierced the dry earth around it stuck out like two splayed legs. Between the root-legs and from the ground upwards was a dark rent in the trunk, like an inverted V. Mrs Puck bent down in front of the oak, offered up a whispered prayer and crawled on her hands and knees into the darkness, until she was fully inside. The boughs, branches and twigs of the tree gave a sudden and windless vibration and then were still.

CHAPTER TEN

Simon Hay sat nursing his fourth tea of the day. Not that he was a tea-pot, but it got him away from his over-loaded desk and down to the tea-point at the end of the corridor for five minutes.

Janice, his immediate boss, and her boss, the *Lecherous Keith*, as he was known by most of the office, had both dumped piles of new work onto his old work, burying him in reports, paperwork and invoices. Now he sat always having to remember to sip at his tea now and again before it got cold, trying to put his workload into priority piles. This alone had taken him twenty minutes and all this was without checking his 100 plus email in-tray on his PC. Not for the last time that day, he wished Sarah wasn't off sick and Jim wasn't on that training course all week.

Simon was amazed he had the wits about him to do this much after the incident at lunchtime. He had popped out of his office to escape the deluge of work and try and clear his head in the park where he sometimes ate his lunch. Putting aside his working class anti-snobbery and bought his overpriced drink, sandwich and crisps from one of those French titled sandwich shop chains in a vain attempt to cheer himself out of his gloom. The food was great, but the price overinflated for what it was, and the crisps always tasted a bit soft to him.

He sat in the London park, with a few tourists and joggers about. Luckily the benches were mostly free, even though the sun shone brightly through the canopy of the tree line path above onto his bench, where he thankfully sat alone. He was trying to think of his book and the history of Hedge End where he lived, but work problems kept butting into his thoughts, making him even more depressed. He was minding his own business, watching the grey squirrels bound across the grass, when an old vagrant suddenly appeared from a tree next to the litter bin to the left of his bench and shuffled over to stand right over Simon.

Simon nearly gagged at the smell of the grey bearded old tramp, which was a mixture of vinegar, pepper and urine, fermented over the winter with cold sweat and a dash of Special Brew. With a disgusted look on his face and trying to breathe out of his mouth, Simon looked up from the tramp's too small and ripped trainers, up his body to look at the wild-eyed man's dirty face.

"Excuse me, please, I've got to get back to work," he asked politely, knowing standing up would bring him within a centimetre of the funky fellow of the streets.

"Fast as Quicksilver, he runs and flies, bird in the hand until one will die," said the tramp in a faint Cornish accent, his eyes not looking at Simon at all, but past the trees to the pond beyond.

"Look, you smelly old git, I've got to get back to my shitty office job, okay?" Simon got halfway to standing before the tramp gripped his left shoulder and pushed him back down on the bench with great strength.

"Look, you Hagrid-resembling retard, let me up."

The tramp did not reply, not in words anyway. He reached into his old dirty black torn Mac and pulled from a deep pocket a small shiny bird, like a small thrush or starling.

"For you, hay man." The tramp smiled at the offering he pushed towards the startled younger man, showing blackened teeth and many gaps.

"Get away from me with that."

Simon stood up fast and pushed the old tramp back, causing the vagabond to fall backwards onto the path. He lost his grip and released the young bird, which squawked once and flew off over the tree tops to safety. Simon turned and hurried away from the tramp, who just lay where he had been shoved and bellowed, "Sharpen your axe, woodcutter, and be on Jack's side of the hedge."

"Did you just deck that old tramp?"

Simon looked round to see three schoolboys of about thirteen years of age staring at him open-mouthed, with their ties loose and trainer laces untied.

"He attacked me," Simon replied, moving past the boys back down the path towards work.

"Kewl," the boys all cooed and ran at the prone tramp to each give the old man a vicious kick to the ribs before running off the other way out of the park, laughing.

Simon just shook his head in bewildered shock and hurried from the park before any wandering police came along or were called. He got back to the office early from lunch, headed straight for the nearest men's toilets and locked himself in a cubicle, where he sat on the seat. He was shaking, he realised. Coming slap bang into the seedier and violent and mad flip side of London life was always something he failed to cope with. He just wondered about the old tramp and why he called him the hay man. Did he know his name was Hay, or was it one of those weird coincidences that you never get to the bottom of?

His last fight was at secondary school, with a kid two years younger, and he only won that by accidentally elbowing the kid in the nose, causing it to bleed, while he had been trying to defend himself. A win was a win, his friend Michael had said to him that day and the mini-legend was born that Simon Hay was not to be messed with. Well, at Hedge End Secondary School, anyway.

He got up after ten minutes, pushed the silver button on the top of the loo just in case anyone else was using the toilets and saw him leaving without flushing. He headed off to make a cup of tea and then went and unlocked his office and sat down to hopefully lose himself in meaningless work.

By five o'clock he had pinged off some holding replies, answered five of the worse priority emails, transferred one chunk of work to accounts, knowing he would get it back, but by the time the internal post delivered it, we wouldn't see if again before tomorrow lunchtime. With no staff and no help, he gave up for the day and headed for the exit, saying goodnight to the guard, Steve, who was on duty today. Simon was always polite to the security staff, because you never knew in a crisis they might save you before the bitch from floor 4, who never even registered their existence.

He was back in time to catch the 17:25 train back to Hedge End and pretended to doze off as so not to have make eye-contact with any of his fellow crammed-in passengers. The sun was getting lower as he walked through the copse coming down from the station on top of Hanger Hill and he breathed in and felt relaxed for the first time since he passed through this morning.

A half chewed lady's shoe, with a broken heel lay on the path before him and with a run up he booted it high into the air to land with a small crash and rustle in a gorse bush to the left of the path. With a chuffed smirk he headed off for home down the hill, hoping Lucy had not cooked dinner and he could order up a comforting chicken curry takeaway instead.

CHAPTER ELEVEN

Geoff Hoonan wasn't feeling very well. In fact, he felt like death warmed over, which made him chuckle through the heart burn he was feeling as he walked past a graveyard on the way back to his flat.

He had earlier met up with a couple of Geordie ex-pats mates and headed into Surbiton from his place in Berrylands to go for a meal and a pint or twelve. Geoff had been fine at first, his usual life and soul of the party, in the half-price for cash curry house they ate in first. He felt a little flushed during the later stages of the meal, but put that down to the warm restaurant and the lamb vindaloo he was wolfing down.

They adjourned to a pub up the main shopping street opposite a supermarket and found a nice corner to sink some pints of Youngs and chat about the plight of Newcastle United. Within an hour, Geoff's heartburn had increased and his face felt both hot and cold at the same time.

"You alreet man? You look as white as a ghoust."

Geoff looked at his mate Bazza and blinked. "I feel like shite."

"What's wrong wi' ya?" asked his other friend, Paul, putting down his pint on the stained pub table.

"I dunnos, I'm all hot like and got wicked terrible heartburn. Maybes I'm coming down with flu or something?"

Geoff looked at his half-drunk pint and his belly flipped over and it was like he was staring at a glass of pure poison and not his favourite beverage.

"Youse better get off home, Geoff." Bazza nodded and drank some more of his beer.

"You want me to call you a taxi?" Paul asked, pulling his mobile phone from his jacket pocket.

"Nahs, I'll walk. I feel as hot as hell. The fresh air will do me good. Must have been that curry, lads."

Geoff got up and exhaled for two seconds, then grabbed his coat, but did not put it on.

"Take care now," Paul said as Geoff waved listlessly and left the table.

"Give us a ring when ya better, mate," Bazza added as Geoff left the humid confines of the warm brightly lit pub.

"Lightweight," joked Paul, and Bazza laughed into his ale, causing bubbles to explode up into his nose.

The cold night's air seemed to have done the trick instantly for Geoff and he headed home. He had just got back to the Berrylands area when his heartburn returned with a vengeance and he developed a tick in his left eye that fluttered away like a newly pulled up set of blinds.

Geoff took a deep breath and stood up straight and realised he wasn't far from home now. He cut though a dark alleyway, with high wooden fences and overhanging trees, that would lead him past the church and graveyard only a stone's throw from his flat.

Pinpricks of dotted drizzle began to hit his flushed face, which felt good on his burning hot skin. The low wall of the raised graveyard was ahead now, and he crossed the quiet road in between dark parked cars to skirt the old wall boundary of the church to his three storey block of flats. He coughed loudly and found that it was suddenly difficult to stop, like some sort of whopping attack on his respiratory system.

When the coughs finally died away, he found he was next to the graveyard wall, bent over, his left hand on the top of the cold stones to steady himself. He had to get to his bed, maybe take a few aspirin and a bucket load of water too. The rain became harder, tapping here and there on the top of his head, and a sound like a creaking door made him straighten up and look over the raised wall and murky graveyard beyond. A dark leafless tree stood bent and gnarled, not more than five feet away from the low boundary wall, its branches creaking in the strengthening wind and rain. From its side another shadow detached itself from behind the wide trunk and headed towards Geoff.

It was dark and the nearest orange street light was back across the road, so Geoff had to squint through the darkness and rain at the advancing figure. There seemed to be something wrong with the person. It had the shape of a man, but shuffled towards him.

Must be worse for wear, Geoff thought *and gone for a slash behind the old tree.* He had done it a couple of times himself over the years since he moved down south after his divorce.

The man, because it looked like a man from where Geoff stood below on the pavement, continued his slow walk toward him and the edge of the raised graveyard, his right arm rising and reaching out to swish at pelting rain before him.

"Youse okay, mate?" Geoff managed to croak out and then tried to clear the knot in his throat, which seemed to tighten for no reason and slowing his breathing to shallow husks. The man came into view now and the arc of the orange glow of the street lamp finally illuminated the shambling figure to Geoff.

No words or even screams would escape his tightening windpipe as he saw the staggering man. Half his face was eaten away, showing dirty bones and skull beneath. One eyeball was missing and the thing had no nose, just the short empty black cavities, where worms lived and burrowed into its dead brain. It wore the ragged remains of a burial suit, the left sleeve of the jacket gone and through the tattered remains of its dirty covered once white shirt, a skeletal arm dangled, with only flaps of skin like yellowed parchment in places. It ended at the wrist and no hand of any type remained at all.

Geoff heard a low moan and realised it was he who was making the sound. Behind the first walking corpse, two other shadowy figures shuffled across the wet graveyard towards him. He turned and to his horror saw that two more dead people, a near skeletal man and jaundiced skinned girl, were crossing the road to cut him off from the way he came

With a burning sensation in his solar plexus, he turned and

ran towards his block of flats, the heavy rain stinging his wide, terrified eyes.

The dead followed him at their own pace.

He finally made it to the shared glass doors of his block of flats, pulled opened the door and raced up the concrete step to the top walkway. He turned left and ran past only one other door to get to his. Geoff risked a look over the balcony and saw the dead people from the graveyard were still slowly following him, soaked in the rain. No one else was about. He fumbled his keys from his coat pocket and stabbed the key toward the lock, only to drop it with trembling hands onto the rain speckled doorstep. Glad of the round walkway lamps, he picked the keys up again, just in time to see the first walking corpse crest the last step of the concrete stairwell and set foot on the same walkway as him. This time the key did go into the lock and he barged into his dark one bedroom flat and turned to lock and double bolt his front door.

Dead people almost immediately appeared at the frosted glass, filling it with corpse faces. Geoff backed away down his hallway to his living room area. The whole flat was in darkness, but the curtains were drawn and some ambient light from other flats filtered through. All Geoff could hear was the scraping and clawing at his front door and the rain on his window panes and the thump of his heart trying to escape his chest.

Only now did Geoff scream, for through the shattered front door the corpses walked, like ghosts. And so many of them. A hoard of the walking dead filled his hall and walked towards him with jerking movements until there was no way of escape.

Geoff turned and ran just before the skin stripped bony fingers could reach for him and crashed through one of his tall rectangular side windows. His chest pain now gone, he fell head first on the side of the shed where the bins were kept and broke his neck with a sickening crack. His limp body fell onto the wet path below and lay still. Above in his flat, it was as silent and empty as the grave.

CHAPTER TWELVE

Mrs Puck was mildly shocked to find it was dark when she crawled out of the hole in the base of the ancient oak tree in her secret rear garden. Her nails were half-broken and laden with crescent lines of brown dirt. Her blouse was torn and ripped in places and she had scratches on the inside of her thighs and her glasses were now missing. She walked stiffly back down her grove of cherry trees, winching at the deep pain between her legs.

The pain would be worth it in the end, because she knew that barriers were falling and the old confined ones would soon be loosed from their long exile.

CHAPTER THIRTEEN

Tony McGann awoke with a start and found himself alone on the sitting room sofa, the television showing a rainy East London football pitch in the second half of an evening kick-off. His post dinner nap had done him no good at all. His vision was blurry, his brain ached like a headache was coming on and he had a chronic attack of acid indigestion.

It was still relatively early and the kids must have already been in bed, when the door opened and his wife, Julie, walked in. "Hard day, love?"

"Yeah, but I'm not feeling too well, as well," Tony replied, using his hands to move up to a straighter sitting position from his slouched nap.

"Ain't got that flu bug, have you? Half of Jamie's class are down with it." Julie McGann walked across the room past her husband, heading for the door that led to the kitchen. "Do you fancy a brew?"

"Yes please, and a couple of headache pills."

"Blimey, you taking paracetamol? You must be suffering."

"Pills, Julie," he stated in a curt, suddenly angry voice that was not like him at all.

"Okay, keep your hair on, love." Shaking her head and muttering under her breath, she headed into the kitchen to put the kettle on and fetch a couple of pills from her bag on the marble counter next to the mug stand.

Tony fumbled for the TV remote, turned down the sound of the football match and put his head in his hands. His feet seemed to be spinning around, even though he knew he was perfectly stationary. He closed his blue eyes and rubbed his temples, trying to get any feeling of normality back into his mind. He cautiously opened his eyes and was relieved to see the world had stopped spinning. In the kitchen the kettle rattled on its stand as it boiled, sounding overly loud to Tony. He looked up to find the football match was no long showing. Instead he saw two naked men, one dirty and painted with weird blue squiggles, the other tanned and oiled, hacking at each other with short swords. Blood flew from deep wounds until suddenly the blue man lopped off the other's arm at the elbow, sending it flying towards the TV screen. Blood seemed to hit the inside of the screen and Tony hiccupped down a little of his own sick. He put the television onto stand-by and turned as he heard his wife re-enter the sitting room.

Yet it wasn't his wife. Yes, it had her shape and clothes but her pretty head had been replaced by a blue-ish purple tinted turnip of a face. Twigs seemed to be sticking out of the top of her bald round head and her nose was a long snout. He recognised the face. It was Raggety, a woodland troll that used to scare the wits out of him as a young boy, from the *Rupert the Bear* TV series.

"I've not forgotten you, Anthony," croaked the voice of the Raggety creature.

"Get away from me!" Tony cried. He leapt up and ran wailing for his life up the stairs.

Out of Stuart's room a twiggy-fied boy in pyjamas emerged. "What's going on, Dad?"

"What have you done with my family?"

"Tony, what is it?" His wife's voice called from the stairs as he backed up to the bathroom door in mystified revulsion. Yet it wasn't his wife that came into view onto the landing. It was the Raggety twig version of her again. A twig version replacement of Jamie came out of his room, rubbing at black large pupils of fried egg sized eyes.

"Get away from me,"

Tony rushed forward, pushed the Raggety figure dressed in his wife's clothes out of the way and belted down the stairs, taking two at a time, opened the front door and fled into the drizzling night. He ran down the front garden path, his socks crunching on the pebbled drive, past his car as his Raggety replacement family came into view at the lit open front doorway. In fact, he was looking back at them when he ran into the road and the dark blue Mondeo hit him, sending him flying back to land onto the bonnet of his wife's silver Fiesta.

CHAPTER FOURTEEN

Kat got back with a white van about six. Dusk was settling over the city, with red and orange tinted clouds reflected off the windscreen as she parked in their empty designated parking bay, minus Matt's sports car.

She turned off the engine and the radio set to Kiss FM died with the motor, but she did not climb out. She rubbed her cheeks, running her hands over her temples and through her long dark hair with a hint of tonged curl to it. She rested her elbows on the large steering wheel and put her chin in her hands, leaning forward to gaze up at the balcony of the luxury apartment they were about to be evicted from. She felt sad that Mathew had lied to her and sad that she would lose the best studio she ever painted in. The early morning light streamed into the place and it was always a joy to create there.

The painting she had done with rage and boiling passion today, her last at the apartment, was a mystery to her. She normally had some inkling of what she was going to paint, but the greens and reds of the painting and the macabre images were not her usual style at all. She knew she could not stay in the van indefinitely, yet as long as she stayed in the cigarette smelling van she could pretend none of today's events after her jog had happened. She wondered where they would be sleeping tomorrow night. She would rather book a reasonably priced hotel in the outskirts of Greater London than stay with Mathew's odious father.

She saw the light of the living room flick on and knew she had to go up and face Mathew again and the hard realities of life. Taking the keys from the ignition, she hopped out, reaching back to gather her jacket from the passenger seat, slammed the door closed and locked it with a press of the key-fob. She shook her hair back and walked tall like her papa had taught her after her mother's death at the age of only 31 of bowel cancer and headed for the entrance.

"I've got the van. Took me much time because of the type of van you want," Catherina called out, tossing the van keys onto the kitchen counter and then draping her jacket over one of the breakfast bar stools. The living room light was on, but no sound or illumination came from any of the other ajar doors in the apartment. "Matt-chew?"

"In here," he called in a low voice from the bedroom and she crossed the wine stained carpet to the bedroom door with a few long strides.

She pushed it open, noticing more flecks of green paint on her fingers. Mathew had clearly been hard at work since she had left over two hours ago. An old duvet cover was wedged into the curtain rail of the curtain-less window. Small tea-light candles covered the surfaces of the empty bedside cabinets and the cheap IKEA dressing table she loved and Mathew hated with a passion.

She smiled, a dimple pressing in her left cheek as she looked down at her boyfriend lying on the mattress with a bottle of Moet opened in one hand and two champagne flutes in the other. On one of his laid out white work shirts were plastic dishes with cold meats, cheese, grapes and other such fare.

"Just imagine a bit of Verdi playing in the background," he said, patting the space next to him on the low mattress. "They took my iPod and dock, you see, but I could hum it if you wished."

Catherina gave him one of her probing stares to see if he was for real and slowly walked around the mattress to her normal side of the bed. She stopped at the edge of the mattress, looking down at him and he smiled that deal clinching grin and rose up to offer her some red grapes.

"So what is going on here, Matt, are you a Roman Emperor now?"

"What, like old Julius Caesar?"

"I was thinking of more like Nero, playing with his fiddle while Rome burns down around him."

"Well, Rome has already burnt down and this is all the vittles I could muster for our last banquet here, or two person orgy if you prefer."

"You have champagne, Matt-chew. This is no time for celebration. We are up to our necks in the shit, as you like to say." Catherina put her balled fists on her slender hips to emphasize her growing displeasure. Mathew noticed the signs and patted the empty space beside him once more.

"Sit down. Beautiful. I know it hasn't been our greatest day ever, but I have a glimmer of good news."

Catherina stayed standing for a few seconds, pouting in thought and then gave him the benefit of the doubt and sat on the low mattress. "Go on?"

"I bit the bullet, excuse the military pun, and phoned the Colonel. And there's good news and bad news." Mathew held out a glass to her, which she took with tentative suspicion.

"No, no, tell me we are not having to stay with your shit of a father."

"The bad news is that he still hates my guts and never wants to see me again, which if also great news if you look at it, and we won't be staying at his place."

"Thank the holy father. What is this good news then?"

"Ah." Mathew paused to pour half a bubbly glass of champagne into each of their flutes. "He informed me in his inimitable way, that my great uncle left me his house in Hedge End when he died."

"So we have a place to go tomorrow, then?"

"We do indeed have a place to go tomorrow. I phoned the family solicitors and we can pop there first thing in the morning to collect the keys, sign a few papers and then bugger off to Hedge End and Jim's old place."

Mathew clinked his glass against hers and they both took a relieved sip of bubbly.

"You came through for us. I like," she purred and lent forward to kiss him with Moet tasting lips.

"No, I rescued us from a situation that I should never have gotten you into. No more secrets after this. If things are going tits-up I will tell you everything, my love." Mathew lowered his flute to rest on the bed and they kissed again, longer and with added passion.

She smiled at him, that thin long smile that told him that she loved him and trusted him once more. Catherina reached down and picked an olive from a jar and popped it in his mouth with a giggle. He chewed and dangled the grapes above her lips for her to bite one off.

"So we okay now?" he asked after spitting the olive stone into his palm, cooling down the moment a little.

"I love you, Matt, and your business was getting in the way of that love lately. Maybe this is a good thing, a new start for us."

"This is why I love you so much, and at least now that I'm out of a job we can spend so much more time together."

"What will we do for money? I have my money saved from the sales of my paintings."

"And that's your hard earned cash Cat. I'll get by, don't you worry. Can't keep this boy down for long."

"I have one question though."

"What's that?"

"Where the hell is Hedges End?"

Mathew nearly spat out his champagne as laughter burst from his lips and it was so infectious that Catherina joined in with him and a great stone weight of worry left them for a while.

CHAPTER FIFTEEN

"This is just what the doctor ordered," Lucy said, stuffing a mixture of chicken Korma, Pilau rice and Bombay Aloo into her mouth in one go.

Simon nodded, his cheeks full of Cobra beer he had just swigged from the table next to the sofa. Both sat with trays on their legs eating the takeaway Simon had ordered when he got home, finding no dinner on and Lucy cat-napping, her work gear still on the sofa. *Emmerdale* was on the television as they scoffed their respective curries.

"Good day at work then, hun?" Simon asked between nan bread and his prawn madras.

"The shits, Si. I'm nearly thirty, working as an assistant manageress in the same shoe store that I worked in when I left school and old Polish Pollyanna or whatever her name is cheeses me off no end."

"Hmmn, sounds as good as mine, except I got accosted in the park at lunchtime by a piss-smelling old vagrant," he said in a considered tone.

"Oh, did the nasty tramp try to touch you up in the bushes again?" Lucy mocked, a wide Korma grin on her perked up face.

"Not that again. I was a kid at the time. He said he had a puppy to show me. I was a naive young virgin then. How was I to know he was going to flop his syphilitic penis into my palm. Wish I hadn't told you about that now. I'm mentally scarred up here, you know." Simon tapped his temple several times and then reached for his lager again.

"Naïve? You were fourteen."

"Thirteen and a half actually, and I still get night terrors from it."

"Baby."

"I'm so glad I bought you this vast banquet of Indian's finest foods and saved you from another night of slavery in the kitchen, just so I could be mocked in my own home."

"That's not fair. I mock you outside the home and in public places and besides the Raj is hardly the most exotic of restaurants. The bloke who owns it is from Corby, not Calcutta."

"Hmmn," Simon snorted through his nose and fixed his eyes on the latest young soap star of the Dales that caught his eye and would make it onto his PC background for a while.

"Don't get the hump. The food was a nice idea, thanks." Lucy leaned over and kissed his left cheek, leaving a mixture of lipstick and korma sauce behind.

"Yes well, I should think so too. Now a bit of bedroom appreciation later wouldn't go amiss." He turned his eyes towards her without moving his head.

"If you want sex, Simon, just ask. Go on say the word. It won't bite." She pointed a potato laden fork at him. "But I might." She winked.

"I prefer to refer to the coital act of joining as love-making. It's not my fault I have a delicate and sensitive soul." Simon waved his arms about in an airy-fairy way to belabour his point.

"Oh, my cousin Kerry has invited us two up to Kingston to see her beau DJ on Friday night."

"Hang on a minute, what has that to do with the S-word? And beau, really, Miss Gaskell, you'll be saying that with have to hang with her homies next in da hood."

"Least my musical tastes are not still stuck in the mid-nineties, boy!"

"Can't make it Friday night. I have a previous engagement, Miss Gaskell," he continued in his plumy upper-crust voice, which used to make her laugh when they were first courting as he called it.

"Like what, a Dungeons & Dragons night with James or train spotting with Daddy?"

"Your mocking tones wound me. No, I'm popping round

Mrs Puck's place. She's helping me research the ancient history of Hedge End."

Simon scrapped up some rice and stuffed the hot food into his mouth and waited for the onslaught.

"You'd rather go see weird Mrs Fuck and talk about old shit than go to a club with me?"

"It's been arranged for ages and it's on the calendar in the kitchen."

"Well, I hope she fucks you, because your chances tonight, Si, are less than nil." With that she got up holding her tray and stormed off to throw the rest in the bin.

"What about sex, then? See, I can say it, Luce. Lucy, come on, hun. Bollocks." He gave up just as the end credits for *Emmerdale* began to play. Putting down his tray on the sofa Simon headed into the kitchen to see what was wrong with Lucy and if he could grovel enough to make her feel better.

He found her viciously scraping the remains of her curry into the food recycling caddy, which sat on the work surface by the back door of their two bedroom terraced house.

"Hey, what's the matter, Goose?" he asked, using his pet name for her.

"You."

"Well, I'll take that as a given, really, but anything in particular this time?"

"I'm nearly thirty- "

"Twenty-eight, come-on- "

"Do not interrupt me." Lucy turned. The dull blade of her knife, from an old set bought a Woolies ages ago, was pointing at his general direction and she was crying.

"Okay." He raised his hand in surrender, causing her to look down at the brandished knife and lob it into the kitchen sink to rattle about.

"You work in London, Si. Least you can look at all those saddo comic shops and book shops you love. I'm still in the same job I did when I was in Mrs McHenry's class at Hanger Hill Secondary School. I'm tired of it and tired of this pokey little two up and two down. I want more and I want a baby so much."

Simon's face hardened as she shouted all her woes at him and he was fucking sick that it was all his fault once again.

"Well great, everything is my bloody fault, eh? Why don't you get off your arse and get a better job? Why is it always me who has to work my bollocks off for another promotion in a job I hate to my very core? And we've talked about kids. You know the plan is to wait until you're thirty." He for once did not back down or slope off to end arguments, because he hated confrontation. This time as with the baby issue he stood his ground again and argued back.

"Fuck the plan, Simon. I want a baby and you ain't even man enough to manage that!"

"Pardon?"

His voice was calm now. All the anger was shocked from his voice, and the rage sunk to his belly and burned, waiting like a volcano to erupt again.

"Just go away, Simon," she replied. The anger had left her voice and been replaced by sheepish avoidance.

"No," he said, grabbing her arm and turning her away from the back door to look at him face to face. "What did you mean I'm not man enough to manage that? Manage what, Lucy?"

"Nothing, I was just hitting out, that's all."

Her tear filled eyes avoided his, and he knew she was lying.

"You're lying. What's going on?"

Lucy felt his grip get tighter on her arm and she was a little afraid of her boyfriend for the first time ever. She knew she had pushed a little too far this time, that even the timid history buff and book loving gentle Simon had his limits.

"I…" She paused to look up at him, making eye contact for the first time in the argument. "I stopped taking the pill eight months ago."

He let her arm go now and backed up two steps. He felt betrayed and humiliated both at once and the convergence of these feeling made him turn and leave the bright kitchen and walk out into the hall. Lucy followed him and watched in remorse as he kicked on his work shoes and reached for his jacket from the wall coat rack.

"Simon, don't be silly, let's talk this through, okay? I'm sorry."

Simon wrenched on his coat and turned to point a finger an inch from the bridge of her nose, the volcano boiling up inside his chest wanting to shout every expletive under the sun at her. But in the end he just snarled, grabbed his door keys and left the house.

He heard a wailed, long "sorry" as he walked up the tiny front garden and out onto the dark street and pounded off toward Green Street. He paused outside The Green Man pub, his local, but carried on, knowing if Lucy came after him she would look there first. Instead he walked down the length of the street to a crossroads, and on the corner with Bates Road was The Cricketers, so he went in there. It was a much lesser pub than the Green Man and the ales were very commercial, so he ordered a pint of Tetleys' and made for a dark un-crowded corner to wallow in his bitter thoughts.

CHAPTER SIXTEEN

Mike Jackson sat in the flush dining room of his large four bedroom house and waited. His lovely wife of thirty-six years, Doreen, was in the adjoining kitchen plating up his dinner of lamb chops, mashed potatoes, carrots, peas and cabbage, and he waited contentedly, his knife and fork in his big hands itching to tuck in. He looked around at the gentle decorations of the dining room and the paintings, all originals of various country landscapes, of home and their many holidays abroad. This was a house that he had built from nothing and it had taken ten long years of scrimping, saving and living in a cavern on site until he had finished his luxury house, build to the design he had done.

The land he had bought first in a posh area of Long Ditton, and it had taken him two years to sort out the plan and get the money together to lay the foundations. Then every Saturday he would work from 7am to 7pm to build his dream home on his own. Sometimes he got some of the men from the various sites he worked on to add their expertise, like chippies and sparks, but most of it he had done. Five years it had been finished and now on the weekends apart from tending the garden he and Doreen could relax. They never had been blessed with kids, but they enjoyed each other's company so much it didn't matter. Doreen had done all the interior decorating while he worked and supervised plumbers and decorators if required. Now they had a palace of their own with interior pool, a snooker and cinema room and every modern luxury known to man.

Jacko put down his knife and reached over to drink his wine, but found that his glass was empty. His throat felt somewhat dry and he had been drinking and pissing like a bitch since he got home from work. His hand extended for the white wine but he only managed to miss the bottle and knock it over onto the table cloth.

"Bugger." He grabbed the bottle and righted it, but a large chug of wine was quickly seeping and spreading out on the table cloth and under the cork dinner mats that depicted scenes of Venice. "Reeny, I've split the bloody wine."

"Oh you clumsy sod," she said as she appeared at the dining room door carrying two hot dinner plates, held with a tea towel that they had bought back from Lisbon. She put the heated plates down on their respective mats and used the tea towel to mop up the spilt wine.

"Sorry luv, I must be tired," Jacko said.

"Least it isn't red wine, Mick." She smiled at him and winked, reminding him of how he had spilt a large glass of red over the living room carpet the Christmas before as he struggled from the sofa to salute the Queen during her annual speech. "I need some kitchen roll to get all of this. You start your dinner."

Doreen left the tea towel scrunched and half wet from wine on the table and to get the kitchen roll the elephants used in those adverts. Meanwhile Jacko resisted the urge to tuck in. Doreen had cooked his dinner as she did every night. The least he could do was be a gentleman and wait for her.

He stared at the tea towel and frowned as he swore he saw it move a little. He leaned forward over his plate, feeling the steam from the gravy rise up to warm his chin. Then he flinched back as the tea towel jumped a little, leaving a small cave like opening facing him. Jacko gripped his eating utensils hard on the bone handles as first one leg and then several others of the arachnid family followed. He sat open mouthed in bewilderment as a fat bodied spider tip-toed out from under the cloth. Its many bulbous eyes seemed to stare right at him. The light from the chandelier above the table was reflected in each of its shining eyes.

Then it suddenly pounced, landing right on Jacko's large nose, its legs on his lips, teeth and pointing into his eyes. Jacko dropped his cutlery and flung himself backwards, to escape the large spider, but only tipped his dining room chair over.

Doreen came in to see her husband fall back in his chair and hit his head on the parquet flooring, knocking him senseless. She rushed forward, a wad of kitchen roll in her hands, and fell to the hard floor on her knees beside her beloved husband.

"Mike, speak to me! Come on, love," she begged his ashen face, but his eyes were screwed shut and his body did not move as she touched his chest. Always a practical doer of a woman, she put the wad of kitchen roll under his head, where a bloody bump was already forming, rushed over to the phone on the sideboard and dialed 999.

CHAPTER SEVENTEEN

Julie McGann was surprised to see Doreen Jackson rushing into A&E next to a trolley with her husband on it, a bandage on his head, but awake and screaming to high heaven to get the spiders off him.

She stood in the doorway of a little room for patients being treated, near the waiting room, reception and the accident and emergency cubicles used for treatment. Her sister Janet was home looking after the boys. She lived nearby and was there before the ambulance arrived. After Julie's hysterical call on her mobile.

Her husband's boss was pushed through some plastic doors into the treatment and triage area and a nurse stopped Doreen Jackson from pushing her way after him.

"Reeny?"

Doreen Jackson spun round at the sound of her name and saw Tony's wife, Julie, standing by the door to the family room.

"Julie?"

The hugged each other, their eyes red from tears, trembling with delayed shock.

"What's wrong with Jacko?"

"I dunno. He fell off his head, I mean chair and hit his head and was out cold. He woke up in the ambulance screaming his head off saying that spiders were crawling all over him."

"Tony went funny in the head tonight as well. He suddenly got up and told us to get away from him, then ran out and got hit by a car. He's broken an arm, leg and two ribs. The doctors say he should wake up, but at the moment but he's just getting worse."

"Oh Julie, what we going to do?" Doreen asked and hugged Julie again as a brown haired nurse approached them to take patient details from Doreen.

"His BP is low, he's tachycardic, but his heart is in fine working order. The drugs we've given him should make him better, but he's just started to get tremors in all his limbs, and his skin is cold and clammy to the touch." the young doctor explained to the on-call consultant, Mr Mannard.

"His skull shows no fractures, and his scans show no hematomas on the brain or any swelling. What do you suggest we do now?" the senior doctor asked in a haughty teaching tone.

"Repeat the test? Maybe he's suffering something viral?"

"Wrong, we speak to the patient's wife. Emergency medicine is sometimes more detective work than just fixing broken bones and writing pill prescriptions, my boy," Mister Mannard patted the younger doctor on the shoulder and headed out of the cubicle area to the family waiting room. His junior looked at the patient and hurried after the senior consultant.

"Mrs Jackson?" the consultant asked the two women sitting together in the family waiting room.

"How is he, doctor?" Doreen said, standing up.

"We're doing the best we can, Mrs Jackson, but your husband's condition is giving us a few anxious moments, as is your husband's condition, Mrs McGann." Mr Mannard looked past the upset Mrs Jackson, to Julie.

"What do you mean? Tony got hit by a car."

She too rose and stood next to Doreen and put her arm through hers in support.

"Yes, he was, and those injuries are mendable and non-life-threatening, but it's the pre and post incident symptoms that concern us. Erm, sorry, do you two know each other?" The consultant asked, a new train of investigative thought entering his disciplined mind.

"Yes, my Tony works with her husband for the same building firm." Julie nodded toward Doreen as she spoke.

"I see, and are they working on a site together at the moment?"

"Yes, an old church refit, turning it into luxury flats," Doreen replied.

"Have there been any problems at the site today or recently, gas leaks, erm, asbestos or any other hazardous materials or waste found?"

"Mike said that Tony and another guy called Geoff Hoonan had found some mercury in the crypt of the church and would have to get special people in tomorrow to clear it away."

"Mercury poisoning. That explains everything. Exposure can cause many different reactions, including coughing, impaired cognitive skills, tremors to the extremities, chest pains and in some occasions delirium, hallucinations and even suicidal tendencies." Mr Mannard clicked his fingers and turned to his junior.

"They'll be okay then?" Julie asked what Doreen was thinking.

"Yes, now we know what poisoned them, we can start them on the right treatment right away. Doctor Vaas, start them on a treatment of British Anti-Lewisite and N-acetyl-D-L-penicillamine."

The young doctor nodded and hurried off to get the right medication and check what dosage to administer.

"Now, if you excuse me, ladies, I have to help treat your husbands and make them right as rain again" Mr Mannard nodded to each with a little bow and headed out of the family room, pulling at his bow tie. He headed first to the admin reception to ask them to see if any other cases had been reported tonight and to check if they could get in touch with the third exposed builder, called Geoff Hoonan, to see if he had been admitted to this or any other hospital. Then he needed the emergency number for the Environment Agency, so they could shut that building site down until the mercury could be safely extracted.

CHAPTER EIGHTEEN

The blinding light of a new day poured through the gaps in and around the makeshift curtain that Mathew had used to cover most of the bedroom window. He had an erection and an aching need for the toilet, so he rolled off the low mattress and stood up, letting the warm morning sunlight play on his chest.

He padded off to the toilet and performed one of those awkward hunched over stiffy pisses that men had to deal with sometimes, his eyes on the bath/shower, wondering if he should have a slash in there before he left the place today. Maybe he'd do a big steaming dump and not flush, just to welcome the next set of occupants. He washed his hands, stared at his dour morning face and bed hair in the bathroom mirror and then with half-open eyes padded out into the kitchen.

Matt was shocked to see that it was only half-six and cursed that his body-clock was still on waking up for work time. He smiled lazily. He had no work to go to now, and the bailiffs had taken his alarm clock. Scratching his ball-sack without consciously thinking about it, he stared out over the skyline of London. The sun shot its rays over the grey buildings, giving them a golden look that the most squalid parts of the capital did not warrant. The haze of pollution was already there, giving a brown smudge to the misty concrete and brick horizon.

Up and awake now, he decided he wanted to be out of there before the bailiffs returned at ten. He rubbed at his sleep crusted eyes and padded his bare feet into the open plan kitchen area. Matt decided tea was the prime requisite of the day, so he filled up the kettle and put it on to boil.

He woke Catherina with a kiss, a cup of tea and a just in

date Penguin he found at the back of the empty cupboards. She looked up at him with the cutest half-asleep smile, and a surge of love, much like heartburn, hit him in the chest and throat area. He wasn't usually an emotional man, passionate yes, but living with the Colonel had taught him to hide that side of him. Only during his summers at Great Uncle Jimmy's was that side of him released, but those summers had ended over a decade ago.

"A girl could get used to this kind of service in the morning," Catherina purred in her morning voice, all gruff and rich like Golden syrup, as she sat up and leaned her back against the bedroom wall.

"It's what you deserve, my Italian princess, and when we get to Great Uncle Jimmy's place, I'll wake you up like this every morning, I promise."

"I will keep you to that."

"Do, because I need you and," he paused to inhale through his nose, "I haven't got a job to get up for."

"What are we going to do for money? You know I have plenty to get us by for a while."

"Well, I do have an emergency plan C."

"And what is that?"

"I'll tell you after this."

"After what?"

Mathew just smiled, put down her tea on the carpet beside the mattress and slipped over the duvet to join her.

"Capisco," she murmured, before his ardent kisses gave her mouth something better to do.

They showered, dressed and packed what remained of their stuff, mostly Catherina's' and put it in the boxes Mathew had gotten from the corner shop yesterday. Because of their early start, they had loaded the van up by a quarter past nine and were now in the empty white and cream apartment, going through every cupboard one last time to see if they had missed anything.

At last they were pretty sure everything they wanted was loaded in the Luton hire van, though some rubbish and crap they had stored away was strewn about the place. They stood on the balcony for the very last time, leaning on the metal and glass railing and looking out over the city.

"Are you going to miss it?"

He turned to look at her, pondering the question. "What, London and its foreclosing banks, wide-boys and backstabbing business bastards? A bit, but this place was only luxury because we lived in it. Otherwise it's just a jumped up, over-priced flat."

"Was that a yes or a no?" She frowned, drawing sharp lines next to her down-turned lips.

"Can't change the past, old Great Uncle Jimmy used to say. Just press on with the future."

"You really loved your Great Uncle Jimmy, eh?"

"Guess I did," he said and then stood up straight. "Come on, let's not waste any more time here. We have a new home and a new future to build together."

"That's more like the Mat-chew I know."

"Come on," he said, taking her hand and leading her back inside the apartment.

"You not going to close the balcony door?"

"Nah, fuck it."

"Time to go then," she said with one last look around their first home together.

"Oh, I just need to pop to the loo first."

CHAPTER NINETEEN

Simon sat by the dining table, a half drunk tea and crusts of toast on a crumb littered white plate before him. He was pulling on his work shoes when Lucy came downstairs still in her nightwear.

"Why didn't you wake me?" she asked, tying up her hair behind her as she entered the dining room.

"I didn't know if we were on speaking terms or not," Simon replied in a neutral voice.

"I messed up, I know. My ticking hormonal clock messed with my brain. I know I shouldn't have gone off the pill without telling you and I'm sorry about what I said last night." Lucy sat down on the chair next to him, failing to make eye contact as his were trained on his shoes.

Simon got up a few moments after she sat down, and took his cup and plate out into the kitchen without a word.

"Simon, come on, we have to talk about this."

"Look," he said, scratching his scalp, "I have to get in early to work. I've got a pile of work to get through today. We'll chat when I get home."

"Okay, I'll cook us something nice, steak n' kidney maybe." She followed him out into the hall where he tugged on his coat and picked up his small rucksack, which held his book, railcard and sandwiches.

"Okay," was all he gave her, and she watched him from the cold doorstep as he strode off heading for the railway station. It was very hard work for him to be so cruel to Lucy, but he needed time to think. He knew he would probably cave in to her baby demands and that nagging little voice in the back of his head would diminish even further, the one that said get out now, while you have no ties but the house.

Yes, he probably would give in, but for today at least he could think of other possibilities and other avenues of life and regain some semblance of being a real man and in charge of his own destiny.

Meanwhile at home, Lucy managed to get back into the warm living room before bursting into tears. She had never seen such a cold streak to Simon's side before and it hurt her deeply. Lucy called the shop and left a message on the answer phone, saying she had been throwing up all night and was going to be off sick today. She had never ever done this before, pulling a fake sickie, but she just could not face the shop today and the teen mums with their different fathered broods.

She ate a breakfast of chocolate, had a large milky coffee and curled up on the sofa to watch GMTV. She would watch *Dirty Dancing* on DVD later, and then cook Simon's favourite meal tonight. Maybe, and it was at present a maybe, she'd put on that tacky dirty underwear Simon had got her for Valentines' three years ago that had never left the confines of its box. Oh, she would turn Simon around to the baby idea, for she had many womanly weapons in her arsenal.

CHAPTER TWENTY

With her husband, Stephen, already out the door by half-seven, Sophia Browning went upstairs to do a job more difficult than when Jesus raised Lazarus from his tomb. She had to shake her wild teenage daughter from her pit. Hannah had not come home for dinner last night, but Sophia had lost count of the times her 18-year-old daughter had not joined her and her husband and youngest child, Luca, for meals. She hadn't come in as of half-ten, when she and her husband had headed off to bed, but this again was not unusual for party-girl Hannah.

Sophia knocked on her daughter's bedroom door, holding a cup of coffee in her hand. She knew the intrusion might not be welcome, but the caffeine would. Getting no answer, she went in anyway and was surprised to find the curtains already drawn and the bed made by her own hands had not been disturbed since she made it yesterday. The bed, so the deal went between mother and now grown child, was the only thing in the room Sophia Browning could or would touch. That's the way Mrs Browning liked it also, ever since she found the empty packaging for a butt plug in her then 17-year-old daughter's knickers drawer.

"What are you up to now, mia figlia?"

Sophia Browning shook her long brown curled locks, fished her mobile phone from her skirt pocket and dialed her wayward daughter's mobile number.

Simon Hay pulled his collar up. Even though the sun was up, a cold wind was gusting down Hanger Hill with a vengeance. He would be glad of two things today, to get into the cover of

Woodhouse Copse and to be going to work, where the mundane ever increasing pressures could dismiss any thoughts of the Lucy/baby conundrum. His mobile was off and even now his mood towards Lucy was wavering. He had put up a good show of resistance, but in the end he knew he would give in on the baby front.

Simon loved Lucy, but always thought that there was some spark of passion missing from their safe little world. He knew now after ten adult years that nothing better was likely to come along, and if he did would be brave enough to take a chance? He never did join his mate Tom on that Kibbutz, never had a threesome involving two hot girls, never wrote that comic with his arty friend Justin at college. What he would do was finish his book. He would offer himself marriage, kids and years of drudgery for his book and there he would pitch his flag in the dirt.

He looked up and found he was already half-way through the woods and had been thinking so hard, that even the tranquil surrounding of the place had not fully traveled from his senses to his brain. He always felt at home here and maybe his hard work would pay off enough to buy his dream place, Hill House, with its large back garden that backed onto the thin line of the woods that ran down behind all the houses on Hanger Hill Road and that bordered the railway lines.

Then he realised that he could hear the sound of a mobile phone ringing somewhere, just like the old landline telephones used to sound. He looked from one side of the fern covered path to the other and as he walked the sound of the ringing grew ever closer. He even checked his phone for reasons unknown. His ringtone was *Song 2*, by Blur at the moment and he knew it wasn't his mobile as the rings came from somewhere in the trees and green foliage.

Then it wasn't there anymore, just the rustle of the leaves in the wind and with a bemused shape to his lips he headed on along the path towards the train station.

Deep in the festering holes beneath the great oak's ancient roots a mobile phone lay in the stygian dark, smashed into pieces by an old branch that was as strong as stone, wielded by unseen inhuman hands and next to the hollowed out corpse of Hannah Browning.

CHAPTER TWENTY-ONE

Mrs Puck woke with a stiff pain in her inner workings and it took a long soak in the bath and antiseptic cream afterwards on the scratches on her legs before she felt anywhere near comfortable. Her chest infection had vanished overnight, as she knew it would after her visit to the grove at the rear of her house.

She stared at herself in the mirror of her bedroom. It was full length, and she was still pleased at what she saw for a woman her age on the cusp of the big five-o. Her over-ripe breasts were sagging a little, but with the support of a bra they still were an eye-popper. Her legs and thighs were still her best assets thanks to all the walking she did, for she did not own and could not drive such an air polluting thing as a car. She pulled at the lines that were forming at the edges of her mouth and eyes, thinking maybe she should have surgery done and then laughed at such a frivolous girly thought.

She pulled at her dark brown hair and noticed the roots needed doing again. She thought about letting her ever spreading grey hair show, but that would just give the locals more ammunition for the strange hermit witch rumours that were already flying about her. Mrs Puck didn't care what they thought, or their petty religions or prejudices towards her. She had her views and ways and they had theirs. She knew she was following the correct path and that just made them and their religions based on solid brick churches, wars and empire given convictions, more laughable to her.

She and few others knew the real truth and soon she was sure a tide of changing faith would soon spread out from this sleepy little Surrey town. She just hoped she was still alive to see it. Rose Puck parted her scratched thighs and pressed the two middle fingers of her right-hand inside herself and pushed until the pain inside turned to dull pleasure and a smile crossed her parted lips.

CHAPTER TWENTY-TWO

The van journey out of London was a nightmare, but they had the radio on and were still in quite a buoyant mood, even though the trip that should have only taken an hour and a quarter took nearly two and a half due to the crawling M25. The stop-off at Mathew's father's oily solicitors to collect the keys and deeds to the house had taken longer than expected. When they came off the motorway they stopped at a pub near Oxshott, a large old Tudor place near the woods.

They had soft drinks and ordered a couple of lunches as it was only twenty minutes to midday. They were not far from Hedge End and the sun still shone on them. It was jumper and not coat weather now.

Mathew was coming back from the men's toilets when he stopped by what he needed, a pay phone out of the sight of Catherina.

The phone was answered at the other end on the seventh ring, "Hello, Sprinkle's Farm, Tim speaking."

"Tim, me old farm muck spreader, it's me, Matt."

"'Ello mate, ain't heard from you for a while. Get it? Herd?"

"Your jokes don't get any better with age, Tim."

"What do you want anyway? I've got a fence to mend, mate."

"I need you to sell the herd and take a ten percent cut for your trouble," Mathew said, looking around to make sure no one was listening to him.

"Blimey, emergency plan zed, eh? Make it fifteen percent."

"Twelve."

"Deal. I'll sort something out by next week. Should net you around twenty-five grand, mate."

"Just what I need. Cash only, remember, Tim."

"Wouldn't want the fucking tax men to get wind for either of us. I'll ring you when it's done."

"I'll call you at the end of the week. I've broken my mobile and need to buy another one."

"Sweet as a nut, mate. Seeyas."

"Yeah and thanks for this, Tim. You're a real life saver."

"Of course," Tim replied, and the line went dead.

"You were gone a long time," Catherina noted as he sat down. The food had already arrived and she had not waited to tuck into her crayfish salad.

"Funny tummy," he replied, rubbing his midriff. He sat down to drink his Coke and tuck into his steak, chips and peas.

Finally, at around ten to two, Mathew drove the van down the London Road over the bridge, over the railway and back into a place that held many fond childhood memories. He went around the round-a-bout and down onto Hanger Hill Road, past woods on both sides at first. The high hedge on the left-hand side gave way to plush town houses while the woods on the left just continued to shadow them down the hill.

"Not far now," Mathew said over the chatter on the radio.

"Good, cos I need to pee."

"What, again? Oh bollocks, that was it," he cursed as an overgrown paved turn-off with overhanging elms trees flashed past on his right.

Catherina craned her neck to see a gloomy opening in a break in the woods, with a low brick boundary wall, diminish from view behind them. Up and across the road to the right was a small road, marked with a sign saying Wood End Lane. Mathew turned into that road, which led to some houses and flats. They had to go to the end to find a place to turn the van around.

"I'm glad you know where you are going." Catherine smirked at him and his huffy annoyed face, lined with concentration.

"Hmm," was his only reply as he signaled left back into Hanger Hill Road and waited for a sudden rush of traffic to go by.

At last there was a gap after a TNT lorry. He turned left and then quickly moved to the centre of the lines dividing the road and turned right into the estate of his late Great Uncle Jimmy. Low hanging elm branches bounced upon the top of the Luton van as he drove along a weed covered paved private road that went past another immensely tall elm and round in front of the large house. The road ended at a single garage separate from the house, which now stood forlorn, dark and empty, even on such a sunny day.

The busy road could not be seen now as trees and tall laurels gave the house on the cusp of Leggett Woods near total privacy. Both driver and passenger opened their doors and jumped out. Catherina had to come round the front of the van to see their new abode.

"Oh," was all Mathew could say.

"It is, as you English say, a bit of a shithole," Catherina commented and put her arm around Mathew's shoulder.

Great Uncle Jimmy's place had never been the tidiest, and that's why Mathew loved it. Years of enforced cleanliness to the point of cruel obsession from his army father had made summers at Hedge End a place to get scruffy, leave your room a mess and keep your pants on day after day if you so wished. Now after years of neglect and then no one living there, the woods had tried to take back the place.

Mathew counted at least six broken window panes, and ivy was so dense on the left-hand corner of the house that it half blocked one window and looked like it was creeping inside the house itself. The roof looked in okay shape, but the rose bushes, once small and tidy before the windows in long lost beds, had grown up to block out two sets of windows by the peeling painted brown front door.

"Nobody ever gets anything for free," he said as he patted Cat's behind and headed for the door.

The old brass lion door knocker hung down on an angle now, fixed by one lonely screw, and Mathew noticed that the bottom of the door seemed like it had been a little burnt on the outside. He fished the door keys that his father's creepy lawyers had handed over in the morning and unlocked the door, but it did not move.

It took a small shove with his shoulder to send the old weather warped door juddering inwards about a foot and then stop dead. A musty damp smell escaped the hall, like it had enough of the funk of the old place. Mathew looked down and saw a huge pile of letters, junk mail and free local newspapers were blocking the door from opening further.

He had to bend down and reach around the door to push and toss the paper debris back so they could open the door wide enough for both of them to squeeze in. The hall was even smaller than Mathew remembered, and it was dark and dingy for it had no light coming in apart from the half open front door. No light came down the stairs in front either, and a brown half-light existed permanently in the hall, stairs and landing above. Mathew moved in to let Cathernia follow him and tried the light switch on the wall. The light bulb in the dangling socket of the hall was smashed, but a covered light worked on the first floor landing when he tried the switch.

"At least we have electricity," he said, turning to face Catherina, but her frown and nose wrinkled in disgust at the smells it had to endure were not the spirit of adventure and hope he was looking for.

Two doors stood closed on either side of the hall. With a nod of understanding Catherina took the one on the right and Mathew the one on the left and pushed them open at the same time. Catherina on the whole had the luckier choice. Her door opened into a huge living room, not that you could tell from the lack of furniture. A tall impressive fireplace stood against the inner back wall, oddly placed to the left, while a door stood closed to the right along the same wall. Light came in through a smaller side window that had all its glass intact. The main large window was covered with overgrown rose bushes, which had at least kept any rain damage through broken panes to a minimum.

Mathew on the other hand had entered something of a Dickensian slop-house, filled with rotted sodden carpets, rat droppings and ivy that had invaded through the broken window panes and was running away up one wallpaper-rolled-down wall. He had to hold his nose because of the smell, which reminded him of the mushrooms and puffballs he and his brother used to find in the woods that backed onto Jimmy's back garden. Green slime seemed to cover the wooden window frames that woodlice had made their own, and half up the corner and bare plaster walls.

He moved swiftly to the door in the far wall, glad to escape. The room though had other ideas.

"Bloody fucking hell!"

Catherina heard the cry of shock just a second before the door she was trying to get through in the living room fell off its hinges with a bang that made her shriek and jump back a foot. She turned and hurried back through the hall to the room Mathew had entered. She found him before the other door of the slimy pungent room, his foot swallowed up to the ankle between two rotted floorboards.

"You okay?"

"Do I look okay?" he shouted back. "Be careful where you step, Cat."

Catherina gingerly walked up to his left side and held his waist as he extracted his ankle and shoe from underneath the rotten floor. "I think you better come this way with me, okay?"

"Safety in numbers. I think you are right."

Mathew tested his ankle and it was fine. The wood was so badly rotted that it did not even scratch his skin, and they made their way back to the living room and the fallen-in door. A dining room lay ahead and it still had a large table intact and a chair and a welsh dresser. This room had fared much better than the front-facing rooms of the old house. A connecting door lead to an outdated, but relatively intact kitchen devoid of any appliances. The gaps for them made the place look worse than it really was. One of the other two rooms on the ground floor was what they used to call the boiler room. It was still in good repair and had a wood or coal burning boiler, which used to heat the house and give hot water for baths. The other room was a small windowed library, with shelves still filled with dusty worm-eaten hardbacks on subjects that made little sense to either of them.

A large upstairs guest bedroom over the damp parlour room below was also damp from a fault on the corner brickwork somewhere, but it was the worst of the bedrooms. The master bedroom was damp, but just needed superficial repairs and a bit of decorating. A study area still had Great Uncle Jimmy's old desk in it, but his Admiralty chair was missing, all the drawers were locked, and no sign of a key could be found. The bathroom looked like it hadn't changed since Queen Victoria was a young monarch and was the abode of spiders.

The last room, apart from the downstairs loo and cellar, was the bedroom Mathew shared during holidays with his brother. He-Man wallpaper was still solidly fixed to the walls and the bunk bed still in good working order.

"So what do you want to do, find a cheap hotel nearby for tonight and come up with another plan?" Mathew asked.

Catherina moved into the bedroom and her fingers brushed some words that had been etched into the side of the wooden bunk bed about four feet up.

MR & SH BEST MATES FOREVER

"No, we will stay here. This is a part of your childhood, something I will never know of you, but being here and clearing it up will make up stronger, together."

She turned and her features showed strength greater than he could possibly manage and he was glad. Of all the things he had lost, he still had her.

"It's gonna take a shit-load of money to do this place up."

"You gotta better things to do, Matt-chew?"

"Hmmn, apparently not." He shook his head. "We better figure out what to do and where to put all our gear before it gets dark."

"We get the mattress up here and sleep here tonight. Most of the back rooms are not so bad."

"Okay, we'll both get the mattress out and our few boxes, then I'll drive down to the B&Q down the road and get some wood and nails and cleaning stuff. Oh and paint and floorboards. Anything else I missed, miss?"

"A cooker and refrigerator." She prodded him lightly in the chest.

"Glad the van doesn't have to be back until tomorrow, then," he said and they both went down the stairs and out to the waiting van.

CHAPTER TWENTY-THREE

By mid-afternoon Sophia Browning had exhausted all the numbers of Hannah's friends and a few ex-boyfriends (too many of these) and her first call to her daughter's place of work brought only questions of *where was she?* before she could ask them.

She rang her husband at his place of work half-crying with worry. "I'm going to phone the police, Steve."

"Wait until I get home, okay? I'll leave at four today," was his reply, his usual reply: wait and see how things pan out first.

"I'm worried about her, Steve," she sobbed. She had a mother's instinct that something was very wrong.

"Have you tried *her* yet?"

"Oh Steve, that was just a phase. She was the student and Hannah hasn't seen or mentioned her since she got the sack from college. She moved away, I'm sure of it."

"A phase. Our daughter has the morals of an alley cat. Sometimes you should take off those rose-tinted glasses you wear when it concerns Hannah."

"Well, thank-you for the help!" Sophia angrily turned off the phone and put it back hard in its cradle. She headed off to the living room dresser to find any recent photo of Hannah and head down the police station before Luca came home from school.

The phone rang just as she was pulling on her leather coat and scarf. She looked at the screen to see it was Stephen phoning. She snorted, ignored the ringing pleas of the telephone and headed out of the door up Church Lane past St. Peters' and the short distance to the High Street. She crossed at the pedestrian crossing next to Boots, the chemist, and walked up the concrete disabled walkway to the local police station.

CHAPTER TWENTY-FOUR

They had unpacked their things by three thirty, man-handled the mattress into his old room and opened the windows to air the whole house. Most of the boxes were in the drier downstairs rooms, like the dining room and library.

"Right." Mathew kissed her cheek. "I'm off to B&Q to get a shed load of stuff for the house."

"Okay," she smiled back. It was cold in the drafty house with the windows open in early spring, but knowing they would spend so much more time together warmed her heart.

Mathew got to the kitchen door before he pulled out his wallet and opened it. With an embarrassed grin on his handsome face he turned back to Catherina. She smiled not only because she knew what he was about to ask, but also because an old cobweb had floated down from the doorway to settle on his short black hair.

"I couldn't borrow your Visa card, could I? I only have a hundred and fifty quid on me and I need to buy a new mobile phone as well, just a cheap pay as you go one."

"D'accordo," she okayed in Italian and went over to the leather handbag on one of the kitchen worktops to fetch it for him. "You know my pin?"

"It's your birthday, isn't it?"

"Yes," she said, handing it over. "Don't forget, bin-liners and a bloody bin also, eh?"

"I'll be as quick as I can, okay?" He kissed her again and left her to her thoughts in the house by the woods.

"Ciao," she called after him. Then she laughed and shook her head. The grey cobweb was still in his hair and her wicked side had kept quiet about it.

She put down her handbag and headed over to the dirty but still usable Belfast sink. She turned the cold tap and was surprised that after three rattling vomits, clear water ran fast. Her hand moved to the hot tap, but only a trickle of brownish ice cold water flowed, however far she twisted. Still, they still had the kettle from the apartment. They could boil water and make tea or coffee to warm them, maybe cuppa-soups and pot noodles would be their staple dinners until they got a cooker.

Catherina shook her head, trying to forget about food before it made her hungry. She took an old newspaper they had gathered from the hall and wet two pages to try and clean the dirt, grime and spider webs from the kitchen windows, so she could look out onto the overgrown garden. She cleaned four panes, until they were as good as new and stared out into the back garden and Leggett woods beyond.

Catherina wondered how this quaint English wood got such an Italian sounding name. The Italian for wood was *legno*. Or maybe it had once belonged to someone called Leggett. She had a quick look outside, while the sun still shone. She unbolted the backdoor and turned the large key in a huge rectangular black lock, but still the door would not budge. In the end she gave up and had to go out the front door and around the side of the house to get to the garden.

The large lawn looked like only an old fashion scythe would be needed to cut it down to size, as it stood tall and over knee height. The red and black brick wall that circled the back and side of the house and grounds was tall and still in good shape, but could hardly be seen behind overgrown shrubs and low hanging tree branches. She beat a path through the tall grass, glad she was wearing boots and jeans today. The garden had a simple design, three side borders, now lost to wild and cultivated border plants, a large square lawn in the centre. Yet at the back Catherina found evidence that there was a stone path, glimpsed in places beneath the overgrowth that meandered this way and that sloping down to the back wall of the garden. She moved to her left and squinted through the ivy and Virginia creeper covered walls to just about see a wooden gate, almost hidden from view in a tunnel of vegetation.

As she pushed past the overhanging downward boughs of a weeping willow to get nearer the back sloping path, a harsh croaking cry came from above.

She looked up to see a bird sitting on the top of the ivy covered wall, staring at her with beady black shiny eyes. Its feathers were a pale hazel colour with green tips and it had a red crown on its head. It might be a woodpecker as she had on rare occasions seen them around the farm back in Italia. The bird croaked at her once more and then flew off into the woods beyond the house.

"Bloody bird," she whispered and headed back to the side of the house to gather old fallen branches from beneath the tall canopy of trees. She had spotted the old boiler in the back room and decided her next job was to warm the place up a bit and get the damp and cold out of the walls.

She put old newspapers and the leaflets of pizza delivery places into the boiler and heaped the driest pieces of wood on top. The greenest ones she put next to the side of the boiler to dry out, and she headed back outside to find more wood. She felt glad that her rustic farm skills were going to be of use here and it reminded her of her simpler life back home. The gathering of wood, the dodgy water supply, the woods and feel of nature made her feel at home, like London never had.

On her next foraging trip she discovered a more open piece of bramble and nettle covered land, on the other side of the right-hand wall of the garden, beyond a line of trees and scrubs. Near the corner of the brick wall was a small dilapidated shed. A waist high lean-to was at one side and under a faded blue tarp was half a stack of cut logs.

Peering through the window she could see an old petrol lawnmower, spades, fork and other garden equipment. This, she deduced, had once been a vegetable patch. She cradled the top five logs in her arms and headed back to the boiler room, hoping the woodlice would not crawl up to her neck by then. She placed four of the logs on spread out newspapers and just one above the paper and branches inside the boiler. Then she stood up, dusted herself down and stared at the open door of the boiler.

She clicked her fingers, opened the iron grate underneath and pulled out a metal tray half full of old grey ash. Catherina dumped this on the roots of the roses outside the front door, as it was good for them, and she hoped Mathew bought some pruning shears while he was out. She returned to the boiler room, rubbing her hands together at her cleverness and then stopped dead in front of the open door as an important though came to her.

"*I fiammiferi*," Catherina cried out and clapped her hands together once and turned on her heal and walked back into the kitchen.

"Matches, matches, matches," she chanted to herself in English as she went from cupboard to drawer, trying to find something or some way to light the fire. They had no cooker, so that was out and she and Mathew did not smoke so they had no lighter. There was a drawer of cutlery, but no matches so she added this to the list of things she hoped her boyfriend would bring home with him. She even thought to call him from her mobile and then realised he had no phone at the moment.

She exhaled and went into the living room to try the lights, but she found the kettle straight away and cleaned the kitchen as best she could and at least found the cups, coffee and sugar and a place to plug the kettle in. As she filled the kettle and looked over the garden, the rushing water from the tap sent messages from her bladder to her brain to inform her she really needed to pee.

After setting the kettle down to boil, she pulled open the untried downstairs toilet door and pulled the cord just inside so she could see what she was doing. The scream that erupted from her lips Mathew heard from the van, with the doors shut and radio on as he pulled up in the drive-in front of the house and garage.

CHAPTER TWENTY-FIVE

Luca Browning came home to find the house empty of life and a devilish smile crossed his 13-year-old face. He rushed in, dumped his school bag, coat and shoes in a heap in the hall, and dashed to the kitchen to fetch a can of Coke from the fridge and a Wagon-Wheel from the cupboard under the microwave.

Luca took his vittles upstairs on hurried grey sock covered feet and made for his older sister's bedroom. He knew she would not be back from work for at least an hour and a half at the earliest and he wanted a crack at her laptop before Mum and Dad showed up. He had cracked her password only the week before and had a certain website of school ground legend that he wanted to browse for certain reasons. Reasons that would probably involve a wad of toilet paper and his trousers and pants being at his ankles.

He was in for a disappointing shock. When he opened her door, he found her standing naked at her window, staring out through the net curtains to the street below. Interest at the nude human form gave way to instant sibling disgust, but then thoughts of blackmail entered his younger brother mind and he whipped his mobile phone out of his pocket.

"Oi Handbag," he called, wanting her to turn so he could snap a more embarrassing photo of her.

When she did turn, he clicked his 5 mega-pixel phone camera before his vision settled on her body, or what was left of it. Her face and breasts had been completely eaten away down to the raw red bone and a cavity had been hollowed out of her stomach, where remains of innards glistened with blood.

Luca Browning screamed until his lungs burnt and felt

like they were stuck in-between his ribs, and when he stopped the corpse of his sister had vanished. He ran down the stairs, dropping the Coke, chocolate and his phone, and reushed babbling and wailing into his mother's arms as she came through the front door.

CHAPTER TWENTY-SIX

Mathew rushed into the house, nearly slipped on some of the papers that remained in the hallway, went into the old treacherous floor boarded parlor, did a U-turn and raced through the living room. He ran through the dining room and into the kitchen to see Catherina standing in front of the toilet door, her long fingers over her mouth and nose.

"What is it?"

Mathew went over to her and put an arm around her hip, but Catherina only pointed to the toilet door with a trembling hand.

"Okay, I'll have a look. It's not spiders, is it? You know I hate spiders."

Catherina shook her head, her mane of brown hair shifting from one side to the other like a shampoo advert. As he got closer to the door, she backed away until her backside bumped into the sink. *Please don't let it be spiders*, he thought and then yanked the toilet door open.

The ill smelling downstairs loo was small and oblong and at first, because there was no natural light apart from what entered from the kitchen windows, he could not see much apart from something dark and odd shaped in the toilet bowl. A pull-cord brushed his right bicep and he reached up to pull the cord, which had a waxy unpleasant feeling to it.

The light came on. He saw what was down the toilet bowl, a little submerged in brown dirty water. "Oh no, that's fucking gross."

Sitting in the fetid loo water were four huge rats, all deceased and in varying states of decay. All had their tiny jaws open, like they were waiting for someone or something to feed them and it being a toilet, Mathew dreaded to think what that might be. He turned off the light and closed the door again and let himself breathe through his nostrils once more.

"You want me to check the upstairs loo for you?"

"*Disgustoso.*" She shivered and Mathew took her in a full embrace to comfort her.

"Don't like rats, eh? And I hate spiders. You sure you want to stay here?"

"Once you get rid of them, I'll be fine." She squeezed him tighter and kissed his stubbly neck.

"Lucky me," he joked. "At least I got bin bags and lots of rubber gloves in the van. You want to come and look?"

"Yes." She took his hand and squeezed it hard. Then she left the kitchen and went out of the house via the dining room. "Ever since we had a big flood at my father's farm once as a child I have hated rats. They er, invaded the house because of the rising waters. It was so *disgustoso.*"

"Least they're dead ones," he replied and opened the back of the hired van to reveal all he had bought with her credit card.

There were mops, two brushes, bin bags by the dozen, rubber gloves in packs of two, gardening gloves, a shiny red toolbox filled with everything you could need, a drill, saws (three different kinds), sprays for the floors, insects, damp, paint, anti-damp paint, filler, plain wallpaper, pots of white paint, brushes, tarps… The list went on.

"I didn't buy a television or anything too expensive. I'll get them another day, ok? With my money, when I start earning again. What do you think?"

"Not bad shopping for a man. You have to show me where this shop is before you take the van back to London tomorrow."

"Yeah, there are also more shops than I remember, coffee houses, clothes shops, bars and all that. Not as backwater as I remembered."

"Come on, let's get this in and get to work. I want the bedroom, kitchen and the room with the boiler cleaned up before it gets dark. *Merda*, did you get any matches, for lighting of the fire?"

"No, sorry, there's a garage with a little shop just down the end of the hill. It's not far. I'll go get us some."

"No, you get rid of those *ratti*. I want to have a look at my new home town." She waved to him and went back to the kitchen to get her handbag.

"Better pick up some rat poison when I'm out tomorrow," he said as he entered the kitchen, carrying bags with various cleaning things in them.

"Ciao then. I'm off to get some matches. Be good." She blew him a kiss and he caught it and followed her lovely rear out of the house to fetch in some thick sheets of ply wood to go over the dodgy parts of the floorboard, until they could be replaced.

She pulled on her jacket, hung her bag over her shoulder and walked out the house, down the gloomy tree covered drive to the road and turned left. She headed down the slope of the hill. The sun bathed her face and made it feel warmer than it was. She passed a few squashed together town houses and beyond them, divided by a small road, was a large garage with six petrol pumps and a small grocery shop with newspapers in a stand and charcoal brickettes outside.

She decided to walk past the petrol station. She rounded the corner and saw the High Street of Hedge End. She stopped and saw a pizza place, a curry house a small supermarket, solicitors, a wedding dress shop, cafe and newsagents, all in the first few stores on either side of the main road. She was at a crossroads, with a bank across the road to her right, a pub diagonally across from it. The pub backed onto a huge green field, with a playground at the fore.

She did not venture any further, but turned around to head back to the petrol station grocery for matches and some basic food supplies, bread, butter, bacon, eggs and of course, chocolate. She picked up two bottles of wine and two of water. They had no matches, but on the counter were some lighters, so she bought two and paid for everything with cash.

Her arms were aching by the time she got back to the place that was now her home. The sun shone into her eyes and she felt good for some reason. Maybe because nature and real life were closer to their back door now (inside if you counted the parlour) and it felt a little like being back on the farm in Italy again.

Mathew was just locking up the van again when she rounded a green barked covered tree. He looked up and saw her and smiled broadly. He had dirt and grime on his arms and forehead, but to her he looked more handsome now than any time when he had worn the shirt and tie of a businessman.

Mathew rushed over to grab the heavy bags from her. His shoulders sagged and he pretended that his legs nearly buckled under the strain. "Jesus, what you got in here? Those matches must be heavy."

"Food, my darling, something you forgot." She grinned back at him.

"You look okay with all this, better than me anyway. This is going to work, isn't it?"

"It just needs a woman's touch and a man's hard work and it will be *fantastico*."

"Bloody hell, I wouldn't go that far. The petrol fumes must have got to you."

"Did you get rid of those rats?" she asked, turning to face Mathew as he struggled through the door, bashing the heavy bags on stretched plastic handles against his shins.

"I did. Bagged them up and threw them over the wall into the woods."

"Good, now let's get cleaning this place up."

"Yes marm." He nodded and followed her back into the kitchen.

CHAPTER TWENTY-SEVEN

It wasn't until late afternoon that Mrs Puck could understand the nagging feeling that had heckled her subconscious all day long. It wasn't connected in any way to her religion or the secret grove at the back of her secluded garden, which made it more strange and annoying to her. Something was missing elusively, and it agitated her so much, she smoked her daily allowance of cigarettes by four o'clock.

she was annoyed now that she had to pull on her coat and walked down the hill to the petrol station to buy some more, when all she wanted to do today was rest and let the pain in her inner thighs slowly dissipate. A walk down the hill was okay. It was the walk back up Hanger Hill that would hurt like a bitch.

When she got to the end of her drive, she found the explanation to the antsy feeling she had all day. The church building site was closed and silent. Only one van was parked outside, and no sounds of work or digging or machinery that normally polluted the air of the hill could be heard. A square white sign had been plastered on the temporary high wooden door of the site:

CLOSED FOR INSPECTION by the authority of the Environment Agency

It was the lack of all that noise that had blighted her hearing for the past few months. A return to the tranquil peace and quiet on the hill had been the answer. She wondered what was going on and if this was all part of the plan they kept telling her about. Mrs Puck had waited years, always listening to them and seeing the signs, and she knew things were coming to a head. She took one last look at the sign and then headed off over the bridge towards Hanger Hill Road.

CHAPTER TWENTY-EIGHT

Both his bosses had been away at a meeting in Norwich, so Simon ignored the piles of urgent stuff on his desk and the constant pinging of immediate emails and left work early, advising his staff to do the same. His train got in to Hedge End station at ten to five and unlike the overcast London he had left behind, the sun was still shining low in the sky as he went up the lane to cross over the road and enter Woodhouse Copse.

Only then did his thoughts turn to home and Lucy, who would be waiting for him. He looked at the deep green ivy and wondered why life, as in nature, could get so tangled. He edged past a holly bush that was invading the path, the sun making him blink as it peeked past branches and newly formed leaves. Sometimes he wished he could stay here forever, as it seemed the only place in tune with him. He felt like he belonged.

Yet sooner than he liked, he left the path and the soles of his shoes once again, pounded on concrete as he walked down the hill with the tall hawthorn hedge at his right for a while. Then that too ended and houses, including his favourite, Hill House, began. He continued down until he came to the crossroads next to the bank and waited for the green man on the crossing signal to show the way.

He sighed at his front gate, put on his most neutral and expressionless face and headed up the side to get to the front door. His key was only an inch from the lock when Lucy pulled the door open and his neutral expression left him and his mouth fell agape.

She stood in the basque and lacy panties that she had sworn never to wear since he got them for her one Valentines. She had painted her nails deep red to match her lipstick and put her blonde hair up in the style she knew he liked, but rarely saw.

"Come on in. There's steak and kidney pie in the oven. But we have a while until it's ready, if you fancy starters," she said softly in a husky voice he had never heard her use before.

They were upstairs in seconds and any plans to make her suffer in his silence went out the window. His fate, he knew, was sealed as he pulled the laced strings to reveal her breasts.

By the time they came down the pies were a little overdone, but he ate his with ravenous gusto. Tonight the usual *Emmerdale* they watched together for years was forsaken in favour of dessert and not the ones you get from a store either.

CHAPTER TWENTY-NINE

Mathew and Catherina made good progress during the couple of hours light remaining in the day. She had cleaned and scrubbed the upstairs toilet, sink and bath into usable states and sprayed the bunk-bed bedroom for carpet mites and fleas. Then vacuumed with the Dyson the bailiffs did not take for some reason, even though it cost more than their Blu-Ray player.

The fire was burning well in the boiler room and Mathew was pleased that the old radiators around the house had begun to warm up, and there were no leaks in the old solid pipes. The radiators in the master bedroom and dining room did not come on at all, but they might need bleeding and he never picked up the right key to do that at the DIY shop, or even thought about it.

He had cleaned both the boiler room and the kitchen in his own time and Catherina had caught him a couple of times playing with his new cheap pay-as-you-go mobile phone. He put a large inch-thick ply wood sheet over the rotten floorboards and cut back the invading ivy and taped up the broken or missing window panes with plastic sheeting he cut with a Stanley knife.

The official time for the sun to go down was just after half-seven, but with the surrounding trees so close and encompassing to the house that it was getting dark inside at about seven. Even though they were exhausted from their day's endeavours they had one last job to do, and that was to replace any broken light bulbs around the house with new energy saving ones.

They sat on two wooden chairs from the library in front of the open door of the boiler and warmed their hands against the cold of the oncoming night, huddled together like two snow-bound Canadian trappers in mid-winter.

The house was warm in places, which was comforting, but also showed up the damp more in certain rooms and sent a musty funk circulating around the place. They toasted bread on long forks that they had used on Sunday roasts, but burnt four out of five attempts and decided to use the toaster and microwave from the apartment to make beans on toast. They followed this up with cuppa-soups and Mathew promised Catherina that they would either find a local restaurant or use one of the many flyers in the hall to get a take-away tomorrow night.

The woodpecker watched the two humans inside the house so long deserted, clinging to the thick overgrown branches of a large buddleia. It could see them in the glow of a warming fire, through the recently cleaned windows. The bird could see their mouths opening and closing but could not hear the crowing of their voices through the frozen ice that held firm even in the warmest days of summer.

It had seen enough. It took off from its perch with a cry and flew over the garden wall into the heart of the darkening woods beyond. Then it circled over a thicket of brambles and down it landed and carefully made its way under the barbed weeds until it stood upon the moss covered stone lip of an ancient and forgotten well. The woodpecker flew down four feet, as far as it could go. The roots of a tree had blocked ninety percent of it over the last two thousand or so years since it had been dug out.

Yet the resourceful woodpecker hopped through a gap at the side and used the roots as a natural stairs, until it got to clear space and fluttered down the last forty feet in total darkness to the tunnel that lay at the bottom of the long dry well.

It gave out a cry of warning and respect and waited in the dank darkness for her to arrive. After a time, she came to listen to the woodpecker, through tunnels long hidden beneath the woods and roads of Hedge End and Hanger Hill and was pleased after all these long untold years of waiting by what the woodpecker had to impart.

CHAPTER THIRTY

Of the numerous households in and around Hedge End, most had comfortable nights. Some, like Simon and Lucy, had fantastic nights, while others, like Angela Pratchett, had a lonely night, after her husband had left home and set up in his boyfriend's love-nest.

Yet in the Brownings' house they suffered more than anyone in the town. They had to get the doctor out to see Luca in the end, who had to give the poor child valium to calm him down and get the terrified boy to sleep. Sophia had refused such medication. She needed her mind clear when the police detectives came round to visit at eight. She and her husband, Stephen, went through the morning before, when they had seen Hannah last. Stephen's sister and Sophia's good friend, Rebecca, had also arrived to lend moral support, better than her silent brother could muster.

At least now they were taking the situation seriously, though their questions were still about where she might be, with a boyfriend, girlfriend or a long one-night stand, which finally woke Hannah's dad from his silent brooding to protest.

They took a few pictures of Hannah for reference and asked what she was wearing, something Sophia, nearly as fashion conscious as her daughter, knew in every detail, even down to her killer new shoes.

They left an hour later, leaving a card if Hannah turned up or anything else useful sprang to mind. Stephen was crying his eyes out after they had gone, but the sister-in-laws were already being proactive, printing out Have You Seen Hannah? flyers to give out first thing tomorrow around the town and the railway station.

No one apart from the drug-calmed Luca slept much that night in the Browning household and at first light they were roused by the screams of Luca coming out of a nightmare about his corpse-like sister. Luca and his father took some flyers and drove to look around some of her old haunts and visit friends and old lovers. Meanwhile Sophia and Rebecca walked the route Hannah would have taken to the railways station, giving out flyers to every person that they saw.

They stayed at the station until ten and then caught a train to Waterloo to carry on her route to work and give out more flyers. They scoured the London streets and side alleys off the roads to Hannah's work and gave out flyers on the tube, trying to find any clue to her whereabouts.

Someone had to have seen her and had to know where she was, yet truth be told, there was now little of her left to find.

CHAPTER THIRTY-ONE

Simon Hay did not see Hannah's mother and aunt that morning, giving away flyers at the train station. He would have, they were there early enough, around the time when he caught his usual train, but today he wasn't on it. Simon could have told them nothing much anyway. He had obviously noticed her before in the carriage going to work, because she was stunning, but she had that haughty look of the beautiful that read, don't even bother talking to me unless you're rich or handsome.

Simon was neither, but that had not stopped him having the odd early morning fantasy about her peeking over the Terry Pratchett book he was reading on the train at the time. The only time he had spoken to her was to say, "after you," as they departed the train back home at Hedge End station one early evening.

Simon was in fact making breakfast in bed for his now fiancée Lucy, after leaving a cowardly I've-got-the-winter-bug message on his boss's answer phone before anyone in the office would be in. He knew he had a vital meeting to go to and a stack of work, but he just didn't give a shit today. Lucy had done the same from her mobile, saying she was still up-chucking for England and hoped to be back tomorrow.

Simon had asked Lucy to marry him this morning after another vigorous bout of extremely dirty love-making. She had always avoided the connubial question, saying there was no need, but this morning she had said yes quicker than a whippet snatching a treat from its master's hand.

They had both given in at last to their fates and Lucy was glad that their child would eventually come from wedded bliss, though she had never thought it essential. While Simon was downstairs humming and making breakfast for them in bed, she lay naked under the heavy togged purple patterned duvet and reached over to her bedside cabinet. She opened up the drawer and pulled her diary, covered with cutesy puppies on the covers and wrote ENGAGED on the Wednesday am for this week in early April. Then underneath in the pm she wrote Lucy Dawn Hay, just to see what it looked like and then giggled to herself like she was twelve again and slipped the diary back in the drawer.

But the time Simon came up with the tea and breakfast things, she was feeling horny once more and kicked the duvet over to his side of the bed as he entered the room. Tea and breakfast got luke-warm, but it still tasted to them like food of the gods this morning.

CHAPTER THIRTY-TWO

The dark blue tarp over the window and the fact that the sun rose on the other side of the house, plus their exertions of the previous day, gave Mathew and Catherina a well-deserved lie-in until she twisted and turned into consciousness at about five to nine. She looked up at the bare blue ceiling and wondered for three seconds where the hell she was.

Catherina turned into her mass of hair and saw He-Man wallpaper through the strands of her locks and she suddenly remembered that they were in Mathew's great uncle's house in Hedge End in the county of Surrey. She could see another sunny day through the gaps where the rigid tarp was tied by string to the empty brass curtain rail. She yawned and moved up onto her elbow and prodded her hair from her left eye and cheek. Only Mathew's short dark hair was visible under the duvet. She slipped sideways off the mattress without his stirring and shivered, as the carpet was cold and a draught danced around her ankles, sending goose-bumps up her long legs.

She had been warm last night and had slept in her dark blue Italia football shirt and thin panties. Now she wished that her boxes of clothes were not downstairs and she had socks on. Folding her arms, she tip-toed out of the cold bedroom onto an even colder landing and into the bathroom, which had scrubbed up well, to take care of her morning toilet business. The floor was black and white squared linoleum, and when she felt the radiator under the towel she had placed there last night before bed, it was stone cold.

She washed quickly, surprised that hot clear water came out of the red topped sink tap. She washed after using the loo and hurried down the bare wooden stairs to find her boxes of clothes in the dining room. Her feet were blocks of ice by the time she found a clean pair of thick socks and a pair of jeans to slip into. She could not find a bra or blouse quickly so she just pulled a thick woolen cardigan over her football top to keep warm.

Still shivering, she proceeded into the kitchen to fill the kettle and quickly see to the stone cold boiler, which was just grey ash in the grate. A look into the garden showed the long grass was covered in silvery glistening frost and there, perched on an ivy smothered sundial, was the multicoloured bird from yesterday.

It looked keenly at Catherina through the boiler room window and she waved her hand dismissively towards the bird. *"Vattene,* shoo, go away."

The woodpecker seemed to Catherina to bend one pipe-cleaner thin leg and bow at her, and then it hopped into the air and beat a swift retreat on its wings back to the woods.

"Bloody strange bird," she muttered as she bent to roll and stuff another local paper into the boiler and get some heat around the place before Mathew woke up and the kettle boiled.

Mathew kissed her goodbye at ten and got into the hired van to drive it back into London and then catch the train home again as soon as he could manage it. Catherina, with a hastily drawn map from him, was going to explore the town and get a few things from the DIY shop, maybe even invest in a cooker and other such essential appliances.

The day had clouded over by the time she left and strolled down Hanger Hill to explore the shops of the High Street. Her first stop was a clothes shop. She could not resist two pairs of jeans in a sale and two jumpers to keep out the Spring cold and dampness of the house. Catherina found an electric appliances shop and felt like a kid in a candy store. She had never had to buy a cooker or fridge before in her entire life. The fridge was easy. She got one of those huge American style double door ones with an ice maker in the front and she got a cheap colour printer for Mathew so he could print endless letters to the local council, banks, water, and electrical supplies, plus the phone people to get a landline and broadband connected as soon as possible. Her only slight problem came with the cooker as she set her heart on an old Arga type double oven with six rings.

"Would you like a gas or electric one?" the young sale assistant asked, trying not to lick his lips at the huge sale he was about to make.

"God, I don't know if we have gas or not."

"Better go for an electrical version then. It's not quite the same, but just as good." *And just as pricey,* the salesman thought to himself.

"Okay, we will go for that, yes," Catherina replied, after seeing the electrical version.

"Excellent." *What a day, and she's hot,* he thought.

"Now, when can you deliver?"

She got some more supplies that did not need a fridge to keep cool and picked up a bin in the DIY shop and a few other things that she put inside the bin to struggle home with. It started spitting as she walked up past the garage, but any heavier rain kept off until she got back into the house. As she entered the kitchen it seemed gloomy and depressing and the rain began with a vengeance outside. She put down the large kitchen bin and pulled out her shopping, including two plastic buckets, which she took into the parlour and the bedroom above it to catch drips from the leaky roof. The boiler had died to embers while she had been out shopping, but a few rolled up pieces of newspaper and then twigs from outside brought it back to life enough for her to add bigger branches and then a log. It was well after twelve by then so she turned on the kitchen light and made herself a jam sandwich and ate it watching the rain.

She had forgotten to get a television and DVD player, on purpose really. Mathew loved buying that sort of thing and it felt good to go without it. It would just interrupt the intimacy of their new start together.

In the garden, at the door set in the far ivy covered boundary wall, a large snout sniffed at the bottom right-hand corner where the wood had rotted away or been eaten by woodlice.

CHAPTER THIRTY-THREE

Angela Pratchett looked out from the attic room window across the road, just watching the day go by. She was not sure how long she had stood there, ever since she had risen this morning, and not bothered to dress. Angela stood in her dressing gown and slippers, her face slack with lack of thought or emotion. She felt like an old hollowed out tree that had fallen in the woods. The dog was downstairs barking for her breakfast and a walk, but Angela felt like she had nowhere to go and nothing to live for.

She had seen with a twitched eyebrow that had a van had left the old house across Hanger Hill Road that backed onto Leggett woods. No one had lived there since that scruffy old hermit she only knew by the name the local kids used to call him, Dirty Jim. She never had much to do with him in life or death, but always wondered why no one had ever moved into the place or knocked it down to build a whole street of houses. Apparently, so the gossip mongers said, he not only owned the house and its gardens, but most of the wood as well.

She watched a dark haired rather chic and attractive looking woman go down the drive a minute ago carrying a large bin and some shopping bags. The rain on the attic window got louder and the whines from downstairs more intense as her dog hated the sound of the rain on the conservatory roof, where she was locked at night.

Angela Pratchett looked at the knife she held in her hand and let it drop to imbed in the polished floorboards. She wasn't going to kill herself today, or tomorrow. She needed to print out the evidence of her husband's gay affair, get dressed and head down the hill to her solicitors and start divorce proceedings. That's what she would do today. After she had fed the dog and let her out to shit on her husband's neatly tendered lawn first.

CHAPTER THIRTY-FOUR

Angela Pratchett just missed the police car and van that drove past her house with sirens and roof lights off. They parked inside the entrance to Woodhouse Copse, before a row of wooden poles to stop people from dumping illegal rubbish there.

The detective leading the case of the missing teenager, Hannah Browning, stepped out of the lead car and turned up his coat collar against the heavy rain. He and his team of boys-in-blue piled out the van, armed with sticks and evidence bags. There formed a wide line and stared to beat their way through the spring foliage, cast slick and shiny by the rainfall from one end of the copse to the other. A taxi driver had seen a woman fitting Hannah's clothes and description entering the woods alone early on Monday morning, as he drove up the hill back to the railway station.

A cry of pain went up from the last policeman in the line, nearest the mesh fence of the railway tracks. Detective English ran over, but only found another bobby pulling the younger colleague out of a rabbit or badger hole his shoe had plunged into,

"Over here, sir," came a cry from the other end of the line of wet uniformed policemen, and Detective English ran over to a tall bearded copper.

"What you got, Henderson?"

"A woman's shoe sir, looks a bit battered, but could belong to the missing girl."

"Jenkins, get my brolly from the car. I want you to stand over it and keep the rain off it until I can call the forensics guys in."

PC Jenkins hurried off to the car as English bent down to look at the shoe. It was chewed in places like a dog or wild animal had savaged it, but the beige sole underneath looked like the shoe had been barely walked in. If this was Hannah Browning's shoe, then his and the parent's worst fears would come true and this would go from a missing persons case to an abduction or murder hunt.

CHAPTER THIRTY-FIVE

The heavy rain lasted no longer than forty minutes and by the time Mathew came strolling down Hanger Hill from the railway station the dark clouds had rolled away to the east and the sun was threatening to come out.

He had spoken to his friend on the farm again and the herd he secretly owned would be sold no questions asked to a buyer over the weekend and he should have his money the week after. Mathew was glad. He didn't like the idea of being poor and the £100 in his wallet would not last him long.

He crossed through the station car park and passed the taxi line, ignoring the lazy London side of him who wanted to get a taxi down the hill, only five minutes' walk away at tops. He crossed over Woking Road, which led down the other side of Leggett Woods and to the DIY superstore and onto Hanger Hill Road. He was now on the same side of the road as his new house and walked hands in pockets avoiding the puddles in the uneven rented pavement.

Something white caught his eye to his right, across the road in the copse on the other side, hedged by that huge hawthorn barrier he remembered so vividly from his youth. He couldn't see much, but it looked like a tent was inside the copse and there was a lot of movement around it. It wasn't until he got further on and saw the two police vans and a car, that he realised something was amiss. Then he remembered the missing person's flyers on the window of the station, by the sliding doors. A pretty young woman had gone missing two days ago.

He shook his head as he passed the entrance to Woodhouse Copse. It seemed you could escape London, but shit things still happened, even in the leafiest suburbs. He rang Catherina on her mobile to ask to put the kettle on. He had a burger and a coffee at Waterloo, but was gasping for a cuppa now.

He found her emptying two half-full plastic buckets of water on the overgrown rose beds as he rounded the tree and crunched up the drive to his new abode. Shame it leaked like a sieve.

"Ciao Bello," he cried in his best take on an Italian accent.

She looked up and smiled. "Hello handsome, come to help me clean up this bloody water leaking house have we?"

"Tea first, then I'll get into Bob the Builder mode."

He reached the step and kissed her lips, then he patted her nice arse for good measure.

"Bob who? But if you can fix the windows and floorboards I would be molto happy."

They went inside, the buckets empty of rain water now, and headed for the kitchen to partake of their tea.

Up the hill in a thick bough that over hung Hanger Hill Road the woodpecker perched, its eyes fixed on the doings of the blue and white coated men below. Unease made it shiver from beak to tail feathers and it looked up to see a raven watching it from its perch on a tree branch in Woodhouse Copse.

They exchanged the blackest of stares and then the woodpecker hopped back nearer its side of the road. It flew off to tell the She-Mother that there were ravens back in the divided woods that the woodpecker knew never to enter or even fly over.

The raven watched the woodpecker go and then took off itself and flew over the railway tracks in the man-made valley below, to the other part of the woods divided for over a century. It found a hole in the trunk of a large oak tree near the top and entered the dark oval opening.

CHAPTER THIRTY-SIX

Simon and Lucy ignored the telephone until it began to bug them and put them off their stroke. This is why you should never have a phone in the bedroom, he thought, as he answered it through gritted teeth, knowing it was work.

"It's Judith. Sorry I know you're poorly, but it's all gone pear-shaped here today. The gruesome twosome are after your guts, Simon, I thought I'd better ring you and give you the heads up."

"What's gone wrong now? Can't a man vomit in peace anymore?" he said in a tired weak voice to his colleague, but then winked and smiled at Lucy.

"The Cold Fire project has gone belly—up, something to do with inaccurate budget figures and our beloved bosses, they of the slopey shoulders, are letting the blame settle on you, dear, which isn't right because you're not here to defend yourself." Judith sounded angry and tired and hated her job even more than Simon loathes his.

"Well, they approved and signed off on them. Look Judith, keep your head down and I'll be in tomorrow to sort them out, okay, and try not to worry."

"Simon, get well soon and don't let them get to you."

"I won't, Judith, thanks for the call. I better go, I feel a little queasy again."

"Okay, bye."

Simon put down the phone and exhaled.

"Can't cope even a day without you eh, fiancée.?"

"Apparently not, fuck 'em, or maybe you." He turned and tickled Lucy's inner thighs and bum, for nothing was going to spoil this day.

CHAPTER THIRTY-SEVEN

Detective English took pictures of the shoe back to the Brownings' house and made sure none of them showed the brown stain on the back of the inner heel. The shoe itself was wending itself to the labs for every test known to science to be done on it, while he stood at their front door, in his rain sodden coat, a buff large envelope of misery in his left hand.

A couple of local reporters were already at the boundary of the house, being kept back by a young bobby. If a teen girl, no scrub that, if a pretty white teen girl goes missing, it's big news in such a small relatively serious crime free place like Hedge End. He paused at the front door, in an indifferent mood. They had found no other traces of Hannah Browning. The detective was only 43, but his job was aging him prematurely. The long hours and poor diet played havoc on your family life and waistline and health. He was mentally tired also. The never-ending stress of seeing all that is bad in human nature was taking its toll, and maybe he'd take the family away for a long holiday soon, or ask for a transfer to another department.

Licking his nicotine tasting teeth and longing for another cigarette, he knocked on the Brownings' door and a young WPC opened the door after a few seconds. He entered, gripping the envelope of photographs and feeling like Typhoid Mary entering a nursery of newborns.

CHAPTER THIRTY-EIGHT

Jacko hadn't cried in thirty years, not since his dear old mum had died. Now, lying in his hospital bed, he sobbed like a baby, turning in his pillow to the blind covered window and letting his tears wet the cotton pillow cover.

At least he had the strength of will to wait until his wife had left to visit Tony and see how his family were doing. Tony was slowly getting better, but was plastered up and set with screws and bolts to keep his broken bones together. But he was alive after his ordeal. Geordie Geoff had not been so lucky. Jacko had worked with Geoff for over ten years and Tony nearing sixteen. They were both good men and now one of them was dead, because of that bloody mercury.

The worst of it was he felt like he had let them and himself down somehow, but they had not been in contact with the mercury for long and he had done the right thing by calling in specialists and closing the crypt down. Maybe they should have all gone to the hospital first for a check-up, but he had felt fine and well until dinner time.

Jacko hated fuck-ups, but what frustrated him to tears was there was probably nothing he could have done to change the situation. But that just made him feel worse. He wiped his eyes on the drier end of the pillow-case and mentally slapped himself. He was ill and self-pity was only getting to him because he was at a low-ebb.

Tomorrow, he'd get a nurse to wheel him round to see Tony and tell him his job would be waiting for him when he got better, however long it took. That was as magnanimous as Jacko could muster, sort your work life out first and the friends and family shit would have to play second fiddle. It was the way that he lived and no tragedy or accidental poisoning at work would change him. He was too old for that.

CHAPTER THIRTY-NINE

They made some progress in the hours before darkness took hold over the house again, but every problem solved or found usually highlighted several more. Mathew had risked life and limb up in the loft, as there were only four loose planks to balance on around the hatch, and the rest of the place was bare joists with itchy old lagging in between.

A hole the size of his head was visible at the far front right corner of the roof. The papery covering had long since fallen away to reveal that ten or so roof tiles were missing and water was seeping into the bedroom underneath and the parlour below that. He laid one of the planks across the joists like a bridge and gingerly made his way over to the hole, holding onto the sloping roof timbers as he went.

Mathew could see the tree tops and the orange street lights on the road outside. This was priority one on the to-do list and as he made his way back to the loft hatch, newly bought torch in hand, he prayed it did not rain again until his cash came through. He sucked at his teeth and swung his legs down onto the fold-up ladder below. Maybe he might have to sign on for a while and take back some of that business tax that he had had been forced to pay.

He covered the broken windows securely with wooden boards before his stomach and aching arms told him it was time for food and rest. They called in a curry from one of the most recent flyers that had some through the door and he paid, leaving him just over £70 to his name.

They ate in the dining room, which Catherina had cleaned up, with the old door re-hinged by her own fair hands at the expense of one of her precious nails. She didn't mind, for the impressed look on Mathew's face made her feel like the sacrifice of a nail wasn't in vain.

She had sprayed and vacuumed the carpet, polished the table, chairs and Welsh dresser and lit some scented candles she had brought from the apartment and put them on the window sill and the table. It brought a comforting soft glow to the room and more importantly covered up smells coming from other rooms.

"So what are we doing tomorrow?" Catherina waved her hands expressively in front of her face, showing she meant the house.

"No point replacing the floorboards until the roof is done, and I don't think the seventy quid in my pocket will cover that. I might start hacking those roses back and maybe even beat a path down to the gate in the garden so I can show you the woods."

"I would like to see the woods." She nodded. "What about the cellar and downstairs lavatory?"

"The cellar can wait. I'll try and clean the downstairs bog up."

"Is the cellar big then?"

He waited to finish the chicken tikka in his mouth to reply, "Big enough. Dirt floor and full of bloody spiders."

"So you will be leaving that to last, eh?"

"Yes." He nodded, tearing at his nan bread.

"When our cooker arrives, I will cook you my grandmother's spaghetti and meatballs," she offered, filling her mouth with the remains of her prawn passanda.

"Sounds great, Cat, and thanks."

"For what?"

"For sticking with me after losing the apartment and the business and my money." He looked down at his food and pushed it from the centre to the side of the plate.

"*Stupido*," she chastised, her brown eyes wild. "I love you because of you and who you are, not because how much money you have in the bank. Anyway, I have had many offers from men much richer than you, Mat-chew Reynolds."

"Offers for what?" He smirked and then had to duck as she threw the remains of her nan at him.

"Careful, or there will be no more mattress fun for you tonight."

"Do I have to pay now, then?"

"I warned you, now we have a problem," she said, rising quickly to run around the table to sit on his lap. He turned his chair out to meet her.

"What are you going to do with me, then?" he asked, raising his wrists up to her face, close together in the mimicry of invisible handcuffs.

"I shall have to spank your *il sedere.*" She eyed his and raised her open right palm.

"My *il sedere* eh? Will that be painful or pleasurable, mistress?"

"For most people pleasurable, but for you I will make the exception." She bit her bottom lip and aimed a whack at his rump.

"The countrified air must agree with you, then?" he said, pushing his lips up to kiss her.

Catherina put her palm in the way so he only kissed her fingers, which he took in his hand and held tight, feeling the warmth of her skin reassuring and comforting.

"Well, I have always fantasised about making the love in the park where we used to live. Now we have our own private woods, I think I would like to try that." She smiled at him and Mathew felt like he was melting like an ice-cream on a hot pavement.

"What, now? Might be a little cold."

"*Stupido.*" She cuffed his head lightly as she stood up and headed for the kitchen, but stopped in the doorway. "I want to feel the sun on my naked body as we make love in our own woods. I want the bird to watch us and fly away with embarrassment, but you know what I really want from you now?"

"No, but I have a few ideas of my own," he replied as she held onto the doorframe and pouted, her body arching into a seductive shape.

"I want you to...do the washing up." She laughed, wiggled

her fingers in a wave and disappeared into the kitchen to boil the kettle to make coffee.

"Hmm," was his only reply.

CHAPTER FORTY

"Meisha, shut up, darling. Mummy is trying to do something here."

The cocker-spaniel did not heed or understand Angela's request, nor was she put off by her tone. She hadn't been taken out for a walk in two whole days and it was a break of routine that drove the poor little dog nuts with frustration.

She barked, wagged her little tail, pulled at the long silk pyjamas her owner was wearing, but all to no avail. There seemed to be no walkies coming again today, as it was already dark outside and Meisha was in desperate need of a toilet trip.

She gave-up on mewling and whining and began to growl, knowing if she did crap on the carpet, the male, less friendly owner would hit her nose with a rolled up newspaper again. Not that he and his odd scent were around at the moment, which also confused her.

Meisha growled and then barked and barked and barked at her mistress, who sat in a chair in the man's study.

"For god's sake girl, shut-up."

Meisha had had enough. She ran forward and gave Mummy a quick nip on her exposed left ankle.

"What do you think you are bloody playing at, you stupid little bitch," Angela screamed. She picked up the cocker-spaniel by the collar, went to the living room and threw the dog out of the French window and locked it shut behind her. Angela Pratchett pulled three tissues from a scented box on the side and dabbed at the small wound. Then cursing to high heaven, she went back to the study to finish booking flights and a hotel in Tobago, leaving on Friday.

Meisha ignored her choked throat and sore paw from her rough landing and raced to the end of the long garden to dig a hole in the bare earth of the empty vegetable patch behind the wooden shed. The relief was like heaven to the poor dog and once finished she took great care in burying her mess under as much loose earth as she could manage.

Right at the end of the garden something small, round and colourful lay in the long grass that poked up from under the back tall back fence. She bounded off to find it was a tennis ball that must have found its way over from next door somehow. Once she had nudged and sniffed the alien object, another deeper, meatier smell entered her nostrils. It was coming from the corner of the fence that backed onto the copse behind.

Meisha soon found a hole in the earth beneath the fence that a fox must have dug out to gain access to the Pritchetts' garden. She had smelled fox many times before, but there was another bloodier meaty, bigger smell coming from behind the fence. Meisha dug some fallen earth away with quick ease and then bent and wiggled her way down the hole. It did not come out the other side, but went deeper and Meisha crawled further down on her belly, the smell of ripe bloody meat filling her nose and all her thoughts. She was hungry as hell, another new neglect from her normally fastidious owner.

Suddenly the tunnel opened out into a much wider opening and Meisha could now easily trot forward in the near dark in search of the elusive fresh smelling meat that made her drool with hunger. The earth beneath her feet now gave way to clay and stone and she could see a much larger place ahead, with a dim glow about it. Another smell entered her snout, something elusive and smelling of pine trees and bees, something that made the hair on her back stand up on end.

No fresh meat was worth this risk and with a built-in sense of inherent danger, she turned and high-tailed it back to the small burrowed hole that led back to the safety of the garden. She had to crouch and wiggle to get back inside and her progress was slow. Up above she could smell the fresh night air, and then something with piercing claws grabbed both her hind legs and with eager force pulled her back down the tunnel, leaving the drag marks of her paws in long lines in the earth.

She only managed a solitary yelp before something unknown to her bit her spine in two through her fur and flesh.

CHAPTER FORTY-ONE

Simon Hay woke one minute before the alarm was due to go off and he cringed inside as he stared at the red illuminated lines that formed such an ungodly hour to wake up. It was still pitch black outside and his eyes would not leave the unmoving red numbers as his mind pondered whether to take another sickie.

The alarm jumped alive and still shocked him with its invading beeps, even though he knew it was coming. He reached over and switched it off as Lucy murmured something he could not understand and turned over to face the window. He dithered for a minute and then swung his bare legs out from under the womb-like warmth and safety of the duvet and rubbed at his stubbled cheeks.

He padded towards the door in the blue darkness of pre-dawn and headed for the bathroom, not knowing if he was staying or going. He still had to have a piss, whatever the outcome. A sickening dread filled his stomach at the prospect of not only another day at a job that he hated, but also that he knew he'd get a bollocking. He moved over to the shower and reached in to turn it on. If he delayed his return it would only make things worse. He straightened the ruffled up mat next to the shower, pulled off his nightwear and stepped into the warm steaming jets of water.

CHAPTER FORTY-TWO

Catherina Di Marco woke from a dream so vivid she thought that she was still outside in the dark woods that slumber had visited upon her. She sat up and slowly became aware of her surroundings again, in the small bedroom, on their mattress on the floor.

The images of the dream were fading fast as her mind woke up, but she still recalled she had been happily running around the woods behind the house, naked as a newborn infant. Yet she had not been alone. She could not recall Mathew being there, but she remembered a bird of some kind that called to her in Italian, and of something else dark and sinister running around the edge of her vision, low down on all fours like a lion or a dog. Then out of nowhere two small boys appeared, dressed in clothes of various hues of green.

She remembered holding their hands and dancing around and around, one second in the woods and the next on a hill inside some sort of ancient fortification. She had been dancing with them, their perfect white teeth smiling at her, when from the corner of her eye, she saw all the trees had turned into squat headless shadows, which startled her back into the waking world. She had known that it was the woods behind the house somehow, even though she had not even set foot there or seen the place for herself.

She got up and headed out of the bedroom without waking Mathew and went past the bathroom to the other rear-facing bedroom, so she could stare out of the curtain-less window. It was still dark outside and she could see nothing through the dirty glass. She turned to head for the toilet when she thought she heard the sounds of children singing outside. She turned the window handle and with three hits with the butt of her palm it opened three inches, wide enough to let the cold air tickle her neck and face as she leaned forward to listen.

The words she could not make out, but the tune seemed familiar to her somehow, something from her childhood back in Italy. Then the singing ended and she heard at least two children giggle somewhere just beyond the boundary wall of the garden and go silent.

Catherina closed the window and headed down the stairs, trying to be speedy and quiet at the same time. In the dining room she pulled an old pair of jeans from a box and tugged them on, then kicked on a pair of old jogging trainers and her blue thick padded coat and made for the back door. To her surprise it opened with ease and she stepped out into the pre-dawn, wondering if Mathew had fixed the door or the cold of the night had un-warped the wood for a while.

She ignored the wet grass on her jeans and hurried down the garden to the wooden door that sat covered and recessed in the ivy gripped wall. She got as close as the vegetation would allow and whispered softly, "Hello, is there anyone there?"

"*Entrare*," whispered two young voices as one and she was not sure if they came from girls or boys. But they definitely came from behind the wooden door that she could not get through.

"I cannot enter. The door is shut and overgrown. Are you Italian?

The giggles from right behind the door started high and then began to descend in intensity as if the children were walking away and back into the woods.

"*Ritornare*, come back," she said louder to the ivy hung door, but no sounds came from the wall or door beyond the garden. She tried the door but it was stuck fast and would need to be attacked with shears before it could ever open.

Catherina turned and saw that the blue night now had smudges of red and orange to it and that the dawn was coming. A mist was starting to form and hover on the tall grass of the garden. Feeling cold and slightly unnerved, she headed back to the house to light the boiler and heat her new home for the coming day. She stood at the open back door for a while, but no further sounds came from the woods beyond, and as the dark slowly gave way to the morning's first light, the mist grew higher and thicker.

The cold bit at her face and hands and eventually she retreated back inside and lit the boiler and boiled the kettle, always with one eye to the garden, but this soon faded from view as the mist turned to fog and the house became enveloped in a ring of grey nothingness.

She had coffee and toast to warm her by the fire of the boiler and Mathew did not come down for another two hours, having been woken by the clanking of the radiators as they slowly heated and expanded. He cuddled her from behind as she washed up last night's dishes and they both stared out into the thick pressing fog.

"Looks like a real pea-souper out there this morning," he commented, "and I don't get to say that often."

Catherina just snuggled back into his embrace and said nothing about her dreams or the children's voices outside, because she knew he believed in nothing religious or spiritual at all. He was an atheist capitalist man and had no time for such ideals. She had once been very religious, well, until her mother had died so young, but it was still inside her somewhere. With Mathew, he had left God behind in his childhood, with ghosts and Santa Claus as things that he knew did not exist for him.

CHAPTER FORTY-THREE

"Do we have to go back to work today?"

"You know I don't want to but I must if we're to save for a wedding and babies and you've already had two days skiving," Simon replied as he knotted his dark blue tie in front of the mirror in the hallway.

"I suppose you're right," she said, downcast, still in her dressing-gown as she only lived five minutes' walk away from the shoe shop.

"Oh God." Simon pulled at his cheeks with both hands, dreading the day ahead.

"I'm sure it won't be as bad as you think. Stand up to them, Simon."

Simon pulled his coat over his jacket and reached down to grab his sandwiches and book laden backpack off the brown hallway carpet. He leaned down and kissed Lucy's forehead and she gave him a hug of encouragement. Then he turned and waved and headed out the front door into the fog. Lucy turned on her heal in her bed socks and headed back into the kitchen to rustle up some breakfast, bacon and eggs, she ravenously craved, instead of her usual bowl of bran flakes.

Simon loved the walk up the hill in the fog. It felt to him like some primeval force had suddenly descended on Hedge End and he half-expected to see long-legged dinosaurs pass him. He was shocked to find that the copse on the top of Hanger Hill was roped off with yellow police tape and his usual route to work was blocked by a couple of cold and grumpy looking policemen. He didn't ask what it was all about, just walked on the pavement alongside the immense hawthorn hedge, and when he got to the station, he soon found out why they were there.

Hannah Browning's disappearance had jumped from local news to the nationals in one day and the finding of one of her shoes in Woodhouse Copse and pictures of the gorgeous teenager were splashed inside and out of the front covers. Simon bought the Sun and the Telegraph so to get the full range of the details of the story and the flyers all around the station made him feel like he had woken up in some strange off-kilter parallel world.

He read the papers column by column until the train reached its final destination at Waterloo. Even the normally silent carriages were filled with chat of the missing girl and not the usual coughs and irrigating drone of personal music systems.

He got into work early and was bemused and slightly unnerved to find his bosses were already in situ. They headed to Keith's office and Janice closed the door behind Simon. Both sat waiting for him to sit with serious faces on.

"So what's the problem, then?"

"Well, if you had been here yesterday you would have found out Simon," replied Keith with a terse frown.

"Yes," nodded Janice with pursed lips.

"The chairman was cracking our heads, Simon, because the Cold-Fire project figures were two million pounds out and not in our company's favour. He was made to look a right Charlie in front of the board and then passed his wrath down the chain of command to us, but they are your figures, Simon." Lecherous Keith pointed one stubby red finger, which was missing the tip after a car door accident seven years ago when he was pissed out of his brain.

"My fault? I gave those figures to you last week and flagged some things that didn't add up and you signed them off, both of you," Simon cried back, his voice rising in self-defense.

"I don't think so," Janice said, shaking her head.

"Can you prove it, Simon?" Keith asked, leaning back on his executive cream leather chair, his fingers pressed together. Well, except one.

"I have copies of the bloody documents in my cupboard."

"Do you really, Simon? Well, let's have a look at them then?"

Keith smiled widely now, his hands wide apart, his face doing the best slimy crocodile impression Simon Hay had ever seen.

"Right, I'll go and get them now, shall I?"

"If you would," Janice replied.

Simon stormed from the room, back to his office to find Jim there opening the cupboard and getting the trays and files out for the morning work.

"Simon, you're back. Feeling better?"

"Fucking back-stabbing backsliding bastards," was all Simon grunted in reply as he tore through the cupboard searching for the hard photocopied figures and graphs his two shits of bosses had signed off. But they were not there.

"The Cold-Fire figures, the copies, where are they, Jim?" Simon turned around, panic rising like the gorge in his windpipe.

"Dunno. Should be in there," Jim stated, moving closer.

"Has anyone else asked for them or been in this cupboard?"

"Janice was rooting away in there yesterday lunchtime, Sarah mentioned."

"Those fucking treacherous cunts!"

"What have they done now?" Jim asked, knowing whom Simon meant straight away.

"Sold me down the fucking river, fucking bastards." Simon smashed his fist into the cupboard door, which flew in and rebounded back.

Simon stormed back to Keith's office and nearly kicked the door in. "Well, my back-up signed copies have mysteriously vanished."

"Oh dear," Keith replied.

"So Simon, I am sorry to say that after this heads must roll, but we would like to reward you for your hard work and dedication to the office these past ten years."

"What?"

Simon looked from Janice to Keith, shaking with rage and the total unfairness of the political life at work in a large corporation.

"Simon, if you leave today quietly without fuss or phone calls to unions or commissions for unfair dismissals we will give you a one year 35k handshake and a glowing reference from us both."

"And if I fight this and go right to the CEO and chairman, hell, the board itself?"

"Then without a shred of evidence, they will sack you for incompetence and you'll get piss-all," Keith replied, placing his hands on his desk." I know this must be an upsetting shock for you, Simon, but you're still young and can bounce back from this."

Simon could do nothing by stare at the treacherous twins of evil that were his cowardly back-stabbing bosses. No words would come out. He just turned and left the office, slamming the door so the whole of the third floor could hear it, even through the fire-doors.

He rushed back to his office and ransacked his desk and searched through every email and letter he had on the project, but came up blank on anything that showed that either of his bosses had signed the figures off. He stone-walled poor Jim and Sarah's questions as he held back tears of rage.

He was well and truly fucked over a barrel and both his bosses, with years of experience, had made good and sure that the blame went past them and fell firmly on Simon's shoulders. He left the office and headed upstairs to see Judith and tell her all. Yet on the way he saw the office for what it really was, a prison, one that sapped the very core from his soul, with the payoff being he and Lucy could take a year's break from the working grind, have a couple of holidays and he could finish his book.

When he entered Judith's room, she rushed forward and gave him a hug of solidarity and said she would back him in any way she could in fighting this work injustice. But he had already made up his mind by then. He would take the money and run and worry about the drudgery of work in a year's time. No, this would work out fine. He knew it.

Brian from HR came to him with the contract to terminate his employment, which he got everyone to check, even Trudy, the lawyer. He was guaranteed this month's and next wages in full and a one off thirty-five thousand pound pay off, as long as he did nothing to jeopardise it by going to arbitration or suing the company at a later date. He signed it in front of Jim, Judith and Sarah and packed up his things in two carrier bags and his rucksack and was out of the building by twelve thirty. Janice and Keith had made themselves scarce for the day and Simon left the company he had worked for over ten years with no regrets at all.

Simon did not go home at once. He visited his favourite bookshops and had promised to pop back at a later date with his old work friends for a farewell drink after work. He got on an empty carriage, on a near empty train at five to two and was surprised to see the fog had lifted as the train passed Wimbledon and they had none at Surbiton. The train shot past Esher and the Sandown racecourse, Hersham with its shitty station on stalks and then finally past Walton to Hedge End.

The copse was open to the public again now and Simon walked through the grey trees, carrying a decade's worth of work crap in two plastic bags. It made him smile, even though it was a bitter and twisted one. Life, like the woods, had many paths in it and he had just wondered off the largest one now, onto an unbeaten track.

In the branches of the oak tree above, the raven eyed Simon Hay as he walked past underneath. and the raven knew the time was soon swiftly arriving like an eastern breeze and he would come with it, for good or ill. Simon trudged on down Hanger Hill, letting the slope and downward momentum of the hill make him feel like he was half-floating above the hard pavement.

When he passed his dream home, Hill House, his attention was captured by a tall dark woman in her thick cotton dressing gown and matching slippers, bending over to peer around her various coloured topped bins. She was calling out the name, "Meisha," over and over like a mantra for the lost. Simon wondered what had happened to the little rat sized excuse for a dog he sometimes saw her drag through the copse now and again. He had seen her many times, and sometimes in the company of a tall, jowly man, but he never knew them by name, only sight. They were Mr & Mrs Hill House to his mind.

Simon walked briskly, turning on an extra gear of pace before the woman could turn round and enlist his aid in searching for her prized child-supplementing pooch. He kept to the right-hand side of the road and down the hill, crossing by the bank as usual and past the cenotaph, the Cricketers pub that both backed onto the May Day Field. Then across the road past the Green Man to his and Lucy's place. He got in and stopped in the hall. The house seemed grey and dull like unpolished metal and he did not want to be there. It felt wrong like he was bunking off school. He went upstairs and pushed his rucksack and two plastic bags under the bed and hurried downstairs, not wanting to disturb anything, not even the dust on the radiator cover.

He left and locked the house and retraced his steps back down Green Street, his shoes nearly wandering into the pub, but he hadn't even eaten his lunch and beer would be only a temporary solution, with longer less happy consequences. No, in the end he cut across the dirt track between the May Day field and the cricket pitch and pavilion that took him into Hay's Street, then up over the bridge over the railway to an old house, still with its blue door that had welcomed him home every childhood day.

He knocked twice, using the old chrome knocker, for the blue doored house had no bell, and waited on the crisscross rubber mat that had seen many a muddy shoe and better days. The door opened after twenty seconds and an older shorter version of him, with glasses and a claret pullover, appeared.

"Hello Dad."

Jerry Hay peered over his glass to the hall clock and then back at his son. "Early day, is it today, son?"

"Every day will be an early one from now on," Simon said, his mouth taking on a sour droop.

"Sounds like I need to get the kettle on. Come in, Simon. Come on in if you're coming. Don't let all the warmth out, mate."

Jerry Hay turned and headed in his socks through to the kitchen, leaving Simon to close the door after him. He instantly knew he had made the right decision in coming to see his dad, rather than sulking at home, or boozing the afternoon away.

"So when you going to do your master plan then, Dad?"

They were in the upstairs spare bedroom of the three bedroom family home, which now only housed his father's trains since Simon had moved out. Simon leaned against the door frame sipping his half drunk cuppa, while his father tinkered with his latest model railway steam engine. A rounded L-shape of a huge railway diorama was set up on three levels with hills, bridges, waterways and scale houses and more from next to the back facing window to round to the bedroom door.

"You sure you don't mind? It is still your old bedroom, son."

"Leave the bed then and work around it, just in case Lucy chucks me out tonight then."

The grand plan was to knock two holes in the dividing wall between the space and Simon's old room, and make tunnels so Jerry could set up another track next door and the trains could pass through.

"And you can help me do it, if you're taking a year out like you say. Sounds like a plan to me. Give you time to get down that gym and get that History of Hedge End book you've put off for years."

Jerry sat down on a long stool and picked up his tea to continue drinking.

"Plus, we can have the odd pub lunch now and again, maybe pop up to the Oval as well." Simon was convincing himself more as he spoke. The only blip on the horizon was Lucy's reaction.

"Sounds good to me, Si, so how do you think Lucy will react?"

"Well, I finally got around to asking her to marry me yesterday. This would give us time to plan that and afford a nice honeymoon."

"Go with that, son, good plan of attack. Maybe pick up some wedding magazines in Smiths on the way home." Mr Hay senior pointed at his son and sipped his tea.

"You crafty old beggar, I like it."

"I have my uses."

"Just need to get you paired up. How about Mrs Puck?, She's available."

"She'd eat me alive, that one. Quite a looker for her age, but not my type, Simon," Jerry drained his tea and put it next to his OO scale railway set.

"Do ever get the urge for…" Simon smiled and winked at his 60-year-old just retired father.

"Simon, please." Jerry raised his hands, finding the turn of conversation rather embarrassing.

"Don't you get lonely though, Dad? It's been, what, twenty odd years since Mum, you-know." Simon shrugged and nearly spilled his tea on the faded green carpet.

"After your mother left me, it kinda put me off women for life, son. Anyway, I have the Railway Enthusiasts club. I'm chairman now, you know."

"Okay." Simon glanced down at his watch. It was nearly five. He finished off his second cup of tea of the visit. "I better get those wedding mags, maybe a nice bottle of cava."

"Simon, don't be a cheapskate. Get her bubbly at least, to soften the blow," Jerry said as he stood up and moved over to his son. They embraced and then headed down the stairs to say good bye.

The journey back was colder and Simon used the pavement, taking the Bates Road and less muddy way back to town. Luckily W H Smith's was three shops before the shoe shop where Lucy worked and he picked up three wedding magazines, honeymoon brochures from the travel agents on the way back on a clever whim and a bottle of champagne from the small supermarket.

He was smiling by the time he got home, placed the champagne in the fridge, scattered the magazines and brochures on the coffee table and set about cooking Lucy dinner.

Lucy got home at five-thirty-five. All she wanted to do was have a bath, throw on her bed things and curl up in front of the television and watch her shows. She'd only just dropped her handbag on the radiator cover and was hanging up her coat when the sounds and smells of cooking registered with her.

She rushed up the hall and into the kitchen to find Simon lighting a gas ring under a covered saucepan.

"What are you doing here?"

"Wait," Simon said and turned to put his finger over her lips to silence her questions. Then he grabbed two champagne flutes from the draining board and opened the fridge to pull out a bottle of champagne.

"Simon, what's going on?"

"Hold please," he answered and pushed the glasses into her hands and then proceeded to unwrap and uncork the champagne, with minimal spillage.

"It this to do with getting engaged? Maybe we should do if more often if you're going to get home early every night to cook me dinner."

"Nothing to do with engagement. Well, not directly anyways," he replied as he lifted the bottle to fill the glasses.

"Why are you home early?"

"Shssh, all in good time, my love."

"You haven't got the sack have you?" she joked. She took a sip of champagne, the bubbles tickling the end of her nose.

Then she saw his face fall like he had suffered a mini-stroke. A sickly feeling appeared in the pit of her stomach and she instantly knew why he was home early to cook her dinner.

CHAPTER FORTY-FOUR

Mathew and Catherina had worked hard all day and reclaimed the master bedroom and living room from the spiders, dirt and elements. On Cat's insistence he had rung round for a couple of quotes from local builders for repairs to the house and roof. The electrical shop rang to inform them that the fridge was coming tomorrow and the cooker next Tuesday, so things were moving in the right direction.

Mathew had not cleared away the vegetation from the garden gate yet, so Catherina promised herself that was first on her list, followed by the lawn and the roses that covered the windows at the front of the house. They sat now in front of the open roaring boiler trying to warm up, Catherina on Mathew's lap as they tried to toast bread on long carving forks with little success. They sipped hot chocolate off a top of a box of stuff from the apartment as they held each other close to warm the chill from their spines.

"I could get used to this," Mathew said, pulling his toast out of the fire before its blackened side caught flame.

"What, burning bread?"

"Her-her, funny. No, this, the simple life, with no deadlines and bank managers, and having you here makes it doubly worthwhile."

"The hard-nosed business man is not going soft, is he?" Catherina turned on his lap so her face looked down into his eyes from only three inches away.

"Soft, not when you're around, Cat."

"Hmmn, I can feel that." She laughed and holding his handsome face, she kissed him, her lips sucking at his bottom lip as they parted.

His hands popped open two buttons of his old shirt she had borrowed to clean the house and slipped his right palm and fingers into her bra to cup her breast. Breathlessly she kissed him back, their passions rising to the fore, before Mathew's new pay-as-you-go mobile phone went off.

His fingers left her warm boob and pulled the phone from his jeans pocket, while an annoyed Catherina moved back and pushed at her mane of hair. He saw who was ringing and turned to Catherina with an apologetic look on his face. "I have to take this, sorry."

Catherina got off his lap and watched him leave the room as he had done so many times in their relationship, leaving her both annoyed and frustrated. Crossing her arms over her unbuttoned blouse, she moved towards the window to stare outside, as dusk settled over Hedge End and Leggett Woods. The woodpecker sat upon the old bird bath watching her intently and then flew off to perch on the wall over the garden gate. There it wandered up and down before flying into the woods two minutes later, when Mathew re-entered the room.

"Who was that on the phone?"

"Bit of business. Just cashed in some secret shares that the taxman doesn't know about. It should give us some cash to live on and smarten this place up."

Mathew moved up behind her to embrace her and tried to slip his hand back under her blouse again. She blocked this with her crossed arms and then turned and headed into the kitchen leaving him trailing after.

"Hey, you okay, Cat?"

"I am fine. I just want a bath now before bed, okay? Make sure you put more wood onto the fire," she said. Then she left the kitchen to dig out some towels from a box and stomp upstairs to the bathroom.

"Great timing, Tim." He cursed at his mobile phone and then shoved it back into his pocket and went to feed the flames of the boiler.

CHAPTER FORTY-FIVE

Angela had searched all day in vain for Meisha.
As the sun set over her garden, she headed up the path to the rear of her property, with a torch in her hand, trying to find the place where her dog had escaped from the garden last night. She had found a rabbit hole at the rear of the boundary fence and had called down that for an hour in the afternoon after the fog had lifted, but to no avail.

She had searched out front and then finally got dressed and walked up to the copse, but no trace of her little Meisha could be found. Dusk was fast descending and she checked every one of her dog's hiding places without any luck, before heading up to check the rabbit hole once again. Maybe the silly thing had gone bunny hunting and got stuck down there and if she was stuck, how would Angela get her out?

She wished her anger had not caused her to snap and shut Meisha out all night for nipping her ankle. It was all her husband's fault, but she had put paid to him. Taking the largest suitcase she could find, she put a load of his clothes inside and taken them all down to the nearest local charity shop.

"Meisha darling, it's Mummy. Come on, baby, time to come home," she half-sang, half-said to the greenery as she moved up the path to the rear fence.

Then she stopped dead, where there had been a rabbit hole this morning was a bloody great excavation large enough for a man to fit down. This must mean Meisha surely had been doing the digging. The hole still kept its width all the way down it seemed into the bowels of the earth. She felt like someone had walked over her grave for a moment and she shivered. The night was drawing in around her and the temperature was falling fast. Then just on the edge of her torch light she caught a quiver of movement.

"Meisha, is that you?"

Angela Pratchett leaned down as far as her balance would allow and a whiff of sickly sweet figs or honey hit her nose from the hole below. All movement had stopped, but she was sure that just at the edge of her vision, something was down there, maybe Meisha, unable to climb out. She stood to her full height again and wondered if there was any rope in the shed she could lower down for her dog to bite and let her pull her up.

A swooping movement in the ever darkening sky to her left caused her to turn sharply. Something dark and full of feathers and claws crashed into her face, scratching deep furrows of agony into her skin and scalp. Angela took one step back in retreat, pin wheeled for half a second and then fell backwards down into the hole.

The raven did not linger in the garden. It screeched once and flew off across the railway tracks and to the safety of its bolt hole high in a tree trunk overlooking the now defunct Catholic Church.

Angela wrenched her neck badly as she slid and finally came to a halt ten feet down the wide hole, wedged in with arms and legs a tangled mess. Her face stung like cold icicles had been laid on her cheeks and she spat out earth that had flown into her open crying mouth as she fell. The torch had skittered down to land with a bump on the thing she guessed was Meisha trapped. But she had been dead wrong.

She moved her head sideways to look down and her body sunk two more inches, causing her to cry out in fear and pain.

"Someone, help me please. I'm down this frigging hole," she called up, but her nearest neighbours were both still at work.

Movement caught her eye below and she could hear something was clawing its way up the dark passage towards her. Each time the thing below clawed the earth to propel itself upwards it caused little falls of dirt to slide down to wherever the hole led.

"Mary mother of Jesus, protect me, your humble servant,

oh lord, please hear this prayer and forgive me." But her prayer faltered and there was no one to hear her cries for help or confession.

The smell of honey and overripe fruit was making her gag now, for there was another smell beneath it all, a smell of sweat and putrid gases. Warm breath caressed her forehead as a grunting thing heaved itself to her line of sight.

Angela screamed and every last breath emptied from her burning lungs at the creature that her brown eyes beheld, but not for long. It bit deep into her large fleshy lips and tore them from her surprised teeth and mouth with a savage shake of its human sized head. Blood flew around the cramped confines of the hole as the lipless woman screamed again, only for the human-like thing to bite off her tongue and chew it in front of her eyes, before she passed out from shock.

The creature took her nose next and then with ten fingers grabbed at her head and twisted it round until it heard a crack of vertebra. A leg and then an arm had to be bitten through before Angela's dead body could be dragged down into the hole to be reunited with what remained of her beloved Meisha.

CHAPTER FORTY-SIX

Mrs Puck stood up from the upstairs toilet, wiped herself dry and shivered like a thousand frozen corpses had marched across her future resting place. She pulled her knickers up over her pale goose-bump covered legs and pushed down her hitched skirt.

Something felt very wrong. Her hands trembled and the tips of her long hair felt like they had been plugged into the mains. She rubbed urgently at an icy ache that had suddenly come on at the nape of her neck and left the bathroom. She crossed the second floor landing toward the picture window that took up a great gap in the wall next to the stairs leading downward.

She peered out. Dusk had nearly taken on the black mantle of night and her garden below was festooned with dark shapes and wanton shadows. From her vantage point she could see over the wall into her secret grove beyond. The tall ancient oak dominated her vision and she could see down the line of smaller cherry trees right to the even darker feminine cunt like slit that led to places only she entered and even then with growing trepidation.

Her eyes closed to slits as she tried hard to get her half-century old eyes to work harder and pierce the umbra shadows that covered the base of the trunk. She moved her body and head closer to the glass at the far right of the window frame, trying hard not to fog the pane with her breath. There it was again. She was sure this time. Movement around the base of the tree. Something raised its head into a less shadowy part of the oak's bark and she knew by the shape of the head and movement of the figure that the children of Lugus were testing the boundaries of their fading prison confines.

Mrs Puck had not called them. They were breaking free of their own accord and that meant only one thing, human blood had been spilt this night and the final battle lines were being drawn. She knew somewhere on Hanger Hill or more likely in Hedge End, only one of the Roman blockades remained, where once there had been four, and its power could not fully hold back the children of Lugus.

She also knew from spoken word and then clay, then slate and finally paper that when only one block remained, filled with his life blood, he shall return, raise up his long sleeping followers and sweep all other gods and deities before him in his rage and anger. Mrs Puck rushed for the stairs, taking them two by two until she reached the ground floor, a tad out of breath and hastened into her large volume filled library. She reached not for any books of ancient lore or etched wooden tablets. No she made for her late father's globe drinks cabinet and poured herself three fingers of brandy.

CHAPTER FORTY-SEVEN

The convincing part had not gone as well as Simon had hoped. Big oral expressions of love and explaining his feelings were harder for him to do than giving a training talk at work to 30 odd colleagues.

Shock had turned to hugs and then interrogation, too much swearing, to "wadda-we-gonna-do-now" wails and then endless sobbing. He hated when Lucy went into one like this. It made his ears vibrate painfully.

He sat next to her and put a compassionate arm over her shoulder, only for her to duck, shrug and move a few more inches to the right onto the settee. Changing tack, Simon reached forward and picked up a honeymoon holiday brochure and opened it to a couple getting married on a white sandy beach, next to a clear blue sea.

"Look, we can have a year, maybe a year and a half off, just the two of us, time to get married, make babies and enjoy being young while we still can." Simon pushed the glossy holiday brochure under her eyes and slowly let it rest on her lap.

"But that was such a great job, Si. You had status, a management position and I could boast about it to my friends and family," she sniffed and dabbed at each watering eye with a curved forefinger.

"Well, imagine boasting that we're taking a year off to travel and get married and have not the slightest money worry. I could even slice ten grand off the mortgage and still have money in the bank to last a year of indulgence."

"Sod the mortgage, Simon. We have years to pay that shit off." Lucy palmed her drying tears from her cheeks and her red-rimmed eyes focused on the cotton suited man and the white dressed woman barefoot on the beach.

"Just imagine no more pongy feet to touch, no more Chavs on benefits buying shoes you can't afford." He took her hand and smiled. "You could do a course at home even and go into a new career of your choosing, Luce."

The feet part swung it. "And no more getting up early. Imagine that, Si, long sexy lie-ins."

"Until the baby turned up."

"Yeah." Lucy took his face in her hands and kissed his lips hard.

"That was a good start," he said, his face still close to hers.

"Tomorrow I'll hand in my notice and you can start by taking me out to dinner Saturday night, as you're visiting old Pucker tomorrow night, you bookworm."

Lucy smiled and let him kiss her this time. He could have his book, if she was getting the beach wedding and the baby she always desired. They went and ate their luke-warm dinner and then cuddled up in front of the telly, drinking champagne and talking of plans for the future.

CHAPTER FORTY-EIGHT

Catherina went to bed early and sleep came upon her swiftly, even with the faint smell of paint and moldy underlay coming from the main bedroom. Mathew worked on, seeing he had no television to watch or any chance of any other fun tonight. He just wanted to clear the bedroom, get it painted and then get some people in to add modern heating and new carpets to the place and fix all the leaks in the south-east corner of the house.

He finally finished undercoating the walls at half-past-nine and dumped the smelly old carpet outside to the side of the garage. A skip was added to the ever growing list of things to do in his mind, but at least soon he would have the hard cash to make his great uncle's place habitable for a while. At the very least it would increase the sale value of the place, or maybe in time he could sell off the woods for housing and keep the house for him and Catherina. His mind was working over-drive in business mode again. He could just set up his next business in her name and all the people he owed money to, including the taxman, could go fuck themselves.

He put his roller in the sink, covered it with washing-up liquid and blasted the white paint off it. The red washing-up liquid and the paint made his fingers go pink as the undercoat eventually gave way to yellow foam.

He had just wrung out the roller with icy cold hands and put it on a newspaper on the floor to dry out when he heard a knocking sound once, and then again from behind the cellar door, which he had yet to open. He wiped his hands on an old t-shirt he was using as a cloth and stood up facing the cellar door.

Old childhood fears returned to him as the naked light bulb above him flickered once and then went out, leaving him in near darkness. Only the glow from the fire through the open boiler room door cast a small cone of light to the right of him. He had hidden down there once during a game of hide-and-seek with best-mate, back then in those hot pre-teen summers that memory always cast in sunshine to him. They stood out as beacons of love and normality he never got at home or whatever barracks they were stationed. That was when his father had him and his brother with him at all.

It had been raining that day though, constantly, from the day before dawn to that evening and all of their outdoor and woodsy games and adventures had been lost to them. Hide and seek had been the last choice, but Mathew really enjoyed it and was easily the better at finding places to hide. The cellar was out-of-bounds to him, his kindly, if eccentric great uncles only edict, and so made it a perfect place to hide. Jimmy was out in his shed and out of the way, potting up veg and Mathew opened the door and crept down the stone steps.

Even though it had stone walls, the floor on the far side was bare cold earth and all manner of junk, which is ever so interesting to a boy of eleven, was dotted about the large cellar. He had squatted behind an old beer barrel, feeling rather pleased with himself and pretty sure that his friend would never enter the dark cellar to look for him. After fifteen minutes, the cellar door opened and the light went on, three bulbs linked by looping and dangling cables around the cellar.

"Matt, you down there, mate?" his friend had called and Mathew had pulled his arms around his tucked up legs behind the barrel.

Hearing not a sound of encouragement, his friend left to search the living room again. Mathew smiled with cocky relief and turned to look about the now lit cellar. Immediately next to him they stood, tiny hands held tightly together as they stared at him with inquisitive eyes.

Jimmy caught his screaming fleeing figure as he came in from the wet outside. He saw instantly where the boy had come from and that had brought Matt's friend skidding round the corner to see what all the commotion was about.

"Simon, get your coat and go home now," Jimmy said in such a stern voice that young Simon fled without a goodbye, grabbing his coat and running down Hanger Hill to his house. He was crying for some reason, not for him, mostly for Mathew, his best friend.

Mathew had been used to corporal punishment from his dad, but a shouting at from Great Uncle Jimmy seemed much worse somehow, even though he laid not a finger upon him. He had been sent to bed without any dinner, sobbing not out of fear, but of the realisation that he had let his great uncle down somehow. It was only when the sobbing into his wet pillow has ceased in the dark of his bedroom, that he recalled the two figures he had seen and their odd grey-green appearance that had brought wails of fear out of him. He slept little that night and kept his Star Wars torch on under the covers, as he shivered with the cold of evening and fear of the cellar. The next day the padlock had appeared before breakfast and things in the house had returned to its normal free and happy status quo. His uncle bore him no undue malice and cooked him a hearty fried breakfast to make up for missing dinner the night before. As for the cellar, it was never mentioned again and Mathew never went within two feet of the door if he could help it.

Yet now as a man, he stood only inches from the old wooden door, his eyes on the old padlock, his ears straining for any new sounds from beyond. He was about to walk away when he heard the creak of bending wood and then shuffling footfalls of more than one person ascending the staircase beyond the dividing cellar door.

Mathew could not help himself and leaned closer, his earlobe only a hair's breadth from the wood. Beyond the door the footfalls reached the top step. Only the thump of his heart could he hear as he held his breath as long as he was able. Only when he knew he could not wait to exhale any longer did two voices speak as one from behind the two inches of solid wood.

"Lo zio." The words were spoken in his ears, but he was not sure that sound waves had carried those ghostly falsetto voices to him. Or had they appeared in his head? It did not matter, for when he calmed himself to a panting shivering mess of a man, he found he was upstairs and in his old bedroom, with nothing but panicked flashes running in his scared mind.

Mathew undressed quickly and lay next to the sleeping Catherina, wanting to wake her to see if she knew what the Italian sounding words meant, but too scared to do anything but hold the duvet over his head and beg for sleep to come.

CHAPTER FORTY-NINE

Catherina was up with the lark, or the woodpecker, that Friday morning, dressed in two jumpers an old coat and a matching set of woolen gloves, scarf and hat of vibrant green. She leaned against the worktops by the kitchen window, munching on the last of her toast and sipping the dregs of her black bitter coffee.

A low mist covered the frosty tall grass of the garden and her gaze wandered down to the shining new shears next to her breakfast plate. The fire had just been rekindled and she felt cold all over, especially at the core of her lower back where her t-shirt beneath her jumpers had ridden up out of her jean tops. Her mobile told her it was barely past eight in the morning, but she had been in bed early and upstairs her partner still snored.

With a last swig of coffee she grabbed the shears and made for the front door. The roses that blocked half the light from the front windows would be her first gardening experiment. If the delivery van with the cooker arrived, she would be there to catch it. She started the daunting task at one corner by the garage, where the roses once crept in through broken panes, now boarded up with hardwood.

By the time she finished the first bed up to the front door she wished for thicker gloves, for she had three scratches or thorn pokes already. She looked at the debris on the gravel drive and wondered what the old brown rose branches would smell like if popped on the open fire of the boiler.

With one side done, it gave her a good excuse to pause for a loo break. She took a few cut twigs inside to toss on the fire and to catch a little warmth back, as her very soul felt frozen.

Mathew had not surfaced yet and she kindly used the grottier kitchen loo so as not to wake him. She gingerly sat down on the freezing wooden seat and tried hard to think of anything but rats coming up the bowl to nibble at her tender bits.

"You sure this is the best of plans, Noel?"

Noel Pratchett looked around on the door step of Hill House and put his thin fingered left hand tenderly against the younger man's cold red cheek. "I need some more clothes and some bank stuff, okay, Rupert? Come on, be brave for me."

The younger, taller man leaned forward, kissed his older lover on his thin lips and gave a wavering grin back, as it was all he could manage. He hated confrontation and one with Noel's Caribbean wife of many years was one he greatly feared. The front door was open now and the die was cast. He followed his man over the threshold and into the hallway.

"Angela, are you home?"

Rupert cringed inside at the sound of his lover's yelling at the top of his voice. The place looked very sterile to his interior designer eyes, not a home at all, but a cold mausoleum to a slowly dying marriage. The light in the kitchen was still on, but the heating wasn't, and not for the first time the French windows of the conservatory were shut but unlocked. Noel could see no one outside, nor any sign of Meisha, so he headed upstairs to the main bedroom.

"What the blue-blazes?" Noel exclaimed, seeing a large section of his clothes were missing from his wardrobe.

On further inspection the large suitcase and some of Angela's clothes were also missing, leaving a small mystery.

"What's going on, Noel?"

"I'm not sure, let's check the study." Rupert followed his older lover down the stairs to his study.

"Her passport is not in the usual place we put them and the computer has an email on our joint account confirming a plane ticket back to Tobago." Noel spun around on his swivel chair to look up at Rupert, who was standing against a low sideboard, trying not to look bored.

"Don't blame her, hun. If you dumped me after x-amount of years, I'd piss off to the Caribbean also."

"Means we have the house to ourselves." Noel's thin lip curled up to match his left eyebrow.

"Now you're talking my kind of house warming, darling." Rupert gave his big bottom lip a slutty look of desire that he knew drove a certain type of gentleman wild, and unbuttoned the fly of his tight black jeans.

In the back garden of Hill House, the low graveyard mist hugged the ground to its bosom and covered the hole near the fence from all but the closest inspection.

CHAPTER FIFTY

A mixture of guilt, routine and a strange feeling like he was bunking off school, made Simon get up and make Lucy breakfast as she took a quick shower.

"You should have stayed in bed, Si. You didn't have to get up early just to keep me company."

Simon sat down at the table and poured her a glass of apple juice.

"Routine, I suppose. I can always head back under the covers when you've gone."

"I would. Got any plans for today, then?"

Lucy grabbed three pieces of toast and scraped marmalade over them, with no butter or margarine underneath, as was her usual method.

"Dunno, sort my questions out for Mrs Puck tonight, bit of daytime TV and general slobbing about in my jammies I think are the order of the day," he said before sipping at his tea, which was too hot to drink as of yet.

"Lucky fella."

"Thought you might be a bit pissed, seeing that you have to go into work and I don't."

"No way. This is going to be one of the best days of my life, handing in my resignation. Here's to us and our future, without meaningful employment," she said and raised her juice glass to tap against his tea mug.

"Well, Juicy Lucy, I wish you well with that."

"Thank you, Haystack. I can't fucking wait to get into work for once."

"You're up early."

Catherina stood up from where she had kicked the rose bush shoots and twigs into a rough pile with her long old black boots and saw Mathew poking his bed tussled head from around the front door-frame.

"Lots to do, sleepy-boy," she replied, brushing at the green stains on her jeans.

"Well then, this might help the worker," he said. Coming out of the door, she saw that he had two steaming hot cups of coffee, one in each hand.

She smiled despite herself, and went over to kiss his warm cheek and take one of the offered coffee mugs with a quick thank-you very much, "*grazie mille.*"

"That looks better. What you going to tackle next then?"

"If you keep an eye of for the cooker delivery man, I will sort out the garden and see what tools are in your great uncle's shed." She nodded for them to go inside and they both retired to the empty living room to sip at their coffee in only a slightly warmer place.

"While you're here, you ever heard the words *lo zio*? Is it Italian?"

Mathew was looked out the now brighter rose-free window, trying to seem as nonchalant as possible.

"It is Italian. It means uncle. Why? Where did you hear it?"

"Something I heard on the radio this morning, that's all," He looked down at his swirling brown coffee. "I have to pop out later, about lunchtime. You'll be okay here on your own, won't you?"

"*No problema*" She smiled back warmly. She was itching to explore the cellar and the woods that led off the garden and she wanted to be alone for some odd un-shakeable reason.

"Fine, I'll better get-" The ring of his mobile interrupted him and he looked down to see a number he did not recognize, so he put it to his ear to answer.

Catherina left him to it and went into the kitchen to find a biscuit or three to nibble on, as the gardening had made her stomach rumble and her throat feel a little sick. She was on her last one, catching crumbs with her hand, when he entered the kitchen, his phone down by his side.

"That was the cooker people. There's been a cock-up and the bloody thing won't arrive until Monday morning now."

"Well, that gives you a good excuse to take me out for dinner Saturday night. Somewhere that is not a fish and chip shop or café, okay?"

"Okay." He nodded, knowing he would have hard cash and lots of it when Tim turned up at noon.

Mrs Puck did not leave the house that morning, nor did she venture anywhere near the grove at the far end of her long garden. She had remembered that Simon Hay was coming over to chat about local history. This, she decided, was no mere accident. It was part of what was slowly happening to the place. The Hay family line was just as long as her own and for generations they tendered the great hawthorn hedge that had squared off Woodhouse copse, when it had been a huge wood. The coming of the railway diagonally through the woods had seen the end to that line of work and the houses soon followed, until only isolated remnants of the original hedge remained.

Mrs Puck looked at her well tendered body in the full length mirror inside her walk-in wardrobe adjacent to her large bedroom. She was dressed down in a simple long skirt and blue blouse, her bushy auburn hair tied back, giving her features a harder look. This would never do. She undressed until she stood naked before the mirror. She would run a bath, do her hair and wear something that would show off her best assets and squeeze in the rest.

Mrs Puck knew that Simon Hay was going to be a part of the unravelling of the ancient guards that held her gods so long imprisoned and she wanted him on her side of the hedge. She squeezed the large nipples on her ample chest and dark unnatural thoughts came running from the squalid gutters of her mind.

Now that the cooker wasn't coming today, Catherina set off to the shed at the rear of the property and found some shears, a push-along hand mower, a sledge hammer and an old farming scythe like her grandfather had rusting away in an old barn back on the farm in Italy. She had to use the shears to free a weed and bramble tangled upturned wheel-barrow, so she could put the implements in it and wheel off with a high-pitched squeak to the back garden.

She started with the shears. They worked okay, but would take ages even to clear the simplest path through the high grass and tall weeds. She used the scythe next and once she got over the awkwardness of wielding it and the pull on muscles she had not used in years, she was soon hacking and slashing away like the Grim Reaper after dead men's souls.

After a while she had a path to the end of the garden and used the ungainly scythe to cut down the vegetation that blocked the old door in the red brick boundary wall. That only got her so far and shears were followed by hand-to-hand fighting with the twisted vines and weeds that kept the door from opening.

After another half an hour of finger aching shears work, she had severed every root and vine that crossed the edges of the old doorway. Now it should open and she could see what lay beyond the confines of the overgrown garden. She lifted an old black painted catch and had to hit it with the palm of her gloved hand to get it free. There was no handle, only the rusted shape and four sets of screw holes where the handle had once been. Seeing that she could not pull it, she would give it a good push to see if it opened that way.

"Whatcha doing?"

Catherina jumped out of her tanned olive skin and turned to berate her boyfriend, who stood behind her with an evil grin on his handsome face.

"You fucking *idiota*, you scared the *merda* from me. Don't do it again, silly boy." She finished her verbal rebuke with a whack of each of her hands to his upper arms.

"Sorry, Cat, I couldn't resist." He retreated back a couple of steps until he bumped into the overhanging willow tree. "Let's have a look before I shoot off. It's been years since I've been through that door."

"It looks like years since *anybody* has been through this door," she added.

"I always thought it was an entrance to Narnia or Middle Earth when I was a kid."

"You were once a child? I thought you came along all grown up, Mathew," she teased. She pushed hard at the door in the wall. It resisted for two second then a hidden creeper gave way and the door shot inwards into a scene from a book that Mathew had just described.

An earthen path led downwards on steps made from trees roots and dirt that had collected. The trees were small and close-knit and towered over by larger ones to give the place a dark tunnel effect. Green mould adorned every bough and branch and the tree trunks where covered like clothes in ivy from the tops of their boughs to their roots. High bushes of camellias filled in the rest of the gaps, with pink spreading flowers that seemed out of place in this dank enclosing avenue of trees.

"Well, that doesn't look as inviting as I remembered, but I suppose things never do look as good when you see them through adult eyes."

"Where does it lead?" Catherina asked, putting her gloved hands on her cheeks and then lips: It seemed to her that she had seen this place before, in a dream or quite possibly a nightmare.

"Down to a little dell and then it opens up a bit and the place becomes less dense with trees. It was a great place to play when I visited. Looks a bit shabby and miserable now."

"I think it looks inviting," she murmured under her breath.

"What did you say?"

"Nothing," she replied and pulled at her glove so she could stare at her watch. "Shouldn't you be going soon?"

"Blimey, you're right." He took her in his arms and kissed her long on the lips. "I'll be two hours tops, okay?"

"I'll be fine. I will go explore our enchanted forest."

"Well, don't get lost, and don't let the Hagmen get you."

Mathew turned and using his arm ducked under the willow's branches.

"Who are the Hagmen, Mathew?"

"Dunno why I mentioned them really. Standing here again

just reminded me. My great uncle said every time we went in there to be careful of the Hagmen because they have no heads and faces in their tummies and will eat little boys if they misbehave." Mathew shrugged and shivered, and then turned to leave again. "Later, babe. Ciao."

"Ciao." She watched him trudge off round the house and out of sight.

Catherina stared into the tunnel of trees and bushes and even though she'd never been here before the place somehow seemed oh so familiar to her, though she could not figure out how. Grabbing the wall, she ducked down to avoid a branch and entered Leggett Woods proper. The flowers pink and wide seemed so beautiful and the green of the ivy and mould on the trees gave it a fairy feel to it. She daintily stepped down the roughhewn natural steps and followed the tight path until it turned away to the left. The open doorway soon disappeared from sight and she moved onwards in wonder at the magic place where she now lived.

She felt no unease, and it seemed strangely like home, even though it looked like no wood she ever had visited in the surrounding area of her home town. The close tree lined path soon widened out into a round dell when no trees grew and the woods opened out. Ivy and dark green bushes covered the mattress of the woods apart from the earthen paths. She picked one such spur and headed south-west, away from the house.

When she had gone the woodpecker flew down from its perch where it had kept its beady eyes upon her in silent vigil. Then it flew to the floor of the woods and under the coverings of the lost Roman well, to inform the watcher that she walked abroad in the woods.

CHAPTER FIFTY-ONE

"So how was your wander in the woods? Any good?" Mathew asked as he came through the living room door to find Catherina sipping a coffee in the dining room.

"Very good, thank you. I love this place and woods, Mathew." She held her steaming coffee near to her cold cheeks and lips, as if to steal any warmth from the mug.

"Didn't get lost, then?" Mathew asked, putting an old blue sport holdall on the dining table.

"No," she replied, her brown eyes staring at the bag. "I walked so far I left the woods on the other side and found a road and a hill with something on top like ancient ruins or something. I was getting cold so did not go up for a proper *guardare*, erm, look."

"That is some old Roman ruin or something. Maybe one of your long lost relatives built it, eh Cat?" He smiled his cockiest grin and fiddled with the zip of the holdall.

"Okay, you win, I have to know what is in the bag?"

Mathew's grin pushed up in such a chuffed way, his cheeks ached. The sight of her gesticulating hands made the teasing even better. "This is our emergency house repair fund."

"*Cosa*? Why do you speak in riddles? What is inside the bag?"

"Have a look yourself, beautiful," Mathew said and stepped back to let Catherina come round the table. She set down her coffee mug, unzipped the length of the bag and pulled it open to find it was filled with rubber band rolled wads of fifty pound notes.

"What have you done, robbed a bank?"

"No, don't be silly. I had an emergency fund hidden away so the taxman couldn't seize it with all my other assets. My friend Tim was looking after it for me and now we can use it to get the builders in and buy one of the huge fuck-off-and-die wall tellies the size of a small cinema."

Catherina picked up a wad in each hand, holding them with her long fingernails. "So this will help, erm, decorate the house and make it a home for us both, so we do not have to leave for a long time?"

"Yes, and give me something to start up a new business venture, once I find something else to get my business teeth into. So you okay with this?"

"If it means you and I get to stay here and be together, it is *d'accordo* with me."

Catherina turned and jumped into an embrace that nearly sent Mathew flying, but he caught her under the bum as she kissed him ardently.

"Everything will turn out brilliantly, I can feel it," he said between kisses.

"Mathew, shut up and take me to bed."

Mathew uttered not another word for an hour at least.

Simon Hay did not bother to dress until well after lunch. He had a long soak in the bath, shaved and then dressed in a casual grey shirt and black jeans for his chat with Mrs Puck, the local historian, tonight. He did an hour of research on the internet and jotted down some questions about the local area that he could put to her. After that, feeling a new sense of freedom, he surfed for porn, football and books, in that order of preference.

He relaxed after that by watching a couple episodes out of the *West Wing* box set he had got for Christmas and never had time to watch. He ate biscuits on the settee and drank two cans of Coke one after the other. He still hadn't shaken off the feeling that he was playing hooky from school, but he was doing his best to embrace the situation he found himself in. Simon tried to imagine what he would be doing now at work during those dragging hours after three in the afternoon which made him chuckle aloud with relief. He popped back into the kitchen to get some Ready Salted crisps to celebrate his new life.

Lucy had texted him in her lunch break with lots of smileys and *I've done it xxx,* so everything he had termed as Operation Joint Leisure was going according to plan. Simon smiled and dived into his open crisp packet and ate three at once, loving the salty taste of his work free fingertips.

CHAPTER FIFTY-TWO

An overexcited Lucy kissed Simon hard and long before he left at half-six to have his audience with the most notorious widow in Hedge End. Since her much older husband had died over twenty years ago, many stories, rumours and teenage legend had been told of Mrs Puck, who lived on the top of Hanger Hill.

Yes, the town had invested many hours of gossip in the glamorous woman, giving her a black widow legend even a celebrity PR man or government spin doctor would find hard to shake off. It is said she offed her old hubby for the money, and that her late husband was her father's cousin. She was also a Wiccan, pagan, god hating witch. The younger generation told tales of some unnamed mate of their older brother's turning up to offer to clean her garden and receiving payment in many lewd ways, which got more pornographic with each retelling.

Lucy was in such a mood she did not care that he was visiting the vamp of the village, another of her names. She decided in the end to go on the razz with her cousin and drink till she puked up whatever burger or kebab she could find open at two in the morning.

The air was damp and chilly and Simon had on his long wide collar army surplus coat and a cap to keep his head warm. Once past the sights and sounds of the town, he made his way up Hanger Hill and noticed a mist was forming ahead and slowly coming down the hill. He resisted the urge to go through Woodhouse Copse tonight, after that missing woman business. Plus he had his best work shoes on and did not want them to get wet and mucky. By the time he passed the hedge and got to the roundabout where four roads intersected the mist had gotten thicker, especially around the edges of Leggett Woods and the copse. He pulled his collar up again for the fifth time that night and crossed over the bridge that spanned the railway tracks and across the road to where Mrs Puck's grand old three storey house stood on the peak of Hanger Hill, opposite the old Catholic church.

He pushed open her gate and his shoes made a crunching sound as he walked up her drive to the small porch. A feeling of excitement flowed through him. He remembered all too well the sex rumours of his youth, about how Mrs Puck was supposed have given blow-jobs to every member of the Hanger Hill boys under 16's league football team.

He cleared his throat and raised his hand to grab a brass knocker on the centre of the door, but the door opened before his fingertips could touch the cold metal. Mrs Puck stood there in a long purple dress, with some kind of sparkly stitching, that flowed up from her stockinged feet to a bodice top with long sleeves that was slashed to near her navel, revealing a large, wondrous cleavage for a woman her age.

"Simon, come on in, dear. Let's get you out of the cold," she said, her voice throaty and deep as she stepped aside to let him in.

She had certainly gone to some effort tonight. Her dark auburn hair, normally scraped back and tied, had been styled and let free to have a life of its own. Simon blinked and stepped inside. The heat of the house after coming in from the misty cold made his head spin for a second or two.

"Let's get you out of that coat." She mothered him and quickly pulled it from him as soon as it was unbuttoned to hang it on an antique looking coat stand. He put his cap on top and followed her down the long corridor with its black and white mosaic floor, through one of many doors into a huge library, with pulled velvet red drapes across the window at the front and another pulled set that only half covered another door in the opposite wall.

"Drink, Simon?" she asked, opening an old globe to reveal

decanters and glasses and a few bottles of old reserve whiskey and brandy. "What's you poison? I always find a brandy goes down well to settle the nerves and warm the body from the cold outside."

"Yep, yes, erm, a brandy will be lovely," he stammered. He could not believe how different she looked compared to when he had introduced himself in the high street only two weeks before to ask her about local history and ancient sites of local interest for which she had long campaigned.

"Take a seat, the green one by the fire. Then once we're comfy we can get down to business," she purred. Simon gulped hard and headed where she had pointed. Two high leather wing back chairs stood a few feet away on a rug facing each other in front of a roaring fire like something out of the old Peter Cushing, Christopher Lee Hammer films he used to love to watch as a kid. He sat down and the cushion deflated to half the size instantly.

She joined him and when she leaned over to give him his brandy he wasn't sure whether his eyes or her breasts would pop out first. Luckily his blinking eyelids and the tight material of her purple dress both did their intended jobs.

"So, you're writing a book about the history of Hedge End and Hanger Hill, my favourite subjects. How far have you gone back and what help do you want from me?" Mrs Puck asked, speaking her last few words into her glass before drinking.

"Recent history of how Hedge End became a town and the pre-wars years is easy to collate. What I'm after is the more ancient history of the place and how it got its name and the significance of the hedge. I know before the railways were built it was a near impenetrable square that hid the woods inside from the outside town, or village of that time, but there are no records of any ruins or buildings of any type being inside the hedge's borders?"

"Well, I see we are going to enjoy ourselves tonight. The hedge, hill and village all go back a long time before records were kept, but I have delved deep and found out the beginnings of our town, that even the scholars and historians have never ever learned."

Simon pulled his biro from the top of his notepad and tried not to watch as Mrs Puck crossed her legs, revealing an unseen long slit in her dress that showed off her legs right up to the edges of her stocking tops.

"Excellent. Now Mrs Puck, I have a few questions I prepared earlier, just so I don't get dis- "

"Call me Rose, please, Simon. Mrs Puck makes me sound like some dirty old whore madam, don't you think?"

"Rose it is, then." He smiled back, then darted his eyes to the warm flickering fire and cleared his throat.

"Did you know before the eighteen hundreds and before the hanging of highwaymen, Hanger Hill was called Hay's Hill?" she asked, interrupting his chain of thought.

"Yes, my grandfather used to proudly tell me that, and in the Magna Carta Hedge End was called Hay's End. Maybe I should be up for a lordship, Rose?" Simon laughed, but seeing only a polite tight smile back he gulped at his brandy.

"I love a man who has deeper knowledge than his outward façade betrays," Rose said. She reached over to squeeze his knee, her hair tumbling down over her face like a shampoo ad.

"Thanks," was all he could reply before clearing his throat again.

"But did you know before it was called Hay's End the Anglo Saxons called it Haga-End, which means the same thing. Though time changes its name, it always comes back to hedge time and time again."

"So why was the hedge ever built? It seems pointless to hedge in a wood for no reason."

"Good question, Simon. It's the one I hoped you would ask. It all stems back to the dark ages, some call it, before the Roman invasion of Briton. Long before when the Celts migrated and came to live in this area, there lived a tribe of forest loving and worshipping men who were truly the most ancient of all the natives of this land we now call England. They spoke in a language unknown to the Celts, who left them to dwell in the woods near their new settlement. These men were shorter than the Celts and had black hair and wore little clothing. The Celts traded in the daytime with these men and called them simply the Dwellers. None of the Celts dared to enter the woods at night, for it is said the Dwellers' blood was mixed with Faye people and earth creatures and their gods ran wild and naked in the night. Each kept to their own patch of land and nothing much changed for countless years until the Roman invaded."

"So there was no hedge at that time?" Simon felt more relaxed by the brandy and the drowsy warmth of the open fire.

"No Dweller or Celt grew it, Simon. They both loved and worshiped the land and even began to believe and worship the Dwellers' gods, especially one they called Lugus."

"What were the tribes called, do you know?"

"That's where we have a slight problem. No Celtic names of tribes were ever recorded. The Dwellers were simply called that and the Celts called themselves the Settlers. When the Romans invaded, they called the Celtic settlers of Hedge End the Atrebates."

"What did the Romans call the Dwellers then?"

"Sadly, they were never given names. The Romans were scared of these strange wood Dwellers and after quickly subjugating the Atrebates, they killed every single Dweller they could find."

"Why?"

"Because they feared them. They were different and cohabited with the creatures of the trees and earth and streams. The Dwellers would never bow to Roman rule so all were crucified in a square around the woods. But then came the attacks at night, Romans and Atrebates would be found torn limb from limb, their remains found dragged to the woods themselves. So the Romans cut down a swath of trees and planted a hawthorn hedge the Celtic priests said would keep the spirits and god of the woods trapped inside. Then the Romans called up the power of their gods to keep the Dwellers and their gods trapped inside with unknown alchemy. The Romans, it is said, raised their own army from the underworld and sent them into the woods to capture Lugus himself. A great battle raged in the woods between the Wuduwosa, the servants of Lugus, and the Anthropophagi the Romans had risen from the earth of the trees from another wood they had blessed and imbued."

"What happened then?"

"No one really is sure. The Wuduwosa and the Anthropophagi were immortal beasts and even though the battle raged for many years, no creature on either side could die. The Romans had a cultural trait when they conquered new lands they called it the *Interpretation Romana,* in which they took the local gods like Lugus and took them to be their own gods. Lugus's name was banned on pain of death and replaced with the Roman god Mercury. Saddened by the death of the Dwellers and after year upon dark year his worshipers died out until he fled the woods broken hearted. The Anthropophagi retreated from the woods, their job done, and went back to the earth to sleep until such time they may be called upon again to fight. The hedge grew taller than the height of three tall men and the Wuduwosa were trapped inside and slowly went out of all tales. The men of Hay, your descendants, cared for the hedge, the Romans left, the Anglo-Saxons appeared and Haga-End became Hay's End and then eventually Hedge End."

Simon looked up from his scribbling, nearly five pages of notes, and saw that Mrs Puck was staring down at her empty glass. Her face looked sad and old for the first time tonight.

"Woodhouse Copse, inside the hedge, that's derived from Wuduwosa, surely," Simon said aloud, breaking the silence and crack of the fire.

"Wuduwosa Woods became Woodwose Woods and then Woodhouse Copse. History is all round us, Simon, if we look deep enough with open eyes." Rose Puck's voice was softer now and she crossed her arms over her exposed cleavage like she was suddenly cold or embarrassed by her under-dressing.

"Blimey, Bates Road, from Atrebates. What else can you tell me about the town? How did Leggett Woods get its name?"

"Oh I think that's enough learning for one night, don't you?" Mrs Puck said, rising, wiping at the edges of her eyes.

"That's a shame. It's still early yet," Simon said daringly. He had no idea where his train of thought was leading, towards a dangerous path he thought, but he had an excited devil-may-care edge about him. He was finding out new things about the place where he had always lived and about his ancestors and he wanted to know more. And something else inside wanted something to happen between him and the well preserved Rose Puck.

"Let's try something more frivolous if you're game?"

"I'm game for anything," he replied and then mentally slapped himself. This wasn't him. It must be the brandy and the sight of Rose Puck's enormous chest that were spurring him on.

"Really?" Rose Puck winked. "How about I read your fortune, then?"

"Okay," he replied with a grin.

"Follow me then, Simon" She turned and sauntered towards the other door like some fifties Hollywood movie star. She opened the door into a smaller parlour with hanging drapes of thin satin, red and gold flock wallpaper and only the single light of a tassel shaded lamp from above. It was low and shone down on a small hexagonal table, covered with green baize like a snooker table. Two antique wooden chairs stood on opposite side of the table and she beckoned for him to sit across from her. Once seated, she pulled open a little drawer on the side of the table and took out not tarot cards, but cards carved from thin wood. They were about 5" x 3" and about a quarter of an inch thick. They were of some polished or lacquered orange-red wood and had no marking or designs on any of them, on either side.

"They're a bit different," Simon ventured as his eyes adjusted to the dimmer and slightly colder confines of the smaller room.

"They are called the Leaves of Lugus and were carved long ago from an ancient and most sacred sycamore tree. Do you wish me to proceed, Simon?"

"Yes," he nodded.

Mrs Puck slowly shuffled the wooden cards and then placed them in line with her cleavage on the green baize before her. "Pick just three. Turn them over in a line on the table."

Simon picked up the strange deck of cards, knowing his hands were inches only from her round tempting and most bountiful orbs of delight. He picked three out of the pack at random and set the rest back on the table before her. Mrs Puck picked up the rest of the wooden deck, put them back in the draw and closed it.

"Then let the Leaves of Lugus tell us the fate that awaits you, strong young man of Hedge End." She placed her two forefingers on the first card on the left. "You will in time sire two children, twins. This is a powerful and good start to your reading."

"Anything else?"

"Let us move on." Her fingers now moved to the centre wooden card, which, like the others, had no marking except the ones that the knots and years lines of growing naturally gave it. "Ah there is more here." She tapped. "The twins will be born far away, from a dark haired woman, who comes from the land of our bitter enemies."

"Eh, Lucy has blonde hair. That's not right."

"The leaves do not lie, Simon. Your relationship with Lucy will sadly end."

"But we've only just got engaged, I love her."

"Let us move on the last card. It may clarify the other two." Once again her fingers shifted to the last card and she let out an audible sigh, like one of post-coitial lust.

"What is it?"

"He's coming back, Simon, and we must prepare. The bonds are severing, and he will save us all."

Before Simon could say anything, she lurched forward, knocking the table sideways, and grabbing onto the side of his face, kissed him deeply and passionately.

CHAPTER FIFTY-THREE

Simon Hay was in total shock. He hadn't even realised he had crossed the fog-covered Hanger Hill Road until the pavement hit his left shoe. Luckily for him, the amount of cars on the road was virtually nil and the few that were there were travelling slowly because of the reduced visibility.

One such car came slowly down the hill inching through the heavy fog at twenty miles an hour. Simon turned, shaken from his pondering by the car going past him not more than five feet away. Yet all he could see was a silver ghost of a vehicle, its fog lights burning back the dense grey shroud that covered the road and pavement. He ran his hand through his hair and stopped dead on the pavement that he could barely see.

He was trying to remember when the night took such an erotic turn from the ancient history lesson. That seemed right, but who was to say it wasn't all fantasy and a little fact. Then the strange wooden tarot cards and then the woman old enough to be his mum pouncing on him. That shocked him, as he was far from being a catch, yet he had gone for it too, like Lucy didn't exist. He remembered tearing at her dress to free her huge soft breasts and her rubbing at his stiff cock, and then, when he reached between her legs, she gasped and retreated from their passionate embrace.

Hurried apologies had come from both. She grabbed a cardigan to cover her chest, which had flamed with embarrassment. She showed him to the door and as he left she said, "Don't let this lapse of discretion stop you coming to me again if you need help again, Simon. I am a useful ally."

Useful ally. What a strange thing to say at that moment. At least it wasn't *we still could be friends,* he thought as he walked down the hill. He was glad of the fog that covered him, shrouding his guilt from any car or truck that rumbled past infrequently. He had been in the den of a living local legend and survived. God, what would Lucy think?

Simon stopped outside the drive to Leggett House and checked the time on his mobile phone. It was a somehow a quarter to midnight, but he couldn't have been there that long, surely. He turned sideways and thought he saw a blink of a light being snuffed out in the lower windows of the long vacant house. Had the old place been bought, or more likely squatters moved in? *Good luck to them.* The place always scared the willies out of him. He continued on down the pavement to town and avoided the drunks and vomiting micro-skirted girls. As Friday night turned into Saturday morning, he finally made it home.

Lucky for him Lucy was still out gallivanting with her cousin. As he sat down to turn on the telly, his phone chimed as a text arrived from his fiancée, which read:

I fucling lub you my finance and whant to make babies tonitee when i get in xxx

Lucy

"Fuck me, she must be so drunk," he said. He rose from the sofa, went into the kitchen and fetched the bowl from under the sink next to the cleaning and toilet stuff. He knew what drink did to his Lucy, and he took it upstairs with a bottle of mineral water and the latest Bernard Cromwell book and waited.

Lucy, his Lucy, at that time was being pulled off some game handsome nineteen-year-old lad she had been French kissing by the toilets, by her pissed off cousin.

"What's the matter?" she slurred and tottered as the youth turned to his mates and giggled over him pulling an older bird.

"Time to go home, cousin," Kerry urged, wishing her useless boyfriend would come over and give her a hand.

"But I wanna stay and play with Dave." Lucy smiled at the youth as she tottered again, blinking as if it would aid her addled eyesight.

"Dean!" shouted the angry youth, giving his real name,

as his mates around him cracked up. "Stupid old bitch" He stomped off with his crowing mates in tow.

"Where's he gone?"

"Lucy, you're twenty-eight and engaged to a nice bloke, remember. Now let's get a taxi and get you home, okay?" Kerry tugged Lucy's arm toward the decks where her DJ boyfriend was finishing his set.

"Kerry, I'm gonna be sick," Lucy foretold. Shame it was only two seconds into the future as she vomited in the corner, slashing her shoes with vile alcoholic concoctions.

"Lucy, fuckin'ell," Kerry moaned.

"Oops," Lucy managed between spitting.

In the house, which lay enclosed on three sides by walls of trees, bare footsteps ran up the stairs and the back bedroom door opened with a stilted creak of age.

"Thank you, darling," Catherina purred, half-asleep as Mathew hopped back under the duvet next to her and handed her a bottle of mineral water.

"That was some nightmare you had. Can you remember it?"

"Not really." Catherina sipped at the water. "Something about being in the woods and a large dark shape was circling me, like a big cat or wolf or something."

"Probably the walk in the woods sunk into your subconscious or something. You gonna be okay now?"

Catherina put the water on the floor next to the mattress. "We need to go order a bed tomorrow, okay?"

"Change of subject, but okay." He shook his head, loving the way women could jump from one subject to the next and expect men to keep up.

"Good, now hold me close and keep the bad dreams away."

"Good as done," he replied and inched up to her back and held her as their bodies spooned together in the dark house in the even darker woods.

In the garden of the house, the door in the wall that lead to the woods stood open and a dark shape with four paws stood watching the lightless windows of the house and waited, as it had done for countless years.

CHAPTER FIFTY-FOUR

When dawn came that Saturday in the waning days of April, it was hardly seen due to the all-encompassing fog that covered the whole of Hedge End from far up the London Road to past the leisure centre far off down the Woking Road.

Mrs Puck lay sprawled in her four-poster king-sized bed, with silken sheets and not a stitch on. A huge black dildo lay discarded after use on the floor, attracting dust and fluff from the carpet.

In a direct line down as the woodpecker or raven flies, Angela Pratchett's husband and young lover lay in her old matrimonial bed, having broken it in with some pleasures it had not been witness to before. They lay buttock to buttock, Mr Pratchett in his pin-striped pyjamas, while his young lover opted for Mrs Puck's choice of bed attire.

In the garden of Hill House, covered in a blanket of fog, nothing stirred in the hole and the woods of the copse were deathly silent, as if waiting for something.

In Leggett House, Catherina and Mathew slept on, with no more dreams to remember, holding each other against the biting cold of the poorly heated old house. In the garden the wooden door that led to the woods was once more shut. While in the cellar two tiny sets of feet shuffled nervously, an uneasy atmosphere rising from the cold earth like an itch in the centre of your palm that you just can't scratch away.

Further down the way, Simon was up and awake. The smell of the brown and yellow vomit in the plastic bowl on Lucy's side of the bed was making him feel ill. So he left her there lying on her front in her bra and knickers, snoring away like a Canadian lumberjack on overtime. Half a glass of stale water, smeared at the edges with the remnants of last night's party-pink lipstick, stood on the bedside stand next to her sleeping head.

Simon went downstairs in his t-shirt and shorts, the cold rising up to tickle the hair on his legs, before he entered the much warmer kitchen. He re-filled the kettle and set it to boil. Then he pulled a mug out and dropped a t-bag and two sugars in, with questionable accuracy. He sat on the sofa and yawned so wide that his jaw cracked a little and ended with a shake of his sleepy head.

Lucy, his fiancée of only two days, had rolled in at about half-one, with the aid of her apologetic cousin Kerry, and immediately confessed in a sobbing remorseful drunk voice that she had got off with some lad at the club and could he ever forgive her. Not that she gave him much time as she ran upstairs to puke in the bath, because for once he had left the toilet seat down.

Kerry waved him goodnight with a fixed embarrassed grin and fled back to the taxi and waiting arms of her boyfriend, DJ Stevie J. He closed the door to the sound of retching from above, not blaming Kerry. She was only twenty and not nearing thirty like her somewhat less drink-wise older cousin.

Simon had to stop recalling how he had showered away her vomit down the drain and helped her to undress and fall into a catatonic state on the bed. Her only craving was the blackness and relief that sleep would bring for a few hours, before the real morning after suffering would begin. He hadn't heard her being sick in the night, but the bowl was magically an inch full this morning.

Simon exhaled and headed into the kitchen to eat a slice of plain bread just to settle his stomach. He seemed to be suffering a hangover by proxy. The kettle boiled and the tea made him feel better and then he wondered if she would remember imparting her cheating ways to him and if she did, he would have no choice but to confess his own?

Neither of them had gone the whole penetrative hog so to speak. Would the two wrongs cancel each other out, or would he keep his lapse secret and use the confessions of his drunken fiancée against her? He did not know. He would play it by ear when she awoke. As he finished his tea, he pulled the blinds in the kitchen and saw that the fog had not lessened since last night. In fact it seemed eerie and denser and their pocket hanky back garden was enveloped in white, so much so he couldn't even see the bins only four feet from the back door. He washed his tea mug, decided not to go through his notes from last night, and then stuck on the next episode in sequence of West Wing.

The roar came in waves of sound, some thin and dragged out, others loud and heavy. The roaring sawing meaty sound came through the fog before anything could be seen, like a warning to the road users ahead that it was nearing. Not that there were many people about at six am on a Saturday morning to see the customised Triumph motorbike coming charging out of the fog down the London Road past Mrs Puck's large house and the still shut Catholic church worksite. A train leaving the station blew its horn like it was trumpeting the arrival of the motorbike as it went over the bridge over the railway tracks below.

The motorbike hammered down Hanger Hill Road, ignoring the blinding fog, past Hill House on the right and then Leggett House on the left, until the traffic lights at the crossroads of the High Street forced the denim jacketed rider to stop. His green helmet was still as he waited for a couple of cars to pass and the lights to match his crash helmet before carrying on at a lower speed down Green Street. Across the rider's back was a guitar case and apart from a box at the bike's back, he had no other luggage. He rode past B&Q's and stopped his mean machine outside the Green Man pub, not far from Simon and Lucy's two up-two down.

He turned his helmeted head and raised the visor to look at the pub, which was still hours from opening. The man with green eyes read the sign by the saloon bar, that rooms were available and then shut his visor again. Then he roared the engine of his bike from an idling purr, did a U-turn in the road and headed right from Green Street into the High Street, searching for someplace to breakfast.

Mrs Puck woke up with a start and rushed to her bedroom window. She watched in fascination as the thick wall of fog began to roll away down the hill, clearing the London Road, like someone was pulling it down like a bed sheet. She rushed across to a front upper bedroom and saw that the road outside was now clear and the church building site was visible again. Mrs Puck strained forward, her boobs hampering her efforts, as she saw the fog retreat back into the thin wedge of Woodhouse Copse on her side of the railway tracks. The dawn could now rise properly and the sun broke from thinning clouds high above and shone down on the wet roads like the fog had never existed.

CHAPTER FIFTY-FIVE

Simon watched the news after *West Wing*, which surprised him by showing a reporter at the edge of a fogless Woodhouse Copse, talking about the latest non-developments on the case of the missing Hannah Browning.

Frowning, Simon got up from sofa and walked into the kitchen. He saw that the fog, which had only an hour before had consumed the garden in its grey cover, was totally gone. The news had flicked now to Hannah's parents at a recorded police press event, begging with tear-filled eyes for the safe return of their beautiful daughter. Simon turned the television off. The pain and proximity of this crime were just too much for him.

Instead he phoned his friend Paul, catching him on the way to work as a fitness instructor at the local leisure centre. They chatted and joked for a while and then Simon gave him his good news, tinged with the job loss incident in full blow-by-blow back-stabbing Technicolor. Paul's reply was one Simon saw coming a mile away and he smirked into his phone.

"Now you have no excuse to lose that spare tyre around your gut and join the gym, porky-pig."

"Is this the usual way you drum up business, walking the streets of Hedge End, insulting fat people until they join your gym out of shame?"

"Pretty much, yes," Paul laughed back down the phone at him.

"Well, I might even take you up on that. I'll pop in and see you sometime next week one lunch time for a protein shake or something?"

"Make it a pint and you're on, mate."

"Good as done, I'll bell you."

"Seeya, Si."

Simon rubbed at the stubble on his chin, wondering whether to cancel the restaurant tonight he'd booked yesterday for him and Lucy. Then he decided decisions were for the gainfully employed and headed upstairs to check on Lucy, have a shower and get dressed.

Mathew and Catherina woke in each other's arms, bathed together and ate cereal at the same table, then headed off strolling arm in arm down the hill to check out the latest bed shop sales, in a shop that was bound to be bust by next Christmas. They picked out a large double bed, with iron railings. Cathernia had to remind him as he went for his cash that a new bed needed sheets, pillows, pillow cases and duvet and covers, times three at least.

They popped into the local Italian restaurant, booked a table for tonight and then trotted down to B&Q to pick up rolls of wallpaper, paint and other stuff to decorate the main bedroom before the carpets were ordered.

Catherina made them lunch while Mathew searched through the internet for two or three builders to ring and come give them an estimate on repairing the house. The roof and walls were vital. Then he would get best prices for the damaged floorboards downstairs and then for redoing the bathroom and kitchen. He would see what all that cost before spending any more of his cash.

Mrs Puck stared from the bedroom window that overlooked the drive and gate of her house at the road and church site beyond. She was half-dressed now, in a robe at least. The supermarket had delivered by van yesterday morning, so Saturdays were quite her own and peaceful. She sometimes went to watch the local rugby matches if they were on, the grunting and sweating of muscular men did something for her.

"Ah, there you are again," she half-sang in a low voice.

A figure dressed in a large Mac walked past her gate and then was lost for moment, before he crossed the road to re-read the Environment Agency's sign, saying the site was closed.

"Father, dear father, you just don't know when you are beaten, do you?" she chuckled to herself.

The motorbike and its rider were back and in the pub car-park just as the doors opened. The rider took off his green helmet and put it on his arm, like an old woman carrying a handbag. Adjusting the guitar case on his back, he got off his bike, pulled it back on its stand and then headed for the bar.

Sinead Flaherty was on shift that Saturday morning, with the owners and brother Bill and Ted Bishop, two large men who hailed from Wandsworth and negated the need for bouncers at the Green Man Inn.

She was pouring pints for the usual old locals that had nothing better to do than spend every waking hour in the pub or the nearby bookies. She looked up as the saloon doors opened to see an average height man, with long wild black hair, in a denim jacket and jeans enter. He carried a green motorcycle helmet on his arm and had a guitar case on his back.

She was taken slightly aback. The stranger seemed somewhere in his early forties, with a look of Mel Gibson in his *Lethal Weapon* days, and though she knew nothing of him except his craggy features, mop of hair and green smouldering eyes, she instantly took a fancy to him.

She had to concentrate and patiently wait to serve the pints she was doing and grab the slowly counted payment while the stranger made his way to the bar and waited, four feet away from the old gentlemen who smelled of piss and bitter. Bill was upstairs, but Ted was at the far end of the L-shaped bar chatting to another regular, and she hoped that he would not steal this customer from her. She managed to put the money in the till and pop the change on the bar near the old man's hands and rush to serve, as Ted finally noticed the denim clad custom himself and moved towards him.

"Can I help you?"

Then man looked at her freckled nose and bright pleasing smile and nodded. "I hope so, love."

The man's voice had a strange accent, something of a kindred

Irish lilt to it, or Welsh, smothered with a North American drawl.

"Pint is it, or food maybe?"

Sinead found herself skipping from foot to foot hidden by the waist high bar and she could not fathom why she felt so giddy.

"For starters, and a room for while if you have one."

"Guinness?"

"You read my mind, lovely, and Smokey Bacon crisps if you happen to have any?"

"We do. You sound like you have touch of the old country in your accent there?" she asked, getting a proper glass to pour the black stuff into. "Ted, this customer needs a room," she called over to one of her bosses.

"A touch and many other wild places besides," he replied, as Ted came over to help out with the accommodation request.

"I can always tell." She winked as she poured.

"How long are you wanting the room for?" Ted asked, coming to tower over the willowy barmaid.

"For a month at least. I don't mind paying in advance, cash."

"I'll get the green room ready for you. Do you want me to take any baggage up now for you?"

"Nah, I've only got what I've tossed up in this morning." His reply made Ted frown at his choice of words, but his brown eyes widened at the roll of twenties the man pulled from a jacket pocket to pay for the Guinness and crisps.

"What name should I put in the register, Mister-?"

"The name's Jack, Jack Lucas, and it's a pleasure to be here again."

"You've been here before?" Sinead asked, putting down his pint and taking one of the offered twenties.

"A long time ago now. Used to play my old banjo around this neck of the woods a while back. Thought I might stay here a while and enjoy the Mayday celebration if you still have one." Jack Lucas took a long swig of his cold stout and smiled a white foamed satisfied grin of contentment.

"Yep, bigger and better. We and the Cricketers always go head to head with our beer tents, trying to outdo each other. Last year we had a steel band dressed as Morris dancers, very

ethnic and diverse." Ted bellowed out a laugh that made his
meaty pecks and deltoids jiggle.

"Got any music for this year, then?"

Jack looked up at the pub owner. He pulled open his packet
of crisps, picked one up between his first two fingers and twirled
it into his waiting mouth.

"Not yet. Our Abba tribute band pulled out last night. Why,
you offering?"

"Ah well, if you really want I can give you a private rendition
of my finest pieces tonight and you can decide."

"Can I hear?" Sinead asked.

"Nothing would give me greater pleasure than to requite
one of my lovely old Celtic love ditties for you."

"I look forward to it," Sinead replied with starry eyes.

"So do I," said Ted, a little disappointed that this Jack fella
had jumped the queue to get into little Sinead's knickers.

Simon plonked the coffee mug down on the bedside table with
enough forceful noise to wake the sleeping Lucy, still in the
same position he had left her in three hours earlier.

A tortured moan escaped her dried lipstick plastered lips.
Her head rose four inches, her eyes opened and then she turned
over.

"God, what was I drinking last night?"

"Only you know that answer," Simon said, bouncing on the
bed with all his weight just to annoy her.

"Oh, don't do that. I feel like shit," she croaked. She put her
arm over her eyes to block out the sunnier day Saturday had
become.

"Must have been what you had last night."

"Can I have some water, please?" she asked through half-
closed blinking eyelids.

"You've got some next to the coffee."

Lucy sat up and winced at the feeling in her empty stomach
and the tap-tap-tapping pain in her cranium. She reached over
shakily to grab the glass and then noticed the bowl of vomit by
her side of the bed. "Oh God, take it away, Simon."

"Don't think God can help you now, Luce," he said in an

odd voice. He removed the bowl from the bedroom and headed downstairs. She sat up slowly on her pillows, resisting the urge to call down the stairs after him to explain his off-hand comment. Then a memory whizzed into her booze addled mind of the young fella she had snogged the face off of and a very vague memory of apologising to Simon about it,

Lucy Gaskell groaned again and put her cold hands over her empty stomach. She rushed to the bathroom and managed to open the toilet seat this time before she vomited.

CHAPTER FIFTY-SIX

"So when are you going to open this cellar door then, darling," Catherina asked. She was holding a mug of coffee near her face, the cuffs of her pullover up over her fingers, as she stood no more than two feet from the old door.

"Dunno, hadn't really thought about it much," Mathew replied, leaning the butt of his jeans against the Belfast sink, sipping at his coffee.

They had had a quick sandwich out and now home with the morning just peaking over the rise into the noon, they stood in their kitchen wondering what task to attempt next.

"I think the builders will want to check the floor and walls down there," she said and turned to face Mathew.

"Bloody hell, that reminds me, I better start getting some quotes for the building repairs." He pointed his finger like a pistol at her. "Thanks for reminding me, Cat."

He kissed her right temple and left the room to turn on the laptop on the dining room table. The phone lines were on now and they only had dial up for the moment, but broadband and television channels would come in time. She didn't mind not having the internet and television for a while. It reminded her, like this house and surrounding woods, of her childhood at home and happier times. Catherina looked at the padlocked door again and frowned, as Mathew had managed to avoid the cellar subject once more.

She put her half-drunk coffee down on the counter, next to the large pristine fridge that stuck out like a sore thumb in this rather old and shabby kitchen.

Next to the kettle and the toaster were three different sized screwdrivers, which she collected in one hand and moved over to the cellar door. Three of the screws holding the padlock bracket in place had Phillips heads, while the other looked much older with one slit, covered by white gloss paint. Slowly, as Mathew tapped away next door, she selected the right screwdriver for the first three screws and began to unscrew them all, one by one.

"The creature emerges from its pit at last," Simon commented and got up from watching *Football Focus* as the just showered Lucy, hair lank and down over her face like that girl in *The Ring*, entered the room.

"Do us a bacon sarnie, will you, Si?" she asked in a croaky voice, which she cleared several times before sitting down at the dining table.

"You up for one, then?"

Simon walked past her into the kitchen with a quizzical look on his face and reached down to open a cupboard to get a frying pan out with lots of added banging and crashing.

"Yes," she groaned, "and I know you're making that louder than normal on purpose."

"Me, love?" He feigned shock. "Would I do that to you?"

"Yes, you bloody would."

"One greasy bacon sarnie, coming right up," he said, turning on the gas.

"Kill or cure, Simon, I don't want to miss our meal out tonight."

"Blimey, I didn't think we'd still be going the way you were up-chucking last night."

"You ain't cancelled it, have ya?"

"No, my dear," he said, getting the oil down from the shelf and then bending down to grab the Tupperware with bacon from the fridge. "So did you have a good time last night, then?"

"Yeah, I think so."

"Not regretting anything?"

"Only drinking too much."

"Okay," he whispered, but his words were drowned out by the bacon going into the pan and sizzling and him turning on the extraction fan to full over the cooker.

"What did you say?"

Lucy pushed her damp hair back off her face and turned to look at her fiancée. as he bent down again to grab the bread and butter from the fridge.

"Nothing." He smiled and that was it, the moment gone. He knew bringing up her club snog-fest with some guy would be pointless and as he had done much the same with Rose Puck, his victory would only be a hollow one. So they left it. She did not venture the information, and like a petrol stain in a puddle, time would soon wash it down the drain.

Lucy put her fist to her mouth and nose, moved into the living room and lit one of her rose scented candles, trying to escape the smell of the frying bacon and keep her stomach contents inside her, like her secrets.

Catherina winced. Her palms hurt as the last and different screw was hard to budge and took all her effort to undo. She put the screwdriver with the others on a nearby counter and then held the padlock bracket with her right-hand and unwound the last screw with the fingers of her left.

Mathew was still tapping away next door and writing phone numbers and information on a notepad in the dining room, a dividing wall hiding their activities from each other.

At last the screw was out and the bracket and padlock sagged a little in her hands, making a little sound, but bringing no attention from the adjoining room. She could swing the bracket and padlock round to the right now and then reached forward to grab the cold round brass doorknob.

It twisted easily to the left and she pulled the door to the cellar open, inch by inch, hoping the hinges would not creak too much. The door was open not more than an inch when a great onrushing wind hit the back of the door with tremendous force, knocking Catherina to the kitchen floor and the door wider, painfully digging into the back of her legs.

Catherina's mouth was open in shock as the tumultuous unnatural wind flowed over her. She thought she heard the word *liberto*, spoken in a stretched whisper on the wind. She

turned her head as the back door flew open like the warped
wood had never forced it shut and tremored in the gale as the
rushing air left the cellar, and finally the house.

Catherina's hair fell back over her face as the noise of the
door opening and her fall brought a shocked Mathew running
in from the dining room. He had witnessed nothing and only
saw the cellar and back doors open and his girlfriend lying on
the kitchen floor in distress.

He rushed forward and knelt down, pulling her into his
arms. "What the bloody hell have you done, Catherina?"

His words were harsh and this shocked Catherina more
than the cellar wind. She had expected compassionate words of
comfort. She pushed him away and got to her feet alone, tears
running down her cheeks now, not of fright, but of anger.

"What have I done? Bloody hell, Mathew, a great *vento* comes
out of the cellar and smashes open these fucking doors, and you
ask what I did? Unbelievable!"

Catherina was in wild gesticulating mode now, her hair
flying.

"Calm down. What came out of the cellar? I saw nothing. I
only heard the doors bang."

"*Meraviglioso.*" She shrugged, "A great bloody wind come
out of the cellar and pushed me to the floor and opens doors by
itself and you see *niente!*"

"Look, calm down, Catherina." He stepped forward, but she
only retreated one step back, "It must be some vacuum effect
like back draft, because the door hasn't been open for years."

"I am not a child, Mathew. It was a great wind and it knocked
me over and opened the back door that even you could not open
because it was shut, and it whispered to me as it flew by," she
raged back at him, spitting a little.

"The breeze from the cellar spoke to you?"

"Yes," she replied, sticking her aquiline chin out at him.

"And what did the wind say to you?"

"It spoke in Italian and it sounded like it said freedom." Her
voice had lowered now, choked with emotion, knowing that her
words sounded mad, even to her as she spoke them.

"Listen to yourself, Cat. You opened the door and that can

affect the air balance in an old house like this and open and close other doors. I've seen it happen in our old house in Suffolk. You're scared, I understand that and the doors and wind gave you a fright. Did you bang your head when you fell?"

Catherina's hands had dropped now and she let Mathew inch close, his arms wide and his words softer and comforting.

"A little, but I know what I heard." Her tears ran from her eyes and his open arms looked so inviting.

"Come on." He beckoned and she gave in. He drew her into a warm enveloping embrace and she sobbed into the collar of his polo-shirt making it sodden. Already in her mind the events seemed less than they were, as if Mathew was helping her to re-write her memories. His explanation seemed more logical as the minutes in his strong arms went on. But one thing that did not was the word freedom, spoken in her native tongue, that still echoed around her skull for many hours after.

CHAPTER FIFTY-SEVEN

Mrs Puck could not put it off any longer. She changed into her jeans and thickest coat and headed down the garden to her hidden grove. The weather had turned now, and the mid-afternoon sun beat down on her dark auburn hair hotter than any other time that year. The fog seemed to have pushed the cold of winter away.

Even though she felt hot and uncomfortable in her heavy coat, she wanted a barrier between herself and what dwelt below after last time. The air she breathed deeply into her lungs seemed to have changed like Spring was finally on its way to Hedge End. Hot weather and even hotter times were to come, she thought as she walked purposefully up the avenue of cherry trees, full of pink and white blossom, leaving a trail of petals for her to walk upon. Soon they would bear fruit, like her long labours. Something had changed dramatically this day, and she had to find out what.

She bent down at the crack before the great oak and said a silent prayer of Celtic protection. Then, with green stains on her knees, she ducked and entered the dark confines inside.

Father Carmichael shivered in his seat in the corner of the Cricketer's pub, by the edge of the May-Day field, even though the pub was warmly heated and his long Mac was still on. His third whiskey of the day stood rigid in his old right-hand, the amber liquid sloshing like a tidal sea, circling up and down the sides as he tried hard to control his tremulous lower arm. Finally with the help of his left he pushed the glass to the round mahogany table where he sat. He ignored the stares and whispers of the bar-staff and patrons who knew his profession.

Something felt different about the town he long served as a priest, the town that had taken his sobriety and then his church and now bit deep into his faith, something he could not afford to lose so late in his life. He had to find out what had shut the re-development of his old church and why he felt without the protection of his church something darker and insidious had crept into the lives of all who lived in Hedge End.

Mrs Puck emerged from the dark slit in the oak both dirty and disappointed. The holes and tunnels she could manage to fit down were dark and empty and stank of honey and rancid pork. She had no idea what this could mean, and it only added to her questions. She stood up, the sun glaring in her eyes. She picked the dirt from her nails as she walked back to her house to have a long soak in the tub and think. She wondered whether to text Simon Hay on his mobile but dismissed this as just her growing libido, which she had long covered in crude drab clothes in her campaign to shut the Catholic church opposite.

Now nearing fifty, she was a woman re-born, or sexually awakened again, but for what purpose, and who would benefit from it?

CHAPTER FIFTY-EIGHT

Catherina had tried to forget about the cellar for a while. She had taken her easel and painting things up to the small back bedroom, on the other side of the bathroom from the one they slept in. She tried for a while to sketch the front of the house from memory, but her artistic heart just wasn't in it.

The episode with the cellar door and Mathew's reaction had put her in an off-kilter, sad, reflective mood, which was never conducive for working on a new piece. Seeing that nothing was coming, she tidied and readied her art work and paints and brushes, which made her feel at ease when she did get the artistic urge once more. The light from the windows wasn't the best and maybe she would move into the damp front bedroom that got the morning sun, once it had been repaired.

She was squatting on her heels, pulling canvases out of a special large carrier box, when she came across the last painting she had done, just before they had left the old apartment. So shocked was she at what the picture showed she rocked back and fell on to the seat of her jeans, just staring at the images she had painted in anger the day the bailiffs had arrived.

For now she recognised the opening she had painted, the laurels and the foliage in a tunnel leading down into the red gloom and those two children holding hands. It was the view from the gate in the wall of the garden that led into Leggett Woods. She stared long at the painting, now seeing something she'd not noticed before. Hidden in the spinning bushes and trees and leaves was what looked like the head of a large wolf.

"Mamma mia," she whispered to herself, her long fingers going to her cheeks.

Catherina exhaled, not knowing what to think. How could she have painted a picture of a place before she had ever visited it? Goosebumps covered her bare arms and she had to cover the painting with another canvas.

She wasn't sure what to do. She could not tell Mathew. He would just shrug it off or explain it away somehow. She knew she had to take a look in that cellar tonight if she could, or get up early Sunday morning before her English lover awoke. She stood and headed into the bathroom to run a bath. They were going out for dinner in Hedge End tonight for the first time since they had arrived. Maybe a long soak and glamming up tonight, with good food and plenty of *vino*, would help things look different in the morning.

Mathew came up later with information on the builders, two of which could do the work and would come over Monday to quote room by room for decorating and repairs. He had offered wine and then coffee, but she refused both as she sank deeper into the bubble covered tub.

Mathew kissed her wet lips and headed downstairs, to see where their nearest carpet shop was, as Hedge End did not have one. He found one in Addlestone, some megastore, and noted down the address on his long to-do list. He rubbed at his jaw. It felt over-stubbly so he fished out his electric shaver from a cardboard box and pulled out a favourite lilac shirt to iron and a suit to wear for their night out.

Simon Hay was amazed as that evening Lucy stood before him in her favourite dining out red-dress, her hair done, and her face prettily cast with glittery make-up and pink lipstick that suited her to a tee. He had pulled on his brown jeans, an old shirt and a jacket: smart for him, but no match for the gorgeous blonde fiance on his arm tonight.

"How do I look?"

"Amazing, but how do you feel?"

"Like I need the hair-of-the-dog and some food inside me. Come on, let's go, Si." She took his hand and pulled him into the hall to get their coats.

"What's the rush?"

PETER MARK MAY

"I feel fine now and want to get to the restaurant while that still lasts, okay?" She giggled and pulled him down by the neck to warmly kiss him.

"What was that for?"

"I love you, Simon, that's all."

"I love you too, Luce."

"Come on then, be a gentleman and fetch me coat." She smiled widely and patted his bum for god measure as he fetched it off the peg on the wall.

Mathew Reynolds felt lucky as he sat opposite his Italian girlfriend in the Venice House restaurant in the middle of the High Street. After what had happened with her and the cellar today, he had been worried that this night out would be a complete wash-out, but Catherina had other ideas. She was dressed in her most eye-catching plunging black short dress that showed off all her lovely assets, but it was the sparkle in her hazel eyes that took his entire attention. He had lost himself in them.

They had only ordered red wine so far, but the candle on the table and the low lighting gave everything a duller edge and only his Catherina was in sharp contrast to the surroundings.

"So do you miss the car?"

Her question woke him from his lovely daydream, which was not like him at all and he had to take a sip of wine before he could reply. "The status and the usefulness of going places, but not as much as I thought. I have everything here I need, I think."

"The material boy melts away and has a heart of a romantic at last," she said with a wide and captivating smile. She took a sip from her wine.

"I have my moments, signorina Di Marco," he replied. He would have said more, but the tall, moustachioed waiter returned to take their food order and both turned their eyes to the white menus before them.

Catherina ordered first and then Mathew did his thing, where he quizzed the waiter on every aspect of the three dishes he had in mind to see which he would order. She was used to this minor annoyance of his and her eyes wandered around the restaurant. Another couple about her and Mathew's age were being shown to their seats four tables away behind Mathew's head. She wore a girly red dress that suited her blonde hair and small features, while the man seemed to have a bashfully awkward air about him and smiled a lot at the other waiter on duty.

He was nothing like Mathew. He had a kinder, more worn look, with green soft eyes that seemed to dazzle in their insecurity, but also created a vulnerable mothering feeling in Cat's empty stomach.

"-bread?"

"Wha?"

"I said do you want bread, Cat?" Mathew asked for the second time.

"*Si*," she said in her native tongue, drawing her eyes back from the other couple, who were settling in now and picking up their menus.

The Italian waiter's eyes opened wide and he launched into questions in Italian, asking where she was from and telling her he had a cousin that came from there. It wasn't the quiet intimate meal that she had wanted and the owners and staff made a fuss of them all night like long lost relatives. Yet Catherina could not help staring at the other couple, even though the place was full of other patrons. She had no idea why.

"I need to visit the little boy's room," Mathew said, standing up after finishing off his dessert and draining the last of the second bottle of red wine.

She was still only halfway through her tiramisu and just waved him off with a full, shut mouth. She looked over at her favourite couple again. They seemed to be having a good time also. Then the man got up and headed off toward the toilet, not a few moments after Mathew. But not before he noticed the beautiful brown hair and olive skinned woman that seemed to be smiling at him as he left his seat. Her cleavage was something to die for and with many impure thoughts he followed the suited chap that had been lucky enough to dine with her into the men's toilets.

When the guy held the door for him, a flicker of recognition came to Simon's mind, like he'd seen the bloke before somewhere but could not place it. They both made for the urinals and stood one urinal gap between them. They unzipped as one and began to do their business, Mathew looking at the tiles and upwards. Yet Simon could not help transgress the bloke's unwritten lavatory law and stare at the other guy about his age as he pissed.

In Mathew's peripheral vision he could see the guy he had held the door open for was staring at him as he peed. Because of all the wine he had tonight it was taking him a long time and still the oddly familiar man was looking at him. Maybe he'd seen his face on Crimewatch or something, or the other guy was Hedge End's serial willy watcher, just his bloody luck.

"Look, I'm flattered, mate, but I ain't interested, okay?" Mathew said and wished he had butched his voice up a little, because it kind of squeaked out and made his message come across less authoritative than he wanted.

"Yes you are. You're a big fat gay, Mathew Reynolds," the other man stated and zipped up his fly, turning towards him.

"Wher, Simon, Simon Hay!" Mathew finished his business and moved forward to hug his old childhood friend, from his summer stays at his great uncle's house of his youth.

Just then, as comic luck would have it a large man as round as he was fat opened the door to the men's room, saw them hugging and said, "excuse me," and hastily retreated to use the disabled toilets instead.

"How long has it been?"

"I dunno, ten years, twelve, maybe more. You ain't changed a bit, Simon, except you're a bit more tubby in the gut department." Mathew smiled and hugged his old friend again. Simon was really the only best friend he'd ever had growing up.

"And you're still a handsome git that talks shit," Simon laughed. "What you doing here?"

"I've moved into Uncle Jimmy's place. Had a bit of money, job and housing problems in London and the old bugger left me the place in his will."

"I went to the funeral, but didn't see you there."

"I had a fight with the old man and left before it all happened, really," Mathew explained.

"Still the army jack-ass, then?"

"Even fucking more so, mate. How's your dad, by the way?"

"Still at number 42 Hay's Street, still messing with toy trains."

"Love to see him again now that I'm back in town. God, I only been back a few days and never thought you'd still live here. Always thought you and your mate Paul would go travelling and conquer the world."

"He did for a while. I stayed here and got a shitty office job in London."

"Come on, we better not hang about in the loo all night. People might think we're cottageing or something. Who you with?"

"My fiancée, Lucy. And you?"

"My lovely bit of Italian womanhood, Catherina."

"Does she have brown hair does she and rather large, erm — eyes?"

"That's her. That's why we got on, Si, we had the same good taste."

"And the fact you were sad little Nobby-no-mates," Simon joked, the old double act just clicked back into place, like the intervening years had never existed.

"This should be fun," Mathew said as he and Simon left the toilet together. And at two separate tables two women glared quizzically at them.

CHAPTER FIFTY-NINE

Bill was downstairs with two other bar-staff, so Sinead lead the way up the narrow stairs to the first floor landing and the guest accommodation. Ted had a nice view of her arse as he followed close behind. Shame it was covered with both dark tight leggings and denim shorts. Her mid-drift was showing as her small green shirt did not cover even her belly button. He had to shake these thoughts from his mind as they reached the door to Jack Lucas's room, and she turned to smile at him and rapped her knuckles on the door.

After thirty seconds, which seemed like an age to the publican and his barmaid, the door finally opened and a sleepy-looking Jack opened the door, dressed only in his denim jeans.

"Not too early or late are we?" Sinead inquired, sizing up Jack's wiry frame, taught abs and hairy chest.

"No, perfect in fact. I just rested the rest of the righteous and am ready to play, if you are?"

"Yep," Ted said in a deep rich voice that was coated with a Jamaican childhood, Newham teenage life and Croydon adult life, before he and his brother bought the Green Man three years ago.

"Well, in you come. Not that I have to offer as it's your place anyways, Edward." Jack opened the door to let Sinead dance past and Ted squeeze his big muscular frame through.

He closed the door and pointed for them to both to sit on the bed, which seemed to Ted tidy and straight and un-slept in. Jack Lucas picked a black t-shirt off the back of a chair and pulled it on. Much to Sinead's disappointment.

"Health and safety," he declared, staring into the barmaid's clear eyes. "I once got my chest hair caught in the strings of me guitar. I screamed like a French woman getting a wax that night, I can tell ya."

Sinead giggled, but Ted just raised his eyebrows. He wasn't a prude in any way, but his mother had taught him and his brother not to be rude in front of a lady. Well, not until you got them past your bedroom door that is.

With a wink and lop-sided grin, Jack grabbed his guitar case from against the dresser and unclipped the catches in the black worn case, which had seen better days. Inside was an acoustic guitar made with some orangey-yellow lacquered wood, with a neck made from a darker wood and inlaid with green tortoise shell type triangles.

"What do you fancy, then?" Jack stared long into Sinead's eyes and then quickly flicked to Ted, the man who ultimately had the nod on him getting the May-Day gig.

"Something lively," Ted answered.

"Got just the thing, Edward, my new friend," Jack smiled and launched into a feisty little song full of life with folksy vigour and a hint of Rock N' Roll.

My friend Jack says he not coming back, my friend Jack put his clobber in a sack,
He went on down, to the edge of town, nothing left there but a hole in the ground.
There has to be, a better place for me, and off he went to sea-o-sea.

It wasn't what Ted or even Sinead expected, but they liked it for some reason and both felt a warmth in their chests as the song went on about Jack and the hole in his sack. Images seemed to flow and form in their heads, seeing Jack's journey through the song.

So when the song ended, the audience of two seemed to deflate back down into themselves a little and the world spun back to its normal dreariness. They both sat in silence. The quietness in the room seemed deafening now and devoid of the joy they felt when Jack played.

"Did you like?"

"Yes," squealed Sinead and she leapt forward to bend over and kiss Jack's left cheek.

"That was payment enough." He smiled at the girl as she sat back down on the bed. "And what about the boss-man?"

"Not my usual thing, but it was good. Made me feel…" Ted trailed off, trying to put into words what the song did to him, but his explanation was elusive.

"Like you were a kid again?"

Ted's brown eyes fixed on Jack's green ones and he smiled. "Yes, it made me feel like I was back in Jamaica again."

"Can you play something else?"

Jack looked at Sinead and her willowy beauty and said, "Something to seal the deal?"

"Yes, romantic if you have one?"

"What about you, Edward sir? What will convince you to give me the gig?"

"Something that will charm any lady into my bed," Ted replied and then laughed with fruity force, feeling embarrassed at what he had said to this near stranger.

"I think I get your meanings. I call this one, *A Rutting in the Dirt*." And he began to play again, but a different tune, as different as the sun is from the moon. It was slow and thick with vibrating sounds and had no words to it. Instantly both Sinead and Ted were caught up in it.

As it went on the bass sounds from the strings seemed to get deeper and louder like the beating of two hearts, with heat rising in it like a tropical storm. Sinead and Ted swayed in unison on the bed, inching nearer as the rhythm of the sound caressed them and pulled them closer, until they turned and their lips were inches apart. Then Jack started a louder more urgent part of the song and Ted and Sinead where swept away together in a warm sea of emotion. Their bodies crashed together like the buffeting waves of a tumultuous raging sea in a high wind.

Jack played on as they tore at each other's clothes and Sinead pushed Ted down onto the bed, pulling aside her moist panties to lower herself down on his ebony length. Still Jack played on. The sound of his guitar was the universe, and nothing else, not even his presence, registered to them as the song carried them to heights of pleasure and lust that their ears had never heard before, except in the warmth of their mothers' wombs.

Jack watched them fuck hard on his bed and smiled. The gig was in the bag.

CHAPTER SIXTY

"I get it now. You are the, erm, letter carved on the bed in Mathew's old room." Catherina waved her arms towards Simon, nearly spilling her coffee as they all sat around in Lucy and Simon's living room.

They had had a couple of drinks in the restaurant and then headed back to the house off Green Street to have a coffee and a chat.

"Inseparable we used to be over those summers." Simon nodded, remembering all the things they used to get up to.

"Well, we can all be friends now, *si*?" Catherina said, looking around at the group.

"I'd like that." Lucy beamed She sipped at her coffee, her eyes on Mathew.

"I can't believe you pulled Juicy-Lucy Gaskell, Simon," Mathew stated "We used to go into that crappy shoe shop in the High Street and pretend to look at trainers, just so Si could get an eyeful of this blonde beauty he was so in love with."

"Sssh," Simon hissed and waved a finger at his old friend.

"Stalkers they were. I remember Mr Jamison threw them out in the end because he thought they were shoplifters. Not that I knew them at the time. Simon was in the year above me and I didn't know Mathew from Adam." Lucy looked up from the floor, where she sat between Simon's legs and gave him a wink.

"So where do you work now then, Lucy?"

Lucy sucked at her teeth at Mathew's question and Simon didn't help by going into fits of laughter behind her.

"What?" Mathew looked from Lucy to Simon.

"I still work there, but only for a couple of weeks. I put in my resignation. Now Simon has got the sack, we can spend a lot more time together."

Simon smirked and Catherina smiled at the false spin Lucy was putting on the situation, but it was not fair the boys were making fun of her.

"So Simon, what are you going to do now for work?"

Simon's laughing ebbed slowly so he could answer Catherina's question and try hard not to stare at her impressive Italian rack. "I got a great redundancy package, so relax for a while, holidays, plan the wedding and write a book about the local history of the area." He finished his sentence in a lower less confident voice.

"Sounds nice." Catherina smiled at him. "So what is your book a-"

"Hey, hey, you and Mathew should go into business together, as you're both at a loose end," Lucy interrupted, whacking Simon's left leg twice with her free hand.

"Reynolds and Hay," Mathew stated, his hands pulling apart to represent a shop or company logo.

"Hay and Reynolds," Simon corrected.

"But what would you two do?" Catherina asked, looking from one man to the next.

"Porn film producers," Simon and Mathew replied in unison and then held their sides as they split with boyish laughter.

"Men," Catherina said, shaking her head and looking down at Lucy.

"Boys more like," Lucy replied.

"I'll see ya Monday." Simon tapped at Mathew's coat and Simon turned at the front door to shake his old mate's hand.

"Sounds like a plan," Mathew replied, buttoning up his jacket as the past midnight air had turned chilly.

"While I slave away at work. Typical," Lucy tutted. She folded her arms to keep out the night air as they said their doorstep farewells.

"It was fantastic to meet you both." Catherina came forward and kissed Lucy on both cheeks and then crushed a surprised

Simon in a warm embrace and kissed his cold cheeks. The press of her boobs against his chest made an unseen flush rise to his cheeks and made his penis twitch into life in his pants.

"It was great to catch up and I can't wait to see the old place again," Simon said, stepping back into the hall to aid the goodbye process.

"Wear some old clothes though, Si. Many hands make light work."

"One of your great uncle's favourite sayings, if I recall rightly?"

"Yeah, they surface from time to time." Mathew smiled in the light of the street lamp. "We better get going, though I'm not sure if the old house is going to be any warmer than being out here."

"*Arrivederci*," Lucy said. She remembered the Italian word from a weekend trip to Rome she once took with her parents.

"*Grazie*, Lucy, *buona notte* and good night," Catherina replied, and she and Mathew turned and headed off down the quite street towards home.

"Bye."

"Night."

Then the cold night was shut out as the front door closed and Lucy and Simon walked up the hall to the kitchen.

"Well, that was a nice surprise," he said, picking up coffee mugs in the living room.

"Yeah, they are a nice couple, just our kind of people, charming and beautiful."

"Mathew is beautiful?"

"You know what I mean, handsome and fun, and Simon?"

"Yes dear?"

"And if you're gonna stare at her tits all night, please make it a little less obvious," she said softly and kissed his cheek. "I'm off to bed. You coming?"

Simon nodded, knowing any reply would probably be the wrong one. And he could hardly plead innocent, when he was guilty on all counts. He put the dirty mugs in the sink and turned to follow Lucy up to bed, yawning loudly.

CHAPTER SIXTY-ONE

Rupert sat up in the darkness and looked around the very unfamiliar shadows. Panic took hold of him until he slowly remembered where he was, and whose bed he was sharing. Noel, in his pristine pyjamas, was snoring on his back next to him. Had that woken him up?

He grasped his gaudy two-tone watch from the bedside stand and illuminated the face. It was just after three in the morning. He sat up on his elbows, the sheets falling down his tanned, hairless chest, and glanced over to look at the shape of Noel next to him. Noel snorted and turned to his side, his back now facing Rupert.

Rupert sniffed and thought about giving his older lover a reach-a-around, but then remembered Noel's snoring had probably woken him up in the first place and he lay down on his back in the comfortable large bed. He was absently playing with his shaven balls-sack when the sound of breaking glass downstairs made him bounce up onto his elbows once again. Even Noel shook in his sleep and turned towards him.

"Noel, did you hear that?"

"Hear what?"

"Breaking glass. Shit, I think we've got intruders, or even worse, your old woman might have returned," Rupert whisper-hissed and banged at Noel's hip with a soft fist three or four times.

"Angela!"

Noel shot up in bed, in more of a panic at that than the thought of knife wielding burglars could be roaming his five bedroom house in search of valuables and sick torture fun.

He jumped out of bed, kicked on his slippers and grabbed his dressing gown that had been draped over a chair in the corner of the main bedroom.

"What are you doing? Call the police, Noel," Rupert said from the bed, pulling the covers up to his chin.

"I'm going to fetch my cricket bat from the other room and go and have a look. You stay here and don't worry. I won't ever let anyone hurt you, my love."

Pulling on his dressing-gown, Noel Pratchett opened the bedroom door and disappeared into the darkness of the landing. Rupert felt both afraid and warm inside from the words his lover had spoken. No one from his parents to friends and a string of lovers had ever cared about his as much a Noel had. He heard footfalls and another bedroom door open and saw a shadow pass by the main bedroom door again. He assumed it was Noel heading to the stairs.

Rupert's ears strained to hear anything, but apart from the creak of the odd stair, the house seemed silent as the grave. Rupert shivered and wished for once he had nightwear on. He got out of bed on tip-toes, went to the pile of clothes on the bedroom carpet and found his pants and t-shirt to throw on. Then, like a fawn in a fairy-tale, he moved across the bedroom silently and listened at the open bedroom door.

"What the fuck!" he heard Noel exclaim from somewhere on the floor below, and then there came the sound of wood whacking something hard twice, something falling and then crazy child-like titter and the dark world of Hill House on Hanger Hill fell into silence once more.

Rupert Albertson-Smith stood at the bedroom door in his t-shirt and pants and shivered with cold and fear for an age untold. His mind and body were frozen and a sickly feeling welled up from his empty stomach. His hand rested on the door handle, but nothing moved except the rise and fall of his chest and he breathed through his nose. It seemed forever to him, straining to listen for any noise or the return of Noel, but nothing came except the odd unrecognisable sound.

"Noel," he finally whispered after five minutes, but it barely registered in his ears.

Noel did not reply.

Mustering all the courage he could, and doing the bravest thing he'd done since he left home at sixteen to escape his brutal, homophobic father's fists, he left the relative safety of the bedroom and moved onto the landing. No lights were on anywhere in the house, and nothing stirred or could be heard from below.

A sudden thought came to mind, that Noel might have just fallen over in the dark and bumped his head and might be lying in a pool of his own blood, his life ebbing away while Rupert dilly-dallied upstairs. Holding onto the banister, he headed downstairs step by step at a slow pace until he reached the foot of the stairs and the large hall, with its cold floor. Fear gripped at his tender parts and tailbone like a vise of terror.

He pushed all thoughts to the back of his mind. The man he loved might be injured, so he headed into the immense living room, which ran from the front to the back of the house. He could see that something was not right with the French doors. Rupert moved forward, past the grey-blue shapes of furniture, closer to the windows, and saw that one of the lower window panes was indeed smashed and muddy splodges of mud, like an animal's footprints, could be seen leading into the house and over the pale carpet. He stepped forward, inch-by-inch, until his foot suddenly retreated from a pool of liquid on the carpet. He could see from what light that did filter through the windows that there was some sort of trail behind a long sofa leading around into the kitchen.

Rupert wiped his foot on a clean piece of carpet and swallowed down some rising bile, as a sickly sweet honey and plant smell assaulted his nose. Trembling all over, he walked parallel to the dark stains in the carpet. It looked like something wet had been dragged across. As he reached the open doors that lead through the dining room to the kitchen, he stubbed his toes on something hard but yielding on the carpet.

He reached down and his hands found the rubber grip of Noel's cricket bat. He picked it up with a massive sob.

Something ahead in the kitchen skittered like a dog's wet claws on a slippery laminated wooden floor. Dark liquid dripped from the raised bat onto his bicep and Rupert could not take any more. He rushed forward with a howl of adrenaline fuelled rage and into the huge kitchen. He flipped on the light and screamed with high-pitched fright at the gore splashed scene his eyes witnessed and his mind could barely comprehend.

Noel lay on the kitchen tiles, where his blood oozing body had been dragged, his legs facing Rupert. His stomach had been gutted and ransacked and his organs eaten away to leave his eviscerated corpse lying in an ever expanding pool of vibrant red lifeblood. Rupert dropped the blood splattered cricket bat onto his foot and hopped in pain. Then he ran into the dining area, only to fall when his injured foot gave way under the stress.

Then they were upon him, out of the shadows, thin creatures with rough bark like skin and heads with wide eyes and razor sharp teeth. Three and then five jumped upon Rupert's back, crushing the air from his lungs. He tried to turn to fight them off but his raised left arm was bitten through by two of these nocturnal nightmares and fell useless and bloody next to Rupert's face.

His scream was stopped by a heavy hand gripping his head and smashing his face into the floor, breaking his nose. His throat began to fill with blood and white pain ran from his back down to his assaulted legs. Then Rupert spat out blood and called Noel's name one last time as wide jaws bit down on the back of his neck and tore the life out of him. He was instantly paralysed and only his eyelids fluttered as death's savage veil covered him and his red clouded eyes faded to see only black.

In his room above the pub, Jack Lucas awoke from a troubled dream and to his shock found that he had been weeping in his sleep. He pushed his long hair from his eyes and sat up in his bed. Then he reached across for his guitar case. He unlocked the catches and played himself a low lullaby with soft fingers so as not to wake the other inhabitants of the inn. Its soothing melody stopped his flow of tears and after a while he felt sleep tugging at his eyelids once again. He put away his guitar after ten minutes and fell into an easier dreamless sleep.

Hill House was now devoid of any living thing. The corpses of Noel and Rupert were no longer where they fell, yet the bloody signs of life-ending struggle still remained. In the garden there was no longer a hole of any shape or form. The earth had been scratched and patted back and covered with leaves so no sign of it ever existing remained.

Down deep in the tunnels and burrows beneath the roots of the trees of Woodhouse Copse, where no man could ever reach, the Woodwoses' slept in a communal huddle in a great cavern of earth, their minds and stomachs sated for the present.

CHAPTER SIXTY-TWO

Catherina awoke dry of mouth at a quarter to six that Sunday morning. She left the mattress with Mathew still asleep and headed to the bathroom to empty her bladder, and then trotted down the cold stairs to get a bottle of mineral water from the fridge.

Dawn was on the verge of arriving and the open fridge just made her feel colder. She turned her eyes and caught sight of the door to the cellar. Closing the fridge door, she opened and drank nearly half the small bottle of water and stared across the kitchen, as outside the dawn tried to decide what weather it should wear that morning.

She rubbed at her bare arms and walked into the dining room, which doubled at their box storage room, and rooted around for something to wear. She found some old DM's and thick socks, then some old jeans she liked to paint in and an old puffer jacket she'd not donned for at least three years. But she was not on a Milano fashion catwalk. She needed warm clothes in this heatless house.

Catherina walked toward the cellar door and, sucking at her top lip, pulled it open and stepped back quickly. No wind or atmospheric disturbance happened this time. The door did not even rattle a quarter inch. She crossed herself and reached through the doorway, finding a dust and cob-web covered pull-cord. Grimacing in disgust at the feel of the dirty and greasy cord, she pulled it down hard and two out of three bare lightbulbs came on in the cellar. Thankfully, one was over the stairway and another somewhere down below.

The stairs down were of stone and not wood, which

surprised her. She started down into the cellar, taking the old steps carefully. The floor around the steps seemed of rough ancient stone, as was the lower half of the walls nearest the steps. The rest of and most of the upper parts of the cellar walls were of newer brickwork patched and built on top of the older stone. Most of the floor was of long compacted brown-grey earth and boxes. Tea-chests and one old looking trunk stood up against the wall to her left. The place was dry and not that dirty and looked quite unremarkable.

Catherina saw no holes or doors or tunnels from the cellar, which left her wondering where the wind that had knocked her flat before had come from. She wandered over to look over the few boxes of junk and clothes that were there and was reminded of a cellar on the farm back home. That had been darker and danker than this and her father and uncle had grown mushrooms down there. She had hated the place because of the musty fungus smell and the ever present threat of rats.

This cellar was clean, dry and compact by comparison. She moved the dry boxes from the top of the trunk, which looked the most interesting of the boxes down there. Catherina flipped the catches with her thumbs and lifted the lid to reveal reams of papers, mostly black and white photographs and things that must have once had sentimental memories attached to them.

She knelt and rummaged through the life of a dead man, and came across a wooden box that opened to reveal World War II campaign medals and pictures of a man she assumed was Mathew's great uncle in uniform during the war. She was smiling looking at him standing in a desert with his Tommy shorts and socks on and an Arab headdress. Then she flipped to the next faded photo and went rigid in shock. The next photo was not from the deserts of North Africa, but from somewhere much closer to home. Captain James Reynolds was still in uniform, though this time in darker long trousers and he was smiling widely. Standing next to him was a beautiful woman in her late teens, in front of a farm house that was unmistakably Italian. Unmistakable because it was the very farm she grew up on in her youth. She hurriedly turned the photo over and written in pencil was only one word, Sophia, and the date 14th April 1944.

The world spun for a while as the name and date sank in, and she had to sit back on the floor as she gazed upon the picture, her mind whirling inside her skull. Her grandfather's sister had been called Sophia. She had fallen in love with an Allied officer during the war and they had married quickly, before he had to leave and continue to fight the war. She had sadly died in childbirth in early 1945 and her child died with her.

Her husband never saw her again before she died, or even knew she was with child. It was all very sad and her grandfather did not like to speak of it much, because it caused him too much pain. Could it really be that her Mathew's great uncle Jimmy was the man who married her own great aunt?

Could it be that the man in the bed two floors up was a cousin by marriage? How could this happen? Surely by no stroke of fate. Was she meant to meet Mathew? Was she meant to come to Hedge End and discover this, and for what purpose? She shut the trunk and carried the picture upstairs to the kitchen, turned off the light and closed the cellar door behind her.

Catherina was sitting by a nearly made fire in the boiler room, with a half-drunk coffee next to her, still staring at the picture, when Mathew finally came down. She quickly hid it in her jacket pocket for some reason as he entered. He looked down at her and smiled as he entered the boiler room, and she looked into his eyes, like both their relatives had done over sixty years ago.

CHAPTER SIXTY-THREE

Sunday dawned with an orange and red tinged sky. The sun broke through the cloud cover at ten and never looked back. By noon it was pleasantly warm, and the Met Office said it was set fair for the coming week leading into the long May Day weekend and Bank Holiday Monday. Winter, it seemed, was finally retreating and the flowers and trees were bathed in the warming Spring sunshine. Hedge End startedpreparinh for the usual Pagan May-Day parade, culminating in a bonfire, fireworks and festival of new life on the May Day Field that lasted into the early hours.

Mrs Puck woke late and opened her bedroom curtains to revel in the enveloping warmth of a sun-kissed Sunday morning. She stretched out her limbs in an X-shape and let nature's greatest ally wash over her naked body. She couldn't help but smile, even though events around Hedge End had her concerned about the plan that she was only a small part of.

Mrs Puck folded her arms over her chest and rubbed at them. It was only a week and a day before May Day and she knew she had lots to do to in organising the parade and the flowers that would go up and down the length of the High Street, and then the big event at night, which she always was heavily involved with.

She did not dress, but walked naked down the stairs to her dark study to grab her May Day folder and make sure things were in order and running to plan. She would phone Councillor George Saunders, her biggest ally and head of the town planning department. He was old, fat and rude to the point of racist and up for any scheme, bribe or sexual favour his piggy little fingers could snaffle up. Yet even though he was on the local C of E parish council, she knew what gods he really prayed to.

She picked up her mobile and rang him, knowing he'd be on some golf course somewhere this time of a sunny Sunday morning. She knew he hated to be disturbed, but she called anyway. This year she had a feeling Hedge End would get a May Day that it would never forget.

Lucy and Simon's Sunday was a lazy affair, sleeping in until the clock ticked one minute past the noon and then showers and dressed to meet Simon's dad for a Sunday roast at the Green Man at one. Mr Hay senior was surprised to hear that Mathew Reynolds was back in town with an Italian girlfriend in tow and living at Leggett House again.

"Italian girl, you say. She should love it here, with all the immigrants that settled after the war around Hedge End, quite a large community for some reason," Mr Hay imparted, polishing off his last roast potato.

"But why here? Why not London?"

"Dunno, Simon. Really, they were farmers mostly and found work first as fruit and veg pickers on the farms when we had some around here. Hard-working chaps your I-ties."

"Dad, please try and remember what century you live in sometimes." Simon shook his head in embarrassment at his old man's choice of words.

"Hmmn," his father responded and washed down the last of his beef by draining the last dregs of his pint of Directors.

"You want another drink, Jerry?" Lucy asked, just to have something to say. Her father-in-law to be wasn't your first choice of company if you were drawing up a dinner-party list.

"Directors," Jerry replied with gravy dripping onto his chin as he stuffed some broccoli into his mouth.

Lucy raised her eyebrows at Simon, who did the same back. Living alone for so long did nothing for his dad's table manners, it seemed. "What about you, Si?"

"I wouldn't say no to another pint. Directors, just to make life easier." He smiled up at her.

"Life easier, you." She winked and sauntered off to the bar.

"You sure you want to marry her, Simon? You could do better," Jerry said and elbowed Simon's upper arm.

"Dad, please." Simon shook his head again and drained the last of his lager.

"Old Jimmy Reynolds had an I-tie wife, it's said. Died during the war or something. They make good wives, I hear. Maybe you should invest in one, Simon." Jerry Hay leaned back and wiped the gravy from his chin, chuckling at the face his only son was making.

"Do you want to drink or wear your next pint, father?"

Jerry Hay just stared at his son and chortled on. "So how was your evening with the sexy older lady? Is she as salacious as the stories that are told about her?"

"Wearing your pint." Simon pointed at his father and clammed up until Lucy returned with the next round of drinks and the pudding menu.

Catherina and Mathew's Sunday was less relaxing. They had to get the painting finished in the master bedroom before the carpets and the bed arrived. They had Cat's iPod on and were enjoying decorating together, even dancing a little to the music as the tunes helped the work get further along, faster. She had nearly mentioned the cellar and the photo twice, but had held the revelation back for some reason even she could not fathom. So they were 2nd cousins. It did not affect things. They were not siblings or blood relatives, so what was her worry?

The longer the day wore on and the more fun they had working in close proximity, the more she pushed the photo further back in her thoughts. Why spoil the day? The windows were open, and the sun was streaming in and she was surprised how warm this old cold house felt with a new lick of Sunshine Breeze paint.

Jack Lucas wasn't in his room when Sinead came on shift and popped up to knock on his door. Wherever he wandered that day, his guitar case still in his room, only he knew and no one bore witness.

The woodpecker sat on top of the lamppost on the eastern edge of Leggett Woods and watched the copse across the road with keen interest. Nothing stirred in the sun dappled woods and no animal moved along the fern and holly edged paths. Not even the raven could be seen today, either perched on guard or flying over the railway tracks in search of field mice.

Yet still it watched.

CHAPTER SIXTY-FOUR

Monday dawned with dew on the grass and no clouds in the clear blue heavens. The day began fine and got warmer as the morning progressed. Catherina sprayed deodorant under her armpits and under the line of her bra for the second time this morning and then rushed downstairs to rejoin the hectic pace of the day.

The bed, the carpet people, cooker and one of the builders had all turned up within ten minutes of each other and she and Mathew were running around the house like tits in a trance, trying to answer questions, make tea and show where everything had to be put or installed. She had just jumped down the last three steps when there came another knock on her already wide open front door. She looked up and to her delight saw that it was Simon and not another tradesman.

They smiled, and she pulled him roughly towards her as a bed delivery man wandered in with the side to the new bed, nearly knocking into him.

"Sorry mate," the young shaven headed man stated and headed up the steps with the metal frame as Simon stood close in Catherina's arms and waited for him to pass.

"Have I come at the wrong time?"

"Not at all, Simon." She stepped back from him and pushed the parlour door open to reveal a flustered-looking Mathew and a tall builder in coveralls looking at the damage by the window.

"Hello, Simon mate. You okay?"

"Yeah mate. You look a bit busy?"

"It's a bloody madhouse this morning. Cat will look after you until I'm finished here, okay?"

"No probs." Simon gave a thumbs up and turned to face Catherina again.

"Would you like a coffee? I seem to be forever boiling the kettle today."

"Make it a tea and you're on."

"Tea, that is fine. I am well learned in making tea after this morning." She laughed softy and lead Simon through the living room and dining room, to the kitchen, where a man knelt pushing a large steel cooker into place after removing some cupboards and adding to the plastic, cardboard and polystyrene on the floor.

"Bit busy, are we?" Simon pointed to the new large cooker, which seemed out of place in the run down, out-of-date kitchen.

"Yes." She nodded, a little lost for words or what they were translated from Italian into English.

Simon stood back out of harm's way by the downstairs' toilet and watched as Catherina boiled the kettle and washed up a mug for him to use. Finally they stood together watching the man putting the finishing touches to the cooker installation.

"So you used to visit here much then when you were childhood friends with Mathew?"

"Well, during the summer when he and his older brother Tom used to come and stay with his Uncle Jimmy. I never came here when Matt wasn't here. His great uncle made odd reclusive hermits look odd and the place is a bit creepy," Simon said, blowing at the film on his badly made tea and sipping at it.

"Creepy? Like a haunted house, maybe?"

"Yeah, especially down there." Simon pointed behind Catherina to the cellar door.

"You and Simon used to play down there?" Catherina turned to face Simon and to glance over to the cellar entrance.

"No, it was out of bounds, really." Simon shrugged. "After Mathew got the frights down there, it was always padlocked up and he was scared shitless even standing next to the door and never went down there again, or even near it if he could help it."

"What did he see down there, a ghost?"

"He said he saw two young boys down there."

"What did they do to him?" Catherina moved closer, eager to hear more.

"Nothing much, they were just holding hands and staring at him. Creeped the shit out of him for ages, it did."

"Do you think this house is haunted then, Simon?"

"I dunno. There are rumours, but Matt was just a kid, and probably imagined it. He clammed up after that and refused to talk about it, and I never pressed him because he used to Woody me until I shut up." Simon sniffed and drank some more of his tea.

"Woody?" she asked, imagining all sorts of sick sexual connotations to the word.

"Hitting on the head, with your bent middle fingers. A deadly weapon in the right hands. Matt learnt it at boarding school probably."

"All done, love." The cooker installer stood up, wiping his dirty hands on his jeans. "You want me to show you quickly how it works?"

"Simon, you don't mind, do you?"

"No, erm, go right ahead." He smiled and watched as the man explained how the cooker worked and how she should turn on the ovens one at a time for twenty minutes before she first used them. Simon just watched Catherina as she talked and the gentle movements of her body, before Mathew appeared from the dining room.

"Sorry, builder was in to give me quote for repairs and renovations." Mathew thumbed a hand behind his head.

"Not a problem."

"Carpet's done. You wanna come and have a look?" came an unseen male voice from the doorway of the living room.

"Sorry, Simon, back in a minute," Mathew said and hurried off to see what the master bedroom floor looked like and direct the bed men to move right in and start assembling the new double iron bed.

"Not a problem." Simon whispered to himself. He listened with interest when the installer man explained that the splash back part of the cooker and front should be rubbed with baby oil to give it that still new look.

It was well after one when all the delivery men, installers and builders had left the house. A delighted Catherina made pasta and meatballs from scratch, as Simon and Mathew caught up on old times and inspected the master bedroom.

"What you think? More homely, isn't it," Mathew said, looking at the major change a new carpet and the bed made to the redecorated room.

"Homely, Mr Reynolds? Shall I get your pipe and slippers now or later?" Simon commented sarcastically as he moved over to the window.

"Fuck off."

"Need some curtains and maybe a curtain pole too," Simon said, pointing at the old windows.

"There's always something," Mathew said, bouncing up and down on the mattress of the new bed. The windows were open, but the place still stank of paint. Maybe one last night in his old summer bedroom would be best and would give them time to grab some curtains and poles.

"So what are you going to do for work then, start up another company maybe?"

"I don't have a clue at the moment. I got some cash in my pocket to do this place up and then I'll put the feelers out. A plan always comes to mind eventually."

"Well, if you do, I might be interested." Simon nodded towards his old friend.

"Noted." Mathew nodded in reply and the conversation dried up as the midday sun beat down on the town of Hedge End.

"Me and Lucy are going to the May Day thing on Monday. You wanna meet up in the Cricketers at about one-ish? If it's crap we can always drink and eat the day away."

"I'd like that. A bit of pagan British ritual will be interesting for Catherina to see. They don't have many Morris Dancers in London."

"Boys, food is ready," Catherina called from the bottom of the stairs.

"Boys?" Simon raised his eyebrows and headed for the bedroom door.

"Like old times, eh Si?" Mathew clapped his old friend on

the shoulder and they headed downstairs for lunch, the first using the new cooker.

CHAPTER SIXTY-FIVE

The week sped past and the sunny days grew warmer and warmer and it was poised to be a great Bank Holiday weekend for the inhabitants of the town. The disappearance of Hannah Browning faded from the news and front covers of newspapers, yet the police were working hard behind the scenes with little lines of inquiry to go on.

On Wednesday they knocked on every door and rang every bell on either side of Hanger Hill Road, getting no reply from the curtain drawn inhabitants of Hill House. Mathew spoke to a constable at the door as his newly hired builders turned up to start on the walls and roof and building a new kitchen for starters. They had arrived only after Hannah had disappeared anyway, and the police constable was soon on his way with a "thank you for your time."

Great boughs of trailing flowers of red and yellows were fixed upon every pole, lamp post and sign from one end of the High Street to the other, all the way across the junction and down Bates Rood and Green Street, when the parade historically ended. A great fair was being set up on the May Day field from Thursday onwards and a huge pyre was built at the far corner of the field and roped off to stop and yobs prematurely setting it ablaze, which happened back in 1997.

The roads were swept daily and garlands of yellow and blue ribbons were tied under the baskets of flowers. In the centre of the May Day field the Maypole, dating back to 1896, was put in place in its special concrete hole, but the ribbons would not go on it until Monday morning, as was part of the traditions that had built up over the years, but only really dated back to 1954.

Costumes were stored in the village hall and Mrs Puck was seen from the length and breadth of the town making sure everything was going according to plan. She wore a dress of Lincoln green, which was long and flowing and slit up to here. She had her hair done, and it was remarked by many a person that saw her that she looked years younger than her true age and she should dress like that more often.

Rose Puck took the kind words and nodded politely, knowing still that behind her back a few of those very same people would also be saying *mutton dressed up as lamb*, to their other halves.

The woods around Hedge End and up on Hanger Hill were reverently silent, as if they were waiting for something, maybe May Day itself and what it would bring. The woodpecker kept his vigil from Leggett Woods and only spotted the raven briefly during the week, high in the far sky, looking for food.

Leaving the builders to concentrate on work, Catherina and Mathew decorated the bathroom themselves, putting in new cupboards and then moved on to paint the boiler room a warming pale orange. The good weather and the noise and bustle of the house meant Catherina could get into the garden and finally hack down the grass and weeds to get a newly bought mower over it. The borders were hacked back and the shrubs sawn and cut back to smaller stumps with green shoots soon appearing.

Simon popped round most afternoons after working on his book and helped out in the garden or decorating. It was fun for Catherina to see Mathew in a new light with a proper friend and not the dull work colleagues he used to hang out with. She got her painting mojo back and the sunny weather inspired her to paint wide deep scenes of poppy covered meadows and other more restful things.

The site of St Barnabus's church was finally reopened on Friday and Jacko was back at work right away, ignoring his wife and the doctor's pleas for him to take it easy. He was behind schedule now and with two men less to boot. He soon got back to cracking the whip. He noticed that the old priest was back watching from across the road like some lost puppy. Jacko also noticed the swigs the priest took from a silver flask under his coat and shook his head. He jumped over a small drained trench to tear a strip off some idle bastard.

"So you're back at it, then?"

Joe Polanski turned as he pulled a plastic bag of builder's sand from the back of the truck and saw the old priest standing not three feet from him. "Yes, father."

"What caused the stoppage?" The priest pressed, moving closer. Joe could smell the alcohol seeping from the pores of the redundant holy man.

"There was a block under the foundations of the church, which had mercury inside. Very poisonous, some men got very ill, but it's okay and safe now" Joe steadied the bag on his shoulder and moved towards the wooden site gates. "I have to get on now."

"Yes, of course, my son, and thank you," Father Carmichael called after him and with a quick glance at Mrs Puck's house he headed off towards the train station to take him back to his residence.

CHAPTER SIXTY-SIX

May Day dawned clear and sunny, more so than anyone could have hoped for the first day of the month and a Bank Holiday to boot. Even if they were not going to the celebrations, people were just glad of another day off from the daily grind.

Lucy had worked all of Saturday and Sunday until lunchtime and she and Simon had a long and lie-in with bouts of love-making as the sun glowed behind their still pulled bedroom curtains, begging to be let in. They ate a fry up with lots of bread to line their stomachs in preparation for the big day ahead. The temperature being in the mid-twenties and the sun burning high in the bluest of skies seemed to lift everyone after the cold winter and the gloom of Hannah Browning's disappearance. They dressed in their brightest and lightest shirt and blouses and everyone got ready to enjoy Hedge End's special May Day celebrations.

"What shall I wear?"

Mathew was buttoning up a white shirt over his jeans and looked around to see Catherina at the master bedroom door (now with curtains) in her bra and knickers and nothing else.

"Eh?"

"For this celebration of May, what do I wear?"

"Whatever you like. No dress code for May Day, Cat." He smiled at her. "A nice dress, but it doesn't matter. You look beautiful in anything."

"Charmer." She waved and went off to the old bedroom at the back that had their boxes of clothes and her dresses hung on hangers on the side of the bunk-bed. She picked a white floral dress and a white cardigan just in case it got chilly at night. Then with an offered arm, they walked down the hill in the sunshine, laughing and chatting, to meet Lucy and Simon at the Cricketers', before the May Day parade began.

They met with smiles and cheek kisses in the heaving pub. Many a tourist flocked into Hedge End for this experience of an old England that did not exist in many places these days. Lucy and Simon had guarded a place at the bar, as all the tables and seats were occupied. They could barely hear themselves over the hub-bub. Simon ordered pints for everyone from Bernard behind the bar, bitters for him and Mathew, and cider for the ladies. Catherina did not drink much apart from red wine, but the cider was cold and refreshingly sweet and she instantly felt a part of these foreign celebrations.

"So why do you have a May Day? Is it a religious festival to a saint of some kind?" Catherina asked as all four stood on a bench outside the pub to watch the May Day parade and floats turn left from the High street into Green Street.

"Go on, Simon, you're the history freak," Lucy said as she sipped her second cider of the day.

"It's more of a pagan type festival, Catherina, for the end of winter and the new life with flowers and crops returning and to celebrate that, really. It goes way back," Simon tried to explain, but he was a better writer than orator.

"Call me Cat, please," Catherina said, gripping his arm and sipping her cider, which had already started to go to her head.

"Nothing to do with fertility and fucking then, Si?" Mathew joked and Lucy laughed as she sipped her cider and then had a small coughing fit, which sent alcoholic bubbles up her nostrils.

"You can be so base sometimes, Mister Reynolds," Simon said in a mock haughty voice.

"Yep," Mathew replied.

"Oh here they come," Catherina cried as the parade led by Mrs Puck in a blue maid's dress, with flowers sewn onto her collars and with a barrette of tiny blue and yellow Spring blooms in her hair.

She was followed by a crowd of weirdly dressed men and woman in various colourful costumes and clothes. There was the Jack-in-the-Green, which was basically a man dressed up as a cone shaped privet hedge, men and women wearing clothes covered in dark blue rags with blacked out faces and men with hats and masks resembling black feathered crows and ravens. They were followed by tall cat-like papier-mache masked men with no heads and faces in their bellies, with lolling tongues and wide crazy expressions. Then to Simon's surprise was his dad, with a signalman's hat covered in holly, dressed in britches and holding a large axe over his shoulder. The sly devil hadn't mentioned a word to him about it and waved as he passed by the pub.

They were followed by men in blue and yellow diamond waistcoats playing banjos, accordions and lutes and women all in green with green painted faces smashing tambourines against their palms. The Morris men in their white shirts and bowler hats with newspaper strips and bells on their joints followed, to a rousing cheer from the whole crowd. May Day and Morris Men just seemed to go together like eggs and bacon.

A choir from Hanger Hill Secondary School came next dressed like Victorian boys and milkmaids singing old English songs. The primary school came after in fancy dress, so you had cowboys and Jedi in the mix for some reason.

A brass band then came after a few themed floats until at last *she* came. On a throne sitting upon a dais, festooned with spring blooms of every shade and hue was the May Queen to be, Anita Longfellow. With a garland of flowers covering her short hair, looking beautiful as fine porcelain, chosen for her looks and the brave fight she just won over ovarian cancer at the tender age of sixteen. Her smile was brighter than any flower and she got more cheers than even the Morris Dancers had.

All these people now headed around to park in the car park off the cricket pitch and to make their way to the tents, pitches and stalls of the May Field. The edge of the cricket pitch had a fun fair, though the middle was heavily roped off.

"What do we do now?"

"Well, Catherina, I'm bloody starving, so I say we finish these and then head down to the fair to see the May Queen crowned, stuff our guts and drink till we puke," Mathew replied and Lucy gave an arms raised yay and kissed him on the cheek.

"Eat, drink and be merry." Simon smiled at the lovely Italian lady and helped her down from the bench as Lucy and Mathew drained the dregs of their pint glasses.

The crowning of the May Queen wasn't for another half an hour, so the two couples did a lap of the stalls, amusements and fun fair rides, but mostly checked out which gut filling food to partake of. The traditional mutton pies nearly got the nod, but the girls were not so keen. The not-so-traditional curry stall was given a wide berth, and they all ended up at the burger van in the end, having beef and mustard burgers, with thick chips and tomato sauce watered down into a semi-vinegary state.

Normally Catherina would avoid fast-food and burgers like the plague, but today she ate her burger and chips with ravenous gusto. The air seemed charged with light and blossoms flowing on the breeze from the line of cherry trees at one end of the field, and she felt caught up in an event for the first time since she had left Italy seven years ago.

Simon and Lucy were great company also, and everyone in the crowd was smiling and laughing. Children ran around cracking teeth on toffee apples and begging their parents *for just another pound please.*

Having sated their stomachs and laid a fat and bread foundation, they went off to the Green Man's beer tent to get another round of bitter and ciders, served in environmentally friendly cups that looked like plastic but were made from plant stems.

They found the last spot next to the square of rope that held everyone back from the May Queen float in the centre of the field. There was only room for two to stand abreast so Catherina and Lucy sat down on the dry grass and the boys stood over them laughing and chatting about old May Days that Simon had attended over the years. Lucy, feeling less inhibited by her third cider and full of beans, whispered to Catherina about the time she and Simon had done the deed in the ditch at the far end of the cricket pitch one May Day night about five years ago.

At last the mayor, Mr Khan, a shortish man of Asian descent

dressed in a white shirt with strips of the Financial Times stuck to it, climbed up a small ladder with the help of Councillor Saunders and Mrs Puck. A DJ from the local radio station handed up a microphone and with a wail of static he addressed the crowd.

"Thank you one and all for coming today to Hedge End's annual May Day festivities. This is my third year as your mayor and I can honestly say the turn-out and size of today's event is the biggest and best that I have seen in my tenure."

The Mayor stopped as a loud cheer rang up from the assembled masses and had to wave his free hand in a lowering motion to continue.

"I would firstly like to thank everyone in the organising committee, the police and St. John's ambulance and the work of local businesses for their time, effort and support. Then, more personally, I want to thank Councillors Saunders and his planning department. And lastly Mrs Puck, whose tireless efforts each year make this event so well known and so popular. So without any further ado, I will pass you over to Mrs Puck to start the crowning ceremony. Please enjoy yourselves and drink responsibly."

The Mayor, all smiles, passed the microphone over to Mrs Puck as he was cheered and booed from some sections of the crowd. Mrs Puck went and stood behind the throne, with Anita sitting patiently in it, as another lady passed her a garland of pink and white flowers around a gold crown. A few wolf-whistles and laughs came from the crowd as Mrs Puck raised the May Queen crown aloft.

"Welcome all to bear witness to the crowning of the Queen of the May. May her reign bring forth a bountiful harvest and may the summer be long and warm. May this fair child of the green's immolation bring back all that was once good from the trees, to the field and woods where Lugus once trod. I give you Anita Longfellow, our new Queen of the May." Mrs Puck lowered the crown onto Anita's head and a massive cheer went up from the crowd with shouts of hurray, and the poor girl burst into tears of overwhelmed happiness.

"Thank god that's over," Lucy said and sipped at her cider.

"It was beautiful," gushed Catherina. Then she looked up at the boys. "But what did that lady's words mean?"

"Pagan mumbo-jumbo from ages past," Mathew replied, shifting from one foot to the other.

"What shall we do now?" Simon asked of his fellow May Day revelers, pondering the meaning of Mrs Puck's words.

"I need a piss," Mathew stated matter-of-factly.

"Me too," Lucy said, waving her hand in the air, like she was back at school.

"Your best bet is to nip back to our place. The queues in the pubs and the cricket pavilion will be horrendous with these crowds," Simon said. He fished his door keys out and handed them to Lucy, who hadn't brought hers or a handbag to lug around.

"Cool," Lucy said, kissing Simon on the lips and taking the keys. "What about you, Cat?"

"I'll stay here with Simon and look around the stalls, if that's okay?"

"Will be my pleasure."

"Okay, meet you back at the beer tent in about twenty minutes," Lucy said, heading off with Mathew.

"Okay." Simon nodded and extended a hand down to help Catherina up from the grass.

"Bit of a different speech this year, Rose?"

Mrs Puck stared down at Councillor Saunders and just smiled and headed off to organise the duck race.

"Simon my boy, what do you think?"

"Dad, what are you wearing?"

Jerry Hay hauled the axe from one shoulder to the other as he stood before his son and Catherina at the coconut shy. "Are you going to introduce me, then? Manners cost nothing, son."

"I was going to deny you're my parent first," Simon said with a laugh., "Dad, this is Catherina, Mathew's girlfriend from Italy."

"A pleasure to meet you, my dear, I'm Jerry Hay, or the Axe Hayman of the Hedge, one of Mrs Puck's little army of helpers."

"What made you dress up like this, Dad?"

"Life in the old dog yet, son. Rose Puck's idea and she can be very persuasive that woman."

"Nice to meet you, Mr Hay." Catherina finally got a word in edgeways and extended her hand, which Jerry Shook vigorously.

"Call me Jerry please, or the Axe Man." Jerry raised his axe and coughed out a laugh, while Simon watched on in morbid embarrassment.

"You'll all be damned to hell if you stay here!" said a slurred voice down the May Day Fair's PA system and everyone looked around to see Father Carmichael in his priest robes and dog-collar standing on the May Queen's float by a bemused looking Anita Longfellow.

"Get him off!" the mayor cried, and Saunders and Chief Inspector Hayward of Surrey Police rushed under the ropes heading for the float.

"Yes, drink and eat and fuck yourselves to death at this pagan festival, this abomination of a psuedo religious event, while my empty church gets made into flats for more unholy rich imps to suck at the golden nipple of Satan himself!"

This got a huge cheer from the tourists, thinking this was all part of the May Day festival. The Reverend Brown joined the police inspector and the councillor as they clambered onto the float and attempted to wrestle the mike away from the obviously very inebriated priest.

"Death is coming to this town! Don't let Mrs Puck's ungodly words ring in your ears. Run before the Woodwoses get you!" The Reverend Brown and George Saunders managed to get the mike from the drunken priest's hands but not before he punched the Chief Inspector in the nose. Another police constable ran up and with the aid of Brown and the Chief Inspector they wrestled Father Carmichael off the float and through the crowds to the car park and out of sight.

"What a great fancy dress costume he had on. Though it does show that too much drink can spoil your day," Councillors Saunders joked and added, "I'm off for a pint. Have fun and enjoy."

He handed the mike back to the local DJ and had a quiet

word with Anita, who seemed quite put out at all the drunk ravings of the once local priest.

"Blimey, old Carmichael's been on the sauce a bit," Jerry commented. "Never been the same since they closed his church down."

"Got to go, Dad. Meeting Lucy and Mathew at the beer tent," Simon said, and without thinking put his arm around Catherina to lead her away.

"Nice to have met you, Catherina." Jerry waved and headed off into the crowd.

"Goodbye," she replied.

While in the car park, the constable held the drunken, now silent priest by the collar as the Chief Inspector dabbed at his sore nose with a tissue.

"Get a squad car here and take this joker away," The Chief Inspector fumed, more embarrassed than hurt, really.

"Surely we don't have to go that far. Leave him in my care and I'll drive him back to his residence," offered the vicar, trying to calm the situation down.

"We don't really want to advertise this with an arrest, do we?" said the Mayor, who had come over to join the small group.

"I suppose not, but if I see him around here again he's nicked!"

"Understood." The vicar nodded and grabbed Father Carmichael. He held his arm and pulled him towards the vicar's car parked not far away. "Bloody hell, you've really gone and done it this time, haven't you?"

"Death is coming to Hedge End, war, the end of all religion," the priest muttered, as the vicar bundled him into the passenger seat and buckled him up.

"What will they say when they see you like this? We better stop off on the way and pour some coffee and sense into you," the vicar tutted. He slammed the passenger door shut and went 'round to get in and drive the priest out of Hedge End.

Catherina and Simon looked around the Green Man's beer tent and could not see hide nor hair of Lucy or Mathew. Mrs Puck was there at the side of the temporary bar, chatting to a man in denim, who was having a drink and a rest from playing his set that afternoon.

"Not here," Catherina said, and Simon turned and exited the tent, scanning the crowds.

"Shall we have a wander round to look for them or wait here?"

"Wander I think," Catherina politely said, and they headed off into the throng again.

They found Lucy five minutes later, hanging around a hoop-la stall, chatting to her cousin Kerry, who was helping out taking the money.

"Hello Kerry." Simon nodded to the younger of the two cousins. "Found you at last. Where you been?"

"And where is Mathew?"

"Matt's over there talking to that fat councillor bloke, so I was chatting to Kerry. Why, are we late?"

"A little, but it doesn't matter now. What's he talking to that old fart for?"

"Ain't got a Scooby-do, Simon." Lucy offered him a bit of toffee-apple, but he waved it way.

"Get us a pint of cider, Luce," Kerry asked, chewing gum and looking rather bored in her low-cut maid's outfit.

"Sound like a great idea. I'm parched. You two coming?"

Lucy stared at Catherina and Simon, trying to get eye contact, but they were both watching Mathew and the councillor chat as people walked past, and the two exchanged a humorous joke.

"Look, you girls get the drinks in," Simon said. He pulled out a twenty from his wallet, which Lucy quickly snaffled up. "I'll go get Mathew, okay?"

"Okay." Lucy took Kerry's arm and Catherina looked from the girls to Simon and then Mathew before she finally hurried off to catch up with the ladies.

Catherina frowned. Mathew had promised to put business on the back burner for a while and enjoy their time together. She wondered what deal he was cooking up with the councillor and local business man.

Mathew saw Simon coming over and took the card from

Saunders's hand and promised to, "call him next week."

They shook hands and both turned in different directions as Simon came to stand by his old friend. "What was that all about?"

"Just putting out the feelers on a little business idea the councillor spoke of." Mathew clapped his old friend on the shoulder. "Come on, you're wasting valuable drinking time."

Simon shrugged and followed his old friend back to the Green Man's beer tent and the lure of beautiful women and casket drawn bitter.

The festivities went on as darkness fell and after more food and two trips back to Lucy and Simon's place for toilet runs. They had more burgers and beers and the bloke in the Green Man's tent was playing a lively set that just made you want to drink, eat and be merry. They lit the bonfire at half-eight as dusk fell and set off the fifteen minute firework display at nine once it had got fully dark. The guitar work of Jack Lucas had not gone unnoticed and the mayor himself, clapping along to the earthy folksy tunes, asked him if he want to play to everyone from top of the May Queen's float, giving Anita a rest and chance to have a sneaky underage lager.

With a nod of encouragement from his new fast friend and whispered confident, Mrs Puck, he bowed to the pressure of the mostly adult throng and started a set that would go down in Hedge End May Day history, or infamy if you were that way inclined.

Everyone began to tap their toes or even dance. Beer and cider helped, but the more the winding, twirling tunes rang from the guitar over the speakers, the more people just could not resist and joined in.

Mrs Puck joined Jack on the stand and at one point sang a song in Celtic that made everyone get up and join in the dancing, even though nearly no one knew what the words meant.

Lucy, Catherina, Simon and Mathew were dancing too, holding hands and moving their feet as they laughed and cavorted and kicked over their pint glasses. The music would change but not end, and every person on the May Day Field, old and young, were dancing and bumping into each other and did not want to stop. An hour passed and even though some were now out of breath or just plain coughing their lungs out, the music played on and still they danced. Feet ached, shins splinted, blisters popped and bled into the dancers' shoes and still the assembled danced on without any thought of pain. The faster and faster playing rang on into the night, soaring high above into the cloudless and warm sky and still the people of Hedge End danced on.

As the clock neared twelve, Rose Puck whispered over the guitar noise and occasional singing of the tireless Jack Lucas and a wide smiled curved on his face to match the one on hers. She stood, not dancing, and spun around, looking across the crowd of hurting revelers as they could not stop while the tune went on.

"I call this one Rutting in the Dirt," Jack Lucas called out, and with a whoop of primal joy began to play a different tune and watched with a grin on his face as Mrs Puck started undressing beside him. His music had the same effect on the mostly adult crowd around him.

CHAPTER SIXTY-SEVEN

The next day dawned with the same sunny weather that had lasted over the long May bank holiday weekend, yet across the town of Hedge End much had changed.

Simon turned over in his sleep and moved his feet under the sheets, causing a wave of pain to shock him from his dreamlike state. He slowly opened his sand-man incrusted eyelids with difficulty and blinked his blurry eyes until some sort of vision came back to him. The first thing he noticed was that he wasn't in his bedroom, but was staring at the bookcase next to his sofa. The sofa-bed was extended, but why had he slept downstairs? Had he and Lucy had a row, or had Catherina and Mathew stayed the night?

The thought of Mathew's Italian girlfriend brought a flash of memory back to his addled brain, of her naked and him thrusting into her throat with wild sexual abandonment.

Simon rubbed the sleep from his eyes and became aware by the soft movements and sounds of breathing that he was not alone in the sofa-bed. He slowly sat up onto his elbow and was aghast to see Lucy slumped in the armchair not far away, totally naked with her legs apart and her puffy red vagina agape for the world to see. Her head was resting on her side and she was snoring softly.

Images jumped to his mind again of Lucy being taken from behind as he watched and her French kissing Catherina as all four of them played out a Roman orgy two centuries too late. He slipped out of bed and noticed that his feet hurt like hell and were covered in blisters. Lucy's feet were in a worse state and at the end of the bed there was dried blood on the sheets where the sleeping form of Catherina Di Marco lay. Shocked that he had no hang-over and no recollection of leaving the May Day celebrations, he hurried as quietly from the living room as he could.

Mathew wasn't to be seen, so he headed upstairs to the main bedroom and found his old friend slumped face down with no covers, fast asleep on the double bed. There was dried blood on his heels and around his buttocks and Simon dry heaved recalling another dark sexual memory from the fog of the night before. He grabbed some clothes and went into the spare room he used as an office to dress. He collected a spare blanket and went back downstairs and covered Lucy's nakedness. Then he stood there in his front room, fixed to the spot, unable to comprehend what happened after the dancing last night and what he would do next.

He turned and was shocked to see Catherina with the most awful bed-hair staring up into his eyes and it seemed through to his very soul. She touched her bruised bottom lip as a memory came back to her of being taken sideways while she licked hard between Lucy's legs. And she remembered looking back and seeing not Matt, but Simon fucking her.

"Do you want a coffee?"

She blinked several times as her mind had wandered off even though she was still staring at Simon's face. She nodded and he left to go into the adjoining kitchen. Then she heard the sound of a kettle being filled. She sat up and winced at the ache in both her feet and her tender lower parts. She hugged her legs to her body, feeling dirty and ashamed. Catherina knew she had not been raped. She had willingly done these things with Lucy, Simon and Mathew, and she stared at the sleeping Lucy and flexed her right-hand in shock of another vague memory of the debauchment of last night.

The kettle reached its boiling peak and snapped off loudly, which caused Lucy to stir from her dreams. As she awoke, the blanket fell to reveal her small round breasts and erect nipples. She stared at Catherina in dazed puzzlement and then realised she was naked. She pulled the cover up and stared with red eyes at the other woman in shame.

Mathew came down twenty minutes later dressed in his crumpled clothes, walking a little stiffly, but smiling his head off. The three others looked up from their silent coffee drinking and frowned at his excited look.

"Fuck me, we had a few too much to drink last night, eh? We'll have to do that all again sometime, cos it was crazy." He sat down on the bed next to Catherina and kissed her forehead. "Any coffee left for me?"

"I'll get you one." Simon stood and without making eye contact hurried back to the kitchen and filled the kettle up again.

"What do you remember about last night?" Catherina asked tentatively. She had her dress on now under the covers, but her knickers were nowhere to be found.

Lucy stared from Catherina to Mathew, knowing she had ridden her man hard for at least most of the night. She wore Simon's shirt from last night and her panties, which had been pushed down the side of the armchair cushion.

"Dancing way too much," he said, rubbing his feet through his socks, "and then being back here and things got a bit spicy. Nothing to be ashamed of. Can't remember half of what we did, but the stuff I can recall, well, porn films have nothing on us four."

"How can you be so blasé about what happened last night? We all cheated on our partners," Lucy said, the last part of the sentence trailing away to a whisper.

"Look, we're still young and attractive. These things happen all the time. We can either brush it under the carpet as a dirty little secret or just move on with no jealousy and comebacks and just be friends again."

"This never happens again," Catherina said in a firm cold voice.

"It must have been the booze, and that music seemed to will me to dance like I had no choice. After that I wasn't fully in control of myself," Simon said, coming back into the living room and handing a coffee mug over to Mathew.

"I just want to forget it," Catherina stated, looking down at the bed sheets. Then she burst into doleful, sobbing tears.

Lucy pushed her sheet aside and rushed over to hug and comfort her, tears rolling down her eyes also. "I forgive anything you did, and that goes for the rest of you."

"Let's just chalk it all up to experience," Simon added.

"A nice experience," Mathew said, "but it's probably best if this does not go past these four walls and we forget it and move on, agreed?"

"Agreed," the rest of the quartet answered.

Sinead the barmaid awoke in either Ted or Bill's bed in the Green Man Inn, wedged in-between the brothers, like the filling in a sandwich, with the limp penises of the two siblings still deep inside her.

Jack Lucas's room was empty, the bed un-slept in and his guitar gone. Four fresh twenty pound notes lay on the bedside cabinet, half pinned under the base of the lamp.

Chief Constable Hayward awoke in the Green Man's beer tent, with PC Haynes sleeping on the grass naked beside him. His mouth was parched and he recalled certain events of last night that he had only subconsciously dreamt of for years, even though he was a happily married man with three children.

Michael Aldridge awoke to find he was on top of Mrs Fisher in her house on her bedroom floor. The non-breathing seventy-four-year-old widow lay crushed beneath his bulky frame. He sat up, screamed and ran from the house stark bollock naked into the road and was knocked down by a police car from another district, called in to help with the hundreds of 999 calls that had coming in from Hedge End that morning. From rape to missing persons, to naked men and women burglars, people finding themselves nude in the High Street or in the busted windows of the local newsagents with the owner's pet Labrador.

Mayor Khan yawned and wondered why he had slept in the back of his mayoral Bentley. Why were his trousers and underwear missing, and why was the sixteen-year-old May Queen Anita Longfellow naked and asleep, her head on his lap?

Councillor Saunders awoke in his bed, having had sex five times with his wife that night. That was more times than they had managed it in the last five years and also his feet were covered in bloody popped blisters.

And so it went on and then came the fights and retributions on wives, boyfriends, husbands and their children. For the whole of Hedge End seemed to have been shaken last night and turned upside down and where the inhabitants fell, it was only where their own lusts had led them.

Anil Passat, who lived next door to the Pratchetts on Hanger Hill Road, ran harder than any gym session or marathon he had ever done. Away from the Italian restaurant he had woken up in, away from the Jewish girl that he had made love to all night. He hated himself and could not see how Allah could have let this happen. He did not even know if she was of legal age. And on he ran, despite the pain in his feet, as his blisters rubbed and blood soaked into his socks as he neared his home.

He had to get out his prayer mat and beg for forgiveness. Maybe someone had slipped one of those date-rape drugs into his lemonade at the fair and he had to explain to his wife before she found out another way. He fumbled his keys out of his jacket pocket and opened his front door. It was after nine now and apart from the sounds of police sirens and ambulances that echoed around the town, his normally busy house was deadly silent.

He ran upstairs and went to the twins' room first. There were crumpled bedclothes all around covering a blood spot on the carpet, but no twins. He ran to his middle daughter's room and this too as devoid of life. Yet the bed had been slept in. His eldest son's bedroom was the same, and he rushed to the master bedroom. Had his wife found out already and taken the kids and left him? He could not blame her if she had. He pushed opened the master bedroom door, which hit the wall with a juddering bang, and he saw that the bed was empty, the blankets strewn over the floor and the bedside lamp lay broken next to them, a wedding present from his late father.

Pushing his fingers through his hair, he went over to the open curtains and stared down at his garden in despair. She must have left him. He beat at his chest and wailed with anguish, "I'm a good man, a good man!"

He did not notice the hole that had appeared in the rose beds at the edge of his property, in the corner next to the Pratchetts' garden fence.

Rose Puck lay in her four-poster bed, moving her pain-free toes and smiling to herself. Jack Lucas lay in an exhausted sleep on her right bosom, his arms wrapped round her tightly. Things were beginning to happen now and with Jack's help, she could finally tear down the barriers around Woodhouse Copse and let the dwellers free. And with it their god, Lugus.

Father Carmichael awoke later that morning with an awful hangover and a feeling of despair and shame. If he wasn't such a coward, he would have taken his own life by now, but he feared eternal damnation. He finally had a cup of tea and still in yesterday's clothes walked over to turn the television on in his three small-roomed, church-owned residence.

"We are now getting a clearer picture of events here, Sue," said a reporter on the edge of the cricket pitch, with the cordoned off May Day field behind him. Father Carmichael dropped his tea onto the carpet and ignored it as he watched, his fingers gripping his old favourite armchair.

"It seems after a quiet day of May Day merriment the people and visitors to Hedge End in Surrey went on a wide rampage of booze fuelled sex and violence unprecedented outside a sporting event. We can confirm that the Mayor has been arrested for sexually assaulting an unnamed girl of sixteen. The police tell us that least thirty people have reported being raped, including men, women and sadly children. There are reports of fighting this morning, looting and burglaries, by normally upstanding members of the community and even unconfirmed reports of three fatalities."

Father Carmichael put his face into his hands and wept for

the poor people for whom he'd once been their moral compass. Now Hedge End was heading for the same fate as Sodom and Gomorra and only he had the power to stop it. Whether he had the strength, well, that was another matter.

CHAPTER SIXTY-EIGHT

Lucy took Catherina upstairs, let her shower and found her some underwear to borrow. Then Simon drove her and Mathew back to Leggett House. They were shocked to find that the juicy goings-on of the previous night had not been isolated to Lucy's and Simon's house. The May Day field was cordoned off with yellow and black police tape and TV film crews, fire engines, ambulances and squad cars and vans were everywhere. Some shops had been damaged and the whole town seemed like it was suffering the aftermath of a war, not a fun and frivolous festival.

They drove in to find a delivery van with its side open at the door and a man standing at the front door, knocking. Mathew jumped out and signed the guy's electronic pad after he brought out a huge television and a Blu-ray player.

"So do you want us to stay for a while?" Simon wondered, as he stood in the living room after helping Mathew in with the television.

Lucy put down the Blu-ray player box on the floor and Catherina just continued walking into the kitchen and put the kettle on and then began to sob, her hands gripping the Belfast sink's cold hard edges.

Mathew watched her go and then turned back to his friend. "Normally I would, but this morning isn't a normal one, is it?"

"You can say that," Lucy chimed in. She looked from Simon to Mathew and she realised she had screwed both the men in this room and done rather intimate things with Catherina also. Yet it wasn't shame or remorse she felt. It was regret that it probably wouldn't happen again, well, unless…

"Don't worry about it," Simon said and offered his hand to Mathew "Are we still friends after last night, with- with what went on?"

"Best friends share, don't they?" Mathew grinned back and shook his friend's hand.

"No awkwardness?"

"Not from my end," Mathew said and then he looked back to the dining room, worried about Catherina. "Best we give it to the weekend to meet up again and let the dust settle, eh?"

"Yep." Simon nodded.

They said their goodbyes, without disturbing Catherina again, and headed back in the car to home. Lucy and Mathew seemed to have the right attitude,that it happened, it was a bit of a crazy one-off thing and it shouldn't upset the status quo. Simon, though, was worried, deep down about his own moral compass. He wasn't a religious man, being firmly agnostic about most spiritual things, but he felt like he himself was slipping down a path he wasn't sure he wanted to take. He blamed it on the mad few days, having lost his job and daily focus, the fumble with a woman old enough to be his mother and then last night's orgy and making love to his friend's girlfriend, while Mathew was doing his fiancée in the same room, sometimes on the same bed, he recalled.

He phoned his father when he got in and was glad to hear that he had gone home early and missed all the fun, as he put it.

Lucy found herself smiling as she bathed when they got home, her cheeks blushing when she recalled some of her memories of the night before and what she and the others had done. When she closed her eyes and the heat of the water relaxed her and soothed her aching feet, her hand slipped down between her legs and her mind played out certain scenes from last night, mainly of her and Mathew. She felt like some decadent lady of wealth and leisure from bygone times past, with no money worries and soon no job, just enjoying every pleasure, regardless of whether it was sordid or wrong.

Catherina went upstairs and did not want to engage in any sort of conversation. She locked herself in the bathroom, drew a bath and scrubbed at her skin until it was red. She sat hugging her legs and prayed to the Madonna to help her make sense of what had happened last night. Catherina felt a weight of guilt on her shoulders, at both cheating on Mathew and engaging in sex acts with Lucy, something she had never done or thought of doing before. She wondered why Mathew did not seem to share this guilt and was quite happy to pass the night off like nothing had happened. But it had, and she wondered what Simon was thinking right now.

She did not feel like she had been raped. No, something else was bothering her deep down, beyond her religious indignation, something she feared to even contemplate for one second. Once hastily toweldried, she headed into the bedroom, drew the new curtains, pulled on her most-skin covering pyjamas and went to bed to give her troubled mind a rest.

Mathew felt it best to let her be and having electronic equipment and being a man, put the night before out of his head. He set the television up on a bracket on the wall and then spent many a happy hour, plugging cables and plugs in and tuning and getting everything working properly. His efforts were repaid when the BBC news came on and he was shocked to see that Hedge End was the top story, not only on the local news, but the whole country. The reports of beatings, robbery, unlawful underage sex and even two deaths, left him sitting crossed legged on the floor, like he was back at school and the headmaster told them that Mrs Pratt, one of the teachers, had died.

"Bloody hell," he commented. He'd thought the fun he and the others had last night had been the exception, but in the end it was normal in the context of what happened around the town. He wondered what old Great Uncle Jimmy would have thought of it all. Then he sniffed and put on an action film, one of two he had gotten free with the player and the television, and with a swift trip to the kitchen to fetch some crisps and beer he let his mind switch off and enjoyed the movie.

The next day Simon got up and headed to the newsagents, which was shut, so he headed off to WH Smiths and bought every different newspaper he could carry from a rather sheepish looking middle-aged woman behind the till. Lucy had grudgingly gotten up and gone to work. The shoe shop had been closed the day before for unspecified reasons by the manager.

Simon brewed another cup of tea and laid out the papers on the dining table and read the headlines, all of which were centred on his normally sleepy little town, in a forgotten corner of Surrey.

ORGY TOWN — said *The Sun* headlines.

MAY DAY MADNESS — blazed the *Daily Mail*

HEDGE END THE NEW SODOM — wailed the *Daily Express*

ST VITUS DANCE PHENOMENON HITS SMALL SURREY TOWN — the headline of *The Times* offered some explanation

CAN WE COME NEXT YEAR? — the *Daily Sport* wanted to know

MAYOR OF HEDGE END CHARGED AS HIS TOWN RECOVERS FROM A NIGHT OF MAY DAY MAYHEM — reported *The Independent*

SURREY'S PAGAN SEX ORGY SHAME — added the Mirror to the condemnation of the night events.

Simon read every paper with every sordid story and was glad to find that he and his friends and loved ones were not mentioned. He rang his friend Paul, and he was okay. He had been in Liverpool watching Chelsea play and had missed everything. He noted that Councillor Saunders, whom he saw talking to Mathew yesterday, was now acting Mayor, as old Khan had been charged with rape and the Deputy had mysterious resigned for no given reason.

Simon leaned back on his chair's back legs, finished his tea and set it down on the table. "What the fuck is going on around here?"

The builders had arrived, so after a brief chat with Mathew, who was too busy to take proper notice of her, Catherina went for a walk on the morning sunshine. She knew the rough layout of the town south and east of the house, but not north, so she thrust her hands into her hooded sweatshirt and with sore feet headed up the hill.

A police car was parked in one of the drives opposite, she noted, but police cars were now everywhere in Hedge End after May Day night. She kept to the Leggett Woods side of the road. The tall hedge that edged the copse on the other side of the road made her feel uneasy for some reason, like the walls of some high security prison. She reached the roundabout and waited for the traffic to thin so she could cross the Woking Road and then passed the taxis lined up along Station Road. She carried on over the bridge that spanned the railway tracks cut into the hillside forty feet below and was about to turn back, not seeing much of interest or shops, when she spotted the spire of a church above another tall hedge of hawthorn. It wasn't until she was across Station Lane that she saw that the church had a wooden fence around it and men and machinery were hard at work around its scaffold covered exterior.

A wooden sign with faded gold letters on a green background stood fixed to a low brick wall, beyond the boundary of the building words. It read:

St Barnabus Roman Catholic Church in the diocese of Guildford

Catherina frowned when she looked over to see a poster of how the church redevelopment into flats would look when work was complete. Even the faith she was born into could not help her. It too seemed to have been driven out of the town. She was about to turn and head home, when a voice spoke to her from her right.

"You have to go to Woking now, if you want to pray, my child."

She turned and saw a bent and somewhat shriveled man in

a large duffle coat, with a collar visible under it. His hair was thinning, grey and unkempt. His eyes were kind, but bloodshot and he had just appeared from behind a parked white van to her side.

"Thank you, Father...?" She paused, hoping he would fill in the blanks.

"Carmichael, or used to be when I still had a church and a congregation. Now I'm not sure what my purpose is," he said, looking at the building site and not her.

"That is a shame. I think I could do with the peace of a church confessional right now, padre." She glanced quickly at him and then back to where he was staring.

"I thought you were of the faith. I could tell once upon a time. Now I'm not sure of anything anymore, my child."

"What happened? Why did it close?"

"Lack of faith in me and dwindling congregations, and its position wasn't right. It was like it was a holy fort in some godless wasteland. I failed too, because I wasn't strong enough and look what happened on that pagan May Day night. The whole town sunk lower than a grave on its way to hell and eternal damnation."

Catherina looked at the sad, broken man and could see how he would have looked, when strong in his faith and doing God's work. "You could always take my confession, padre."

"Really?" He shrugged. "Yet I may be the biggest sinner of all. I gave in to my demons and was weak in God's eyes and have failed in my task to protect this town from evil."

"Then let us repent our sins together, padre." She smiled and Father Carmichael looked down at his hands and saw for the first time in years they were not shaking from the DTs.

"Thank you, thank you so much, but not here. Let us go to the old Roman fort on the hill. It may not be holy, but it is at least neutral ground, so to speak." They walked off together back over the Bridge Road and down the Woking Road to where a path in the wooden fence of the line of trees led up to the eye-wincing sunshine of the ruins of the old fort.

Mrs Puck had watched them walk off together from her front upstairs spare bedroom window. She was dressed and an exhausted Jack Lucas slept on in her four-poster bed at the rear of the house. She headed downstairs, opened the side gate of her house and wheeled his motorbike in and around the back before anyone noticed it.

"Can I speak to Mr Eversley, please?"

Mathew had been forced out of the house and the garden by the sound of the builders starting working and was now standing in the dappled light-strewn mess that was his late great uncle's weed covered vegetable patch of old.

"Can I say who is calling? He's very busy at the moment," said the tried voice of Mr Eversley's PA, whom he finally got through to after being transferred umpteen times.

"My name is Mathew Reynolds. I'm a friend of Mayor George Saunders and I have a once in a lifetime opportunity for your boss," Mathew replied in his smoothest voice.

"I'll try, but as I've said he is rather busy today."

"Is that a Yorkshire accent I can detect?"

"Erm, yes, I was born in Harrogate." The fake London vowels fell away as her accent of birth came flooding through.

"Thought it was. My dad was stationed up there for three years."

"Did you like it?"

"Bloody hated it, but the people were nice and the girls, oh so blonde and pretty," he said, continuing his smooze assault.

"I'm blonde, you know."

"I bet you're pretty too."

The young woman on the line just giggled, "I can see Mr Eversley is off the phone now. I'll try and put you through, okay, Mathew?"

"Thanks."

The phone went onto a drab rendition of some melancholic Simon and Garfunkel song for a few seconds and then the PA came on again. "Putting you through now."

"Cheers."

"Mr Reynolds, I understand you know George Saunders, but I was surprised to hear he was now Mayor of that, erm, interesting town he lives in."

"Thank you for taking my call, Mr Eversley, first of all. Yes, old George got a bit lucky after all the resignations and suspensions on the council down here."

"Well, I know George. But I don't know you, so if you please, I have a meeting in five minutes?"

"Right. I now own Leggett House and the surrounding woods after inheriting it from my Great Uncle Jimmy. You have offered him in the past to buy said lands and house to build one of your superstores on, but he was never willing to sell."

"Plus the Mayor at the time and his cronies hated the idea."

"Well, times change, Mr Eversley. I am willing to listen to substantial offers for the land I own, which is big enough really to house three superstores, or maybe housing or a leisure complex. Plus our friend Mr Saunders is head of the Planning Department and now acting Mayor, and I'm sure he can help push such tricky planning permission through." Mathew looked up and smiled as a breeze blew up and made the boughs of the trees overhead sway and shiver.

"I think we better set up a meeting, Mr Reynolds. I could even come to you as my own house is not more than ten miles away."

"Probably better if I get the train up to London and meet with you, given what's gone on here lately."

"Would eleven tomorrow morning suit?"

"Suits me fine, Mr Eversley. I look forward to working with you on this endeavour."

"Until tomorrow, Mr Reynolds."

"Until tomorrow."

Mathew ended the call, threw the phone up into the air and caught it with both hands. Singing to himself, he headed back towards the front of the house to see Catherina walking along the drive. He rushed up, picked her up and spun her around, to her surprise and delight.

"What has made you so happy, then?"

"I'm just pleased to see you. I love you, Catherina. You know that?"

"Yes." She curled her lips into a smile and kissed him for the first time since May Day.

A wolf-whistle from a builder grabbing a hammer from his van made them turn and stop, and they headed back indoors and brewed up coffees and teas for them and the men at work.

On the insistence of the Home Office, the detective leading the case of Hannah Browning's disappearance was replaced by a more senior officer from the Met Police. He would take on all the cases for Hedge End after there had been a public outcry at the violent and unlawful events of late in this once quiet end of Surrey. He took on three murder cases, Hannah's case and now the missing family of Anil Passat and many cases of rape, unlawful and underage sex and other deviant cases that did not make the papers.

When he found out that the neighbours of the Passats', the Pratchetts, had not been seen for ages, he ordered the place to be searched. In fact, two bobbies jumped over into the Pratchetts' garden with ease and found the broken French window and the blood trails and stains on the carpets and floors, but not a single body. In the gardens of the two houses on Hanger Hill that backed onto Woodhouse Copse, no holes were there to be discovered.

CHAPTER SIXTY-NINE

After the workers had left for the day, Mathew stoked up the boiler and added more fuel, as Catherina indulged in her second love, which was cooking. Her mother had died when she was eleven and being the only female left, Catherina had taken over cooking duties, while her father and uncle had worked the farm.

She hadn't minded. She loved cooking and somehow it made her feel close to her mother and the small stove in the kitchen was the only place she was happy for a long, long time, until she discovered that she was a pretty good drawer and painter at school.

Mathew told her over dinner that he had to go back to London the next day to talk to the taxmen about the winding up of his company and his declaration of bankruptcy. She nodded, not really understanding or wanting to know about English business law.

"Will you have to pay them back?"

"No, I might even get a rebate," he said, reaching over for some bread to accompany the succulent chicken meal she had prepared.

"Really," she raised her thin eyebrows.

"Maybe." He waved his hand over his dinner. "Anyway, I'll be here to let the builders in, but you'll have to keep an eye on them, okay? I should be back by three, maybe earlier."

"How *emozionante*," she answered, looking up at him as she put her head low over her plate to stop sauce dripping on her blouse.

"Pardon?"

"Nothing." She winked back at him.

He grinned and scarfed her food down like there was no tomorrow. She felt a little better now as the days moved on from that fateful May Day night, and talking to Father Carmichael had helped ease her burden of guilt. He had spoken to her as well of how the pagan elements and moral and holy decline in the town had led to his fall from grace. He seemed to hate this Mrs Puck person who organised the May Day events, and he feared she was leading the whole town down into hell. The smell of alcohol on his breath and clothes had led her to dismiss much of what he had said about certain trees and woods and even birds being evil.

While at the excavated trenches and ruins of the old Roman fort, he had informed her that it was his belief that the Romans, when they invaded, put up the hedge in a great square to keep certain creatures and men of the wild woods from killing their men and infecting the local Celtic tribe with their ancient pagan religious views. This, with some ancient spells or rites that he did not understand, had kept the elder gods trapped within and the demon men of the woods troubled only those who ignored the tales and crossed the hedge or hay as it was then called.

She liked listening to such local folk tales normally, and missed those from her home. London seemed to have ghosts and murders, but nothing of local tradition. She thought it interesting to find markers of ancient peoples and times left behind, like what remained of the hedge and the fort on the hill.

They watched some television and went up to bed together and she let Mathew hold her in his arms again, but they did not make love, as she was not ready yet. It still felt odd that the last person each of them had made love to were Simon and Lucy and not each other.

A noise, maybe the squawk of a bird, had woken Catherina at about three and she trudged off in need of the toilet, as she and Mathew had polished off a bottle of white wine over dinner. She sat down in the dark and did her business with her eyes closed in the blue cast unlit bathroom.

It was only when she was pulling up her pyjama bottoms

that she noticed an odd green glow from outside. The windows of the bathroom were made of rippled glass and all she could see of the distorted light was it came from the far end of the garden. Rubbing her eyes, she padded downstairs on bare feet and headed through two rooms to the kitchen. The linoleum was icy, and the air had a nip to it that made her cross her arms across her chest to keep out the cold. She went up to the sink and peered out the windows. Behind the willow, the back gate of the property was open and the soft green glow seemed to be coming from the woods beyond.

She thought about waking Mathew, but changed her mind. The illumination was not harsh and white like a torch or red like a flickering fire. So she kicked on her trainers, pulled on her puffer jacket and headed out the newly planed and unstuck back door. She zipped up, fully expecting the light to go out and to hear people running away, but that did not happen.

Catherina made her way over the dewy lawn, ducked under the willow tree and moved up to the open gate and the doorway to the woods. The glow made the bushes, trees and flowers shine in the tunnel-like entrance to the woods and down at the bend in the path bobbed an orb of green light. As her eyes trained upon it, it moved out of sight, like it was playing hide-and-seek with her.

She took one look back at the dark house and then plunged through the open gate and down the gentle slope after the strange Will-O-the-Wisp, as it kept to the edge of the path. She only glimpsed it now and again as it led her ever onwards towards the centre of the woods.

Catherina came at last to the small clearing, where the trees crowded around like rugby players in a scrum, but letting the night sky and stars shine down on the clearing, giving it an unworldly feel. The green orb glowed bright for a moment and then shot down into the undergrowth ahead of her and disappeared from sight. The night suddenly encroached as the glow was now gone and she turned around in the darkness, feeling cold and suddenly wary of her surroundings.

She jumped an inch when behind her a woodpecker screeched and flew down to land in the grey-dark blue night and block her path. It was her old watchful friend that she had noticed many times since arriving in Hedge End. It unfurled its wings, and it seemed that the bird bowed low to her.

A snapping of a twig made her swear in her native tongue and turn to where the orb of light had vanished. She staggered two steps back when she saw standing in the same spot a great dark furred wolf. On its back sat two small boys riding the creature like a pony.

The wolf and the boys, who were twins, seemed cast in the same green glimmer of the orb that was coming from the ground below, shining through the undergrowth in a circle like glow. The wolf stepped forward and Catherina shuffled a step back. The twin boys giggled and jumped off the wolf's back and joining hands, walked into the clearing to stand no more than four feet from her.

"*Buonasera,* Catherina," the twins said to her, but she could not see their lips move. Their words were heard only in her head, for her ears picked up nothing but the sounds of the tress rustling on a light breeze and the fast pace of her breathing.

"Who are you?" She surprised herself by asking in English, as she was sure she had spoken in Italian.

"I am Romulus," said the boy on the left.

"And I am Remus," said his brother on his right.

"I must be going insane. You cannot be. Am I dreaming this?"

"This is not a dream, sweet Catherina. We reveal ourselves to you in thanks for setting us free from the house our uncle trapped us in by his death. He was touched by the love of our homeland and so you and only you, a descendant of our Roman line, could set us free to rejoin our Wolf-mother," said both Romulus and Remus in perfect unison. The twins' voices were not in her head now, but spoken in English.

"I cannot believe I'm saying this, but you are the founders of Rome from the ancient legends. If so, why are you here?"

Catherina's hands flexed at her sides. She wondered how she was coming up with such rational questions, while the walls of reality crumbled around her.

"We were summoned long ago and the Wolf-mother carried

us over the seas and lands to raise an army of creatures to combat the Dwellers of the sacred woods yonder." The twins raised their thin arms and pointed up the path towards the house. "Yet wars never solve anything. They just change the landscape and murder the innocent. We rose our unforgiving creatures to fight theirs, yet neither side could prevail, so strong and undying were our armies. Yet time did for us both. The gods of the forest were bound to their woods by ancient incantations, the growing hedge and blocks of stone placed at four corners that contained the blood of the gods. Lugus, the Dwellers' god, was forgotten in time and after three generations of Celts they referred to him as Mercury and prayed only to the Roman deities on fear of death. So our victory came at last. The Dwellers were trapped and Lugus fled in defeat, yet we found out to our cost that victory has its price also."

"What do you mean?"

"Our followers were returned to the earth as their purpose was over. We had made them so strong even we could not unmake them, so we buried them deep and there they still sleep and wait for a time where they may be required again. Yet we too had left it too late. Time passed and the god of the Israelites took hold of our empire and we too, like Lugus, faded into myths and stories and were bound here until the end of days, or until war comes once more to the woods."

"Did Mathew's Great Uncle Jimmy know about you?"

"Yes, his love made us visible again, gave us shape and form, for he carried the essence and love for our homeland in his aura."

"What about Mathew? Does he know about you?"

"We appeared to him once, but his mind is so very closed. But yours is what we have long yearned for. Your blood is strong with the soil and your mind is open to many beautiful things."

"What do you want from me, though?"

"Nothing yet, but the time is coming when we shall call upon you and require your aid. So the earth and the sky will change places. The hedge is now only a remnant of the past and all but one of the sacred blocks has been destroyed. The Dwellers are moving once more, pushing at the boundaries of the prison that has held them for two millennia. Lugus is now remembered and his followers grow strong. If the last sacred block is destroyed or moved, great suffering will come to the people of Hedge End and the rest of Briton."

"So where is the last stone, and what can I do to help you?"

"The time has not yet come to reveal that, but know this; you are bound now to it and your lover. Stay out of the realm of the Dwellers and keep your eyes open and ear to the ground." The twins' voices became softer now and Catherina felt her head swoon as if she had gotten up too quickly or drank too much wine.

"This seems like a dream. Will I remember it in the morning?"

"Yes," they said and their heads drooped with sadness. "We are sorry for this, but it is the only way."

"What do you mean?" Catherina edged back along the path and a squawk from the woodpecker behind made her spin around to avoid stepping on it. Fast low movement caught her peripheral vision, and she turned back just as the she-wolf sunk her teeth into her left hand, causing her to yelp in pain. The twins had vanished and a glow came from the covered well hole. Catherina turned and ran back up the root covered path as the darkness pressed in on her like a black fog and she stumbled on a tree root and felt herself falling…

Falling, as if she had lost gravity, and then her head went into her pillow and her body bounced on the bed, her right arm under her and her left held out over the carpet. Her eyes flicked open in panic and she found that she was back in her bedroom. The dawn sunshine was streaming through the gaps at the side and bottom of the window. She flicked her head to the right and saw Mathew was fast asleep beside her and she reached out with her cold left hand to grab at her wrist watch. Pain lanced up her arm. She looked and saw wide puncture marks of a bite on her hand and dried blood surrounded the deep and ugly looking holes. She bent over the side of the bed and saw her mud covered trainers were on the floor. On the carpet were red and browning drops of blood from her wound.

Holding her throbbing hand so as not to injury it more, she slipped out of bed, gathered her trainers in the crook of her left arm and hurried to the bathroom to lock herself in. She put some antiseptic cream on the four bites marks and then covered the wound on her palm with two large overlapping square plastic bandages. Then she cleaned her trainers with her right-hand the best she could and flushed the dirty toilet paper down the toilet.

She went to the sink, ran the cold tap and splashed icy water over her face with her right-hand, to keep her left dry. She stood up, her face covered in water, her brown eyes staring back at her in the mirror. Catherina raised her wounded hand to her face and recalled most of her weird conversation with the Roman gods that resided in the woods behind her new house, and understood why they had hurt her. It was proof that it happened. Without it, waking up in her warm comfy new bed, she would have dismissed it as a very vivid dream.

A hard thump at the bathroom door made her jump and nearly head butt the mirror in fright. She turned to see the door handle rattle in the lock and a shiver travelled up her body from calves to the nape of her neck.

"Cat, unlock the door, I need a piss."

"Coming," she answered shakily and hurried over to open the door for her lover. She began to use her left hand but then changed over to the right, and pulled the door open to let a near hopping Mathew rush over to the toilet, pull up the seat and urinate.

"Ah, that's better," he sighed. "Hey, what have you done to your hand?"

Catherina stopped, her left hand on the doorknob, as she was about to slip out and get dressed in a thin woolen jumper with long cuffs to hide the wound.

"*Sciocco*, silly me," she answered. "I went downstairs to get a glass of water and fell onto a nail. It's nothing, darling."

"Wasn't a rusty one? Because you might need a tetanus jab." He pulled back the shower curtain from the bath.

"It was shiny new. Nothing really, Mathew. So are you having a shower?"

"Yeah, better look clean and respectable for my meeting in London this morning," he replied, grabbing a large towel and placing it on the now closed and flushed toilet seat.

"I'll put on some coffee, make fry up with some bacon, eh?"

"Cool."

Catherina gathered up the trainers that he had failed to notice as Mathew bent over the bath, putting the rubber mat in place, and slipped downstairs. She put the kettle on to boil and wondered how much an espresso machine would cost. Then she looked out the window and sitting on the birdbath was the ever watchful woodpecker. It unfurled its wings and like last night bowed and flew off up into the sun kissed tree tops of Leggett Woods.

Simon lay in bed watching a freshly showered Lucy get dressed. Her body was red and blotchy in places from the hot shower and he saw more flaws, pimples and moles on her body that never really bothered him before. Her hair was wet. Usually it was one of her best features, but now it looked near brown and unattractive.

"-you going to do today?"

"Eh?"

"You never bloody listen. I asked what you were up to today." Lucy said in a high voice as she leaned forward to pull on her bra, fasten it at the back, then pull up the thin black straps while waiting for Simon to answer.

"You know, I'm not quite sure."

"Well, the grass is growing fast. You could cut that and put some washing on," she ventured, pulling on her shoe shop blouse, and fastened the buttons with her short little fingers.

"So I'm a house-husband now. Next you'll be leaving me lists and Post-its around the place for chores to do."

"What's wrong with you? I only asked what you were up to and the lawn does need cutting, Simon," she said, anger underling her words.

"Nothing much," he stated. He lay back in the bed and put his hands behind his head. "So with Mathew, was it good, different?"

"Simon, where's this festered up from? I haven't got time for this. I've still got a job to go to, remember?"

"Just curious," he said, frowning.

"How was Cat, then?" she spat back, wriggling her navy-blue skirt on and zipping it up at the back. "Did she suck your cock to your satisfaction?"

"No need to be crude."

"You started this, Si," Lucy said, her hands on her hips, in her ultimate defensive mode. "You fucked Cat, I fucked Mathew. It happened. Do you want it to happen again, is that it?"

"No." He sat up, annoyed at the suggestion, and then in a normal voice he said, "It's just messed my mind up a bit, understand?"

"I do if you explain it like that, not in your stupid lad's way. I still love you more than ever, Simon. May Day night was just one of those crazy booze-fuelled things that ninety-nine times out of a hundred never happen, except in the letters pages of dirty magazines. We were all complicit in it and it's something we have to just get over in time and move on."

"You're right. Just ignore me and expect that lawn to be like the top of a snooker table by the time you get home."

"Good," she said, leaning over to kiss his lips. "Now I've got to dry my hair if that's okay with you, Simon Hay?"

"Dry away," he said, raising his hands. He wriggled back down under the covers to watch her do so with half-closed eyes.

"What you doing in here, Sinead? The mixers need sorting," Ted said, coming into the empty room in the inn where Jack Lucas had stayed.

"Sorry." She turned to go past him and then stopped. "I wonder why he left. Did we do something wrong?"

Ted frowned, but Sinead just hurried past him into the corridor outside before he could answer, if indeed he had an answer. After the May Day night fiasco, he wasn't surprised that the guy had fled such a screwed up little town. Yet the Green Man Inn seemed a slightly less sunny place now that he was gone, as if the colour was turned down a notch on the television.

He and Bill had continued to sleep with Sinead over the last few nights, but they could never recapture the wanton rough thrill of the first time and each time the feeling of joy grew less and less. Jack Lucas had left a vacancy in the register of their inn, but also a void deep inside Ted's soul and others who had encountered him.

It took only twenty minutes to cut the small square back garden lawn and ten minutes of that was getting the lawnmower out of the small cluttered shed. Simon was back indoors by ten and sitting on the sofa flicking through daytime TV with a drab bored look on his face. He decided to have a can of lager from the fridge as a gardening reward, to cool him down as the temperature was already mild for early May.

He snapped his fingers after a minute of sitting down and turned on his computer to type up his notes from his meeting with Rose Puck. Once finished, he found himself tapping his finger on the small computer desk, wedged in the corner by the bookshelf. He was just staring at the words he had typed up on the screen, re-reading the near fantasy tales she had told about the history of the hedge and the how his name and family were connected in some way to such tales of long ago.

Simon felt restless. He saved his work, turned off the computer and took his empty beer can out into the kitchen to put in a bag on the back door handle. He sighed loudly and leaned on the kitchen counter. The sun was bright outside, and he was indoors. He quickly grabbed his mobile phone and keys and decided to put on his trainers and go out for a walk.

"Let's cut to the chase, Mr Eversley, shall we? I am now the owner of a prime piece of land you have been chasing for many years. This could help you steal a march on your competitors in the area. Let's talk money," Mathew said, leaning forward in his business suit and uncrossing his legs. He was not one for idle chit-chat when a deal was going down.

"Well, I can't just pluck a number out of thin air, Mr Reynolds. I'd have to get my surveyors to take a look and then come up with an offer," Eversley calmly replied, his fingers on a report with a plastic cover on the table before him.

"Mr Eversley, surely that report you had hurriedly done last night, the one under your hand, can give you a figure. I never went into any meeting without knowing what the other person wanted, or what I was willing to pay first, and I doubt someone who has scaled the management heights here would either."

Mr Eversley grinned and with a nod sat back in his chair, his fingers leaving the report and going to his armrests. "Very well. Seven hundred and fifty thousand for the house and the woods."

"How about one million and a quarter and you can even keep the lampshades and curtains," was Mathew's reply.

"I think you overestimate the value of the land and house, Mr Reynolds. We would never pay that price."

"Your company makes a profit of over a million pounds per day in the UK alone. Your new supermarket, with petrol station and space for other shops to lease in and maybe a housing estate with a few trees kept to please the tree-huggers. You'd be in profit within two, maybe three years."

"I'll tell you what, Mr Reynolds, I'll send my survey team along, on the quiet, not to alarm the locals and then talk to my people. I'm sure we can come to an arrangement to please both parties. We want the land, that is a given, we just have to sort the nitty-gritty, so to speak, in the next few weeks." Mr Eversley rose, buttoned his Saville row jacket and extended his right hand.

"So in principle we have a deal?" Mathew rose and reached over the desk to shake the taller older man's hand.

"Yes, I think we do."

And there they left it, both content in their own way. Mathew knew that he would get the full asking price and Eversley knew he would have gone up to two million pounds to have secured the site.

After Eversley's PA had escorted Mathew down to the lifts, she found Mr Eversley waiting for her by her desk.

"Ah Ingrid, get me Councillor, no, Mayor Saunders on the phone again, please?"

"Right away, Mr Eversley," she replied with a faint Yorkshire accent.

Catherina had been delayed in her plans by the builders' requests for tea and questions about stop-cocks and ring-mains, which were words she did not understand. She shrugged and let the men find these things for themselves. It wasn't until half-eleven that she managed to tell the guy in charge that she was off for a walk.

She hurried down the garden and had to open the stiff gate. The sunlight was lost to her for a while as she hurried down the root littered track into the woods. The clearing was bathed in a ring of solid sunlight, and pollen and flies could be seen dancing in the late spring rays. She walked out of the shady gloom and into the light, which felt like stepping from in front of the freezer to an open oven door in two steps.

The air was still and seemed filled with tranquil peace. She could hear wood pigeons hooting from the tree-tops. She hurried forward and knelt down in the dust and pulled a new pair of gardening gloves from her back jeans pocket. Catherina put them on and leaned forward to pull at the brambles, trailing ivy and holly. She pulled and tugged the vegetation free and even kicked at the harder woody stems, cracking them so she could fold back the holly.

It did not take her long to reveal the remains of an old stone well, parts of which had fallen in over the countless years and blocked it up. She tried to move the top large block, but it was well and truly wedged in and did not even budge an inch even though she pulled with all her might. Her arms were aching as she gripped the earth covered sides of the well. She wondered what was down there and if it had something to do with the twins, the wolf and that woodpecker.

"*Merda!*" she swore under her breath. How could she move the blockages? Maybe with a rope or a spade to lever them up.

"Catherina?"

She jumped not for the first time since she arrived in Hedge End as a familiar voice spoke to her from her right. She scrambled back in shocked retreat to find that Simon Hay was walking up from another path towards her.

"Sorry, I didn't mean to startle you."

"Simon, thank God. You frightened me," she panted, putting her hand to her bosom.

"You found the old well, I see. We used to keep away from the place as kids, me and Matt. We always thought zombies and monsters might crawl out of there at night. How have you been?"

"Well, in my body anyway. My mind, well, I think I may be losing that, as you say." She gave a very unconvincing laugh.

"I'm a good listener. We could chat and walk in the woods if you like?"

"Yes, I would like that." she smiled thinly.

They walked off up the northern path next to each other, but keeping a distance of a foot at all times.

"Mathew not about?"

"No, he has some meeting in London with the taxman," she explained and then looked up at him coyly. "So did you come to see him or me?"

"I just went for a walk, really. Off in my own little world and found myself here, which is to say that I'm still glad I bumped into you, Catherina."

"Calls me Cat, please."

"Okay, Cat, shall I show you the Roman ruins over the road and up the hill?"

"I've already been, with Father Carmichael, but you can show me again if you like."

"Really, did he offer you a drink?"

"No." She turned towards him and stopped between two old elms. "He offered me absolution for my sins."

"I've never been a sin before," Simon remarked and he noticed that the woods seemed to close in on him and Catherina, and the world suddenly contracted into a small bubble that consisted of only their two souls.

She felt him ease closer and found she was somehow moving closer to him. Her heart thumped in her chest when his head inclined down towards her. Her lips parted, wanting to reclaim the sin that could not be washed away by a fallen priest's words.

Something dark swooped down at them and aimed for their heads. They both ducked in time, but bumped each other's heads slightly. The woodpecker missed them by an inch and flew off over the treetops and out of sight.

"What the fuck?"

"I know," Catherina said, standing back up. "Lots of strange things keep happening to me lately."

"It's like the whole town has gone to pot," he said, looking at Catherina and knowing the moment was lost. He was glad in way. He had sinned far too much for his liking lately.

"I think I better be getting back," she said, "to check on the workers."

"Probably best if I head this way," he said, pointing up the track that lead to the Woking Road.

"Yes." She nodded and retraced her steps back to the glade and the house, without a goodbye.

CHAPTER SEVENTY

Rose Puck wandered into her bedroom as dusk finally fell over Hedge End and saw that Jack was standing at the window, staring out over her garden and her secret grove. Deep shadows clung to the bed and furniture like a black skirting and outside the failing light had a purple-pink tinge that gave the garden an eerie, almost mystical feel.

She stood in the open doorway, the lights from downstairs bringing a dull artificial glow behind her. Jack had his faithful denim jeans on, but was shirtless, and fumes of smoke were rising from what must be an unseen cigarette in his lips. They hadn't spoken much since he moved in a week ago. They had eaten and drank and fucked like the world was ending, but discussed nothing. She wanted to ask him why she felt younger each passing day in his presence and why they had become instant lovers, as if she had known him forever, or maybe in a previous life.

"When's a door not a door?"

"Pardon?"

Jack Lucas turned and she was shocked to find he had no cigarette in his lips or in his hands and the smoke she saw had dissipated.

"When's it's a-jar," he said simply and pointed to the open bedroom door, in which she stood.

She closed the door behind her and leaned her shoulders and back of her head against it, liking the feel of the cold gloss paint on her skin. She wondered who or what Jack really was. Mrs Puck had her beliefs since childhood, and then in her twenties everything had changed and she was the new mother it seemed, of something ancient that had suddenly awoken in the deep earthy vaults beneath the woods opposite her house. Her husband, Philip Puck, being also a distant cousin, had died only months after their marriage, which bore no children, but left her the house and the means to carry on the plans that had long been laid out for her.

"I thought you were smoking?"

She pushed herself off the door and moved towards him, to the centre of the bedroom, next to a linen box at the foot of the four-poster bed that they shared.

"Just a little trick I learned from a fakir in Hindustan." He smiled a lopsided grin and twirled his right forefinger next to his head and a wisp of white smoke appeared.

"Who are you, Jack, really?"

"In the glades of a forest long ago I came across a stream of silver, banked each side by pale wands of willow. Through the rushes I saw her fair, with aspects of light and blood flame hair, my forever love, Rosmerta. I made for her a place of peace, where our children danced at our feet and for many moons and harvest suns, we lived in happiness with hearts of one."

Rose Puck could almost smell and taste the air of those woods of long ago; such was the passion and imagery of his words. She came to herself once more and saw that he had turned and was looking out of the window once again.

"I was wondering, when are we going into the woods together?"

She inched forward with every word, walking on tip-toes for some unknown reason in her own house.

"Not yet."

"When then, they're getting restless. Their actions are becoming more reckless. People are going missing. Someone will notice."

"I will go down to the grove tonight and no further. If they come I will talk to them. I hate the dark so," he finished in a whisper.

Rose took off the t-shirt she was wearing, unhooked her bra and let it fall onto the carpet between her feet. She came up behind him and pressed her warm body against his and they waited for the dark to fall, and maybe for the children of the forest to appear.

CHAPTER SEVENTY-ONE

L ike after a wildfire, when all the flames were doused and the ash had settled onto the floor, things returned to some sort of normality. May had given way to June and the numbers of the missing had not grown. The woods were still and full of watchfulness, awaiting the next phase of life or death. The awkwardness between the two couples had been buried deep and they still saw each other mostly at weekends and without the wanton abandon of May Day night.

The guilty were being charged, the dead buried and mourned, and other events around the world let Hedge End slowly become old news and next week's chip-paper. The charges against Mayor Khan meant that George Saunders now took up his post on a permanent basis.

Lucy finally had left her hated job in the shoe shop and she and Simon were trying to adjust to seeing each other twenty-four-seven and forge a new way of life together. The house at Leggett Woods was improving and the old damp parlour and other bedrooms were now water-tight and redecorated. They had nice new cupboards and granite worktops to match their modern appliances in the kitchen.

"What have you done wrong?"

"I don't know what you mean."

"Dinner. You never cook me dinner, not even back in the apartment when we first go out, to impress me." Catherina stared at Mathew across the dinner table at home, as he poured her a glass of chianti and made a fuss over her.

"Can't a man cook his girlfriend dinner once in a while

without having an ulterior motive?"

"In my experiences, no." She shook her head, swishing her mane of brown hair from side to side. "Is it something to do with that package that was delivered this morning?"

"Can't get anything past you, can I?" He winked and the Tom Cruise smile appeared right on cue.

"So are you going to tell me what it was?"

He smiled at the way her hands gesticulated in front of her face and knew that it was now or never. "It was a contract for me to look over."

"A contract for what?"

"To buy the house and the woods from me for over a million pounds." His grin widened. "I'm back, baby."

"But what about you're great uncle's house?"

"Oh, they'll knock this old shithole down and build a fucking huge supermarket in its place. There will be jobs aplenty for the locals and we can buy some nice crib anywhere in the world. You name the place and just enjoy the high-life once more."

"Wait, you want us to leave Hedge End, dishonour Jimmy's memory? What about Simon? Won't you miss him?" She had put down her knife and fork now and simmering anger boiled within her fiery Italian heart.

"Look, we can ask Si and Lucy to stay wherever we go, maybe even do some more of that foursome stuff, if you want?"

"*Merda!*" She stood up sharply, knocking her chair backwards to crash onto the floor. "Why do you always fuck things up, Mathew? I love it here. I want to settle down and marry you and have *bambini* and paint great art. I love this old house and Hedge End and its strange ways. I won't let you do this."

"Too late, Cat, I've signed on the dotted line. We can stay here until the planning permission goes through and then the world is our oyster. I dunno why you're not seeing the bigger picture here."

"So Mathew Reynolds says so it has to be fucking done, eh??" she shouted at him, beating at her chest twice. "It is all about you. What about what I want? I want to stay here and build something special with you."

"Here we go. Why are you determined to hold me back? You're just like my father." He stood, anger causing his shoulders to tense up.

"You bastard!" she screamed and headed for the kitchen.

Mathew grabbed her wrists as she passed and they struggled on the edge of the kitchen entrance, his fingers and her thrashes causing her skin to burn.

"I won't let you fuck this up for me, Cat, d'you hear?."

"Bastard," she spat and kneed him in the balls. His hands went from her wrists to his groin. She rushed past him into the kitchen, threw open the door and ran across the garden and through the already open gate in the boundary wall. She hurried on at full speed and heard the gate smash shut loudly behind her, but she had not laid a finger on it. Down the root strewn path she fled with nimble feet and into the clearing, where she at last cast herself down in front of the well, sobbing her heart out.

"Don't cry, aunt," came two voices as one. She sat up and wiped the tears from her blurred eyes as the twins stood hand in hand just to her right.

"He wants to sell the house and the woods. He has betrayed his great uncle's trust. They will tear down the woods. What are we going to do?"

"If they destroy the house and woods it will be found, the last defence against the enemy. Lugus will be free to return to his home again and all things will fail and he will be a god once more."

"I do not understand. What shall I do?"

"Find the three that are now lost and it will lead you to the last. Protect it at all costs, Catherina. No more aid can we give at this time. We can only help you once more, thrice in all, and then only to raise the Anthropophagi from their ancient slumber and rally them for war. Now go while you can. We will delay him, run!"

Mathew grimaced and stumbled across the lawn holding his aching balls until he reached the closed gate at the end of the garden. He moved past the willow tree and up the two stone steps to reach for the closed gate set in the high surrounding wall. He took hold of the handle and winced at how cold the black painted metal felt, even though the nights were quite mild now, and he pulled. The door resisted his initial efforts, so he arched his back and heaved. It felt like someone on the other side had just given up the ghost and let go, for the gate swung out and he stumbled back, two, three steps and then his shoes slipped. He fell back onto the grass, bashing his right shin, and his head made heavy contact with the hard, dry lawn. Mathew's dark world became inhabited with yellow and blue flashing stars for a couple of seconds, before the silent pre-dusk returned and his vision cleared.

He gingerly stood up, rubbing the back of his head through his hair and wincing at the pain in his leg and the ache at his core. He put his hand on his knees, leaned forward and stared into the dark maw of the tunneled path into the woods and exhaled loudly. "Well, that could have gone better," he said to himself.

He stared down the dark path and shook his head. Chasing after Catherina now would not help matters and he wondered how things had got so heated so quickly between them. Didn't she want to be comfortably rich again? He turned and headed back to the house, recalling that she had no keys or money with her and had to come sloping back before midnight, or spend a miserable night alone in the dark woods.

His name long ago had been Stephen Theakston, but that name and life had long been lost in a twenty year street haze of drugs, booze and bouts of ill-tempered aggression doled out on his body. To most of the street wanderers of London and the charity workers, he was known as the Bird-Man of St. James's Park. He could often be seen, his arms wide like a scarecrow, on the green spaces by the flowerbeds, covered with birds of every variety that the park could offer.

Now he wasn't anywhere near his old haunts. He had begged enough train fare to get him to Hedge End, but had been thrown off at Hersham by the guard for swearing at the top of his voice that death was coming to everyone and that the *wood people* would sort out all his fellow train passengers.

So he had been forced to walk on aching feet, with three toes missing in all from cold sharp winters of years gone past, and it wasn't until nightfall that he finally trudged down the London Road and saw the sign saying welcome to Hedge End. He shuffled on past a building site, taking no notice of the church behind its tall wooded barricade.

A motorbike roared past, its screaming engine breaking the silence of his one track thoughts. He crossed Woodhouse Road without looking, onto the pavement again and then crossed a drainage ditch to enter a small triangle of woodland wedged between the road he had just traversed and the mesh fence that marked the boundary of the excavated train tracks far below. His way was soon blocked by a tall hedge of hawthorn that made his neck ache as he looked up to see the very top. Above his head the thick branches of an old tree towered over him and over hung the hedge by two feet or so.

"I'm here," he said, his voice tight and wheezy. The tramp lifted up his arms as he had done on many occasions in the parks of central London.

He closed his eyes and waited, but after a few seconds only one heavy burden landed on his right shoulder. He blinked and turned to see the large dark shape of a raven sitting right next to his ear. "I am the bird-man. You have nothing to fear."

The bird-man howled when with lightning speed the bird's beak shot forward and pecked deep into his right eye, causing his vision to turn to red and then black. He beat the raven away as it attacked his grime stained hands and he ran for his life. He only got four feet before the silent assassin flew down to stab at his skull through his woolly hat and greasy locks. He half turned to get a fix on it to bash at it and his toe snagged under a root that had grown out of the earth. He pitched forward and smashed his face against the bark of an old Linden tree. His lip split and two teeth came loose in the impact as the bark tore at his bearded right cheek.

The bark next to his face turned inwards and a dark vent could be seen in the lower trunk of the tree. It looked like it had once been burnt many years before and had still grown on, with this gash in its side healed as best it could, but leaving an opening in the trees side.

The tramp wheezed and held his chest as pain burned in his heart and his left arm felt numb and useless. His wounded eye had puffed up now and it felt like it was on fire. He searched the dark woods for any sign of the raven with his one remaining good eye. The small little woody triangle was silent once more and he could see no sign of the bird that attacked him, or hear the flap of its wings.

He pressed a palm into his left side as the pain stabbed at him in knifing waves and he turned his head towards the hole in the trunk of the tree beside him and spat out a tooth onto the dusty earth beside the tree. A darting small hand reached out from the hole, picked up the tooth and held it aloft. The arm was long and sinewy and a sweet smell like bread and honey invaded his nostrils. He turned his head more to let his good eye get a better look and the face of the creature that popped out from the hole, its eyes burning green in the darkness, its head covered with twig like stubbles of hair. Its lipless mouth opened wider than any human in a dentist chair. The creature grabbed the tramp's dirty Mac and slowly pulled him closer.

Stephen "The Bird Man" Theakston's last act was to form a wide O of fright with his drawn back lips, before his heart stopped and his restricted vision faded into darkness that had nothing to do with the night.

The raven watched on from above as the tramp's body was dragged into the crack, with the snapping of bones to get it inside. His old trainers were the last to disappear. Then the raven hopped back into its hole high up on a different tree trunk, bobbed its head under its raised wings and went back to sleep.

Lucy and Simon were all cozy on the sofa, watching a new DVD he had bought that morning when there came a knock at their front door. Both of them frowned, as it was a quarter to ten and a bit late for unannounced visitors. They both looked at each other with *you go* eyes, wondering if it was the old lady from over the street again, who kept losing her front door keys down the lining of her age-old coat. Neither of them moved an inch towards getting up.

"Your turn." Lucy nodded for him to do the gentlemanly thing and get up to answer the door.

"I helped the old lady out last time, and I'm pretty sure there are some laws against young men fiddling with old ladies' clothing," he said back to her.

The bell rang now, followed by another two knocks.

"See, she must have luuuved it, Si, and she came back for more," Lucy teased, tickling at his side.

"Okay," he said finally, getting up after rocking twice to get momentum, "but you owe me big time, baby."

"Stick it on the slate," she said and raised her middle finger at him.

He rocked his head back in mock shock and flashed two fingers back before heading off to answer the door. He was surprised to find Catherina at his doorstep.

"Oh Simon, I am very sorry to worry you so late, but Mathew and I have had a blazing row and I had no place else to go."

From the light from the open door down the long hallway he could see her eyes were brimming with tears. "Erm, no, don't worry, come in, come in."

Lucy appeared, opening the door wide, as Catherina held onto Simon's arms and tears now trickled down her round cheeks.

"God, what's happened?"

"She's had a row with Matt," Simon replied.

"Men, eh? What a useless bunch of bastards," Lucy said and took the upset Italian woman from Simon into her comforting embrace.

"I am still here, you know," he said to his fiancée.

"Well, make yourself useful and get the kettle on and the Sambuca out of the cupboard," Lucy said and escorted Catherina into the living room. Simon paused for a second and then made for the kitchen and grabbed the kettle and filled it with cold water. The television was switched off and the reason for the row spilled slowly from Catherina's lips.

CHAPTER SEVENTY-TWO

Rose Puck, for the first time in many a long year, did not have the slightest clue what to do next. Jack sat in the wing-back chair, watching the fire crackle and spit even though it wasn't cold inside the house anymore. He sat with his jeans on and nothing else, as was his habit since he'd moved in. His green eyes were fixed on the flames.

He had been like this for days on end now, since the Dwellers had come to her grove and conversed with him in a language even she, with an ancient language degree, could not comprehend. Three of the ancient wood creatures had emerged ten days ago, on the night of the last full moon. Rose had hung back at the edge of the line of cherry trees, that now were laden by bountiful dark red round fruit.

She had long communed with these ancient creatures and even let them have their rough way with her to keep them on her side. Now she was a little afraid of them, as they had murdered people and had the taste for blood. She no longer felt she had the same bond and accord that she once had. Jack, though, was different. They had all bowed to him and they spoke in their strange guttural voices for an hour.

The moon was covered by a bank of clouds and with nodding heads and toady-like scraping the creatures retreated back into the oak tree and headed down into their deep underground tunnels.

"What did you say to them?"

But Jack did not reply. He just walked past her like she was another cherry tree, but she could see he had tears in his eyes and his face seemed to have fallen into deep lines of sadness.

The sex had stopped and conversation too. She had shouted at him in frustration at times, but still he would not speak with her and barely acknowledged her presence.

Then an idea came to her, and she rushed upstairs to the bedroom they still shared, now in silence. She grabbed his guitar case and carried it carefully downstairs. She opened the case on the settee, picked up the instrument by the neck and moved over to the fire. His eyes darted up to her as she placed the guitar on his lap and moved his hands to hold it.

It seemed to have the desired effect. His hands rubbed and caressed the wooden instrument, like an old lover that he had taken back into his heart. He looked at her. Life at last had come back into his eyes, but sadness still lingered on his heavily lined face. "What happened to my beautiful children of the woods?"

"I don't understand, Jack."

Rose knelt down at his knee and rubbed her warm hand up and down his jean covered thighs.

"They were so fair once, full of light and life. Now they are tainted by blood and darkness, Rose."

"Maybe without you they had to adapt to survive. Maybe if you were to enter the woods things would change and together we could teach them to be what they once were." She smiled up at him, pleased that he had used her name after days of silence.

"The time has yet not come. Things still have to play out first, before I can enter the woods." His voice was distant, but not sad, and he reached down and put his open palm onto Rose's right cheek.

CHAPTER SEVENTY-THREE

Lucy was feeling rough the next morning, so Simon was the first to get up and dressed, before coming downstairs at half-past eight. He stood next to the dining table, trying to peer through the semi-gloom to see if Catherina was awake on the sofa bed yet. Not that he had a great desire to find out what went on last night. He just wanted to know if he could boil the kettle and make himself a brew.

He stood looking at the shape in the bedcovers, wondering what to do about the situation. The thought of Mathew selling the woods and having them bulldozed down to build a supermarket filled him with horror, and that meant taking Catherina's side against his old childhood friend. He wished she wasn't here and was glad she was, both at the same time, as the intimacies they had shared on May Day night came to mind and to have her lying in a bed not more than ten feet away was giving him certain thoughts.

"Morning," a tired and dry sounding voice came from the covers by the pillows.

"Sorry, didn't mean to wake you. Just wondering if you wanted a tea or coffee."

"You know, a tea would be nice for a change," Catherina said. She sat up in bed and looked at Simon, who was standing like an awkward child in his own house.

"Coming right up," he said, wiggling a forefinger and headed off back into the kitchen.

Simon pulled down two mugs, since Lucy wasn't in the mood for one. Nothing to do with the bottle of wine she and Catherina had polished off during their heart to heart last night.

He was just opening up a new bag of sugar when he heard soft footfalls approach. He turned to see Catherina approaching, wearing her long t-shirt down over her underwear and showing off her long shapely tanned legs.

"You know a lot about the history of this place, don't you, Simon?"

"Yes." He nodded only briefly and smiled at her, and then hurried on with pouring the sugar into the sugar bowl. "Is there something you want to know about?"

"I've been talking to, erm, Father Carmichael and he told me about these old Roman blocks that were placed on the edges of the old hedge to keep bad creatures in or something." She paused to move closer as the kettle bobbled and boiled its way to switching off. "I wonder if you might help me find them?"

"Well, I'll give it a go. I know the woman who runs the local museum and library services quite well and have photocopies of the old maps and some on my computer. But where would we start looking?"

Simon tried hard to concentrate and ignore her shapely legs and soft pleasant voice while his eyes bore into the mugs as he poured the water and carried on making the tea.

"The first stone was under the crypt and walls of the old catholic church that they are un-building now. Two other were, erm, digged up when the railway lines were, erm, built. If we can find out about where they were digged up, we might find where the last stone is."

Simon poured in the milk, took out the teabags and added the sugar as he pondered. "My dad is a train nut, loves the things. He might have heard about these blocks when the lines were laid over a hundred years ago."

"*Eccellente.*" She smiled and he passed her a mug of tea.

"Let's have a look at those maps, if I can dig them out." He pointed to the computer desk, where his files and folders were.

"Thank you, Simon, you are a lovely man for doing this and letting me stay here." She leaned forward and kissed his cheek. The heat of her half-dressed body was unbearable and he just wanted to hold her again.

"I'd do anything for you, to help," he said, adding the last two words quickly to make his words sound less obvious.

He watched her smile, then turn her body towards the computer and monitor. Simon put down his tea next to the monitor and fetched a dining chair for Catherina to sit on next to his old swivel chair.

"So where is Lucy? Having a long sleep?"

"Yes." He turned his computer on. "Well, she's ill, really. Too much vino last night probably."

"Ah," she simply said and blew on the top of her hot tea.

"It's easier to have a look on screen. I've saved some so we can scribble on it and not worry," he said, clicking through some folders to reveal a recent map of the town. He used a bright red computer highlighter to mark certain things on the screen. "So stone number one is under the old Catholic church up here," he said and moved and marked a red dot there on the map on his screen. Then he clicked on green and drew in the remains of the hedge to show Catherina where they would be now, if the hedge had remained intact.

"What did it look like a long time ago?"

"Easy," he replied and he drew lines from the dotted remaining parts of the old hedge and filled in the rough rectangular shape all the way down Hanger Hill Road, to join up on the remains on Bates Road, then along through some newer houses and up through more houses in Wood End Lane, over the railway tracks to join more remains up across Woodhouse Road to join the hedge near the church boundaries. The top of the hedge ran across London Road over the railway bridge to the edge to join Woodhouse Copse again, where it met Hanger Hill.

"That is much better. I can see that the train tracks cut right across the old wood," Catherina said, leaning forward towards the monitor and closer to Simon.

"It must have upset and disturbed a lot of wildlife back then," Simon stated, looking at the green and red overdrawn on the computer map.

"So, if we had to guess, the stones would be roughly here, here and here." Catherina pointed to two places on the railway tracks and one place under the shops in the High street.

"That's if they were placed equally and in straight lines at each corner, which we don't yet know."

"These were my Roman ancestors." Catherina laughed a little. "Straight lines and straight roads was what they did."

"I'll print this out for reference then, and I'll give my dad a call later to see if he can help us out," Simon said, clicking a few buttons on the screen. The printer chugged into life under the desk, at his feet.

"I wonder what mood my Mathew is in."

Simon reached down and grabbed the printed page, the sense of unity between him and Catherina dispelled by one sentence from her.

"Pining for you and feeling sorry for himself, I hope."

"I hope so and I hope he has changed his mind about selling his great uncle's woods," she said, standing. "Can I use your bathroom please now, Simon?"

"My home is your home," he said as she went back into the living room. She grabbed her jeans and skipped past him to head upstairs.

He stared at the screen again and the excitement of a real life treasure-hunt intrigued him. This was more exciting than a dull 9-5 office job any day. He drank the rest of his tea, noticing Catherina had left most of hers, and picked up the phone to ring his father.

Mathew Reynolds turned over and stretched out his left arm across the double bed, but found only cold sheets. At the back of his waking mind, he knew that something was wrong and his eyes flickered open to find out what it could be. It didn't take any amount of IQ to figure out that he was alone in the bed and had been all night.

He groaned, scratched at his hair above his right ear and exhaled, knowing he had not handled last night well at all. He pulled back the covers and jumped out of bed in just his boxers and headed into the bathroom to pee. Mathew then checked the other bedroom and saw no sign of Catherina. He was just starting down the stairs when he heard a rap of the knocker on his new front door, which caused him to rush down the now carpeted steps two at a time. He crossed the small hall and pulled the door open to find the boss of the builders and decorators standing before him with a sheepish grin on his face.

"Having a lay-in, are we?"

"What do you want?" Mathew barked and hid behind the door a little.

"To start work, boss, unless you fancy giving us a day's paid holiday," the stubble chinned man in his mid-forties answered.

"Come in. I'm gonna get dressed."

Mathew turned and headed upstairs as fast as he could go as the gaffer of the builders smirked to himself. "Johnny, get the kettle on. Time for a breakfast brew first, me lad."

Johnny, whose real name was Jarvindar, went past his boss and made for the kitchen and the main stay of any builder, the kettle.

Mathew showered and dressed quickly and started to ring Cat's mobile, until he remembered she had left it behind when she ran out on him last night. Her bag, purse, money and credit cards were also still at home, so he figured that there could only be one place she could have gone. He pulled on his shoes and grabbed his wallet, and after telling the decorators that he was going out, headed down Hanger Hill towards Simon and Lucy's place.

Lucy sat on the toilet upstairs and peed as another wave of nausea hit her and she gulped down a lungful of air to stop anything coming up. This seemed to do the trick and she took slow long breaths for a while.

Simon and Catherina had gone out ten minutes ago to visit his dad for something to do with local history and all that archaeology crap that her fiancée. was into. She hadn't minded a bit. In fact she was very glad to be alone as she pulled the cream coloured electronic pregnancy tester from out between her legs, wiped it with some toilet paper and set it on the side of the bath to wait for the result to come. She had a stack of such testing kits hidden in a shoe box in the back of her wardrobe, ever since she came off the pill eight months ago. Out of the ten that she bought costing her a bomb in money terms, only one remained.

Lucy ran the cold tap in the bath and put her left hand under the flow of icy water and then drew her hand back to wipe down her flushed and hot face. She hoped for once that this sick feeling in her abdomen was just the results of Simon's home cooked prawn Passanda or the necking down of half a bottle of cheap supermarket plonk.

She glanced at her wrist watch and saw the seconds had somehow ticked round to past a minute. With a trembling hand, she grabbed the pregnancy tester and moved it to her face, her eyes screwed shut.

"One, two, three," she counted and opened her eyes to see the word PREGNANT come up on the little screen on the plastic stick. "Oh fuck," she cried and jumped off her seat, spun round with her knickers about her ankles and vomited into the yellow piss water in the toilet.

Mathew adjusted the collar of his polo shirt and rang the doorbell of Lucy and Simon's house. Then he adjusted the other side of his collar as if something was irritating his neck. He waited, in his neutral business state that he developed over the years, like a character actor, used for sacking staff, giving out bad news, or hammering down a new business deal. The anger of last night had now gone. He just wanted to see Catherina again and explain the situation better. Maybe Simon and Lucy might side with him.

He knocked again, just before a change in light and shadows though the mandarin sliced window of the door showed that someone was approaching. A very wan-looking Lucy opened the front door, dressing in slouchy clothes of ankle length combat pants and a big loose fitting t-shirt that must have at some point belonged to Simon. Her hair was scraped back in a single pony tail and seemed more light brown that blonde today.

"Thought it might be you," Lucy said in a tired voice and opened the door wider. "I think you better come in, Mathew."

"Is she here?" he asked as he passed Lucy in the hall.

"She did stay the night, yes, and she was bloody upset. What right do you men have to fuck our lives up, eh?"

Mathew stood fixed to the spot in shock at this outburst, as Lucy closed the door behind them. "I've come to apologise and explain," he said, not liking the whiny way his words came out.

"She ain't here," Lucy informed him. She walked past him into the conjoined rooms that were kitchen, dining and living room. The bed was still out and unmade and Lucy frowned at it and then pull up a dining chair and sat down with a dejected bump.

"Where is she, then? What did she say about me?" he pressed, standing over her from the centre of the small stretch of carpet, between the bookcase, computer stand and the dining table.

"It's all about you, isn't it, Mathew," she said, looking up to his face.

"What are you on about? Where's she gone? Is Simon with her?"

"I'm pregnant."

"Erm, congratulations, I suppose," Mathew said, taken a little off guard by the dramatic swing of the conversation. "Bet Si is over the moon."

"He doesn't know yet," she said in a lower voice, her eyes falling to his shoes.

"Why? I thought you were trying for a baby." Mathew sat on the swivel computer chair so he could be at the same eye level as her. This was all very interesting, but he just wanted to know where Catherina was to sort their little spat out.

"Because you're the father."

"What!" he exclaimed, standing up. "Come on, I know we did it, but that that was just a once off. You must have slept with Simon loads of times around the same time."

"I secretly came off the pill nine months ago, Matt, without Simon knowing and not even missed one period. I sleep with you and *dad-darh*, one month later I'm up the duff."

"That still doesn't mean it's mine. Come on, I'm sure Si's the father." Mathew paced in a short two pace pattern of anxiety. "I just want to know where Cat is."

"How did things get so messed up and complicated? Just as everything was going according to plan for once," she said to her pink furry slippers.

Mathew knelt, grabbed Lucy's shoulders and shook her a little. "Tell me where Cat and Simon have gone."

"Mind the baby, hun," Lucy said, looking deep into his baby blues. He stopped and stood up once again and turned away from her. "They've gone out on some treasure hunt or something. I wasn't really listening. Sorry, I had other things on my mind."

Mathew dragged his hands down over his stubbled cheeks to his jaw and was sure he could hear his father laughing somewhere deep in his brain.

"How is the coffee, my dear?" Jeff Hay asked as he walked from one pile of folders, files and paper piles in his spare room to another to search for something that might help his son and his lady-friend.

"Dad?"

Catherina smiled at the interaction between son and father, sipping at her instant coffee as Simon's father rummaged through another pile of papers and book and railway memorabilia.

"It's here somewhere, lad. I've got a delicate filing system going on here, you know," Jeff said and winked at Catherina He dug his hand deep into a pile and pulled out a sun faded blue folder. "Here we go."

Catherina put down her coffee and joined Simon in moving closer to Jeff Hay, as he opened the folder. Some loose pages from an A4 pad were inside. The second one had three names, with addresses and telephone numbers on them. "This is him, if he's still alive, that is."

"Who?"

Jeff Hay look up at his son and stubbed a finger on the middle address. "Eric Worley. Worked on the trains for years. Must be in his eighties now."

"And he knows about the digging of the railway tracks?" Catherina asked hopefully.

"No," Jeff answered, "but his dad did and he might remember something, if his mind hasn't gone. I'll give him a ring now, shall I, son?"

"Please, Dad."

"Can we sort this later, Lucy? Please tell me where Catherina is."

"Oh Mathew, you're so single-minded and self-centred. I used to fancy you all those years ago, when you hung around with Simon and to tell you the truth I don't give a toss if they cut down the stupid wood."

"Lucy, please, come on, tell me where they went."

"To see Simon's dad," she finally gave up and told him.

"Thank you," he said, but didn't sound that polite or pleased, and he headed for the door to the hall.

"See you soon," she called after him. "I hope things work out," she added sarcastically.

"By some luck he still is hale and hearty and lives in the same house," Jeff Hay said, coming into the living room where Simon and Catherina waited.

"Great, where does he live?"

"Only down the road in Woking. Come on," Jeff said. He pulled his car keys from his trousers pocket and twirled them around his right fore-finger.

"What do you mean?"

"As if I'm going to miss all the fun, son, especially if it has anything to do with trains and railways." Jeff went back into the hall, where the wall mounted phone was and grabbed a light beige jacket and his driving gloves.

Simon and Catherina exchanged looks and shrugs and followed Jeff Hay out of his house and towards his old battered Ford Cortina.

Mathew had used the old shortcut between the May Day field (which was still roped off) and the cricket pitch. It must have been years since he last gone this way to Simon's dad's place. He remembered that his mum had run off with some other bloke when Simon was only a toddler and Jeff had raised him on his own and done a much better job than Mathew's own father.

The sun was warm on his neck as he hurried along the dry

dusty track, with bicycle marks weaving this way and that along its length. Tall dry grass grew up on either side with intermittent hedges and trees. He finally made it across and headed over the street and up the road to Jeff Hay's house. Mathew half expected to see Simon's dad's old brown Ford Cortina outside and wondered whatever happened to it as he walked up the path to ring the doorbell.

He also wondered if Catherina had done this on purpose. Maybe she was embarrassed about last night and couldn't face him. Mathew rang the doorbell again and then knocked on the door. A woman next door came out, with green gardening gloves on. "He's gone out, love."

"Oh, do you know how long ago and where?"

"You just missed them," the woman said over the hedge that divided the two front gardens.

"Them? Was his son, Simon, with him?" Mathew asked, putting on his most sincere fake smile.

"Yes, and some dark haired woman. Do you know them, then?"

"Yeah, we're old mates," he said through gritted teeth.

"Shall I tell them you called?

"No, I'll ring or pop round later, thanks." Mathew half waved and headed off up the street to Bates Road and then headed towards the Cricketers. He went inside to have a drink and try to collect his thoughts.

CHAPTER SEVENTY-FOUR

"Cor, it must be ten odd years since we last spoke, Jeff," Eric Worley said from his worn armchair, next to an old electric fire. He was still in rude health for his advanced years, but the wooden stick wedged in the cushion of the chair and a large hearing aid on his wide ears showed even he needed a little help.

"Yes, maybe even eleven," Jeff, who was seated on the not matching sofa closest to the old man, replied. "You look well."

"And you brought some young folk to see me too. Don't get many visitors at my door these days. Lots of my old chums have pegged it, you see," Eric said to Catherina and Simon, his false teeth causing the odd whistle to be added to each sentence he spoke.

"My son and his friend, yes." Jeff nodded. "Look, Eric, they want to know about when your dad dug the trench through the woods at Hedge End for the railway track and station. Can you recall him mentioning anything about that?"

"Blimey." Eric smiled, scratching at the hair growing from the top of his large nose. "That's going back."

"Did he ever tell you about any stones or strange blocks that they dug up?" Catherina asked, leaning forward and saying her words carefully and with increased volume.

"I'm not deaf yet, lovely. You from abroad, then?"

"From Southern Italia," she responded in a normal voice.

"A foxy looking I-tie woman in my house. Well, I am a lucky old goat," Eric cackled and smiled so wide it made Simon think of the clay models from Wallace And Gromit animations.

"So do you remember anything, Eric, about the excavation

and the track laying?" Simon asked this time.

"Well, I do, as a matter of a fact. My old dad, Richard, but everyone called him Ricky you see, he told me this once and once only one winter's night, when he'd had too many of the old pints of Mild down the pub. Now, he had a mate, see, a Mick called Paddy O'Hara. Built like a brick outhouse, he was, so my dad said, though he died before I was born. They worked on the railways navvying and laying tracks all-around these parts and the south coast. He said that the Hedge End excavation was the worst he'd ever done, not cos it was the hardest, no, because of all the odd happenings and ghosts about the place."

"Ghosts." Simon leaned forward intrigued now.

"Yes." Eric nodded. "They found these strange tunnels under the trees and men got sick and saw ghosts and gremlins and the whole thing took many months to do and things were always going missing or broken. Now, it was Paddy who found the first of them, a square block buried down twenty feet or so, with no other remains or stone near it. This was before they even got past some high bloody hedge, excuse my French, that they had to chop down. My dad said when they tried to get a block and tackle to move it away it fell and broke in half and this silver liquid pours out. Now that night my dad was struck down with a terrible fever and so were many of the lads, but in the middle of the night Paddy O' Hara comes a knocking at his door saying that Lucifer's demons were after him and then ran off into the night. My old dad was too ill to go after him and barely made it to bed before falling into a deep sleep for nigh on two days. When he woke he felt better, but old Paddy was found hanging from a tree, with a rope around his neck right over the trench they were digging in the middle of some wood in Hedge End. But that weren't the end of it. When my dad was better he returned to work, and just before they dug out the place, the station were to go, they found another of these blocks, but they were more careful with it this time, cos the last one had been full of mercury and hundreds of years old, they reckoned."

"What happened to the second block?" Simon asked, liking the old man's ghostly tale of long ago, making a mental note to put in his book.

"Carted it off to some museum somewhere. Don't ask me. But none of the men would work there after dark or even when dusk came around, so my old dad said."

"I don't suppose if I show you a map you could point out where the stones were found," Catherina said and poked Simon to get the map out.

"Be no use. I wasn't even born, love. All I know is one would be just before where the hedge used to be and the other just before the station." The old man shrugged, still smiling.

"Don't worry about it, Eric, you've been a great help." Simon got to his feet and his father and Catherina followed.

"I was glad of the company," Eric said, using his stick to push himself up. "I'll show you to the door."

They left the bungalow, and all got back into the seen-better-days Cortina, the men in the front and Catherina in the back. Jeff peered back over his shoulder to the back seats. "So was that any help to you, Catherina?"

"In a way it confirms where I thought the stones were. I just wish I knew where exactly the last block was and other mysteries."

"Other mysteries," Simon asked, turning to look at her.

"I don't suppose you know about a wolf-mother and Romulus and Remus, do you?" she asked in a non-serious manner, staring out the window at Eric's rose bush fronted garden.

"I don't know about wolves, my dear," said Jeff, pulling away from the curb, "but Romulus and Remus were a twin pair of standard goods locomotives for the Great Western Railways back in the late nineteenth century."

"Does that help, Cat?" Simon asked from the front passenger seat.

"No," she laughed and shook her mane of brown hair, "it just makes me feel more confused."

They went back to Jeff Hay's house and he showed them pictures from a couple of books he had of the two locomotives.

"Did they ever work down here or pass through Hedge End?"

"I doubt it, son." Jeff shook his head.

"Anyway, we've taken up enough of your time, Dad, and Catherina has things to sort out."

"Yes." She nodded grimly, if that was possible for one so fair.

"Is there something you're not telling me?" Simon asked as they took the same shortcut that Mathew had taken a few hours before, but in the other direction.

"About what in particular, Simon?" she said, picking the head off a wild flower.

"About the row with Matt, or the stones or blocks you're so interested in?"

"I like you, Simon, you are so easy to talk to, but some things I am not ready to share yet, okay?" She touched his arm lightly, and they stopped and turned to face each other.

"What sort of things?" he asked, taking her hand in his and looking deeply into her hazel eyes.

"This is a very odd situation, Simon, with us. You are a man I've never dated, but have made love to and given myself in ways I never thought I could do. Mathew is treating me like a foolish girl and I want to stay here in Hedge End, in Leggett Woods, something, erm, magical or supernatural that speaks to my very soul wants me to stay. I need your help and friendship, Simon. Let us not complicate things with feelings and love, please."

"I do and I don't understand, but I'm here if you need me." He smiled down at her, totally at the limit of a man's understanding of how a woman's mind and heart worked.

"*Grazie.*" She winkled her nose and leaned forward to kiss his cheek.

"Oi I fucking saw that!"

They both turned and shuffled apart as Mathew came running down the path from the other end. They were three quarters down the track and had been too busy talking to notice him approaching.

"Mathew, it was nothing but a thank you kiss," Simon said, moving in front of Catherina, his palms out in a peaceful gesture. "Come on, mate."

"You're fucking welcome to her," Mathew raged through gritted teeth and punched Simon on the chin. The shock of it and trying to duck backwards rather than the force of the blow caused Simon to stumble and fall on his arse in the dust. "And just to let you know, your fiancée is probably up the duff with my baby."

"Mathew, stop it!" Catherina moved forward to stand over Simon, who just stared up at his friend in stunned astonishment.

"Lucy's pregnant and she told you first?"

"Yep, mate, you're just not up to the job, it seems."

Catherina pushed Mathew back away from his floored friend, smelling whisky on his breath. "And I'm gonna sell the woods and house and make a small mint. Maybe even take Lucy and the baby with me."

Simon jumped to his feet and dived onto his old friend, grabbing at his throat. Catherina was knocked around in a circle but managed to keep her feet, which was more than could be said for the two men. They were on the floor turning and rabbit punching in the dirt, until the flow of blood and the dust and exhaustion took over and Catherina finally pulled them apart. They sat nursing their wounds and panting, their eyes boring into each other's.

"I think you better go home, Mathew," Catherina said. It was to Simon she went to kneel down and comfort.

"Okay," Mathew said, getting up and wiping the blood away from a split lip, "I'll go home and pack your stuff for you."

Catherina helped a wincing Simon stand up and they watched Mathew walk back the way he came. "Let's get you home, Simon, I think you need to talk to Lucy urgently."

"I'm not sure I want to be in the same room as her. I dunno what to think anymore," Simon replied, as he patted his clothes to get the loose dust off.

CHAPTER SEVENTY-FIVE

"You sure about this?"

"No," Catherina said with a laugh and raised her thin eyebrows at Simon as they stood at the corner of Greet Street that led down to his house. "But you need to talk with Lucy and I need to try and talk to Mathew. We cannot leave things as they are."

"Wish me luck."

"No, you wish me luck." They hugged and went their separate ways for the time being.

Simon watched her bravely walk up the streets to the lights at the crossroads and then she was lost to sight. He turned, thinking of a stop at the Green Man Inn for courage, but then shook his head and walked reluctantly towards the house he and Lucy shared.

Tunnel vision seemed to take over and ignored a neighbour when she said a high pitched, "hiya," as they passed on the street. He did not notice cars, nor anything else and fished his keys from his trouser pocket and put the right one into the lock. There it paused for a few seconds, as Simon did some shallow breathing. Then he turned the key and went inside.

The house was silent. Only the dust motes caught in the rays of sunlight from the window halfway up the stairs were moving in the house. No radio, music or television was on. He approached the hall doorway and pushed it with one rigid forefinger of his left hand. The door swung inwards with a fanfair like squeal of protest and there on the dining table was a white envelope with his name on it, waiting for him.

Catherina's progress was halted and all her carefully thought out words and counter arguments were scrambled and pushed back when she saw Father Carmichael waiting for her just past the garage and in front of the houses before she got to Leggett Woods.

"Padre, I have not seen you in weeks. Are you well?"

"I'm sorry, my dear, I've been weak and lulled back into the bottom of a whisky bottle, and I curse the wood demons and their gods for causing this. We must be strong to fight this evil that slumbers in this town awaiting release to cause the end of not just our faith, but every faith in the world."

"Father Carmichael, calm down. What is wrong?"

Catherina took his arm and wrinkled her nose against the alcoholic sweat that exuded from his unwashed pores.

"He is back," the father said, his fingers going to his face. "The devil Lugus himself is here now in Hedge End and he gathers his demi-gods and denizens of hell around him, waiting to destroy the last sacred block that halts this oncoming unholy war."

"I know more about the blocks," Catherina whispered to him.

"You do? Tell me now." His voice was on edge and his hands shook badly.

"One you know was under your church. Two more were dug up when the railway was, erm, laid down and dug up. The last one, if it's in one piece, is somewhere under one of the shops on the High Street. Look, I have a map," she said and pulled the folded colour map that Simon had printed out earlier in the day from her back jean's pocket.

"It must be buried under some foundation or under a cellar somewhere," he muttered ,tapping at his whisker covered chin.

"How do we know where to start looking?"

"Leave it with me. I have a friend at the local museum who should be able to help me. Come on," he beckoned and started off down the hill.

"I cannot come with you, padre, not now. I have unfinished business to sort out first," she said, looking towards the treetops of the near woods.

"With your boyfriend?" He pointed questioningly towards the woods also.

"*Si.*" She nodded.

"Then, I will meet you tomorrow night at nine, at the old Roman ruins and we'll decide what to do next and share whatever information we can gather." For the first time ever she saw him smile, because he had purpose again.

"Father," she called, "what if I know someone that may help us, someone who is not of the same faith as us?"

"My enemy's enemy is my friend," he replied with a wave and set off down the hill.

Catherina's pace up the hill was slow and she took every step with forced dread as she walked up the drive and up round the front door. Two suitcases where dumped on the front step, next to two large cardboard boxes of her paintings and other odds and ends.

Her pace quickened as her Italian blood boiled inside and she went up to the front door and started hammering on it with all her might.

Simon sat on the swivel chair by his computer, wiping the tears away from his eyes and staring at the short note that Lucy had left for him. His safe job, life and fiancée; all three had been turned upside down in a matter of weeks. The long held wishes he had every day on the train ride up to London and work had all come true, but that still was not a guarantee of happiness. He was out of the job he long loathed and had free time to work on his book, but everything else was crumbling around him. He looked at the note once more and read it again.

My Dearest Simon,

I am writing this because I'm too scared to face you. I'm pregnant and I'm not sure that you may be the father after all we have not conceived in all those months I was secretly off the pill and after May Day night's events, it well could be Mathew's child I am carrying.

You deserve better than me and you deserve a better life than Hedge End or the people here can give you. Get out while you still can, make a new start somewhere else. I love you in my own way, but I'm so scared, please forgive me?

I'll go and stay with Kerry for a while or my friend Julie in Leeds who I haven't seen for years and she is always begging me to come and stay. What I need is time away from this shitty town and everything.

Please forgive me if you can, if not I'll understand.

I'll be in touch soon, when I can say your name without crying.

Lucy

Simon opened the closed palm of his left hand to reveal a gold ring with a diamond set with six smaller ones around it. Lucy's engagement ring.

CHAPTER SEVENTY-SIX

When he had not answered the door she knew it was all over, like a portcullis had come down, cutting their love in half and she was the peasant locked outside and he the wealthy lord sitting on his lonely pile of gold.

Yet that had been yesterday, and she sat upon the sofa bed and looked at her suitcases and boxes with scorn. She had wheeled her suitcases back to Simon's house to find the poor devastated man sitting on his computer chair holding a goodbye letter from Lucy. She sniffed up a tear recalling how they had just held each other and cried into each other's shoulders, then without many words had a stiff brandy and walked back up the hill to fetch the rest of her stuff. Lucy had taken the car, so it was hard hot work and they were exhausted when they got back.

Wine had been uncorked and they had woken up just after six, having snoozed the rest of the afternoon away on the sofa. Catherina had offered and cooked a small meal, which neither of them finished. Only the wine opened earlier had that honour. Tired, they had gone to their respective beds at about nine, each wishing they had the courage to ask to share one bed, not for any carnal desire, but just to hold each other and forget all the worries that lay heavily upon them.

A wind blew up that night, sending whistling noises down the grate of the fire in the boiler room, where Mathew sat alone. He had poured himself a large vodka two hours ago, but not a drop had passed his thin pressed lips. The door of the boiler was open and he watched the flames dance orange and blue around the coal and woods stacked within. The nights now were humid and the fire unnecessary, but he wanted to sweat out any thoughts he had of Catherina. Once his deal went through, women he could have aplenty and better looking ones too, but that did not keep him from feeling like shit now.

Yawning, he looked away from the flames down to the glass and then picked it up and threw it into the fire, which shot up high in an excited woof of flame. He shut the door and went into the kitchen to find some chocolate biscuits and maybe make a cup of tea. Outside it was only just getting dark as the summer days were so long and the wind was pushing the tops of the trees of the woods this way and that.

With a sudden sustained gust of a gale force wind, the back gate blew open and banged every fews second in the wind. The noise was loud and annoying and penetrated the house from outside. Mathew knew he would have no sleep tonight if that kept going, so he pulled on a light jacket and headed out the back door. The air pressure on the door surprised him and he nearly lost grip of the lock as the door wrenched open and he came with it.

He managed somehow to close it again without damaging the frame and pressed on through the wind and across the lawn. Bits of paper, flowers and a shopping bag flew past as he made for the flapping and banging gate, ducking when he went past the old willow tree and up the couple of stone steps.

Mathew had to cross the threshold of the door to grab the black looped handle and as he did something eerie and extraordinary happened. The wind just dropped, like it had changed direction in an instant and the swaying branches of the wood went suddenly still.

Mathew let go of the door handle and looked around the gloomy hollow, down into the woods, as there seemed to be an unnatural glow up ahead. He moved a step forward to peer into the gloom and the gate banged hard shut behind him, causing him to break wind in sudden fright at the loud and unexpected noise. He turned and grabbed at the gate, but found to his annoyance that there was no lock on the far side. Why would there be? Somebody walking in the woods could just open the gate and fetch themselves into your back garden. He gave the gate a good kick with the toe of his shoe, but it was thick and well made and repaired since they first arrived at the house.

He had no choice now but to take the path left and come out on to Hanger Hill Road, then walk back to his house and get in through the open back door. The sky was still blue above the tree-tops and he carefully made his way down the sloping track to the clearing. He was just about to take the left hand path when the glow reappeared from the old well in the ground and he edged left, his eyes not leaving the unnatural illumination.

"Come back, uncle's heir," spoke twin echoing voices from the well.

Mathew had had enough. He had heard those voices before. He turned and ran along the left hand path, but only got four yards when he skidded to a halt. There ahead of him, coming out of the shadows, was a large snarling wolf like creature, bigger than any dog that he'd ever seen. It sprang at him and he turned in terror and ran back the way he had come towards the clearing. He had gotten only a few feet before a weighty impact on his back knocked the wind from his lungs and sent him crashing to the ground.

Mathew closed his eyes tightly and crawled forward, until he got into the clearing again. He could hear the panting and snarling of the wolf beast behind him and dared not open his eyes to see what would surely soon attack his exposed flank.

"We need to talk," said the twin voices again close by.

Mathew opened his eyes and lifted his head to see two young twin boys standing before him, hand in hand, gazing down at him. "Our uncle would be ashamed of you. You scared Catherina away and she was part of our plan. Now you will have to pay the price, Mathew."

Mathew Reynolds's logical business mind could not cope with seeing the twins he'd once seen before in the cellar of the house and he fainted dead away in fright.

"He has the blood, but not the fight in him." The twins shook their heads at the same time. "Who will dig out our pretty little well now?"

The Wolf-Mother grabbed at Mathew's ankle with gentle, but strong teeth and pulled him up through the dust towards the sloping path and the open gate in the high garden wall.

Father Carmichael's mind had not felt so clear in many a long year and he strode up the lane from the train station on Hanger Hill, loathing the fact he had to come so close to the house of that ungodly woman, Mrs Puck. Every step he took up the lane sent confidence into his alcohol dependant body. The need for the next glass had left him and had been replaced by a growing warm feeling of faith that once he had taken for granted.

The loss of his church, the addiction to every label of whiskey from the Highlands to Tennessee had been a test and up to now he had not been up to the job. Now with Catherina's help he had purpose and a goal, to save Hedge End from falling into a religious vacuum and no one, not even Mrs Puck, would stop him.

"Do you have light, brother?"

The Roman Catholic priest was shaken from insular thoughts by a strong rich voice with a hint of the auld country about it. He looked up and to his right and saw man dressed in jeans, cowboy boots and white plain t-shirt leaning back against the thicker bottom half of a lamp post on the corner where the lane met the London Road. He had a thick set of wild hair and was staring at the priest as the sun sunk over the hill, casting crazy long shadows behind the man.

"Pardon, my son?"

Father Carmichael moved closer and saw the man was offering a cupped hand with a thin rolled up cigarette between his fingers.

"Son." The man tilted his head and with that, let the dying sun shine suddenly past to make the priest squint his eyes until they were mere thin slits. "I'm thinking I'm too old for you to be my father."

"I mean in the clerical sense, only," Carmichael replied, raising his left hand to his eyebrows to stave off the harshness of the blinding sunset, "and I'm sorry, but I do not smoke."

"I know," the man replied, pushing himself off the lamp post with the sole of one cowboy boot. He stood before the priest, blocking his way and letting the whole of the setting sun shine behind his head like a burning crown of gold. "Would you take a snifter of friendly advice, Father Carmichael?"

"You have me at a disadvantage," the priest said, feeling unease creep once more into his bones and the tremors tingle on the liver spots of his vein lined hands.

"Yes I do. I have the advantage. in fact, I hold all the aces, so take this from one man of faith to another as a little warning. Go back to the bottom of whichever bottle of Scotch you crawled out of tonight and go home and die of liver failure in ten years' time. Don't let yourself be thrown into an unholy alliance with Lupa and her lot. She can be a real bitch when roused."

"Who are you to threaten me?"

"Threaten? Not me, father. I'm a lover not a fighter as the saying goes," the man said, raising his hands in supplication. "But those who keep the company of the wolf, always meet a bitter end."

The man then turned on his Cuban heels and walked up London road, smoking at the roll-up that the priest never saw him light. He turned at Mrs Puck's gate and opened it to go in.

"You are in league with her, old pagan Puck, aren't you?" Carmichael shouted at the retreating figure of Jack Lucas.

"I'm in league with no one." The man waved and entered the grounds of Rose Puck's house. "Who are you in bed with?"

Father Carmichael looked around and jumped back onto the pavement he had wandered off while conversing with the man in denim, as a Volvo sped past very close, beeping its horn in one endless whine of warning. Somehow he was on the other side of the road, standing on the pavement by the road bridge over the rail tracks below. He hurried across the bridge, his coattails flapping behind him, as the sun gave up on another English summer's day and sunk behind the tree-topped horizon.

With the loss of the blessed sun, an unseasonal chill gripped him as he found himself beside the path that led through Woodhouse Copse. He pulled his old Mac around him and his right hand clutched the silver and gold crucifix that hung out from the neck of his collar. He grasped it and whispered endless *Hail Mary Mother of Gods*, under his breath.

Mr Khan, the ex-mayor, was driving his BMW down London

Road to an extraordinary general meeting of the local town council. He was smiling and listening to Neil Sedaka, as with a few called in favours and back-handers, all charges relating to the uncharacteristic dalliances with the teen May Queen in the back of his mayoral car had been dropped.

Mr Khan was humming away, speeding along, thinking of Saunders' face as he laid his trump card to get his old position back, when through the trees a sharp last ray of the sun went right into his eyes, blinding him for a second. He blinked and saw Rose Puck standing in the road right in front of his fast moving car, and he wrenched his steering wheel to the right to try and avoid hitting her. His black BMW hit a concrete bollard by the crossing and flipped up summer-saulting twice in the air.

Father Carmichael heard the squeal of brakes and had no choice but to run into the darkening woods, just before a black car crashed down on its roof where he had just been standing and slid along after his rushing feet. Luckily for him the car came to a halt against two young looking trees, as he fell forward onto the dusty path winding, himself. Unluckily for ex-mayor Khan, as a low branch shot through his driver's window and entered below his left ear and sent his brains and life blood rushing out the right hand side where his right ear had once sat.

Father Carmichael scrambled round in the dust and saw the ex-mayor's impaled head, blood and brain matter, and ran from the awful crash seen deeper into the woods he dreaded to be in ever since he had arrived in this parish twenty or so years ago. He staggered deeper into the gloomy and tight aired copse, while the car at the edge of the woods exploded into a ball of flame that shot fifty feet into the dusk air.

The mere sound of the eruption sent the priest falling to his knees again on the dusty track far inside the copse. He turned to see the flames and smoke rise high above the treetops.

"Need a hand up, Mister Carmichael?"

The priest turned back and found that Rose Puck was standing not more than five feet in front of him, dressed in a green dress, with plunging neckline that showed off all her well preserved womanly assets.

"Not from you, I don't. Call the emergency services quick,

woman, there's been an accident." He rose to his feet with difficulty and then glanced from his old sparring partner, round to the pillar of smoke rising up into the pink tinged dusk skyline.

"Oh, it was no accident, I can assure you." She smiled and walked. "It's got you right where we want you."

"What are you talking about?" he asked, but then he became aware that they were not alone in the copse. No, other things were in the corners of each eye, hugging the boughs and trunks of the trees and nearly blending in like tall manlike chameleons. Yet Puck and Carmichael, apart from the burning corpse of the unfortunate Mr Khan in his car, were the only two human beings in the copse that early evening.

CHAPTER SEVENTY-SEVEN

Simon and Catherina had spent much of the day on the internet looking up the past of Hedge End and the locomotive engines Romulus and Remus. They found no record of these GWR engines, if they had been used to lay the track, or if they had ever passed through Hanger Hill Station.

When Simon took a break to phone Kerry again to see if Lucy had turned up there, Catherina searched for other meanings for Romulus and Remus. She read Romulus had founded Rome according to legend and then as a man and son of Mars killed his brother Remus. More interesting was a shorter paragraph below, about a She-Wolf called Lupa who suckled the two abandoned twins aided by a woodpecker called Picus. She learned that Romulus never died, but went missing during a great battle when a storm blew up and he disappeared from his beloved Rome forever.

Catherina stood up and watched Simon pace to and fro on his small lawn at the rear of the house, talking loudly with Kerry or maybe the next person who could give Lucy a place to stay. She clicked the page off, headed into the kitchen and picked up the empty kettle. She took it to the kitchen window and tapped on the glass to get Simon's attention and wave the kettle at him. He nodded and smiled a limp, defeated smile and ended his call with a resigned look of frustration.

She had just filled the kettle and set it to boil when Simon came back inside and tossed his mobile phone onto the closest worktop, which went spinning round until stopped by a teacloth.

"Any luck in finding Lucy?"

"Nope," Simon said, rubbing at his unshaven chin and staring down at her feet. "No one seems to have either seen or heard from her. They could be lying for her, but they didn't sound like it. In fact they all seemed shocked that she had left me."

"Tea or coffee?"

"Which will help more?"

"Neither, I am afraid, Simon," Catherina said, and then closed the gap between them and pulled him into an awkward hug. Simon resisted at first, but the smell of her subtle perfume and the feel of her body coaxed him into a closer embrace. "Is that any better?" she asked first to break the short hug.

"A little." He nodded. "And mine's a tea, by the way."

"We are both hurting, Simon. You are not alone in this, okay?"

"I know," he said, leaning back on the washing machine as she pulled two mugs down to add teabags and sugar to.

"I have to meet Father Carmichael later, up at the old ruins," she began. "I would feel safer if you would accompany me."

"He won't try and save my lost soul, will he?"

"Of that I am not sure, but it will get you out of the house for a while." She spooned two sugars into his mug and half turned to give him the briefest of beautiful smiles.

"Then I'll do it for you."

"Good, for I notta take no for an answer, *capisce*?"

"Capisce," he repeated back with a half-grin.

They walked up the hill on the left hand pavement, so that Leggett House would be on the other side of the road as they went. The sun had just set over the treetops when they heard and felt a tremendous explosion up the hill. Dark black smoke could be seen ballooning up like a great cloud at the top of Hanger Hill. They exchanged glances and hurried up the hill past the houses and towards the gap that led up to the copse entrance before the remains of the high hawthorn hedge.

"What am I talking about, he asks, this man of the cloth, this drunken false prophet." Mrs Puck laughed and spun around as the creatures of the copse closed in on the priest from all sides.

"You and your pagan witchcraft do not frighten me, Rose Puck. Let your evil wood-demons do their worst. I have God on my side and the truth," Carmichael said boldly and felt no fear in his old bones.

"Evil. Evil, he says. It was not my church that raped the Dwellers' daughters and wives, and it was not my religion that crucified their own messiah. It was not my faith that slaughtered thousands in the name of their lord. No wars we have had over our faith. No, it was you and your Holy Roman Empire that trapped them here long ago, casting spells to bind the Dwellers to these woods and growing your hedge to keep them in. But the barrier is failing now and the old faiths will have their day once more," Rose Puck spat at him.

"Your creatures are the spawn of the devil himself. Have they not killed in your false-god's name?" he said back to her as the creatures closed in on him. Their arms and legs seemed bent and stiff and their skin thick and gnarled like tree bark. An overpowering sickly smell of hot summers and honey invaded his nose and throat, making him want for water.

"I must admit they have been restless of late and prone to the odd sacrifice." She smiled in the fading light and then walked off down another path past him and back towards the now low burning wreckage of Mayor Khan's car. "I will miss you, Carmichael."

He turned his head and watched her glide past and get lost in the trees, as the Dwellers leapt upon him, grabbing themselves a limb to wrap their thin wiry strong fingers around and lift the poor priest off the woodland floor.

"God help me!" he cried as the creatures pulled at his arms and legs, all of them digging their heels in different directions.

"What the fuck!" Simon exclaimed as he and Catherina stopped dead in their tracks upon the woodland path he had so often taken without fear through the copse. Yet fear hit him and Catherina now, as they looked on with unbelieving eyes while four shadowy creatures pulled at Father Carmichael's limbs and in doing so lifted him three feet off the ground.

"Leave him alone!" Catherina screamed. But they didn't.

Father Carmichael gave a gulping cry as the creature holding his left arm suddenly fell backwards, still holding the priest's blood spurting appendage, which it had just wrenched from his socket. The creatures then dropped their interest in the priest and let his mutilated body fall to the soft earth and turned as one on the two remaining invaders of their territory.

"Bloody run!" Simon yelled and pushed at Catherina's chest and then arms to get her to turn and run back the way they had just come. His urgent shoving made her stumble and forced her to turn as he grabbed onto her right arm at the elbow and shepherded her along the tree over hung path. Then from behind a tree trunk another of the creatures jumped out from its hiding place and blocked their escape.

In the far distance the wail of a fire engine could be heard approaching, but all Catherina and Simon were interested in was the sounds of close pursuit behind them. Looking from left to right, Simon could see no other means of escape so he decided in an instant to charge at the lone creature, this Woodwose that Mrs Puck had told him legends of, and hope to barge it out the way. If it failed, at least Catherina would get to freedom.

But a bird interrupted his heroic charge. The woodpecker dove low and hard, ramming its beak into the left eye of the creature. The Woodwose fell back against the tree trunk, startled by the fierceness of the little bird's attack. This gave Simon and Catherina the chance they needed and they ran past the two unfairly matched combatants and finally out of the copse just as a fire engine, all lights and sirens blazing, speed past. The movement of the air and the sudden noise of it nearly made the fleeing couple stumble.

The Woodwose had gripped with the brave woodpecker and squeezed the life out of it with one and then both hands. Blood oozed between the knobbly creature's fingers, but the sound of the large red machine close by caused it to throw the lifeless bird onto the path and make its escape after its fellow Dwellers, down the hole in the trunk of the largest tree.

Police cars were followed by ambulances and Simon and Catherina retreated across the road to walk up the hill on the

Leggett Wood side to see what would happen next. The fire crews soon had the car blaze doused and were moving into the woods with other emergency service personnel. Soon a cry followed by another went up from the copse.

Simon had to physically restrain Catherina from rushing back into the copse to find Father Carmichael. "We have to see if he's alive!"

"But those things, they'll get us, Cat, it's too dangerous," Simon yelled hard into her face.

"What are we going to do?"

Simon looked around and saw that with the number of police about they would soon be questioned, so he forced the issue. "Come on, let's talk to a one of the firemen, see if they found him."

Green clad paramedics ran past and into the woods as police and the fire crew closed off the left hand lane on the hill near the incident and both lanes on the bridge. Cars and motorbikes were soon diverted down the Woking Road and back towards the far end of the High Street, where they would have to turn right and go through the main road in the town.

"What happened, mate," Simon asked a fireman who was taping off the accident scene.

"Massive one vehicle RTA, driver burned to a crisp and his passenger must have been flung out of the car into the woods. Tore the poor bugger's arm clean out of the socket," the young fireman said matter of factly as he wound the bright coloured tape round a lamp post twice.

"What passenger?" Simon blurted before really thinking, but the fireman didn't notice anything amiss.

"Some vicar or something," the fireman muttered, biting at the end of the tape with his teeth.

"The priest, is he still alive?"

The fireman looked at the slightly wild looking woman and shook his head. "Nah, he died of the shock before the paramedics could get to him. Shock can do that worse than blood-loss or head trauma. But saying that, that drummer from Def Leppard survived a car crash and the loss of his arm. Went and saw them at Earl's Court with my older brother a few years back."

"Did you see anything else in there," Simon pressed the talkative fireman.

"Anything strange?" Catherina added.

"Well, come to mention it, there was this dead woodpecker, lying all squished on the path near the priest. Must have got too near the blast."

"Nothing else?" Simon asked.

"Isn't that strange enough?" The fireman shrugged. "Look, I've got to go, or the guv'nor will be on my arse."

Simon just smiled and nodded and led Catherina away from the scene and across the road again.

"Take me home, Simon, please," Catherina asked, the last word a hitched hiccup of tears.

"Let's go the long way, then," Simon replied, and with his arm around her they took the long route with the diverted traffic down the Woking Road and back down the High Street to get to Simon's place. As they passed the edges of Leggett Woods, two wet wolfen eyes watched them go from the shadows of the closely spaced trees and scrubs. The Wolf-mother pined for the loss of her messenger and friend and vowed bloody revenge on the Woodwoses and their deity.

"Well, that nearly ruined everything. The copse is crawling with police and firemen now," Rose Puck shouted as she entered the spare bedroom overlooking the second floor of her house. Jack was standing at the window looking down at the scene of carnage, his jeans on, his t-shirt discarded on the floor beside his feet. "Trees were damaged, the woods could have burnt down, I could have got run over and the Dwellers could have been spotted."

"It doesn't matter," Jack Lucas replied in a soft voice, his fingers holding the net curtain back, so he could see the goings on across the bridge better.

"It doesn't matter? I don't get you, Jack. Don't you care? When are you going to return to the woods?" Rose Puck said in a lower voice, her anger still underlining her words.

"When the time is right and not before."

"But I don't see why. Explain it to me." She stood behind

him, her fingers reaching out, but hesitating from touching his bare back.

"I wandered lost for so many years. Others claimed me and changed who I was. I was Romanised and then demonised and then worst of all forgotten. This has to be done correctly or everything may fail and I will never find my way back again."

"But we have the Hay-Cutter and the Faye Child. We only need to find the last block and the children of the wood will be free once more," Rose said in a soft voice, her hands rubbing up his shoulder.

Jack Lucas turned on his heel and grabbed at her wrists in a crushing grip. "That's not enough!" he screamed at her and then seeing the pain on her face, let go of her hands. "They are just dark hollow shades of what once they were. They were beautiful once, Rosmerta, and the music they played burned like a sun in the pit of your very soul and their voices were fair like birdsong mixed with honey and scattered upon the slightest breeze."

"But I'm not Rosmerta and the Dwellers have lived below the earth for two millennia awaiting your return. They were changed by the battles then and had to do things, some say wicked things, just to survive."

"But don't you see you can be my goddess and they can be full of light again? If you trust me. If the plan works down to the last action of every man, woman and child involved. Do you trust me, Rose?"

"I trust you with my life," Rose Puck replied in a hoarse whisper.

"Then be patient for a while longer. Soon the time will be upon us and the rejoicing will begin." Jack opened his arms and Rose moved into his embrace.

CHAPTER SEVENTY-EIGHT

Mathew Reynolds had a new tactic. Try and drown the outside world out, with either the television or music from his mobile, with earphones that constantly hurt the inside of his ears. Yet still the noises from outside seeped into the house. The explosion from earlier had rattled the windows in their frames and even he had to peer out the spare front bedroom window to see what was going on. Not that he could see much but a plume of black smoke and the wail of sirens and the flash of emergency service vehicles going up the hill through the trees and hedge outside.

Yet worse than this was the constant howling of that spectral wolf from the woods. It had been fierce at first and had somehow penetrated the wall of sound Mathew had thrown up around him, numbing his brain to the thoughts of ghosts and the loss of Catherina. Now the howling was mournful, like a hound that lay on his master's grave.

Booze didn't help, nor hardcore porn nor bouts of masturbation. Nothing seemed to stop his ears catching the faintest howl in between beats of the music, and he feared that it was just in his mind, and not real at all. Like when you stare hard out of a window on a grey dull morning and think you can see lines of rain where there are none.

Finally, after he had gone to bed, with toilet paper as made-shift earplugs in his ears and still could not get any peace from the haunting howling coming from outside or inside his skull, in the end he got up and pulled on his jeans. He rushed downstairs, pulling bits of stubborn tissue from his right ear and went to the back door and opened it. The clock on the oven showed that it was well after two in the morning and the moon was shining brightly from above, showing him that the back gate to the woods was open again. There, its dark fur cast silver by the moon, was the large shape of the wolf, standing watching him, its head bowed lower than before.

"What do you want from me?" Mathew hissed from grinding teeth.

"We need you to dig," came the voice of the twins from behind Mathew's back, causing him to scream a little his mouth like a frightened schoolgirl.

Simon Hay sat bolt upright in the dark of his house, a faint dream like scream still echoing in his muddled mind. He looked around and found he was fully dressed, lying on the pulled out sofa-bed in his living room.

"What is it?" Catherina's voice came from beside him and he felt the mattress move as she shifted her weight on the bed and sat up next to him.

"Erh, just a bad dream," he replied, remembering that Catherina had asked him to hold her and stay with her the night as both of them did not want to be alone after what they had seen.

"What, about those monsters we saw?"

"No, I thought I heard someone scream, but it must just be a nightmare. Not surprising really," he said, but left out the part that he was sure that Mathew was the person screaming, so as not to alarm her.

"What are we going to do, Simon? Who can we tell about this? They will think us insane."

"I'm not sure. Let's just try and get through the night and then in the morning write down everything we know on a large piece of paper and figure out what is going on in this town, then try and figure out a way to stop it, or find someone that might help us."

"I agree," she softly replied and in the semi-darkness she kissed his lips gently. Without thinking he kissed her forehead and they lay back down together and held each other tight to hold off the darkness and the creatures that hid in its shadows.

CHAPTER SEVENTY-NINE

Mathew Reynolds wandered in through the back door of his house caked in dirt, with enough crud under his nails to plant potatoes. His normally jelled Tom Cruise hair was wild and ruffled and in it he had not only a leaf, but a small spider along for the ride.

His shirt was covered in brown stains and the knees of his jeans had grass and other vegetation stains on them like it was trying out a new camouflage design for the army. He headed to the fridge and pulled a bottle of water from inside, used his teeth to open the top and proceeded to drain the clear bottle in ten mighty gulps. He closed the fridge: leaving brown dirty marks on the smooth new surfaces. His trainers left a dirty encrusted trail of footsteps through the house and up the stairs to the bathroom that even the myopic Mr Magoo could follow.

He showered for half an hour, letting the water slowly lose its heat, until it was barely lukewarm. But the shower had done its job of clearing the dirt and soothing the aches in his biceps and lower back. Once dried off he dressed in clean clothes and grabbing his wallet and keys headed off down the hill to Hedge End to wait for B&Q to open its doors for the day.

He came home laden with bags full of rope, a large iron spike and a couple of kiddie rope ladders for fixing on suitable low trees. Mathew bought a cheese and bacon roll at the garage and consumed it before he'd left the forecourt. He headed home and into his great uncle's garden shed to fetch a pick-axe and a sledge hammer he knew lay inside. These and the newly bought things he loaded into a wheelbarrow and trundled them all through the gate in the garden wall and down through the enclosed tunnel to the clearing beyond, where he had been busy.

Catherina and Simon had woken earlier than their tired bodies had wanted, but the images of the night before would not rest easy in their sleeping minds. After Catherina had insisted on a hearty breakfast and strong coffee, they set to work writing down all they knew on a huge drawing pad Simon had kept from his college art class days.

Simon went through his notes from his meeting with Mrs Puck and they searched online for stories of Woodwoses, being hairy creatures, which the Romans referred to as Fauns or Wood Demons, which led them to stories of the Green Man and also to the name Puck, who was another woodland spirit of Old English mythology. Next on the list was Lugus, the deity that Mrs Puck had mentioned and on the net they found the picture of an old stone engraving taken from a ruined church near Goldalming. It depicted a three headed god, thought to be Lugus, and when the Romans invaded they interpreted his to be their version of their god Mercury. Also they discovered that the consort of the deity that the Celts worshipped was the goddess Rosmerta.

"This is getting too weird to comprehend," Simon said leaning back on the dining room chair, away from the sheet of paper.

Catherina stared hard at the words and tried to figure out what they could do next to stop the Woodwoses from killing more innocent people. She looked over at Simon, who had his eyes closed and was rubbing at the bridge of his nose, trying to get the wealth of information into one cohesive linear tale of events since Hedge End came into existence.

"The Woodwoses and Lugus and all the weird people of the woods are there before the ancient Briton or Celts or whatever come to this place. Then the Romans come along and it all kicks off, bish-bosh, rape, pillage, people nailed to crosses and then they call up their own gods Pinky and Perky and their hired muscle to duff up the ancient wood-weirdoes. Lugus's name is banned and changed to Mercury, they plant a great big bloody hedge and at each corner place mystic blocks with Mercury inside, which keeps the wood creatures trapped inside. Time passes, blar-de-blar-de-blar and the hedge gets lopped down and the blocks slowly get smashed, leaving only one and letting the bad-arse Woodwoses free to go on a killing spree. Did I miss anything?"

"I'm not sure, Simon. I did not understand much of what you said," Catherina said, shaking her head. "Do we have a plan to stop them? Cannot we call the police or army in?"

"The police would at best think we were high on illegal substances or at worst somehow involved in the murders themselves."

"Okay, then what?" She shrugged her shoulders, her palms out in front of her chest.

"The old blocks were filled with mercury, right? Maybe we could get your wolf and twins god chums to bless some stones and we could drill 'em and fill them up with mercury?"

"I suppose we could ask, but that means sneaking into the woods. I am sure Mathew would just laugh at us."

"Where the hell do we get mercury though, steal it from a school science lab?"

"*Aspettare*, wait." She snapped her fingers. "In Leggett house there two of these strange, erm, clock things in the library, with mercury inside. Mathew says they tell the temperature and when it is going to rain."

"An old barometer, I remember now." Simon smiled widely, shaking his fingers at Catherina like he was a darts player without a pint in his hand.

"Bravo," she cried and reached forward, taking his face in her long fingers and kissed him on the lips.

They parted with happy smiles and looked into each other's eyes with softer vision and an altered train of happy thoughts. Simon looked at her beautiful high cheek-boned face and leaned forward again to repeat the kiss, with a longer version of the one that went before.

A knock at the front door, followed by a shrill ring of the doorbell, brought them back to the reality of the grim world they both inhabited. With an exasperated exhale, Simon got up and headed for the hall and front door, wondering who it might be. A brief flash of thought that it may be Lucy came to mind and he hurriedly pulled open the door.

It wasn't Lucy. An older woman with deep saggy lines in her face, like she had recently lost a lot of weight after sixty odd years of plumpness, was standing at the doorstep, clutching a blue A4 folder to her non-existent chest. She looked slightly familiar, but Simon did not know her name, or where he had seen her before.

"Is a Catherina Di Marco staying here," she asked in a prim and proper voice, looking back over her shoulder as she spoke and sizing up the street.

"Yes she is, I can get her if you like?"

"Could I possibly come inside, away from prying eyes, young man?"

Hating the phrase *young man*, Simon still smiling invited her in, even though he had a distrusting itch at the back of his skull. He closed the front door and led her into the dining area, where Catherina turned in her chair and then stood to greet the stranger.

"Are you Catherina?"

"Yes I am, but who are you and how do you know my name or that I was even here?"

"My name is Edith Brown. I'm the old curator of the local museum and Father Carmichael begged me to come and see you if anything should happen to him." The woman looked sad and fail now, as if she had aged to seventy in the short walk from the front door to here. "He begged me to find this and give it to you."

"What is it?"

"I'm not sure why it is so important," she said, handing the folder over to Catherina, "but he was very insistent. It is a photocopy of one of the oldest maps drawn of Hedge End. The original is kept in the British Museum, gathering dust on a shelf somewhere, no doubt, but I've had this at home for years."

Catherina's long slender fingers opened the flap of the folder and pulled a dark toned A4 sized map of the old area from inside. She placed the folder on the table behind her, as Simon came round to look at is. It took a while even for Simon to recognise the rough features of the land it showed. He moved past Edith Brown and picked up the map he had done and laid it on the dining room table.

"Why was it Father Carmichael's dying wish, that I bring it here?"

"I'm not sure, Mrs Brown," Simon answered, as Catherina laid her map down next to his more modern view of Hedge End.

Edith Brown moved to the other side of Simon and stared at the differences with a trained eye. "You can see the old straight Roman built road is the same in both maps. What we call Bates Road and the High Street now and all below it was farmland. The squire's house is long gone and the coaching house up by the top of Hay's Hill crossroad, as it was called then before it went by the more grotesque name of Hanger Hill. Both London Road and the Woking Road have not changed and there on the hill is the church. Next to the old coaching house is the man made hill the Romans built for fortifications and you can see that Leggett Woods is much larger and the hedge is completely intact."

"What are we missing?" Catherina looked up at Simon and noticed his eyes had become fixed on one part of the map in particular.

"Is this old map to scale, Mrs Brown," he asked the older lady without turning his head to face her.

"Yes, as you can see the main roads we have today are much the same as they were over a thousand years ago, why?"

"Well, on this old map, the hedge finishes a good way shorter than the remnants of the hedge alongside Bates Road," he said and pointed at the difference on each map to the two women.

"Yes, people always make that mistake. The old hedge ran along what is now called Wood End Lane. The hedge right on Bates Road next to the bank was only planted around half a century ago by the old Squire Henry Truman. In fact, they used to call it Truman's Folly back in those days, but now it's not common knowledge. I only found out by accident some years ago after reading the parish journal of the Reverend Aubrey White, who was the local vicar back then."

"Thank you, Mrs Brown, you've been a great help." Simon rose to his full height and put his hand on the old lady's arm.

"We wouldn't want to keep you any longer."

"Oh well, I'm glad I could fulfill Father Carmichael's last wish, even though I'm not sure what it's all about."

Simon led her down the hall and ushered her quickly out of the house, explaining that he was writing a book about Hedge End and the late father was helping him with certain information about the old town when it was just a village. With a half-hearted thank you, Simon closed the door on the old curator.

"Well really, young people today have shocking manners." She headed back to her old Morris and drove home to her little bungalow just outside Addlestone.

"Simon," Catherina said as he re-entered the room.

"I know," he cut her off before she could continue. "If the hedge is higher the blocks will be further up the tracks about here and the other block with be here." The last here was approximately where Leggett's House was, or in the garden or the woods behind.

"*Stupido*," she said and banged her forehead with her right hand, "the well in the woods, the twins, bird and wolf all seem to be around there."

"So what are we going to do about it?"

"We have no choice now. We have to go see Mathew and make him listen to us." She grabbed both maps and the information they had gathered.

"What, right now?" Simon said, taken aback, not sure of the type of reception they would get. Or how he would feel about the person who may have knocked his fiancée up and which made her leave the house. Also his growing closeness to Catherina confused things. He enjoyed her company, and they had a shared purpose now. They fact that they had slept together back on May Day night complicated matters even further, which just had to sit in the to-do pile at the moment, as they had the Woodwoses to stop somehow and a very sceptical Mathew to convince.

"You had other plans, maybe?" she jokingly asked, her head tilted to one side, her eyes alive as a grin formed on her perfect lips.

"Only for a long life," he said, "but who needs one of those, eh?"

He grabbed his keys and mobile and they hurried to the front door before either of them could talk themselves out of this next course of action.

CHAPTER EIGHTY

Rose Puck woke late and found the bed beside her an empty tangle of sheets. She got out of bed naked, tired and aching from the rigours of Jack's amorous intensions last night. She certainly felt her age this waning end of the morning and her thigh muscles ached as she walked over to grab a thin silk oriental style dressing gown from her wardrobe.

Jack Lucas wasn't anywhere on the upper floors, so she padded barefoot down the stairs to see if he was in any of the ground floor rooms. A quick search turned up nothing. She hurried out into the conservatory next, with a girlish impatience she had not felt since her wedding night long ago.

The French windows were open, so she hurried out onto the yellowing lawn, the grass tickling her bare feet as she ran along. She had a slight panic now for some reason. Maybe the police had arrested him. But her fears were allayed when the gate leading to her secret grove opened and Jack came striding confidently through, beaming from ear to ear.

"There you are. I've been looking all over for you. Is everything okay?"

"More than okay, my love," he laughed and took her in his arms and lifted her off her feet and spun her around like she was a mere slip of a girl and not a woman eleven years away from her pension.

"Get everyone ready and I mean everyone. Now is the time when all will be revealed. The Faye Child will come to us and reveal the location of the last stone and then the children of the forest will be set free again."

"I'll make sure everything goes according to your plan," she promised.

"This is not my plan alone. Without your sacrifices none of this would have borne fruit. This evening, you will get the final reward and resolution to your long labours, Rose. Tonight you will hold another man in your arms and speak words of love to him."

"I understand." She smiled widely and kissed him roughly on the lips, pulled him down with her onto the grass and tugged at the buckle of his belt. Once his jeans were pushed down he entered her wetness, as her dressing gown lay open upon the lawn, which now turned from dry yellow to wet rippling green. Life spread out from their thrusting bodies, until all the grass had a healthily spring fresh glow to it. In the borders the drooping flowers and blooms, straightened their stems and their colours were heightened two-fold.

Jack Lucas let his seed flow into her for the first time since they had met and the first time she had let any man do so for over twenty-nine years.

CHAPTER EIGHTY-ONE

As soon as they had made their way onto Green Street, they noticed the thick heavy humid air that clung to their clothes and pores of their skin. Clouds could be seen coming from over the May Day field and the atmosphere was of weighty static that they could almost taste on their lips like silver foil.

Gnats formed great long pillars over the trees that lined the shortcut that separated the cricket pitch from the May Day field to their left. When they reached the High Street, they found it was surprisingly empty, like an early Sunday morning or FA Cup Final day.

Simon glanced at his watch and saw it was just after twelve and wondered where all the shoppers were. It also seemed to him that the traffic was far less than it should be at this time of day. They crossed at the lights, just as the sun was blocked by fast moving clouds of grey. Yet not far behind them were low black clouds, heavy with storm and crackling with lightning and rain. Ahead near the top of Hanger Hill, a gap formed in the sheet of cloud and rays of golden sun shone down in at an angle ahead.

Even before they were half way past the exit of the petrol station, there came a crack of distant thunder as the dark storm clouds borne on urgent swirling winds brought an eerie darkness over Hedge End. As they walked past the entrance to the garage and up the hill, they could see thinner, brighter clouds in the distance, but the black clouds were gathering over the town, making it feel like an early blue dusk.

They were only two steps from the gravel drive into Leggett House when a police car, with no sirens or lights on, screeched to a halt by the curb and made them turn around. They were surprised to see the head of Surrey police, the former detective from the Hannah Browning case, get out with two heavy set blank-faced police constables behind them.

"Are you Simon Richard Hay and Catherina Di Marco?"

Simon and Catherina looked at each other confused and then back at the Chief Constable who could barely fit in his uniform anymore, and nodded.

"You better come with us," said the plain clothed detective. "We need to ask you some questions."

"Us, why?" Catherina asked, as the two constables moved onto the pavement blocking the way forward and back.

"Are we under arrest or something?" Simon said with a smirk, trying to look amused, but felt a gallstone the size of a lead football had grown instantly in the pit of his stomach.

"Yes, you are," the detective replied and unbuttoned his jacket to show to them a dark grey handgun holstered on his belt.

"On what charge?" Catherina asked defiantly, using all the Italian bravado she had left.

"For the murder of Mayor Khan and Father Carmichael," the Chief Constable said and signaled for his men to move in with open handcuffs now ready in their hands.

"This is preposterous! We have nothing to do with any murders," Simon stated, as the first policeman grabbed his arm and spun him around to slap the cuff onto his wrists with bone-jarring tightness. Catherina turned to face her advancing policeman, trying to make a possible escape, when the detective drew his handgun and pointed it at her midriff.

"Don't," he said simply with a slight shake of his head.

Above them the thunder rumbled like a stomach before Winter Vomiting Flu struck and another unmarked police car pulled up from the other side of the road and parked before the first one. Out of this one same the Met Police Detective who was now running the investigating and his DS.

"What's going on here?" He stared at the two people about to be arrested and saw the shock and fear in their faces and then he noticed the gun the other detective held. "That's a bit over the bloody top, isn't it?"

"This is none of your concern. Local matter," the Chief Superintendant for Surrey said and smiled.

"You can't just point guns at people even if you're arresting them and they don't look like they are going to resist arrest. This is why we get such a bad rep and sued every other week. What have they done?"

"Murder suspects," the policeman that held Simon said.

"Whose murder" the Met man asked, turning back to the detective he had replaced.

"Yours, sorry," the detective replied and fired two shots into the belly and chest of the Metropolitan Police Detective, who crumpled to the floor in dying disbelief as the thunder snapped like broken wood above their heads. The other Met Policeman got within a foot of his car before the detective shot him twice in the back, as another heavy roll of summer thunder covered the gunshots.

Catherina ran past Simon and down the drive, gravel crunching under foot as she went heading for the back garden. Simon was caught but tugged his copper sideways to get in the way of the detective's line of fire. By the time Simon had been roughly pushed aside, Catherina had already hurried around the side of the house and into the garden beyond.

"Shall I get her, sir?" one of the constables asked, moving towards the drive.

"No need, we've got who he wants," the Chief Superintendant barked. "Get him in the car," he cried over the raging storm above.

"You just shot your own men," Simon said in bewilderment, as the constable pushed him down into the back on the police car.

"They're not our men," replied the constable before he slammed the door shut and went round to the driver's side and got in.

"You better clear this mess up," the Chief Superintendant ordered to his detective colleague, who nodded in reply.

Simon watched, his eyes wide and his mouth agape, as the detective and the other constable opened the boot of the Met Police vehicle and one by one they dumped the corpses inside. The thunder cracked once again directly overhead, yet no lightning or rain had yet come. Simon Hay looked this way and that out of the police car's windows, searching for any other witnesses to the murder: or even a peek from the rows of houses opposite, but oddly no one else seemed to be about. The Chief Superintendent got in the passenger seat and the car did a U-turn and headed up the hill.

Simon could not believe that somebody hadn't heard the gunshots or that no cars seemed to be passing either up or down Hanger Hill in either direction. A flash of lightening ahead somewhere beyond the copse at the rise of the hill, burned blue and then yellow into his retinas for a while and was soon followed by the loudest clap of thunder he had ever heard in his life and he ducked down on the back seat like Chicken Little fearing the sky had indeed fallen in.

"Where are you taking me? The cop shop is back that way," he said from the back seat, his voice just audible over the maelstrom of an electric storm cycloning above them.

"We're taking you home, son," the Superintendent replied, "so don't you worry, you aren't going to get hurt. In fact the opposite. You are very precious to us all, Simon. Now shut up and be a quiet chap, eh?"

Simon felt a sudden urge to be sick, but fought to control it. The wide leering smile of the most senior policeman in Surrey frightened him to his mortal core. If the Surrey constabulary were killing their London counterparts, then the world had suddenly turned upside down. Was this really to do with Lugus, Rose Puck and the Woodwoses he had seen with his very own eyes? The police car crested the top of the hill and he had to wince to block out the bright sunshine the car inexplicably drove into. In fact the whole of the Woodhouse Copse on either side of the railway track and the roundabout was bathed in bright sunlight, while the storm raged over the rest of the town.

Yet they were not alone, as hundreds of smiling people it seemed were crowded on the road and the roundabout and the edges of the pavement near the copse. Simon recognised people he had seen every day for all of his life there. The police car turned left and came to a halt on the road next to the northern pinnacle of the copse and before the bridge. Yet when Simon looked in-between the fluff covered headrests of the car, he saw that the bridge had gone. Grey plumes of smoke rose up in wisps from the edges, but a great twenty foot by twenty foot square piece of the bridge had cracked asunder and fallen on the tracks below, blocking any trains from coming or going into the station.

A man Simon didn't know ran up and opened his door and beckoned him out with a rapturous smile that any religious zealot would be proud off. The two policemen got out of their respective doors, and came round to open the one where Simon sat in reluctant defiance. The constable smiled and reached in and grabbed Simon's wrists and he thought he was about to be forcible ejected from the back of the vehicle. Yet instead, the policeman was just unlocking the handcuffs from his wrists and pulled them out like a Vegas conjurer, leaving Simon to his own devices.

They stepped back out of the way, and Simon saw why: for out of the copse walked the musician from the beer tent at the May Fair, holding hands with Rose Puck. A hush came over the crowd of people young, middle aged and old as the couple approached the car, like they were a regal couple on their way to a coronation.

"Simon, dude, get out of the car, pretty please," the wild haired man asked in the strange sunny lit eye of the storm that seemed not to moving away, even with the high winds generated not more than a hundred yards away.

Seeing there was nothing else he could do, he shuffled along on his behind and stepped out of the car, to be greeted with a loud happy roar of approval from the small crowd gathered to his left and ahead.

"What the fucking hell is happening to this town?"

"Reclamation, recommencement, redemption, three R's, you take your pick, Simon Hay, resident of Hedge End," the wild haired man replied with the twirl of his right hand at the wrist and then he bowed low.

"Who are you?" Simon pointed a wavering scared finger at the man.

"Me? My name is Jack, but once upon a merry morning in the dawn of the world, the good people around here used to call me Lugus." The man smiled in a trusting way. "And to answer a question you have yet to pose, you, Simon, are the Faye Child, and we've been waiting two millennia for you, old son."

CHAPTER EIGHTY-TWO

Catherina had tried the back door, but found it locked and fearing pursuit ran down the lawn and saw that the gate in the garden wall was wide open. She plunged into the unnatural gloom as lightning struck somewhere close and thunder like the ending of the world erupted overhead, making her stagger and hold her hands over her ears for a few seconds.

Then she hurried on down the path and into the clearing, just to see Mathew covered in dirt heave down a long handled sledge hammer into the old well and hit something. Thunder cracked above, as the sledge hammer hit the centre of the last stubborn piece of rock blocking the hole, sending it in pieces to fall to the bottom of the old Roman well.

"Mathew!" she cried out at the top of her lungs over the winds that had risen to bend even the strongest and oldest boughs in the woods.

He looked up at her, his face wracked with pain and exhaustion and sank to his knees with fatigue and let the sledge hammer drop also down the now unblocked well. She rushed over to him and going to her knees cradled him in her arms, as he said "sorry," repeatedly.

Catherina had to lift his head, by putting her right hand under his chin and lifting it to stare into his blank looking eyes, "I forgive you, Mathew, but Simon is in danger. We must help him."

"The time has come at least for the cousins of our homeland to work together, but as you say we have little time. You two must head down the well and help set free the Anthropophagi army."

Huddled together against the raging storm, Catherina and Mathew turned as the rain, long threatened, fell heavily from the dark, swirling heavens. Before them stood Lupa, the Wolf-mother, and on her back sat the twins, Romulus and Remus, yet they seemed little affected by the storm conditions.

"But Simon is back there." Catherina pointed to the right of where the house would be. "They might kill him."

"No, that you do not have to fear, child of our lands. They need him very much alive," the twins answered. "The only way we can save him is to raise our own long slumbering army to take the fight to the Woodwoses and stop their god. You have to go now, down the well into the long forgotten tunnels or Lugus will be reborn and the balance of nature will forever be tilted in his favour."

Without waiting for a reply, the great she-wolf sprang from a standing start past them and head first down the well, with the twins hanging onto her fur for grim death.

"What shall we do, Mathew?"

"Trust in the Twins like Great Uncle Jimmy did, I suppose." He shrugged and reached behind him to grab the kiddies rope ladders he had earlier tied together and secured the two loose end rope around the nearest tree next to the well.

"I like that plan, for he was my great uncle too," Catherina shouted over the storm and helped lower the rope ladder down the well as the rain lashed down on them soaking their summer clothes through to the skin.

"What?"

"I will explain later, *cugino*," she shouted back. "I'll go first."

"Okay," he said and picked up a large torch and handed it to her before she scrambled over the edge holding on to the wet rope ladder.

CHAPTER EIGHTY-THREE

"Look, your little fun and games will be up soon. People will come to investigate the collapsed bridge and the cars will come along down other roads to get here and find you all standing around like one of those flash parties organised on Facebook or something." Simon Hay held his hands to head, grabbing his hair in fists, trying to keep the madness that had affected all these townsfolk of Hedge End. "It's like you've beguiled the whole town, like on May Day night."

"That was rather fun and naughty of me, wasn't it," Jack said, "But look, no guitar," and he raised his arms wide to show Simon. "But no aid is coming. We have police roadblocks stopping anyone entering or exiting town. Terrorist laws can be so useful to quote."

Simon had moved down the Hanger Hill Road now, inching his way along towards the dark stormy world that existed around the bubble of midsummer he was stuck in. Yet the towns' people moved with orders unseen or unheard and closed off his possible means of escape until they formed a rough circle around him, but twenty reverent feet separated him from their human barrier.

"So what's your trick then, Jack or Lugus, whatever you're called?"

"I have no tricks, Simon Hay," Jack began, "I was here at the first dawn, I walked on the first grass, under the eaves of the first forest, before the one you call god was conceived. These good people think it's high time I returned and I will take on that mantle again. I will be their god, for they have become so empty and angry and lost without me and you will help me son."

"I'm not your son," Simon spat.

"Quite right, you aren't my son, yet you are the Faye Child and with the Hay Cutter and The Mother Goddess, you will bring about such a change to these lands that has not been seen since the Romans came."

"Why do you keep calling me that?" Simon asked, anger near the surface, ready to boil over any second.

"Because that's who you are, the son of the Hay Cutter and the Mother Goddess. You are the piece of the trinity that will bring me back to my old self."

"My parents are Jeffery and Annabel Hay, arsehole."

"I see you are a man that has to see to understand and not take people on their word or faith," Jack Lucas said and snapped his fingers.

A few of the crowd parted and relief eased the tension in his shoulders as his father was let through and ran up to give his son a bear hug.

"Dad, I'm so glad to see you. The whole town has gone mad. Please help me," Simon said in a low voice into his father's neck

"I know, son, don't worry, everything will turn out okay." Jeff Hay stepped back and with it he pulled the folded maps of Hedge End old and new from the back pocket of Simon's jeans.

"Dad?"

"Trust me, Simon," his father replied and walked over to hand the maps to Jack.

"Dad, what the fuck are you doing?"

"His duty." Jack smiled and unfolded the maps with a giddy laugh. "Oh I see the error my followers made. Well, we will soon find the last stone and destroy it, setting the children of the woods free again to re-educate any unbelievers."

"Dad, what did you do that for?" Simon asked, exasperated. A cold sweat clung to his armpits as hope of reason and rescue died before his betrayed eyes.

"Oh, let me explain," said Jack pointing the maps held in his left hand at Jeff Hay. "This is your father, the Hay or Hedge Cutter you might call him now, and over here," he turned and pointed to Mrs Puck, "is your mother and my good companion, the Mother Goddess Rosmerta."

"She's not my mother. My mother's name was Annabel Greenwood and she left when I was a toddler."

"Not quite, son, Annabel was my wife, but Rose bore you and is your true mother. Poor old Annabel was just for show really, and when she said she wouldn't go along with the pretence of being your mother anymore, well let's say, steps had to be taken."

"Dad, come on, that ain't true." Simon reached towards his father, tears welling up in his eyes.

"I would take you to see her remains, but the Woodwoses took care of all that long ago. But don't be sad. You know the truth now and your mum is alive. Isn't that a bonus?" Jeff Hay smiled and turned to look as Rose Puck, who was standing behind Jack with a sad look on her face.

"A bonus? You killed my mum and lied to me all my life." Simon felt a tear run down his cheek for Annabel Greenwood.

"I'm your mother, Simon," Rose said stepping forward to stand beside Jack, "and we can be one big happy family again." She smiled and held out her arms to her son.

"You're all sick. We nearly had sex and you knew I was your son? What was that all about?" Simon pointed at her, tears now cascading down his face, much like the rain and thunder storm raging only yards away.

"A mother's love, that's all, Simon," she replied without a blink of her eyelids.

"It won't matter soon, Simon." Jack frowned and nodded, moving a step closer. "It's time for me to return to the woods for the first time in over two thousand years and with your father's help, mother's help and your help, I will be whole once again and not the thrice faced man, exiled to wander the earth alone for all these long years."

"Come on, Simon." Rose and Jeff moved to positions behind their son and the crowd near the hedge parted and one of the local firemen stepped forward and handed a new red handled axe to his father.

"Oh the excitement of it all," Jack cried and spun on the spot. "It would make a wonderful TV show. The ritual begins, with the Hay Cutter and his axe."

Smiling, Jeff Hay walked over to the hedge, leaned the axe down against his right inner thigh and spat on his hands before gripping it again. Then walking forward, he picked his spot and arced, sweeping sideways, chopping strokes at the thick root base of the hawthorn hedge, and the surrounding crowds sent up an almighty cheer as one.

CHAPTER EIGHTY-FOUR

The bottom of the well was a wet mud covered mess, littered with splintered brick and stone and the carcasses and bones of small woodland animals and birds. Catherina and Mathew had to clear rocks and the deep roots of probing nearby trees before they could lie in the oozing inches deep mud. So they could crawl and wriggle like human versions of worms into the tunnel leading off in a northerly direction under Leggett Woods.

The standing water and mud ended after twenty or so feet and their mud encrusted hands knees and feet soon made better purchase on dryer clay like tunnel floor. Mathew followed Catherina and turned his head suddenly to the left as her shoes flicked mud up into his face, hitting his upper cheek and missing his right eyeball by only a few millimetres. She also held the torch up in front of her, making her right hand ache.

Of Lupa the wolf and the twins, she could see nothing but a faint green glow of an orb the size of a cricket ball dancing and bobbing in erratic motions through the darkness of the subterranean tunnel. Luckily for them it carried on straight, never deviating left or right, nor were there any side tunnels or openings either. Catherina wondered if her Roman ancestors had built it and if so, were they the last ones to traverse it since those long ago times.

"How much further?" enquired Mathew's tired voice from behind her .

She extended her torch carrying arm to try and get a better view of where the trilateral orb was leading them and what lay at the end of the stygian darkness of the ancient passage they both crawled through. She heard Mathew curse under his breath as his wet and muddy left hand let the sledge hammer slip from his grasp again: before groping in the near darkness, he found it again and followed Catherina.

She exhaled and resisted the urge to wipe mud from her chin, knowing that would only dirty her face even more: when she realised the green-white glowing orb had now vanished from sight ahead. Catherina cursed in her mother tongue and increased the speed of her hands and knees, until she saw the tunnel widened into a small low chamber not more than ten feet ahead. As she neared the juddering flickers of the torch beam showed that the chamber only widened out a few feet on either side and sunk down three or so feet.

"I think we are near the end of the tunnel, Mathew." She bent her head low to call back between her legs.

"Good," was his only fatigued reply.

The tunnel's dirt covered wall gave way to a brick lined chamber and at the edge she was glad to swing her legs from under her and sit on the edge as Mathew caught up with her. He pushed the sledge hammer forward down into the chamber and then from the tunnel he watched as Catherina slowly moved the torchlight from one side to the other. The dusty red bricks of the side walls gave way to a flat ochre covered dead end of a wall not more than five feet in front of them. Then something showed in the outer gloom of the torch and Catherina swept the light downwards to the far left bottom corner.

A skeletal face loomed out of the darkness, its white bone caught in the beams of her modern torch, given illumination to it for the first time in over a thousand years. Both of them reared back with a start, but Catherina luckily gripped the torch in fear and it did not drop from her grasp. Any loss of light now would mean the end of their little underground trek and they did not want to end up like the remains of the poor unfortunate; half lying and half slumped where he died against the dead end of the chamber.

"So what do we fucking do now?"

Catherina frowned at Mathew's profanity, but said nothing. Instead she moved forward and rubbed her wet hand down the far wall, to see if it felt any different or there was some door or hidden way behind the sickly coloured mud covering the wall in front of her. The wall felt different at least to the hard clay floor or the wet oozing bricks that made-up the side of the chamber. It was smooth to the touch and where her hands had passed the thin layer of yellowy-red mud had smudged away onto her palm and something lay underneath.

"What is that?" Mathew asked, clambering into the small chamber. He came over in a walking crouch to where she sat on her haunches.

"I'm not sure," she said, wiping another part to reveal some green tinge of colour and shape behind. "There is something here. Help me clear the mud away."

Mathew reached to the left and dampened his hands on the slimy ancient brick work and ran them both down the centre wall near to where Catherina had wiped. His wet hands revealed more shapes and colours now, until his hands were rubbed dry. Something like an arm or hand could be seen behind the mud covering now.

Catherina repeated the process again and revealed one face and half of another face. The faces were of two small children and down lower and to the right of the adult larger arm that Mathew had uncovered. They continued wetting their hands and wiping away the millennia of mud until a round shield like shape almost four and half feet in diameter was revealed. They soon revealed what must be a representation of the twins Romulus and Remus under the left leg of a taller near nude male figure. Mathew uncovered some sort of bird at the right foot of the taller painted figure and up their wet hands went uncovering a green and brown lyre in his left hand and a stick or sceptre in his other hand raised up with a symbol like a number eight on its top. A bare pale chest led up to an angelic face, with blond curly hair and a hem of silver with golden wings adorning it. Across his upper right shoulder and sometime much after the fresco had been painted and crudely etched with a sharp point was the Latin word *Mercurius*.

"Mercury," Catherina whispered and turned her head towards Mathew.

"Okay, so what do we do now?"

"I think," Catherina said tapping the shaft of his sledgehammer; "we smash his bloody face in."

"Oh." Mathew exhaled and moved back hefting up his hammer, "It will be my pleasure." And he smashed the weighted end right through the inch thick frescos.

A rush of cool air came through the hole just under Mercury's chin and the sound like the escaping long gasp of a dying man echoed through the tunnel.

CHAPTER EIGHTY-FIVE

"That's the ticket!"

The gathering crowd of likeminded townsfolk pressed closer on shuffled feet, to see the five foot gap that now lay in the almighty tall hedge. The words of Jack sent their peering faces into raptures and caused Simon to look round at them in utter incomprehension.

"Don't listen to him, this is madness!" Simon shouted at the ever nearing crowd, but they only shook their heads and smiled, if they noticed him at all.

He turned back and saw that several of the Woodwoses had crept forward to the boundary of the hedge and were staring out through the gap, like newborn children seeing the sunlit world for the first time. The crowd behind Simon spoke in hushed whispers, but he surprisingly heard no cries of exclamation of shock or fear.

"You see, Simon, all is as it should be, or will be very soon. The children of the woods and the people of Hedge End will be reunited once again and live together under my guidance in harmony, as it once was before the Romans came." Jack held his arms wide and spun once and leapt onto the stump of one of the thick and woody bases of the hawthorn hedge that had been hewn down by Simon's own father and then hauled away.

"But there aren't any bloody Romans about, there hasn't been for, I dunno, over two thousand or more years," Simon shouted back at Jack.

"Ah, but their descendants still live here, their churches still pollute the lands which once were forest. Their blood still runs in my enemies. All this will be swept aside and replaced by, well me," Jack finished and pointed to his chest with a simple smile on his face.

"And how are you going to sweep away two millennia of Christianity and all the other faiths from the land? You look just like an ordinary man with a guitar to me. Your music won't beguile the whole world."

"Well, I'm so glad you mentioned that, m'boy." Jack smiled and pointed at Simon. "I need your help with that, plus your mother and fathers also."

"Over my dead body," Simon defiantly spat back.

"Well, I kind of expected that reply," Jack said, turning his back on Simon and walking into the woods for the first time in over two thousand years. "In fact I would have thought less of you if you'd just submitted. So I've come up with a little insurance policy, to make sure you help me regain my old form." Jack clapped his hands together and then turned back to Simon. "hope you are going to respect the extra mile I go to achieve my aims."

Simon frowned and moved forwards and the crowds behind him shuffled in to close the gap and fill the void of his movement. Then his face turned from a scowl of shock to a tight lined look of blazing anger: as two Woodwoses moved forward on their strange bent legs, dragging a struggling Lucy between them.

"Lucy, God, are you okay?" Simon ran forward and stopped, crushing the fallen leaves of the hedge under shoe, as he stood at the edge of the woods, standing at the gap his father had just cut down. His parents Jeff and Rose moved round to stand behind him now and block off his retreat, and the chosen people of Hedge End shuffled ever closer to the woods, so they stood where the road met the pavement.

"I'm sorry, Simon, they caught me. Don't listen to him and don't do anything he asks. He is the god of all liars."

"Let her go!" Simon strode forward and grabbed at the collars of Jack's denim shirt and pulled him close to his face, spitting anger onto his immortal lips.

The twenty or so other Woodwoses moved with jerky movements towards their god and Simon, until Jack raised a free hand to stop their advance. "Stay where you are, my children."

"I'll give you five seconds to let her go or I swear to God I will kill you."

"It would be fun to let you try, but time is a-wasting." Jack just smiled back at Simon. "Because if you do not let me go and do as I ask, I will let my children take full advantage of poor little Lucy. Then I'll let all the men folk of the town take their turn, then the woman folk with fingers and fists and then the children with sticks and branches until there is nothing left of your Lucy but a wet patch on the earth where she was brutalised."

It was the first time that Simon had seen Jack show any flicker of anger and dark emotion and that worried him. And looking at Lucy's terrified face, he knew even though she had left him, that she had up to a couple of days ago been his whole life. "What do you want me to do?"

"What was that, the rest of the class missed it," Jack asked, shrugging off Simon's loosening grip and pushing him backwards a step.

"I'll do whatever you want, just don't hurt Lucy, okay? Satisfied?"

"Yep," Jack simply replied, "now let you, me, your parents, my children of the woods and town and not forgetting dear little Lucy here, head deeper into this small remnant of my former domain and start the ritual that will bring me back to my former godlike self."

Jack led the way into the deepest and oldest part of what remained of his old woodland realm. Two Woodwoses grabbed at Simon's arms and with strength their thin limbs betrayed, they pulled him forward behind Lucy, with Jeff and Rose behind. Lucy ahead of him began to weep and Simon hung his head and let himself be led forwards, knowing all hope of saving himself had failed.

CHAPTER EIGHTY-SIX

A cave or tunnel cut out from deep into the bedrock and under the hill had been on the other side of the now destroyed frescos. Mathew and Catherina had scrambled down its short length until it came out into a huge natural cavern with rounded smooth walls of grey and bronze. Two Roman pillars marked the end of the tunnel or maybe the beginning of the cavern and Catherina lifted the torch to reveal such a wondrous and breathtaking sight to behold.

Steps of white marble lay before them, neat and squared off like they had been chiselled only yesterday. They led up to two rows of three pillars besides a dark opening, which held up the angled roof of some kind of ancient Roman temple. On the top step sat the twins Romulus and Remus were who were holding hands and giggling: a sound that reverberated and got tinnier as it echoed around the cavern. Seeing Catherina and Mathew they stood up turned and rushed forward to joined the Wolf-mother and all three disappeared into the darkness that lay inside the open temple's interior.

Catherina and Mathew exchanged glances and then hurried up the marble steps to join them and see where they had gone. The air in the cavern and on top of the temple steps was cool and there was a faint smell like wet chalk in the still air. The pillars formed a line four deep and ended at a short black mass of an opening, no more than five foot high and three feet across. No sign of the twins or their surrogate mother in wolf hide could be seen, so they pressed forward; Catherina, trying not to think of what might befall Simon up above and alone on the surface.

The beam of the torch did nothing to dispel the thick

blackness that was the entrance to the inner tomb of the temple, even when they stopped no more than inches away. They clasped hands out of primal fear and closed their eyes. Then stepped through the veil of forever night that hung like a stygian curtain at the entrance to the sacred tomb beyond.

When they opened their eyes again, they were relieved to find themselves through the unnatural dark barrier and in a well-lit bare chamber, square in dimension and lit by four huge braziers of bronze in each corner. Just four feet ahead lay three wide steps leading down to a sunken part of the room, filled with strange odd lunks of rock or statues long since covered with two millennia of calcium. The strange almost human-ish sized shapes were five abreast and five deep and as the two of them walked down the steps to examine them, the twins appeared from behind two of the odd shaped stalagmites.

"Here is our last chance of keeping the status quo between our two factions. Here lie sleeping the guardians of ancient Rome and our mightiest soldiers, the dreaded Anthropophagi."

"How do we wake this army of yours?"

"Catherina, daughter of our ancestors, it takes only one word to raise the most ferocious army of the underworld into battle. Do you still wish us to raise them for their last battle, before eternity takes them?"

"Yes, you must. Can they save Simon?"

Mathew looked over at his ex-girlfriend and saw in her concern and love for Simon, which to a degree he shared and felt a tinge of jealousy. For whatever the outcome of today's events, he knew in his heart he had lost her forever.

"They can combat the Wuduwosa, but of Lugus, it is up to you both to find a way to halt his transformation back into the deity he once was and thwart his plans."

"Get on with it, boys, we haven't got the time for a senate debate about this," Mathew cried out in frustration at the two diminutive children of Rome.

"As you wish," said Romulus.

"*Excito*," said Remus, leaning his head back. and his small angelic voice pierced the near silent temple. On his voice went, getting higher and higher in pitch, until it was a shrill stretched tone that made Catherina and Mathew clap their hands to their ears in pain. Still the voice went on, gladly beyond the ability of the human ear to hear, but its powerful effect on the stalagmites was amazing. Two thousand years of calcium deposits cracked and then broke away slowly at first and then soon, it was happening to all and then the only two humans in the temple saw what really lay beneath. They hugged each other as the true repugnant shapes of the Anthropophagi was revealed and reborn once more for battle.

CHAPTER EIGHTY-SEVEN

Jack Lucas stood with his bare hairy chest on show again, having let Rose Puck peel his denim shirt off his back with slow caressing touches. His shirt lay on a nearby fern, bending it back down onto the woodland floor, as it trembled near to snapping.

Rose Puck and Jeff Hay moved to within a few inches of Jack and their right and left hands clasped one another, fingers interlocking tightly. With their free hands they beckoned to their son, who stood his ground for the time being. The two Woodwoses holding an arm each of Lucy pulled her skirt slowly up her legs. Dark veins like vines of plants throbbed on the lengths of their long and erecting phalluses.

Simon bit his lip and moved forward at last, to save Lucy from the rapist advances of the wood creatures and reluctantly joined hands with his father and then estranged and just revealed mother. Rose Puck then began to chant in a language dead to the British Isles since when Julius Caesar was a lad. A jolt of energy like pins and needles passed through Simon's shocked body, and the hairs on his arms and neck stood on tingled end.

Simon watched on in disbelief at the situation, as Jack glowed with a blue haze, radiated an inch from his flesh and trousers. It seemed to Simon that he was running around Jack or was it he who was spinning, or the world and the woods and the whole of creation. Yellow and gold rays of sun beamed now from Jack, but he was not the Jack that had ridden into town now. He was growing in height and stature before Simon's eyes. Slowly growing into their stretched embrace and getting taller than the trees of the copse like a titan of old Greek myths. But this was a home-grown myth, long forgotten by the majority, now being reborn as Lugus god of the woods of Britain and the earth moved beneath their feet and the long dormant trees of the copse stretched their roots out like a prelude to a new war, from old gods and ages uncounted in the history of this sceptred isle.

He tried to look at Jack's face, but it was a blur of motion and he was sure he saw not one, but three faces whipping this way and that at eye watering speed. Jack's face was in there, as well as a larger bearded countenance, with red cheeks and there was a last face. This face was just a blank smooth out line, with no feature or nose, but just a mass of flesh, like a child's un-modelled clay.

He looked back, unable to break the grip that held his hands to his parents and saw Lucy and his heart sank to his shoes. So there she stood, in-between the two Woodwoses, both her hands pumping on their monstrous organs, as their pitted and rough fingers explored up her untucked blouse. Yet it was the wicked sneer that she gave when she came out of her rapture and saw Simon looking at her mouth agape and he knew then the depth of his betrayal. Everyone he had ever trusted and loved had played him since his birth, to get him to this place and time, to release Lugus and his Woodwoses

Lugus's head now dominated its lesser features, and the transfiguration was nearly complete and the god's laughter echoed throughout the woods. Yet beyond this earth juddering bellow of rebirth, Simon heard faintly at first, another sound. The faint cries of many people, distant at first and then closer and increased like a football crowd had been caught in some fearful tragedy.

A few of Lugus's human followers came running past into the woods against their orders, out of fear of something worse than a vengeful deity. The Woodwoses turned as one and moved forward, sniffing the air and watching as people ran past them screaming in terror. Then they were upon them, hitting like an unexpected tsunami into the woods, the Woodwoses had so long protected.

Short in stature, but squat and wide they were, but that

was not their singular oddity. For they had no necks or heads upon their thick shoulders only eyes and in their chests were great wide lipless mouths bearing razor sharp teeth. The Anthropophagi renewed their war with the Wuduwosa. Deadly hand to hand melee followed, with the two immortal armies ripping at each other's flesh, coating the sacred floor of the once ancient forest with dark red blood.

Simon heard Lucy scream and whipped his head around to see her fall as she attempted to flee the bloody onslaught. She turned onto her back to get up just as an Anthropophagi leapt upon her and bite deep into her un-showing pregnant belly. So wide and so deep was its bite, that when it ripped its head back, it looked like Lucy had suffered a devastating caesarean section and she coughed up a word that Simon could not hear because of the blood that shot from her mouth and her head and limbs slumped to the ground, and her time on earth was ended.

Simon cried out her name and tried to break the spell that kept his fingers fused to his parents, but all was to no avail. The Anthropophagi gathered around them and tried to attack the trinity and Lugus, but some invisible force just kept them at bay.

Lugus roared with bellowing anger at the rape of his sacred wood and the killing of innocents once more, yet he could do nothing until his transformation was fully complete. Then the twins came, riding on the Wolf-Mother's back, gripping her fur and holding on for grim death. She leapt and sank her teeth into the right arm of Jerry Hay and with bones grinding and snarling sawing bites, severed his arm at the elbow and so broke the trinity's barrier around their god.

Jerry fell to the floor and the spell was broken. He dropped to his knees as he tried to stem the flow of precious lifeblood with his now free other hand. Simon shook off his dad's severed lower arm with disgust and fell backwards onto his backside with a bump and scrambled backwards. Rose Puck took one look at Lugus and hitched up her skirts and ran for her life.

Simon looked and saw Mathew and Catherina running through the woods towards the ugly scene of death and destruction. Mathew tried to faint left to avoid the swift arching claws of a Woodwose, but failed, yet still had the strength to run at Lugus and jump, while bringing the end of an old looking barometer into the side of his Jack Lucas head, which burst like an overripe boil. Lugus fell to his knees and hollered with pain and clutched at his missing human face. Then Catherina jumped over the fallen figure of Mathew and smashed a similar looking barometer into the large hairy face of Lugus of old. The mercury exploded into his eyes and bone, blood and brain exploded out in a silent rain of red mist.

She managed to keep her feet and pulled Mathew over to where Simon lay, who immediately saw a large red stain appear in Mathew's clay covered shirt. In fact both he and Catherina were covered head to foot in red earth and clay, giving them the appearance of ancient golems.

As Catherina and Simon tried to stem the unending flow of blood from the deep wound in Mathew's abdomen, they saw a new change come over the thrice headed deity called Lugus. From the flesh of his blank face, one began to form as his titanic body shrank back down to normal human size before their eyes. A long nose and brown eyes formed and a proud but thin lip and on his head grew wings that formed into a cap and curly dark brown hair lay underneath.

Simon focused on the deity now, not wanting to gaze around at his ruined life: from the hollowed out corpse of Lucy, to the death agonies of his dying father, or to the silence but proud death of his once best friend Mathew Reynolds's blood pooled under his back and his face grew deathly pallid.

Instead he looked in wonder upon a new face, but an old face: of Mercury and so did the fighting beasts of both camps and as the Anthropophagi cheered in warbling deep tones, so did the Woodwoses wail in horror at the loss of Lugus once again and they fled the battlefield and entered their tunnels and holes far beneath the woods and roots and earth and huddled long in the darkness of despair.

"Take care of her." Simon looked down to see that Mathew had whispered these words to him.

"I will," was all Simon could say, with a voice hoarse with anguish and loss.

"And tell the Colonel, I fought a good fight," Mathew added.

"You tell him, Mathew," Catherina said, holding his body in her arms, but he never spoke again.

All around the town of Hedge End the electric storms abated and the followers of Lugus ran for their homes and shut themselves in, as the wails of sirens passed the now open local police road-blocks, manned by confused and stunned officers of the law.

"You must leave the fallen and run," the twins said from the back of the Wolf-Mother, as fire-bugs shot forth from the silent god, Mercury. Wherever the balls of fire hit, they caught hold quickly and soon the fire was burning everywhere.

"Run," the twins urged Simon and Catherina again, as the fires grew tall and across the dry woods of high summer.

Simon had to drag her at first, but when a ball of fire hit Mathew's forever motionless leg, she ran, holding his hand like a new spell was forged between them. They made it through the woods, to a path that lined the wire fence that marked the boundary of the railway track below. The fire now was high as seven feet, like a wall of flame cleansing the woods once and for all.

Catherina turned and saw that Mercury, Lupa, Romulus and Remus were now gone or obscured by the searing and smokeless flames. Simon kicked hard at the bottom of the chain link fence, forcing a small gap into one they could squeeze through.

"Come on," he urged as he got on his hands and knees and scrambled through, then pulled at the wire with all his remaining strength to let her follow after. They held now onto trees at first as they scrambled and skidded down the dry earth of the bank that led down to the tracks where a train, stopped by the fallen bridge now waited. The last part of the steep bank was devoid of trees and they had to come down on their behinds, finally escaping the flames above, as they stumbled with blinding tears of loss towards the train carriages.

A door near to them slid open and a guard appeared, looking at them questioningly. "What the hell is going on here? It's like the end of the bloody world!"

"Call the fire brigade, quick!" Simon cried out. "The woods are ablaze."

"Bloody hell, right-ho," the guard said and pulled his mobile from his pocket and dialled 999.

Simon and Catherina turned back to look at the blazing woods, the heat on their skin and smoke in their eyes made them cough and weep, as they held each other so close, while the screams of the dying and burning were heard from one end of Hedge End to the other.

EPILOGUE

The large sleek bird with lacquered black feathers used to visit her once a month. It tapped at the glass of the small high window which was crisscrossed with wire inside for obvious health and safety reasons.

She like her son had escaped the scorching of the copse on the crest of Hanger Hill and the carnage and when they found her hiding in the attic of her house, she had been caught like a rat in a trap. The great oak in her sacred and secret grove had also been incinerated by fire, yet not by fire, but from a bolt of lightning from the heavens.

The statement she gave the police was the whole truth and it at least got her out from standing trial for her crimes. No they sent her somewhere more isolated, on the Isle of Wight, with a sea view; well if she had had the neck of a giraffe the attendants in white told her laughing.

Yes the Faye Child that she bore in secret and was denied access to all her life was safe, in a country far away, where the stain on Hedge End and Lugus could not touch him. She examined her hard-clipped nails and listened to the Raven's tales of long trips to the southern west coast of Italy and the farm he and his new consort bought with the sale of his house and his late father's. How they tended the land and kept animals and had a few groves of grapes and hoped to produce wine very soon.

Two years had passed since that night in June and the jacket she once wore was missing now, which she thought a shame as it was rather cold in her new bare cell. The raven though never visits her anymore and her mental pleading to Jack or Lugus or even the Woodwoses brings only the cold silence of her mind. Maybe the move back from the Isle of Wight to Epsom in Surrey had confused the poor little fellow.

Yet she had not been idle. She had been a model patient and followed every word and edit of the doctors to the letter and it was bearing its own rewards. Tomorrow was Thursday, late night shopping and she and a female guard were off to the new shopping centre just opened in Hedge End, on the old site of Leggett House and woods. Mathew Reynolds had died but his father had readily gone ahead with the sale of the land and woods to the huge supermarket chain. The new portly mayor had passed the planning permission before the protestors could daub the first letter on their protest banners. Yet they didn't care, they needed new work and a change for the stain on the town had run deep and many residents, felt a deep shame over their actions that day.

Thursday soon came and dressed in dowdy jeans and a sweatshirt of faded blue she and her minder headed into the Leggett Woods Shopping Centre, with eyes wide with colours and wonders, her eyes had not seen for so long. Flats now stood where the copse once had been and even though an outer ring of trees were retained, most of Leggett Woods was covered in tarmac, bricks and steel.

Her minder's mobile rang and they had to stop and wait by some sort of up and down crane on wheels, which stood next to a marble edifice two metres tall and on top was a square of blue stone. Two men left the crane and went to fetch another banner for some mega-sale they were put up all around the sides of the glass walkways.

Rose Puck looked sideways at her female companion, whose phone call had gone from lovey-dovey to heated argument in less than a minute flat. The woman nodded and glance at Rose, who smiled back and turned to read the plaque on the marble.

An example of Dark Age Italian stone found under the foundation of Leggett House when it was demolished to make way for this shopping centre.

The first thing the woman escorting her patient heard was the crash of metal upon stone and the cries of other shopper as the stone shattered across the cold floor of the entrance to the shopping centre.

"Shit, got to go," the escort exclaimed and cut off her lover in mid-swear word. She saw the broken blue stone on the concourse floor and the strange silver liquid that oozed out of it, but not her patient. Panic set in until she cast her eyes over to the now moved crane, with Rose Puck at the control grinning from ear to ear, like only the greatly disturbed can manage.

She speed dialed the institution where she worked and ran over to pull Rose away from the two security guards that had run up to apprehend her. Identity cards were then shown and an argument broke out as the woman escorting Rose, just wanted to give the Institute's address and contact details for any claim of damages and leave with her ward. Yet the two paunchy security guards wanted to haul Rose off to a security room and call the police.

All the while Rose Puck stood and waited and whistled a little tune that someone called Jack once taught her.

The screams came at first only after five minutes from the car park and everyone standing next to Rose turned to see people of all ages and sexes running towards the many open doors of the shopping centre in wild panic. The security guards exchange nervous glances and peered through the clear glass to see what had caused such a panic before they reported it in. Then after the first wave of terrified shoppers pushed and ran and bundled through the doors, it became apparent what was causing such a wild frightened stampede.

Twenty plus greeny-black skinned creatures from some dark twisted fairytale came loping through and sometimes bounding over the rows and rows of parked cars. A squeal and smash of metal on metal with tinkering of glass was heard outside, but the accident was unseen from the front of the centre. Then the screams began from behind them and all turned now to see a service hatch in the floor near TK-Maxx explode upwards and up hopped another creature from a dark nightmare, yet these were different, headless things that poured from the hole, with faces in their chests.

The human shoppers were caught in the middle as the two warring factions resumed their two millennia old war, crashing into each other, not caring who they ripped apart to get to their foe. Rose Puck saw her helper run into a coffee shop in panic and just stood and watched the surrounding carnage, whistling to herself and wondering if they would have green or her preferred red jelly on the institute menu tonight.

Simon Hay sat on the small hill next to the farm behind the cover of some bushes, his back resting against an old cherry tree. A borrowed rifle with a scope on his knees that Paulo who worked on the farm with him and Catherina had lent him.

It was nearly dust and he could see the sun casting its last rays upon the roofs of the farm house and out buildings. To his left he could see the port and the little boats that bobbed there and the sea. He had sat at this spot every day at this time for two hours until dusk finally fell, ever watchful, ever vigilant.

Today was the day or dusk. A cry from the heaven told him to get ready and he scrambled to a kneeling position and pulled the rifle to his shoulder like Paulo had taught him. Then his prey saw into sight over the small wood behind him towards the farm buildings. With his right eye to the scope he tracked its progress through the sky as it flew low to circle his new home.

Simon fired. The raven spun in the air twice and then fell like a stone into the field down the hill from the farm house. Simon gathered up his bottle of water and ran down the hill with an athletic speed he had not had since Mr James's cross-country class back in Secondary school. He was fitter and leaner now and the hard work in the farm and the love of a good woman had helped.

He found the raven near the gate; it wasn't dead and lay flapping with one good wing in the dust. Simon put his brown boot on the good wing and lowered the muzzle of the rifle to the raven's head and fired without hesitation, ending the bird's life. The body he left there for the foxes to deal with and putting the rifle to his shoulder headed through the gate and down to the farm house.

He put the rifle in one of the barns, in a secure steel combination cabinet and walked briskly back to the farmhouse back door and his family.

"Good hunting?"

Simon looked up from where he was taking off his boots as his wife, Catherina, entered the room carrying a baby monitor.

"Yes," he simply replied with small grin.

"Good," she said and laid the monitor on the kitchen table.

"The twins go down okay?"

"The usual." She nodded. "I think they might be awake for their papa to gives them a goodnight kiss."

Simon got up and hugged Catherina and kissed her on the cheek and then headed upstairs with pat from her on his behind, to see his children. He managed to avoid the creaky step on the stairs for the first time in ages and pushed open the children's shared room, the light from the landing casting back the shadows of the room. Simon Hay entered the twin's bedroom and found them both waiting for him, pulled to a standing position in their cots, smiling as he entered.

"How are my two beautiful little girls, then?"

ABOUT THE AUTHOR

Peter Mark May is the author of six horror novels (*Demon, Kumiho, Inheritance* [P. M. May], *Hedge End, AZ: Anno Zombie,* and *Something More Than Night*) and one novella (Dark Waters).

He's had short stories published in genre Canadian & US magazines and UK & US anthologies of horror such as *Creature Feature, Watch,* the British Fantasy Society's 40th Anniversary anthology *Full Fathom Forty, Alt-Zombie, Fogbound From 5, Nightfalls, Demons & Devilry, Miseria's Chorale, The Bestiarum Vocabulum, Phobophobias, Kneeling in the Silver Light* and *Demonology* and *Tales From the Lake Volume 5.*

Website: http://petermarkmay.weebly.com/

Curious about other Crossroad Press books?
Stop by our site:
http://store.crossroadpress.com
We offer quality writing
in digital, audio, and print formats.

Enter the code FIRSTBOOK
to get 20% off your first order from our store!
Stop by today!

41354938R00201

Printed in Poland
by Amazon Fulfillment
Poland Sp. z o.o., Wrocław